1

"There's a lot of people walking around, full-grown, and so-called normal-they have everything that they were born with, the right leg length, arm length, and stuff like that. They're symmetrical in every way, but they live their lives like they are armless, legless, brainless, and they live their life with blame."

Wayne Shorter, saxophonist

# Contents

# Forward

When I first thought of writing about the "world's tallest man", I thought of basketball champions, as well as how dominant he could be in so many sports, if he was coached well and took it seriously. That's why I have Dan Johnson become not only a champion basketball player, which is what the world wants him to be, and he becomes, but a champion in Judo and Wrestling, sports I played and loved, but like many kids, could only dream of world championships and gold medals.

This story is about dreams and victories, but the more I wrote, the more I began to see the need to develop stories about Dan, the man, and to find a few interesting people to dig into as well, which is why CANYON grew from what was a short story to a novel.

Yes, Dan likes basketball, but he is a deep, complex person, who spends a lifetime looking for his purpose, whether he has done enough to leave his mark on the world, to deserve his place on the planet. If this man, so accomplished and one of the world's most famous individuals, could have doubts and fears, hopes and dreams, then what does that mean for the rest of us poor souls? Does that mean there's hope yet, or a reason to just give up? I think Dan would say to never stop looking, seeking, whether that's to seek out your fortune, your purpose, or whatever it is that can make you happy, while we are still here. It teaches that every day is a blessing, a day to make your mark, or to just sing a happy tune, because you never know when your time is up, and

CANYON is about that as well. Indeed, Dan often found his greatest joy in simply sharing an inside joke with the short list of people he called friends; a movie quote that only his wife will understand, a nice session of "busting balls" with his friend Tony, or just finding joy in speaking with a delightful personality, like Marvin Middleton or Charles Winfield, former basketball greats who share Dan's interest in humor and activities out of basketball, who share Dan's pursuit of "Renaissance Man" status.

CANYON is about family. It's about stereotypes, why there is truth to them, at times, and why they're also, at times, not remotely true at all. That's the case with the Minnelli family, the real heart and soul of CANYON. The Minnelli's are all the greatest things that America stands for, and the reason me, a kid from Northern New Jersey wanted to write about an Italian American family, people I grew up with, is simple. To me, nobody is fuller of life than the Italians. Life comes in many varieties, hard work, anger, laughter, love. When God handed out hearts and souls, the Italians got to go back up in line a second time. Probably because God liked their food. They have their issues as much as anybody else. Their flaws, their problems, their insecurities, and with the Minnelli's, we explore that, but in the end, there is no family that offers more love, and more life than Jimmy Minnelli and his family. To be in their good graces is to have a strong ally, a loyal friend, and CANYON explores friendship, its RARITY, and how opposites sometimes attract. It's what Dan is envious of, that he sees in the Minnelli's that he feels he lacks passion.

And with Billy Barty, an amazing person who you will find was a real man, a well-known actor and comedian that some of you may remember, Dan finds a mentor. A warm, generous person who had to overcome his own physical challenges, just like Dan, but in a different way, yet with laughter, hard work, and the right attitude, Billy earns respect, and he is, besides his parents, Dan's mentor and despite their large age gaps, a true friend.

Everything Dan does is a learning experience, just like so many of us will find, and as famous and wealthy as he becomes, sometimes life can get no better than lying around on a suburban mountain top with a good friend, drinking beer and discussing life, with the lights of Manhattan in the distance, an event that repeats itself throughout the book. All that's missing is a haunting jazz piano solo from Michel Petrucciani, yet another brilliant, little man who overcame great physical challenges. I challenge you to look him up. It's amazing such interesting men and women could live and do great things, and sometimes even leave us, without us ever knowing about them. We can learn about the battles of war, the victories on playing fields, and other great events, but the best thing to learn about is the greatness of people.

I would like to thank my wife, for the countless hours, and at times, painful, story ideas she had to endure from me, Dr. Larry Kaplin of South Lyon, MI, the many Ann Arbor "Townies" I met online, the comments from former and present North Jersey residents of "the Oranges", my former wrestling coach Jeff Conley, the encouragement of friends and acquaintances that rooted me on as I completed chapter after chapter, and last but not least, in the only totally non-fiction portion, retired Detective Thomas King of Essex County, New Jersey, for his riveting first-hand account of the tragedy of September 11th, 2001. At Eagle Rock Reservation in West Orange, NJ, a place frequented so often in this book, is a monument to the memory of the innocent and brave souls that lost their lives that day.

I hope you find CANYON a great read and remember to keep striving to be your best and never give up on life, because sometimes, the hardest thing to find in life is yourself.


Dave Goren
October 15, 2023

# Key Characters

**Dan Johnson** - World-class athlete with a long list of championships in Wrestling, Judo and Basketball, including NCAA, Olympic and NBA titles. Considered, at eight feet, eleven inches, the world's tallest man. Loves the "Rat Pack", jazz, and movie quotes. Widely known as "The CANYON", "C Man", or "C".

**Dr. Cathy McGinnis Johnson** – Lillian, Alabama native with veterinary degree from Auburn University, and Dan Johnson's mother. Works as veterinarian in Acworth, GA

**Chuck Johnson** – From Cleveland, OH suburb of Parma. Purdue graduate, School of Aeronautics, naval aviator, Vietnam veteran and engineer with Lockheed-Martin company of Bethesda, MD and Marietta, GA. Father of Dan Johnson.

**Franklin Johnson** – Chuck Johnson's Father and Dan Johnson's paternal grandfather. From Cleveland suburb of Shaker Heights. United States Navy. Served on the USS Hornet Aircraft Carrier. Worked on the flight deck during the Doolittle Raid, Battle of Midway, and finally, the Battle of Santa Cruz, where he was rescued by a nearby destroyer as the great aircraft carrier sunk.

**Billy Barty** - Prolific actor, comedian, and activist who starred in over 200 films and TV shows, from silent comedies to fantasy epics. Afflicted with cartilage–hair hypoplasia dwarfism. Founder of Little People of America.

**Anthony "Tony" Minnelli** – Youngest son of James and Carole Minnelli. Doorman, 77 Central Park West Apartments, New York, NY. Graduate, Lehigh University, 1997. Resides in West Orange, NJ. Gregarious personality

**James's "Jimmy" Minnelli** – President of Metro Holdings (formerly Minnelli Masonry). Son of the late company founder, Dominick Minnelli and father of Paul, Gina, and Tony Minnelli. Resides in West Orange, NJ. U.S. Marine veteran with two tours of Vietnam.

**Carole Minnelli** – Wife of Jimmy Minnelli. Originally from Kearney, NJ.

**Paul Minnelli** – Oldest son of Jimmy and Carole Minnelli. Vice President of Metro Holdings. Graduate, Penn State University 1990, MBA, Rutgers Business School, 1992. Lives in North Caldwell, NJ.

**Gina Minnelli** – Middle child of Carole and Jimmy Minnelli. University of Pennsylvania Finance graduate, 1993, MBA, Wharton School of Business, 1995. Senior Vice President, Real Estate, Metro Holdings, Licensed realtor. Lives in Livingston, NJ.

**Luccia Minnelli** – Father of Jimmy Minnelli, Native of Sicily. Now lives in West Orange, NJ

**Martin Kaufman** – 91-year-old Founder and Chairman, Kaufman Homes, Captain, U.S. Army Intelligence, and member of famed "Ritchie Boys" Unit during WWII. Born in Germany and lived there until moving to the United States when he was ten.

**Melanie Jacobs** – Native of Escondido, CA. Graduate and Basketball Player, Old Dominion University, 1999. 1997 NCAA Championship Runner-Up member, Pharmaceutical Representative, New York, NY

**Ed Simmons** – Host, Basketball Tonight TV Show, and play-by-play man. Graduate of Pepperdine University

**Marvin Middleton** –Co-Host, Basketball Tonight TV Show. Colorful, humorous, and sometimes controversial personality. All-American, The University of Arkansas. Nicknamed "Double M".

**Charles Winfield** – Four-time NCAA champion with the Michigan Wolverines and teammate of Dan Johnon. 6'1" point guard from Detroit Cass Technical High School (Cass Tech).

**Ann Karlsson** – Graduate, University of Michigan, artist, inventor and co-owner of the Canyon and associated trademarks, owner, Ann Karlsson Galleries, New York, Beverly Hills, Ann Arbor

**Mike Vance** – Dan's Agent and Attorney

**Larry FitzPatrick** – Dan's Financial Advisor

**Lisa Vickers Sawyer** – CEO of the Vickers Shoe Company, maker of "The CANYON" Basketball Shoe

**Stephon Williamson** – V.P. Marketing, The Vickers Shoe Company

**Thomas King** – Detective, Essex Country, NJ SBON (Sheriff's Bureau of Narcotics).

**Rod Dorfman** - General Manager, New York Knicks

**Remy Garnier** – Vice President, Property Management, Garnier Industries

**Marcy Goodman** – Executive Director of The CANYON Foundation. Over thirty years of executive management for non-profit organizations. Two-time, Non-Profit "Executive of the Year."

# PART ONE

# Marietta, GA and The Wheeler Years

# The Interview

All his life, Dan Johnson knew he would talk about his life, eventually, at the right time, and to the right person, because there had been very few people like him. In fact, there was nobody like him at all.

He walked into the Mission Sports studios in Chelsea. It was October 15th, 2010. He was ushered into the studio where he would have a conversation with Shelly Unger, who had risen to fame from a soccer player in North Carolina, to the #1 rated sports journalist in the country. She had defeated the naysayers that said she lacked the experience, the personality, and the right sex, to become number one in her field. She took a lot of crap during that time, to secure an interview for the ages. Hell, a "no holds" barred series of questions that at least the purists wanted to hear. It might seem logical that the younger generation didn't know about the Canyon, but has anybody ever forgotten Babe Ruth? Well, Dan was bigger, and there were more urban tales surrounding Dan than any person in history, and much of it had to do with the fact that the C Man simply didn't talk much. The money, the inner turmoil, the women admirers. Dan promised to open up as much as he could about it all, and even after all this time, the world couldn't wait. For five years, Dan Johnson had been asked for interviews, and he only gave brief appearances. He had enough stardom, stares, enough fame, enough money, and even enough criticism, to last 100 years. He was happy to hang out down at Lake Lanier, at his amazing Lake House at Flowery Branch, and, to those lucky enough to see it, Canyonville, what some have called the "world's ultimate man-cave." He got out on his own terms. He thought he got out at the right time, at 30. He had many detractors for retiring so early, but he had his reasons. As the years progressed, his knees, shoulders, hips, feet, back, and every other joint would speak to him. He walked fine, that is, on a good day. On a bad day, the plantar fasciitis in his feet meant excoriating pain upon the first step out of his custom-made, ten-foot mattress, probably the 5th version that he had made beginning when he started playing for the Knicks, and he could afford it. Hell, he could afford anything, and after taking the Knicks to the promised land five years in a row, he had them exactly where he wanted them. Dan agreed to stay on for three more years. But it was the Canyon basketball shoe, and some other endorsements, but mostly, the Canyon shoe, that made him a billionaire. But if there's one thing the public likes more than a hero, it's a villain, and there were always some who wanted Dan to be that villain. After all, no man should have the ability, the intelligence, the looks, the fame, and the riches as the Canyon. Was Dan Johnson the best thing to happen to Judo, Wrestling, and Basketball, or the worst thing? There are positions on both sides.

The Canyon. Like Liberace, Madonna, and Oprah, the Canyon was recognized all over the world by a single name. In Dan's case, it was one of several names. Dan Johnson, the Canyon, the C Man, and what his teammates mostly called him, C. Some say he was more recognized than Muhammad Ali. Ali never won a gold medal in three separate sports. Dan travelled to Iran when they saw

America as "the Great Satan" and was beloved by a country obsessed with amateur wrestling. He went to Japan, spoke humbly about his favorite sport, and his attempts at mastering the sport, and his failures, and the people treated him with the adulation normally reserved for an Emperor, or a top baseball player. He travelled to many nations, especially in the years right after his retirement, and was nothing less than a hero everywhere he went. In some places, it was his celebrated humility. Always looking for ways to lift people up, in and out of sports. To help others. Elsewhere, it was strictly his manliness. A man who could bench press over 800 pounds and dominate other men in the manner that he did, and then be willing to shake your hand and speak to you with respect instead of intimidation. That was admired by people the world over. Dan had the essence of a warrior.

Dan had a lot of things going for him. The last man to stand nearly nine feet tall, Robert Wadlow, died at the age of 22. He wore leg braces, and an infection ended his life in his sleep. Dan had no such problems. Well, not in the beginning. Faced with the uncertainty of a Wadlow-like experience, Dan's parents, Cathy, and Chuck Johnson, educated, ambitious, loving parents, were terrified of a baby born at 17 pounds, and what his future might bring. But test after test, and year after year, Dan kept growing, and without any medical ailments. On the contrary, he had just the right physique, perfectly proportioned, wonderful balance, speed, great eyesight. He grew to be an ambitious and shy boy who would as much watch a movie and recite movie quotes, or play jazz or Sinatra, then ever step on a court or mat. But he did like the power he possessed and liked the combat of judo and wrestling. He had excellent coaches who designed the very best moves and strategy to put to full use this Goliath. As early as he began, as a nine-year-old, he might have started earlier. At six, he stood over six feet tall, and later, he had to compete in older age groups, so his parents brought him on slowly. This only served to get Dan ready, eager, and hungry, for when he was released, it was like a tornado. The predictions about Dan's success were incorrect. He surpassed all the expectations to such a degree that the outcomes were, frankly, shocking. Dan's size alone simply could not be handled by competitors, but it was his coaches, who took no chances and always assumed that Dan could be beaten, who took every precaution to help him succeed. In addition to his parents, Dan came to believe that he should not trust most people. This was an unfortunate reality, and Dan wasn't always wrong. Too many people wanted to ride on the "Dan Johnson Gravy Train". Again, Dan was warned from the start, and more than anything else, he could thank a diminutive actor who had been in the business since the age of three and had seen it all. Dan met him by chance on a talk show, and he took to Dan. He saw a man-child that might easily be manipulated for gain by so many, and it was no more than a simple phone call or sit down for a few minutes that often-helped Dan find his way.

Dan was thrust into the limelight in New York, and immediately felt all alone, and this could have been a time when things unraveled, but he found refuge with a New Jersey family that couldn't work out all of its own problems, but gave Dan a refuge, a 2nd family away from his parents in Georgia. The family didn't need Dan's money, didn't want to share in his fame, but felt that this was a boy that needed caring for, a family, and nobody was better than being a family than they were.

A musical theme came up on the screen, like a Cecil D. DeMille classic, showing various images of Dan. Celebrating another NBA title with his teammates. Holding up his Knicks 05 Jersey during draft day. His playing days at Michigan and fans rushing the courts, a tremendous Judo throw, a wrestling pin, his many product endorsements. Dan with the President, Dan with the Queen, it could go on for ten minutes, but eventually there was a close-up of Shelly Unger, with the MISSION SPORTS logo on the back wall.

"Hello everybody, this is Shelly Unger. Mission Sports is proud to bring you an unprecedented event. A rare interview with NBA, Olympic, and collegiate legend, Dan "The Canyon" Johnson. These are the ground rules laid out by the C Man. No audience, no other guests, and no questions shared with our interviewee in advance. Just an honest discussion with a man whose life and achievements many say will never be equaled again in the annals of sports. We've all wanted to speak to Dan Johnson so many times, and Dan can be seen as much as ever, through his product endorsements and work with his charitable work, the CANYON Foundation, and spend time with his wife of seven years, former Old Dominion Center, Melanie Jacobs.

We'll be back with our interview with Dan Johnson, the Canyon, the C Man, perhaps the greatest athlete ever to walk the face of the Earth, and certainly the largest, right after these messages.

The advertising world said that commercial time for these interviews were more expensive than the Super Bowl that year.

In addition, Mission Sports executives were heavily criticized for making this a live event. Despite his somewhat quiet demeanor, going live was always a risk, and it was never certain what Dan Johnson might say. This would be his only interview, or could there be more? What were the producers and executives to do? That was Dan's "take it or leave it offer." All that Dan really cared about at this point was the success of his foundation's programs. That's the strength of a man who has known in his life only championship performances. Dan was to be paid nothing, in exchange for a 30-second commercial for the CANYON Foundation each half-hour. The only thing worse than the wrong words, to the Mission Sports brass, were no words at all.

Fade to CANYON FOUNDATION COMMERCIAL, "Feeding the Nation"

**Project Description**: CANYON FOUNDATION, "Feeding the Nation". Dandick Ad Group, Inc.


Client: CANYON FOUNDATION, LLC
Target market: Men/Women, 35-55
Title: Feeding the Nation
Actor: Actual workers, farmers, warehouse, dock workers, get-togethers meals with guests

Description: Inspiring music, using orchestral (approved) score, horns, and strings. Begins as the sun rises on a field of crops.

Narrator: It's another day in America, children and their families rise, go to work, to school, play. Babies are born, people die. And over 38 million Americans go hungry. Every day. This shouldn't happen. Not here. Not in America. Not in the land of the free. At the CANYON Foundation, we use every resource at our disposal to partner with a network of food centers from coast-to-coast. We feed people with a smile, up to 500,000 tons of food per year, and it's going to take a lot more. Nutritious food, and we hold everybody we work with to high standards, especially ourselves, because in America, nobody should go hungry. But we can't do it without your help.

Cut to Dan Johnson sitting at a table with guests being served a meal, his height clearly visible in the shot: "Please give what you can to the CANYON Foundation and ask your employer to join our team. We work hard at battling childhood illnesses and feeding the hungry. That's what we do. God Bless you and thank you."

The CANYON Foundation logo flashes onto the screen, which is the CANYON "brand" logo, with a red heart replacing the well-known basketball, and the words underneath, "The CANYON Foundation."

# Highlight Reel

"We're back with Dan Johnson, known by even more people as the Canyon or the C Man, and we'll get into that name a little while later. Dan, I wanted to read some random quotes from people we received after visiting some of the areas you've lived in, worked in, spent time in.

First there was a man about your age we found, while in West Orange, NJ. It wasn't hard to discover "Dan Canyon" sightings, and through questioning, we learned that the former door man of your apartment building became a good friend, still to this day, and he took you home to his large family, who became much of a second family to you." "Yes, that's very true", Dan said.

This man, Andy Davis, said "Oh, everybody knew that he hung out in West Orange, and people would see him at the Reservation, just sitting with another guy, drinking beer. Just minding his own business. We'd be bowling and a couple of times drove in, and there he was." The reporter said, "did you talk to him?" "Oh, not at all. He looked like he was relaxing, you know. As any guy would want to do, and he was so famous and hounded by people all the time, so we just turned the car around and left. But I do know a guy, a kind of pushy guy, you know, got out once and started talking to him." What happened?", the reporter asked. "Well, this guy told me that the Canyon shook his hand, asked him where he was from, if he liked the Knicks, and then shook his hand again and thanked him for coming by, and my friend was super happy, you know. Shook the hand of the Canyon, and he drove away."

Another person said they went to the University of Michigan the same time you did. "Yes, we'd see the Canyon on campus, maybe on South U., South Quad, people saw him eating a lot, Twigs, on the hill, at Mosher-Jordan." "And what was he like?" "You know, he was totally famous, from day one. The city, the state, went crazy when he chose the school, and I feel everybody respected him. I never went up to him. I mean, you could see him from hundreds of feet away. I kind of felt bad about that. He stuck out like a big statue being rolled around. I walked right by him for years because I arrived the same year as him. I mean right by him, maybe once a week. He could have left for millions of dollars after three years. I mean, nobody could blame him. A lot of people even gave him heat, but the students and fans stuck by him. I mean sure, we wanted another championship, and he gave it to us. Can you believe going to a big University and getting to celebrate for four years like that? The students said hello to him as he walked, and I suppose he stopped for a picture occasionally. He had to get to class just like everybody else. It was well known that he didn't like to give autographs, but he was humble. He'd always shake your hand and thank you. But I never bothered him. I mean, who would want that to happen to them, constantly. I got to see him walking around and I felt privileged for that."

Finally, a student at Wheeler High School in suburban Atlanta talked to us. "Well, we all knew him from the start. I went to middle school with him. It wasn't that he was almost nine feet tall as an adult. He was six feet tall when he was seven. Do you know what that looks like? He towered over everybody. Even the girls, who at one time were taller than a lot of the boys, but nobody ever came close to Dan. He was quiet. He wasn't famous and he didn't even play sports. He was kind of nerdy and kind of a brainiac, you know. Kids made fun of him behind his back, but he was never bullied. He was just too big, but he wasn't popular except for just being big. He really didn't have many friends. But by the time he started basketball, he was like an instant hero. We never lost, and I mean never. It was hard to get into a game as a spectator. I know he wrestled and was good, but in basketball, it was great to be a Wheeler Wildcat. I mean, some of the other schools were newer and they said better than us, like Walton, Pope, Lassiter, but we had a great school, and then later, a magnet program, so we got some of the smartest kids around, and Dan was already really smart, and it wasn't uncommon to see a TV crew in the gym, even when he was in the ninth and tenth grade. He never acted superior to anybody. He almost seemed embarrassed."

"So," Unger said. "Does that describe you? "Oh yeah, I was shy, very self-conscious about my size. I knew almost from the beginning that if you're extra tall, you play basketball, but I never really took to it right away. My parents never pushed me, not for a long time, and I mostly just stayed in my room and read, played board games, video games. So even when I became famous, I didn't really feel special. Some student stuck his hand out, of course I would shake it and talk to them. I never felt superior. I felt, still, like a freak." "But you almost never signed autographs." "No", Dan said. I always simply felt uncomfortable doing that, and then it got around that I wouldn't do it, so I think people felt an autograph would be more valuable. Occasionally, somebody would get rude about it, you know 'my kid wants your autograph" "And then what?" Shelly said. "Well, then I wouldn't do it, and it was rare, but

26

somebody would call me a rich jerk, once I was a Knick, you know. 'We built your career, and you're too good to sign an autograph, and I've got to explain that I'll say hello, usually shake your hand. Be civil to you. But you can't please everyone, and somebody once told me that some of these people were collectors. A famous actor once said that all you owe people is a good performance. I think I provided that. I did my talking on the court, and on the mat, even though most people didn't seem to care about the mat work."

Dan, you've been away from the game now for five years. So, we decided that would take the next few minutes reviewing the highlights of your career from childhood to your retirement from the Knicks. Then, we'll spend plenty of time discussing your career and whatever else you'd like to talk about, for the next sessions.

It's quite a list of accomplishments:

You were born in 1975 in Atlanta, GA, at Northside hospital, at a hospital record 17 pounds.

> Your parents had planned to hold you back from sports, both from concern over your size and health, and the unwanted attention you might receive, but as a nine-year-old you were introduced to the sport of Judo after seeing a demonstration. That sport is not immensely popular in the United States as it is in Japan and some European countries.
> Four years later, at thirteen, you begin to learn wrestling from contacts made in Atlanta, as you

kept growing at twice the rate of other children your age.

> When it was decided at thirteen in Judo and fourteen years old as a wrestler, that it was time to see how you'd fare in competition, you had already practiced against some top players, and frankly, they were frightened of the prospect of unleashing you. Here you were, thirteen years old, seven feet five, 330 pounds, stronger than men twice your age, and according to experts, exceptional at both sports, with knowledge, speed, and a lot of coaching.

> Your size meant that you had to compete against players several years older than you, in the heaviest, or open categories. A boy against grown men, so it was no surprise that your parents and coaches kept your activity to the practice room.

> When you did begin to compete, you obliterated everybody in sight, so much so that the associations of both sports considered banning you. New guidelines in both sports had to be considered solely for your participation. But you had hurt no one and in fact, seemed to go out of your way to protect your own opponents. In sports based on age and weight, you weren't hurting the chances of young boys or even men at lighter weights, and that eventually was the argument for allowing you to continue. Leaders in both sports spoke of the fact that your Olympic prospects were excellent, and there had never been a men's gold

medal winner in Judo, in the brief time that it was an Olympic sport.

➢ You won your first U.S. Senior Nationals Judo Competition at fifteen, and later that year, you beat Hiro Nukiyama, the current world champion. In 1992, at seventeen, winning a gold medal in both Judo and Wrestling in Barcelona. That had never been done. In 1996 you repeat your gold medal in wrestling in Atlanta, but in what some called a major upset, Nukiyama beats you for the gold, his first and only victory in three attempts, in a close match. You tell the press that you did not consider it an upset, losing to a former world champion. Your competitive career comes to an end in both sports after Atlanta, just before your 21$^{st}$ birthday, so you can concentrate on basketball. That seemed to be a decision that was universally accepted. Many looked at your height and never understood your fascination with other sports.

➢ Let's get to basketball now. Until you were thirteen, you barely picked up a basketball, even though you and your family couldn't go a day without being pressured about it. You finally made the decision to play, but for a year, you got instruction, how to play Center, went to "Big Man" camp, shot thousands of times, practiced with the local high school team in 8$^{th}$ grade but did not play at all then, and finally, when you were fourteen and in the ninth grade you joined the squad at Wheeler High School in suburban Atlanta, and the Wheeler Wildcats went undefeated for four years. During your senior year, you're eight feet seven and unstoppable. Colleges are drooling for the chance to sign you up, and that creates tremendous pressure for you and your family.

- ➢ You choose to play for the Michigan Wolverines, and your play only improves. The Wolverines win over 90 straight games and four NCAA championships. You have yet to learn what a defeat feels like in basketball.
- ➢ The New York Knicks draft you by winning the NBA lottery in the spring of 1997 and sign you to one of the most lucrative contracts in league history, before you even step onto the court.
- ➢ As with the collegiate level, you continue to dominate the courts as never seen before. The grueling 82-game schedule causes the team to let you rest, but you score at will, or pass off to open teammates, and the Knicks win a record 73 games against nine losses, seven of those games you didn't play in.
- ➢ You sign a deal with Vickers shoes to help design and sell "The CANYON Basketball Shoe", and the shoe is a phenomenon to this day, making you a very rich man. You earn other lucrative endorsements not only in the USA, but around the world.
- ➢ The Knicks win a record eight NBA titles in a row, and you announce your retirement during a press conference on June 19th, 2005. In the interim, seven years ago, you marry the former Melanie Jacobs, herself a 6' 1" former center from Old

Dominion University, a powerhouse women's program.

➢ You are not without your detractors in all your sports, for having physical advantages some say take away from the sports themselves, take away from competition, and you also are the subject of an authorized biography that some say was not always very flattering. Rumors of relationships with woman circulate, and during your rookie year, you're attacked by a man with a history of mental illness, and medical experts say you nearly kill him with a single punch, but you are completely exonerated of any wrong doing.

➢ The following year, the year after your retirement, the Knicks went 47-35, and lost in the first round of the playoffs.

➢ Since your retirement, you've put all your efforts into your charitable foundation, the Canyon Foundation, and some people, perhaps not sports fans, say your efforts will do much more than any achievement you have earned on a court or mat."

"Well, I hope so", Dan said. I hope that the foundation helps to do so much more than what I could do shooting a basketball. It has come to mean much more to me."

"Well Dan, did we forget anything?" Dan laughed, "You seemed to hit the highlights, didn't you." "Of course, Dan, there are so many questions beyond the numbers and the wins. You've been a notoriously quiet person, but no man or woman lives the life you've lived without stories, without feelings, and we hope to spend the next hour understanding Dan Johnson the man. What we learn, of course, is up to you." "Well, we'll talk about many of those things soon, right after these messages."

When the lights dimmed for the commercial break, Shelly said to Dan, "Well, Dan, so far, so good. A good breakdown of your career. We thought we'd start off that way, kind of like the Kennedy Center Honors, you know. Put out the achievements, and then go back and examine different aspects of your life, and that's when we're going to dive into your personality and thoughts. That's the real story, Dan. Anyone can look up your record. So, we're off to a good start." Dan said, "That's because I haven't said anything yet," Shelly laughed, but she was thinking the same thing. Holy shit, was this guy going to talk? This was a career make or break move for her, and more than one industry friend had told her, "An hour with a guy that hasn't said ten words since his college days, 13 years ago? I hope you know what you're doing."

# Cathy & Rascal

Young Cathy McGinnis, Dr. McGinnis, also known as Cathy Johnson, was nobody's fool. It's true, she grew up in the tiny hamlet of Lillian, Alabama, sitting right on Perdido Bay, where she could see the Florida shore, just minutes from Pensacola. But her parents, William, and Rebecca, were college graduates, her dad from the University of Alabama and her mom an Auburn graduate, back in the days when women didn't often attend college at all, or went for, as most anyone would tell you, and "MRS" degree. Well, that wasn't the case in the McGinnis household, as her mom was an accountant and her dad, a veterinarian in Pensacola.

It's true, little Cathy grew up in a "house-divided" home. The Alabama-Auburn football classic, better known as the Iron Bowl, was a serious event in a state where you simply didn't joke around when discussing football. The series had its share of great finishes and upsets. Recently, in 1972, Auburn came from behind in the 4th quarter by blocking and returning two punts (and the birth of the phrase "Punt, Alabama, punt!"), the Crimson Tide had won three in a row, on their way to a series record of nine straight wins. Cathy was glad to have a baby in addition to her work schedule, to keep her mind off football for a while. They named him Daniel and called him Danny. Yes, many fights had occurred, from Opelika and Montgomery, to Birmingham, Huntsville, and Mobile, and all points in between, and yet "house divided" families were not uncommon.

As much as William and Rebecca tried to get Catherine to socialize with other children, it turned out to be quite a difficult thing to do. She loved the animals that her vet dad would bring home at times, and they eventually had a mixed breed dog that passed away from cancer when Cathy was six. They had only had the dog for about 15 months, and Cathy never really had much of a relationship, as the dog had been ill for a long time, and her father wanted to give the dog the best life he could during his remaining days. The situation changed about six months later.

William thought that a German Shorthaired Pointer would be a perfect breed for the family, and he found a reliable breeder just outside in Mobile. German Shorthairs, or "GSP's" for short, were natural-born hunters and runners. William was going to extend their fence to give a new dog around two acres to run in, and then try to teach him to recall and return when called. With the abundant wildlife, including birds and squirrels, William wasn't sure that would be possible.

Two passions occupied most of Cathy's young childhood. The first was that dog. Thanks to a Pensacola theater in the mid-50s that always played the Hal Roach "Our Gang" shorts, most from only twenty years prior, Cathy had a love affair with Spanky, Alfalfa, Darla, Wheezer, Farina, Chubby, Miss Crabtree, and the rest of the gang, so when she was appointed as the official dog-"namer" of the new GSP, she proudly said, "I'm going to call him Little Rascals." Her parents laughed, and her mom said, "Honey, Rascal is a great name." "Yes, Rascal", shrieked little Cathy, so Rascal it was.

Little Rascal lived to run, and from early in the morning until the evening, he ran. He had a little door that allowed him to come and go, and a fence to keep him in. He ran so much, so hard, and for so long, that he was extremely thin, but he was also extremely muscular. His skin was pulled tightly over a vast body of muscles, as you could see all his sinewy leg, back. They were amazed, and William assured both Rebecca and Cathy that Rascal's weight was within the acceptable level for a GSP. He was the first dog any of them could remember that put food second to running and playing. He loved to chase balls in addition to animals, and he "pointed" like a star. He was gorgeous, and while he ran all day, coming in for the official licking of faces, at night, he collapsed. From about 6:00 to 8:00, he was a cranky toddler, fighting sleep, finally giving up at around 8:30. He was a champion snuggler at night, eventually sleeping with Cathy, burrowing right under the covers, sometimes stealing important parts of the blanket. It could get so bad that sometimes, a cranky, sleepy Cathy could be lamenting, at 4:00 in the morning, RASCAL!!! Stop stealing the blanket. And Rascal liked to give hugs. Up on his hind legs he'd go, put his paws on your shoulders, and hug you. He would sit and lie in the most crazy, awkward positions, his paws straight up in the air, or his rear end on a chair while his paws went onto the ground. And he would put his paws way up on your shoulders and hug you. Never had the family ever seen that before.

Rascal lived to be 17 years old, and he was another reason Cathy studied hard and became a veterinarian, just like her dad.

In addition to her time with Cathy, she loved to read. From Little House on the Prairie to Little Women, Cathy was a voracious reader. Cathy was also the best student every year in her class, and graduated valedictorian from the Pensacola Christian Academy in 1967. She then left Rascal, still running, albeit a little slower at 12, to attend Auburn University, where she would study to be vet, just like her dad.

As a Junior, Cathy had the option of a veterinary internship at any one of several vets around the country, who applied to Auburn. Cathy found a clinic right in Fairhope, in Baldwin County on the Mobile Bay, which was a great stroke of luck. She and her dad agreed that she'd be better off working for a vet who wasn't her father! She could live with her parents in Lillian and make the 34-mile drive each day to the Bayview Animal Hospital. Further than she had wanted, but so far, her Impala kept running. She would work there, earning both a small salary and credit toward her degree, beginning August 1967, to July of 1968. She was 21 years old and eager for what the future would bring. A year's internship to coincide with next August's fall Semester at Auburn, and one more year for her degree.

On a Saturday, an off-day, and back in Lillian, Cathy was talked into going out for a drink in downtown Pensacola, at a popular bar on Palafox Street. There, she met a handsome flyer named Chuck Johnson. Chuck had quiet confidence about himself, which Cathy liked. They had much in common. A strong work ethic and sports fan, Chuck was a Cleveland man all the way, and didn't "get" college football, and yet now, he was seeing it firsthand, in the land of Florida State, the Florida Gators, and less than ten miles away, crazy football fans from the state of Alabama. Of course, there were the Hurricanes, LSU, Ole Miss, Clemson, and Georgia fans to contend with as well.

Over the next six months, Cathy and Chuck met whenever they could. Several Navy personnel got together to support a former pilot, Bob Snow, who opened an old warehouse he called "Seville Square", including the "Rosie O'Grady's" bar. They had a lot of great times there, and it helped Cathy make a lot of friends, and do a little matchmaking at the same time.

Eventually, Chuck was shipped off to Vietnam, and Cathy returned to Auburn to complete her degree. They would stay in touch and "see where this goes". A lot could happen, they had to admit. Fortunately, for both, things worked out exactly the way they had hoped, for they had both been in love, but rejection and separation also played a hand. Cathy and Chuck probably wondered, as everybody else did, why the game of love had to be played like a hand of poker. In any event, there was school, and there was a war, and either of those things could "kill" a relationship, or worse.

# The Aviator

Chuck Johnson was born in Cleveland and grew up in nearby Shaker Heights. Cleveland was a manufacturing city, a "working" city if there ever was one. Located on the Southern Shore of Lake Erie, Cleveland was founded in 1796 near the mouth of the Cuyahoga River by General Moses Cleaveland, after whom the city was named. Its location on both the river and the lake shore allowed it to grow into a major commercial and industrial center, attracting large number of migrants and immigrants. It grew rapidly after the 1832 completion of the Ohio and Erie Canal.

The city's economic growth and industrial jobs attracted large waves of immigrants from Southern and Eastern Europe as well as Ireland. Chuck Johnson's ancestry included English, Irish, and German roots, and his family made its way to Cleveland, to see work, in the late 1880s, having first spend time in New York.

Chuck's Grandfather on his father's side, Preston Johnson had the good fortune of moving from an industrial job to a position with Higby's Department store, first working at the Playhouse Square Center, and then the Terminal Tower Complex at Public Square, at the Cleveland Union Terminal. Through hard work, including long hours, his grandfather was able to purchase a small home in Shaker Heights, where Chuck's father who was born in 1921, and spent much of his childhood. The store struggled for a time, but recovered and flourished. Ultimately, Chuck's dad, as a teen and then for the rest of his working life, also worked at Higby's.

Chuck's dad Franklin served in the Navy during World War Two, which was the primary reason that Chuck himself became a naval aviator in Vietnam.

Chuck was extremely proud of his father's service aboard the USS Hornet aircraft carrier, where he was on the flight deck to help launch the 16 B25-B aircraft of the Doolittle Raid on April 18, 1942. Less than three months later, he was part of the Battle of Midway, considered the battle that turned the tide for the U.S. in the war against Japan. Finally, in the Battle of Santa Cruz Island, in October of that year, the Hornet, sinking from the result of repeated attacks by Japanese dive bombers and torpedo planes, was ordered sunk by Vice Admiral William Halsey, and Johnson evacuated ship and was picked up by nearby destroyers.

Chuck's father rejoined Higby's and worked there until his retirement in 1981, when he turned sixty. He passed away from cancer in 1989, at the age of sixty-nine. Like many in his generation, he picked up the smoking habit as a teenager, and suffered from lung cancer. Chuck could never look at a logo of Camel's without feeling disgusted, and his dad's chronic cough, which began many years before his death, was enough to keep Chuck from smoking.

After the war, Chuck's Dad settled in nearby Parma, southwest of the city, and soon recognized as the fastest-growing city in America.

Chuck grew up with the discipline that comes with a hard-working veteran father. His dad appreciated physical toughness, but also realized from both his civilian and military life that "brain over brawn" was true most of the time. Nevertheless, Chuck's dad came from an old-school belief that even if you were the studious type, you had to act like a man. The basement of their Shaker Heights home had a punching bag and medicine ball, and Chuck's dad, who learned boxing in the navy, taught Chuck the fundamentals of boxing, such as having the proper stance, footwork, basic punches, like a jab, cross, hook, and upper cut, some combinations, and basic defense. Chuck was fortunate not to need much reliance on his skill, but he always took the time, even during demanding study sessions at Purdue, to take 15 minutes and do some shadow boxing and exercises. It gave him, in addition to a good, quick, intense workout, a way to relieve stress. It also gave him confidence. Chuck would rely on his intelligence first, but if needed, he would be able to protect himself, because bullies respected only strength. He vowed to teach his own children the same thing and had a heavy bag and some other equipment in his house when his own son was born, ready and waiting for the right time.

Chuck was raised to appreciate American history and American know-how, and that included all the technology that was born in America. Chuck played sports. He boxed a little, played some football, and was considered "above average" in size and skill, but it was clearly his brains that would take him somewhere, and his parents recognized and welcomed that. Chuck loved airplanes, and with his admiration of his father's service, decided he would fly planes in the navy. His dad told him that aviators, of which he was not, needed to be among the best and the brightest, so Chuck applied himself through school and was accepted into Purdue University, 336 miles to the west of Cleveland in West Lafayette, IN.

Chuck Johnson, and then later, Dan Johnson, didn't come about by accident, but was the result of planning, knowledge, and desire. It was one reason that Chuck's dad, and later Chuck himself, looked up to Theodore Roosevelt, a Renaissance Man known for his saying of "Speak softly, and carry a big stick. You will go far." Chuck told Dan one day, when was about five, prompting Cathy to just roll her eyes. "Dan, a Johnson carries himself a certain way. He is always learning, always trying to better himself. He treats others with kindness and respect, but also knows that in this world, some do not respect the gentleman, which is why you must acquire the knowledge to protect yourself and to dish out physical punishment, but only to the degree that helps resolve conflict, and brings back normalcy and calm to the situation."

"Oh yeah," said Cathy. "He grasps that."

# Well, Bless His Heart

In November of 1976, baby Dan in tow, Cathy discovered a new playgroup with four other moms. She worked at the animal hospital four days a week, which was a good setup with the three other young vets, two of which went to Auburn, and the third to another highly ranked vet school, The University of Georgia. Dan was 17 months and twice the size of any little toddler his age. At the same time, he walked sooner than most as well, and had, even this early on, great balance, strength, and quickness. Cathy and Chuck loved sports, and just dreamed about where Dan's life would take him, but they didn't want to press him too hard, and had no interest in pushing him into a sport until he was closer to ten, and they, only if "little" Dan wanted it. His medical checkups were going great, and doctors said while there was no way to predict the future growth of a child, their chart, and his current progress, they believed would put Dan at well over six feet and perhaps, even seven feet tall. Chuck and Cathy were simply amazed and yet both weren't too sure that this would be a good thing. "A seven-footer", said Chuck, shaking his head. The kid will be sent to a basketball court at the point of a gun. "Not if it isn't what he wants", Cathy said. Danny is going to do whatever and wherever his heart takes him to, even if that means he studies viruses in a lab and never touches a ball. "Well,", Chuck said, we'll see what happens. They both smiled at the way they were doing exactly what they said they would never do, and that was, jumping ahead to conclusions, but it sure wasn't easy.

Cathy had put little/big Dan onto a large, thick blanket over a wooden floor that the host Mom spread out over, so that the kids, when they inevitably fell, would not be hurt. Much of the time, the kids played alone with the many toys put out for them, or "parallel play". Two of the moms were there, with another just pulling up to the driveway. "Hey Ginger, would you please do me a favor and watch Danny while I use the restroom?" "Of course, honey", replied Ginger. Dan played alone happily inspecting a toy dump truck with a tailgate that opened and closed. It was a great toy to help a toddler with fine motor skills.

Lisa came in and said "Hey, everybody, sorry to be late. There was an accident on Johnson Ferry Road, and I just sat there." "Oh, no problem! Just watching Sasquatch here while her mom is in the bathroom." Each of the three women laughed at the insult intended for Danny. Unfortunately for them, Cathy was already out of the bathroom and just out of the site around a wall, in the hallway. "Well, bless his little heart," came the next sentence from Lisa.

Cathy Johnson was a sweet person and easy to deal with. But she was also a new Mom and while the term "Mama Bear" may not have been used often, that's what Cathy was. She had the Irish blood of her ancestors. Cathy could take a joke with the best of them, but insult her son, and it was "game on".

Cathy came in and picked up Dan, which was getting to be more difficult by the day. "We'll be leaving now". Cathy said. "Why? What happened", Lori, the host said. "Well Sasquatch and I have better things to do than hang around people who make fun of us." "Oh, Cathy, we were just kidding!" "No, no you weren't. We must already start thinking about how Danny is going to stand up for himself when kids get a little older. We didn't think we'd have to worry about what grown adult parents would say." "Cathy, Lisa said, you're taking this too seriously. It was just a little joke." "No, you never thought I'd hear you, and I did, and at least now I know where I stand. Look, I don't know what the future will bring for Danny any more than you do for your own kids, but he'll do whatever he wants to in life, and I can assure you, he'll have the last laugh. He'll be fine. More than fine. At that point, Cathy walked out, and the understanding was that she had made her point clear, and she would not return to any future play date gatherings.

"Honey, you did the right thing", Chuck said. I'm proud of you. "You know", Cathy said, "That thing you always say about Southerners, how they smile at you while thinking about how they're going to stab you in the back as soon as you turn around?" "Oh honey, I didn't mean that." Chuck said, "No, no, yes you did mean it, and now I see that you're right. At least up north they'll tell you off right in front of you." "Oh, I don't know, Cath. I think people are either nice or they're not. They may be sneaky about it, but at the end of the day, most people are nice but sometimes you get a bad apple. Maybe someday, when Dan is famous, you'll have the last laugh." Cathy said, "Oh, honey, I just want Dan to be healthy and have a long life. I don't want him to be famous."

# Marietta

Settlers began to build homes in what is now Marietta around 1824. An early road in what would become Cobb County crossed the "Shallow Ford" of the Chattahoochee River and ran just south of these settlers.

In 1832, Cobb County was established, named after Thomas Willis Cobb, U.S. representative, U.S. senator and Supreme Court judge. His daughter was Marietta. In 1834, the town, already inhabited by many homes, was officially founded by the Georgia legislature.

Three years later, the Western and Atlantic Railroad established a spur that would stop right where the center of town, or square is, and this is when the town began to quickly grow.

The city continued to prosper and grow and was a prominent area during the Civil War. General Sherman took up residence there after the nearby Battle of Kennesaw Mountain, perhaps the last stand of the Confederate Army. The Union Army, soon after, began their devastating march to the sea, destroying everything in their path.

In 1973, when Cathy and Chuck purchased their home east of the Marietta square, the eastern part of Marietta, often referred to as "East Cobb" was being transformed from a heavily forested and farm area separating Marietta from the town of Roswell to a true bedroom community of its own. Homes were going up at a quick pace and the many family farms that dotted the landscape were surrendering their land to ambitious contractors who paid handsomely for the opportunity to divide beautiful land into 1/4 acre lots.

Where there are homes, there are families, and those families need schools, grocery stores, churches, parks, stores and shopping centers, and other varieties of entertainment like drinking establishments. From 1975 to 1987, three high schools alone were built in this relatively small area, Walton, Lassiter, and Pope. With the influx of residents from the northeast, Midwest, and west coasts, in Atlanta for the many Fortune 500 company offices, and more, the schools earned a reputation for being some of the better public schools in the state.

A little closer to downtown, yet still to the east, is where Chuck and Cathy settled, just off Roswell Road, and only about four miles to his office at Lockhead Martin. The plant builds some of the country's most important planes, and yet Marietta, GA is still more recognized as the home to a certain Kentucky Fried Chicken restaurant on the Cobb Parkway, with a 56-foot mechanical chicken sign. "The Big Chicken" is a famous landmark, and residents often reference it when giving directions, such as "To get to that car dealership, you'll pass the Big Chicken, and then it's three miles on the right." New York has Lincoln Center and Marietta has the Big Chicken, but everybody must eat.

Dan had a lot of places he could choose from, to hang out. Marietta had a lot of shopping nearby, and the mall, in the 1980s and early 1990s, was still in full swing, so depending on the mode of transportation, Dan might occasionally take a ride down Cobb Parkway to Cumberland Mall, or Towne Center Mall in the other direction, in Kennesaw, was built in 1986 when Dan was eleven. Six Flags was about 30 minutes way, and White Water, even closer, right in Marietta. Parents would get their kids summer passes and let them hand out there all day. Of course, Dan would be subjected to stares, the older he got, but the larger the crowd from his area went, the more insulated he was. Eventually, he couldn't fit in most of the roller coasters at Six Flags, and without roller coasters, you were out of luck at Six Flags, so he did tend to spend more time at the water park, White Water. Atlanta kids, but the time the '90s came along, weren't what you'd call "southerners" so much. Many of the parents were raised in the northeast or the Midwest. With Dan, he had what his parents joked was a "mixed family." Cathy from Alabama and Chuck from Ohio.

With the I-75 interstate passing right though the center of town, it was easy to drive a few minutes to downtown Atlanta, further south down to Florida, or further north to Chattanooga and into Ohio. You could connect to I-85, which joined I-75 just south of the center of Atlanta, called the "downtown connector" and then branch off again and ending in Petersburg, VA. Yes, Atlanta was a rail, air, and transportation hub, home of the world's busiest airport, huge growth, and even the restaurants were coming to town. Schools were improving in most places, and in GA Tech and Emory, you had two of the finest colleges in the nation. In twenty-one years after Dan is born, 197 countries would converge on the city to participate in the Centennial Olympic Games, and that competition would prove to be an exceptional story for Cathy and Chuck Johnson and their famous son.

# In the Home and Out

For the first few years of his life, Dan stayed near home. His parents made sure he ran and played a lot, and there were some neighborhood kids that the Johnsons felt they could trust. They knew that they couldn't stop the stares, and they had to live. They went over to the local Publix, over to the Cumberland Area, up to Barrett Parkway, over to Johnson Ferry Road, down to West Paces Ferry, walked along the river and took the occasional drive up to Elijay, maybe to the Alpine-themed town of Helen, over to Unicoi State Park to marvel at Ana Ruby Falls, to Lake Lanier, and maybe in the warmer weather, to the laser show at Stone Mountain. They had to live, after all, and Dan was tall, but if you didn't look hard, he could have been a sixteen-year-old who was six feet, six feet five. That was Dan in his early years, and what the hell, he was handsome, and he was graceful. Both Chuck and Cathy felt he would be a natural athlete, but until he was about ten, they felt just healthy exercise, by playing and running, was just fine.

Dan and Cathy were more interested in Dan's mental development. There were lots of board games scattered around the house. Books of all kinds. And music. Today, big band, with Sinatra and Martin, Benny Goodman, Ella Fitzgerald. Other days, a little Mozart, Beethoven. A little jazz, rock and roll, too. Dan was taught what his parents knew he probably wouldn't learn in school. How the U.S. government works. They went to Washington when Dan was eight, about our wars and why they were fought, and about mistakes America made, too, in the way they treated certain peoples, how they corrected themselves, and how there was still much work to do.

# The Gentle Way

Dan was intrigued by a Judo exhibition as a nine-year-old while in New York with his family. It was 1984. As usual, Dan was stared at everywhere he went, this 6-foot-2 frame with the little boy's face. At the Felt Forum, underneath the main arena at Madison Square Garden, an exhibition was taking place, featuring some of the very best area judokas. Sensei's Yonezuka, Shimamoto and Watanabe welcomed some of the best young players in the area and the country. It was explained how Judo "the gentle way", was a sport that taught how to use technique, speed, leverage, strength, and balance, to defeat a person of any size, often using your opponent's own strength against him. Dan was intrigued to see a young boy "flip" a much larger person onto his back. Those demonstrating were all taught how to fall correctly, too, escaping injury. It looked a little brutal, with the grabbing and throwing. Dan's ears perked up when he heard the sensei, or instructor, explain how a "tall man" could be defeated by a shorter man. But of course, that also meant that a skillful tall man could defeat a small man. Much of it had to do with skill, not size. And yet size probably still had its advantage if used wisely. After all, they explained that competitions were held by weight.

# Wrestling Practice

Dan Johnson was 13 years old, standing seven foot three and weighing 290 pounds. He had already been practicing Judo since he was nine. That was four years of steady practice, hip throw practice, hundreds, thousands of times, called Koshi Waza, ground techniques, called ne waza, even chocking and arm bar techniques, the last several months. He loved those, for some reason, and became so proficient at both that his sensei instructed him never to put more than just a little pressure on the throat and elbow joints. When he got a secure grip, he was to let it go, before a practice partner was forced to tap out. Nobody was going to escape it. It was decided that Dan would practice against junior national champions and place winners, whenever he could get away to make that happen. Other players were asked to help develop a judoka of very young age who could be great for American Judo, and by now, he was beating national champions who were 15 and 16 years of age. The bouts were deliberately unsanctioned and unscored, to help all to save face. On the record, it was randori, practice. There were no winners. Nothing counted, mattered, but everybody saw what was going on. A sixteen-year-old jr. national champion was told after a practice. "Don't worry, it was practice. In two years, he'll be 7'5" a hundred pounds heavier than you, out of your class. Right now, he needs competition. A guy like him comes around once every hundred years, and maybe, never at all.

But right now, Dan and his dad, Chuck, pulled into the Atlanta Lovett School's parking lot and walked into the wrestling room, where coach Jim Glasser, himself a former National Champion and coaching legend, was conducting a practice. Of all, places, Coach Glasser and Chuck met at a Marietta coffee shop with Dan and started a conversation. The word was out around town already, and the Coach had invited the two to a Lovett practice, simply to check out the sport of wrestling. Before the practice, he told his wrestlers, many of whom were state contenders, "gentlemen, today, if all goes according to plan, we'll have a visitor from a young man, in fact a 13-year-old from right down the road in Marietta. But he is no ordinary boy. His name is Dan Johnson, and he is seven feet three inches tall. The kids gawked and looked at each other. Somebody said "holy shit" under his breath, and it went ignored. Usually, it wouldn't be. A couple laughed. "Oh, I know this kid, Coach," said one of the wrestlers. The Atlanta Journal did a story on him, and my dad saw him on The Tonight Show. He does karate, right?" "Well, no," coach Glasser emphasized. "He's a Judo player and has been for four years. And he's very good. Because of his size and weight, he hasn't been able to compete against his own age, but later this year, the judo association is going to let him compete in an open category for sixteen-year-olds. But we're here to talk about our sport, wrestling. I met with Dan and his dad about six weeks ago, by luck and Dan wants to take a little primer in wrestling. We're going to have a regular practice, but I'll be spending some time talking to Dan, showing him the basics of the sport, and he'll be watching you, so please, men, good behavior, like always. Nothing will be different." "Coach, will we have to wrestle this guy?" "No, that's not going to be happening. Not today. He doesn't know the sport." "Coach, at 7'3", how much does he need to know?" The other wrestlers laughed. "Hey", Coach Glasser said, "give our sport a little credit. Plus, I understand he beats everybody at Judo, national champs several years older than him, and I've seen judo guys take to wrestling very quickly, so today, Mr. Johnson and his son Dan are visitors to our practice, so it's business as usual. Be friendly and helpful." "Coach", a student asked, "does this mean he's coming to attend Lovett?" "No", it does not mean that. "I've gotten permission to let him visit this one time, and maybe two or three additional times, but you gentlemen are the reason we're here. This is Lovett and we are accommodating, but the focus on Lovett wrestling, as in all sports and all activities, is on the students. Listen guys, Dan is curious about the sport, I am curious, and you should be curious about a 7 foot 3 thirteen-year-old. Of course, I'd love him here because I've met him. He's a polite, courteous young man, eager to do well, and if I wanted him here at Lovett, it would be for those reasons." One of the wrestlers whispered to another, "That, plus in a few months he's gonna kick the crap out of any wrestler in the state."

Dan and Chuck walked in. Dan was wearing a t-shirt, gym shorts, and sneakers. He wouldn't have known what a "singlet" was anyway, which the Lovett wrestlers and others didn't always wear to practice themselves. The group had only just started practice, and were doing jumping jacks to loosen up, a daily ritual, with two wrestling captains leading the way. The entire group stopped, in awe, and looked up at Dan. Dan looked down, embarrassed, but that was Dan. Coach Glasser said "Mr. Johnson, Dan, please, come in. I've already told my wrestlers about your visit. Dan, say hello to our two captains for this year." Dan and Chuck both shook hands with the two captains, which was meant as representing the entire room, to save time. "Dan, Chuck, we're having regular practice. Nothing different today but the three of us will go over some basic wrestling, let you ask questions, and then maybe later you can watch the Wrestling Lions do some live wrestling."

The wrestling session continued, but there wasn't a single Lion who could practice normally that day, as each would steal a look at his huge kid, who was not only 7'3", but had some muscle on him as well.

Coach Glasser took a small part of the mat and started talking quietly to Dan and his Dan. He asked Dan what he knew. "Well, Coach, one of my dad's best friends wrestled for Purdue, so my dad knows the basics. Also, when we knew were coming, we didn't want to waste your time. I know the basic Georgia High School rules, of there being three, two-minute periods. First standing, then in a referee's position down, first one wrestler, then the others. I've learned about some basic takedowns, like a single leg, double leg, fireman's carry. Then on the bottom, escaping for a point when you are both on your feet, in a neutral position. Then, on the top, he told me about ways to turn your opponent over, like a half-nelson, arm bar and cradle. I know that you must keep your opponent's shoulder blades down for two seconds for a pin, but you can get a near-pin for two or three points."

Coach Glasser covered his mouth and laughed. Just the expression Chuck wanted. He wasn't about to let his son go in green. It was six weeks since the meeting up in Marietta. Chuck and Dan had no less than four 30-minute "classroom" sessions. There was a reason that Dan was a straight-A student and Chuck was an aeronautical engineer.

The Coach walked a few feet away and came back, laughing. He handed Dan his whistle, "Here you go, Dan. You're ready to coach. All three laughed. Chuck spoke up. "Coach, all classroom training, textbook stuff. Dan has never wrestled, but we respect your time." "Oh, no problem", Jim Glasser said. "I'm impressed, that's all."

"Ok, Dan," Coach Glasser said. "Today, we're going to simulate some of those moves your talked about, or have you done that already, maybe with Coach Gable out in Iowa City." Dan chuckled, "No, sir". Coach Glasser then went through some basic moves, slowly, and Dan gave it a try. Single leg, double, arm drag, duck-under. "So those are ways to secure to 2-point takedown, and sometimes, you can take an opponent directly to his back." Dan learned how to get into a referee's position correctly, arm placement. Coach Glasser emphasized how wrist control was so important to a match, to escape and to turn your opponent over. He said, "Son, if you can have an explosive stand-up, at your size, you will be hard to stop, but often, you will be pulled back down, and you need to understand how to stay off you back. If you can control your opponents' wrists, you will be hard to pin." They practiced how to stand, perform a sit out, how to pull a "switch". Then on top, some basic pinning combinations. It was a real "speed" practice covering about forty minutes.

"Well, what do you think?" "I love it coach, and I think I can, be good." "Well, son", Coach Glasser said, so do I. Now, I recommend you go to the coach at Wheeler because that's where you'll be. You're always welcome here but I must put the instruction of Lovett wrestlers first. But occasionally, let's bring you in and see how you've progressed, that is, if you choose to wrestle. I'll even call your coach at Wheeler. I know him and he's a good coach." "That's great, coach. I'll do it. I hope they let me wrestle and not wait. I want to compete, not just practice." "Well, I don't blame you, son", Coach Glasser said.

With practice wrapping up, some of the wrestlers headed to the gym to shoot some baskets before their rides came, just for fun. "Hey Larry," Coach Glasser said, "Would you take Dan here into the gym and let him shoot around with everybody, while I talk to his dad?" "Sure thing, coach, Larry said. "C'mon Dan, follow me."

"Hey Coach," Chuck said, "I really appreciate you doing this. I know he's not a Lovett student". "Hey, no problem", Coach Glasser said. "I'm a wrestling fan and I was curious. Plus, I love the Atlanta area and I most certainly love the Lovett School family. I spoke with our Athletic Director, Bill Conley, who is a most generous man, and got his okay. To be fair, I would recommend you go talk to the Wheeler Coach. Of course, if attending Lovett is ever something you might think of, that's another matter, but that was not the purpose of today's exercise. If this young man can do what I think he can do, then all wrestling in Georgia will benefit."

"Well, what do you think?" Chuck said. "You're one of the country's most successful high school wrestling coaches. "Can he win big?" "Let me put it this way", Jim Glasser said. "First, he's smart. Obviously, smart parents. Everything I taught him; he could do right away. He's quick, I watched him, he's enthusiastic. I imagine he's very strong. He needs to have good endurance. And I won't lie. He's massive and if he learns how to use his size to his advantage, well, the sky's the limit. If he's beating national champs in Judo three years older than him now, there's no reason he can't be that good in wrestling, but that's my opinion. It's not the same sport but my God, is he still going to grow? He's only 13!"

Chuck said, "the doctors never give us exact information. They say there's no way to predict exactly, but over the next 3-4 years, we should know. But they feel, based on his records and progression, he could wind up being well over 8 feet. He's growing at 4 inches per year, year in and year out. Normally, growth plates stop growing sometime after puberty, and usually by 18, you cannot get taller, but even at that rate, he'll be about 8 feet, 3 when he's eighteen, and he could still grow for a couple of more years after that."

"And what do you and your wife want?" Coach Glasser asked. Chuck said, "For him to be happy, to be smart, to be well-adjusted. There were no organized sports in his life house until he was nine. Oh, sure, walking, hiking, physical exercise, but that's it. We concentrated on studies, on the appreciation of music and reading. Judo started at nine." "And", Coach Glasser said, "no basketball?" "Well," Chuck said, "that's what everybody asks. Believe me. His Mom and I have spoken with him, that everybody will want him to play, and that he could secure his future, maybe become wealthy, playing basketball. But money's not everything, and we only just got a basket in the driveway six months ago." "So now what?", Coach Glasser asked. "He'll learn basketball from me, very slowly, dribbling, passing, jumping free throws, all the basics. The intensity will increase. But he wants to compete in Judo, in the Olympics. He says that will be 1992, in Barcelona. In four years. He'll only be 17, but every time I count him out, he surprises me." "Well, he does have one of the most incredible size advantages I've ever seen. If he takes to wrestling like Judo, he could be competing some day in two Olympic sports, but I'll deny ever saying that. It's WAY too early."

In the gym, some of the Lovett wrestlers were shooting around with the leftover basketball team members. Practice was now over for both sports, but a handful of kids were shooting around. Dan got the same look of wonderment from the basketball players. "Hey Dan, we'd like to show our new weightroom." Actually, it was the same weightroom but with some new Olympic weights, six benches, a Smith Machine, and a 1,200-pound capacity Olympic barbell.

"Have you lifted weights before?" one of the wrestlers asked as they entered the room, Dan ducking carefully under the entrance. "Actually", Dan said, I just started three months ago. I wanted to lift earlier but my dad said I had to wait until I was thirteen." Trying to be accommodating, at least two of the kids said, almost in unison, "Well, sure, yeah, young kids shouldn't lift." But, Dan said, "My dad was it was fine to do calisthenics, you know push-ups and sit-ups, so right now, I've gotten to where I can do 145 pushups at one time." The other boys just looked at each other.

"Well, how much should we start you with?" one of the boys said, "Well", said Dan. My dad won't let me bench press alone, to be safe." "Well, how much do you weigh?" The other boys leaned in, so they could hear this important piece of information. "I'm 290 right now." "Well, I'd say that a good marker is to be able to bench press your weight. I'm 185 and I can bench press this amount here, 225, six times. But I train all the time, so I'm a little stronger than the average guy." Everybody nodded in basic agreement. Why don't you see what you can do with 225? "Ok", Dan said. "And two of us will spot you, so don't worry, you'll be safe." Dan got down, his legs extending far out from the end of the bench, his rear end just barely setting on the bench cushion. He took the bar and for a second, it went to the left. His stabilizer muscles had to get used to the balancing act. But that stopped and Dan began to lift the weight three times, then six then nine, then twelve. When he got to 19, they said, "Okay, Dan, let's stop there. Nice job." Dan seemed satisfied. "Maybe we should add some more plates."

A few minutes later, Dan and the other wrestlers entered the gym. Some parents were waiting outside in cars. Coach

Glasser was joined by a gentleman with some gray hair, perhaps in his late 50s. "Dan, I'd like you to meet Coach Bill Conley, our Athletic Director. He came down from his office to say hello." Dan said "Hello, sir," and shook his hand. "Well, hello there, young man, and welcome to Lovett. I take it the coach and boys have been helpful to you today." 'Oh, yes, sir. Everybody has been very nice, and I learned some good wrestling moves already. They even took me back in the weight room, and dad, don't worry, they spotted me, so I was safe." Chuck smiled at that. "Well, son, you come see us anytime you want, and good luck in all your endeavors." He nodded toward Chuck and said with a smile, "Mr. Johnson." "Thanks once again everybody," and Chuck and Dan walked out the door. Chuck, in a gesture performed often, had his arm around Dan's waist, like any father might do. He couldn't reach his shoulders." "See ya, Ace!" was Coach Conley's parting shot just before the two walked out the door.

The next scene looked almost scripted by a movie producer. Four boys and Coaches Conley and Glasser got into a loose circle, and Coach Conley said, "Well, what did he bench?" The one boy said "Well, after 400 he stopped, but he didn't seem to struggle too much with it." Another said.

Coach Conley looked straight ahead and simply said what the rest were thinking, "Good Lord."

# Here's Johnny

On Tuesday, October 17th, 1989, at 7:10 PM, the phone rang in the home of Dan and Cathy Johnson. Dan joined his parents at the dinner table, where, as usual, Dan put down enough food for the starting backfield of the Wheeler Wildcats. Tonight, it was seven pieces of chicken, a plate of mashed potatoes, peas and carrots, a salad, fried okra and three slices of apple pie a la mode for dessert. There was no Judo practice tonight. Wrestling practice had not yet begun for another two weeks, but Dan and Chuck went through passing and dribbling drills outside from 5:45 to 6:30. As a 14-year-old 9th grader, it would be another year before Dan joined the Wheeler team, but the coach called Chuck now every week for a status report. This coach was a man who would literally become a slave to the Johnsons if that's what it would take to make sure he stayed in this district and played for Wheeler.

Cathy herself got home that night at 4:45 as part of a staggard schedule at the Acworth Animal Hospital. On Monday and Wednesday, she stayed until 7:00, and on Tuesdays, Thursdays, and Fridays, she left at 4:00.

Cathy answered the phone to the sound of a young, articulate woman. "Hello, is this Mrs. Johnson, Dan's mom? My name is Barb Connelly, and I am the production assistant to Mr. Fred De Cordova, the Executive Producer of the Tonight Show Starring Johnny Carson." Cathy felt her face go a little flush. "Yes, hello", was all she could say. Barb Connelly got right to this point because this wasn't a courtesy call. She had a constant schedule to keep with, but she was at least civil. "Mrs. Johnson, we read an article about your very talented son, Dan, in the Atlanta Journal-Constitution, and would love to have him on the show on Tuesday, November 10th. The show tapes at 5:00 PM. We would fly Dan and one parent, since he's a minor, from Atlanta to LAX, provide transportation from LAX to NBC's Burbank Studios. He would arrive at approximately 2:45 PM, where Mr. De Cordova and possibly I would give him very simple instructions for the show. If you watch the show, Johnny has the most famous celebrities in the world, but he loves to interview interesting people from all walks of life, and he would love to speak with Dan. Johnny does not arrive until approximately 30 minutes to taping, but the day before, he will be given a full briefing on Dan, where he lives, in his case, his school, any hobbies, and of course, the interesting story behind his visit to the show. We know that Dan is fourteen and stands over seven feet tall. My goodness. So, Johnny will talk with him for six minutes. He will be the third guest and come on at approximately 5:42 PM. Following the show, we would take care of your dinner at any one of five very nice restaurants in the Burbank area that we have agreements with, that you can choose from, and then you would stay at the Sheraton Burbank overnight, which is a 4-star hotel. We will speak with the hotel to see if there is anything they can do to accommodate Dan's height, but we cannot guarantee anything. If you choose to bring in this case, a second parent, we will also comp that person's meals but not the flights. In the morning, we would take care of your breakfast, and there is a 10:15 flight that would land at Atlanta's Hartsfield International Airport at 4:47 PM. Finally, Barb stopped talking, presumably, to breathe.

"Mrs. Johnson are you still there?" said Barb to a shell-shocked Cathy. "Yes, I'm here but, please, we have to slow down here." Jesus, that's just what Barb expected. It was so much easier with celebrities. She could speak with agents of publicists. She hated speaking to "amateurs." "Ok", Cathy said. "I am here with my husband, Chuck and my son, Dan." "Honey, who is that? You look a little pale." Cathy moved the phone slightly away from her mouth so she could let everyone listen. "Chuck, Dan? This is Barb, I'm sorry, last name?"

"Connelly", Barb said, impatiently. Cathy continued. "This is Barb Connely with The Tonight Show." "Johnny Carson's show?" asked Dan. "Yes, the one and only. Dan, Ms. Connelly wants to know if you'd like to be on the show and be interviewed by Johnny. They read the AJC article." "It's starting", said Chuck, which he thought he said to himself, but the words came out.

"Honey, is that something you would want to do? It would be next month." Dan responded the way any 14-year-old might. "I don't know, Dad, should I? Can I?" Chuck wasn't sure what to say. He whispered to Cathy. "Tell her we have to discuss it." "Well, Barb, this is a surprise, and we love the show. It's just an amazing thing. Believe me, we're honored, but can we discuss this as a family tonight?" Barb answered. "Discuss, but I have to know by this time tomorrow, because dates have to be filled." And just like that, she hung up. "Wow", said Cathy. "All business-like."

"Ok, everybody, into the living room," Chuck said. "We have to have a talk". He looked at Cathy, "THAT talk." "What is THAT talk," asked Dan. "Sit,", Chuck said, and everyone sat. "Ok, I'll get right to the point. Dan, you're a smart young man. You're seven feet five and you're a national champion in Judo. You start wrestling competitions this fall You're not just extremely tall, Dan, but you're very good in three sports. Wrestling and basketball coaches have seen you. You know that. You could be as good or better in those sports. I wanted to avoid this discussion, but you are, as you know, an exceptional young man, and I'm talking as an athlete right now. You might be winning some big titles in the coming years, that's IF you want it and IF you give it all you've got. And nothing is guaranteed. I know a lot of people know you already, in the Judo community, around Atlanta and some colleges already, but now we're talking millions. If you want the attention, I can think of no greater stage. Do you want that?" "Yeah dad, I think so." "Cathy, your thoughts?" Cathy said to Dan, "Honey, we can't hide you from the world, not that we wanted to ever do that, but your dad's right. This is who you are. If you're going to "go for the gold", so to speak, then why not go onto that show? What matters is what YOU want." Dan said, "Well, it's kinda scary, but I want to do it." Chuck said, "and we'll both go, even if they're too cheap to pay for both of us."

Dan said, "This is our family, right here. We stick together. Dan, this is the hand God dealt you, and it can be a wonderful thing, but it can also be overwhelming. You can quit anything, anytime you want, and we will love you just the same. You can concentrate on one sport, or none at all. We expect hard work in the classroom, otherwise, you can give all of this up." "No," Dan said. It's what I want.

# The First Skit

It was Tuesday, November 10, 1989, and Johnny Carson put the big news in his monologue from yesterday, that everyone in the world was talking about and virtually nothing else. The Berlin Wall came down the day before, and Johnny put his usual funny spin on life.

After that, more talk about the event, a little more serious. Then he said, "Ok, we're going to go to a break and when we come back, we'll hear from the 'Mighty Carson Art Players" and meet an extraordinary young man from Atlanta, GA, a 14-year-old who stands seven and a half feet tall. Ed, someone you can finally look up to.

There was a change in the initial interview from the time the assistant, Barb Donnelly, told the Johnsons. Johnny and Fred DeCordova had their daily production meeting the prior day when they spoke about the next day's show. When they came to Dan, they decided that they hadn't had a "Mighty Carson" sketch for a while. Sadly, Carol Wayne, the blond beauty and fixture on the show's comedy sketches, passed away in a tragic drowning just four years earlier, and the sketches had lost their zing. They decided that Dan's tremendous height might make for a funny "used car" sketch. Fred said, "what about giving Billy Barty a call and see if he can come down and help us out?" Johnny said, "Big guy vs little guy? Can you write it up and make it funny this time?". Fred smiled and spoke. "Just wait, John. It'll be funny even without a dame with big tits."

After about six commercials, the show came back, Doc and the band finishing off some big band tube. Ed had the microphone, "And now, ladies and gentlemen, it's time for the Mighty Carson Art Players and another visit from Honest Sam Sanderson used but not abused cars.

Johnny started, fake mustache already getting laughs, with a set that looks like there's construction going on. "This is Honest Sam Sanderson for Sam's Used but Not Abused Cars." "Pardon our dust while we expand to offer you even more great savings. You know our slogan, our used cars are so nice, they'll only break down once or twice. Just to demonstrate how big a deal you'll get with Sam's, we brought my sister's kid out all the way from Omaha. Come on out, Tiny." And out walked 7 foot five fourteen-year-old Dan Johnson, wearing a cap and overalls. "Now Tiny doesn't say much, but he's here just to show you how big a deal you'll get here at Sam's. Now you might remember that last time, we had Stretch Madison here to demonstrate that you won't pay much here at Sam's." Suddenly, a paint can fell off a ladder, probably done on cue if there was no laughter, and it worked. The crowd laughed. Well, Stretch is away at a basketball tournament, so we had to find a replacement. Suddenly, actor Billy Barty ran in, in anger, shook his fist at Johnny, while the audience howled, climbed a ladder, and threw a coconut cream pie in the face of Dan Johnson, who was doing his best not to laugh, and failing.

"So, big savings or small cost, either way, come by Honest Sam's today."

The crowd loved it. Billy waved to the audience, and so did Dan, and, as promised, he didn't have to talk.

On to a commercial.

When they returned, all three actors were on the coach, and Johnny said, "everybody, Billy Barty", and the crowd applauded strongly. To set things straight for the audience, out of respect, Johnny said. "We called Billy with a fun idea, and to our luck, Billy was available, but Billy, you're a hard-working man." "Well, John", Billy said, I'm blessed, my calendar is still pretty full at my age." Johnny, knowing this answer, said to Billy, "You've been in over 200 movies now, isn't that right, Billy? I mean, Mickey Rooney, Ginger Rogers, it goes back to when you were a kid." "Three years old, John". The audience clapped. Billy

Johnny turned his attention to Dan, knowing he'd have to help the shy young man along, unlike the pro that Billy was.

"So, Dan Johnson. I'm told you are seven and half feet tall. That's really something." "Yes, sir". Said Dan. "Now, slow down", joked Johnny, and the audience laughed. "No, I'm just kidding. I mean, you're fourteen and a lot of people watch the show. Anybody would be nervous." "Hey, kid, Billy motioned, knowing Johnny wouldn't mind a little more laughter. "I still get nervous coming on here. You might say I shrink in fear." The audience and especially Johnny just cracked-up when Billy said that.

Johnny asked Dan about his sports, his judo success, now wrestling and basketball. His titles already and Olympic aspirations. Dan answered with a lot of "yes, sirs." Johnny kidded him a little more about that. Billy said, "Kid, don't you have any 'tall stories' you could tell?" Billy was on a roll, and Johnny appreciated it.

Finally, Johnny said, "Dan, in all seriousness, you are a remarkable young man, and I think that with all you're involved in, we're going to be hearing a lot more about you. Would you come back again?" The audience applauded. Dan finally got a little witty, "Can I have a line in the next sketch." Everybody laughed and Dan immediately felt better. Johnny motioned off-stage and said "Fred, the kid wants a line." Billy, sharp as a tac, said, "Here it goes. It's starting already. Now he wants a line, then he'll want a trailer. Kid, put in a few more years, and you can't use my trailer parked out back. You'd never fit inside!"

Johnny thanked both guests and then said. Let's go to a break, and when we return, Joan Embery from the San Diego Zoo. Doc, take us out. Some great music began and both Dan and Billy walked off stage.

Within ten minutes of the show's ending, Johnny and Billy were gone, but Dan would be back, and he would now reach true celebrity status, good and bad.

# Tough Question

"We're back. Shelly Unger here on MISSION SPORTS with the Canyon himself, Dan Johnson, world champion basketball, wrestler, judo player. What do they call it in Japanese? A player?" "Judoka", Dan replied. "Ok," Unger replied. "Now we know that.

Let's start at the beginning with something. You were a 17-pound baby. Your parents were worried." "Yes, worried to death". Dan said. Everything about it spelled problems in their mind. It wasn't normal. Amniocentesis didn't show anything. They read up on everything. They're smart people as it was. Doctors said they would have to wait until I was born, and when I was, everything looked normal. They looked for signs of gigantism, and I had an MRI a week after I was born. Blood tests, no pituitary issues. Naturally, I don't remember any of this, but they told me that they were always waiting for the other shoe to fall, and doctors could never find anything. They said I was completely normal."

"But", Unger said, here to flush out the Dan Johnson that couldn't be found in the sports stats. She wanted the person who had, so far, refused to discuss personal matters, but agreed to, finally, for this interview. Unger and her team were skeptical. "But sports weren't a big thing in your house when you were a toddler. There was no Tiger Woods, hitting of golf balls at three." Dan smiled, "No, more like Mozart and Duke Ellington and flash cards with numbers and shapes." "Why do you think that was?" Dan said, "Well, I think that's easy. That would have been my parents' choice no matter who their child was, big or small, boy or girl. They're very cerebral. I think they felt that sports were a hobby, but learning was for life, something to start right away. They weren't going to have me shooting balls on a tiny little toy basket when I was two, just because I was tall. They didn't look at things that way." "But they must have gotten questions, comments, both good and bad," Unger continued. "Oh, sure, comments. That's quite a little linebacker you've got. Pretty harmless stuff." "Yes", Unger pressed, but you weren't just a little large, you were tremendous. You were over five-feet tall at four years of age, and what about elementary school, and kids could tease, be brutal? You weren't called names?" Dan got quiet. It's not that Unger wanted to injure Dan, but there was a lot on the line. The risk of the papers, the media, calling this a giant waste of time was very big. Her reputation was on the line, and she didn't work all those small-game sidelines to fail now. "C'mon, Dan. Weren't you an outcast? A misfit? Did kids call you a freak? Call you names?" "Wow", a producer said from the control room. "This is a little brutal." "Dan, nobody anywhere was as big as you, then or since. Did you have a single friend?" Dan got very quiet. "A voice came into Sherry Unger earpiece, "Sherry, lighten up. It's not a courtroom. Don't lose the audience." Dan got quiet, and silence was the deadliest in a broadcast. "Do you need a minute to collect yourself?" Still nothing. Dan took a drink of water. "Let's go to commercial break, and we'll be back with Dan Johnson."

That was about it. Shelly rolled the dice, and it came up snake eyes. Dan shut it down for the final half hour, and the media decided that nothing new was to be discovered about Dan Johnson. "If only Shelly Unger understood what most sports commentators already knew; Dan Johnson was a reclusive and not one prone to 'spilling his guts'.

It was the last big "one-on-one" interview that Shelly Unger had until she left the network to do her own podcasts, ten years later.

# Bob's Big Boy of Burbank

Four weeks later after the used car bit, Johnny gave a quick review to the audience about "meeting a very tall young man a few weeks ago named Dan Johnson. He was a delightful, interesting young man, and he made a big impression on the audience. Well, he's back again, and he'll be here right after these messages." When they returned, the producers and Johnny pulled out a script from the "Mighty Carson" vault, from 1978, the "Female reporter in the locker room" skit, again with Dan and Billy, and to everybody's delight, just like in '78, the female reporter was again Betty White. Betty was in the middle of her starring role on TV's "The Golden Girls", so the crowd went wild when she walked on. This one had some sexual innuendos, and the producers needed to check with Dan's parents. Their answer to the producers, and to Dan was, "Well, if Dan is okay with it." So, they had the skit take place in a high school locker room, and with Johnny, Dan, and Billy, wearing towels. They made strategic use of the word "Johnson", and once again, Bill found a way to pull a cream pie out of a locker, his manhood insulted, and threw it at Dan. This time, Dan had a speaking part. He said one word, "Well", and that was enough to anger Bill and hence, the pie. The funniest line wasn't a line at all, but Betty White looking at Dan when his towel, "accidently" fell, thought it was clear that Betty pulled it down. It was better than the first skit and everybody from Dan's school saw it. Dan was a bit of a local hero since the assumption was that the name Johnson, "fit him." Even Dan's parents, who were backstage, had to laugh. The Johnson's, after all, weren't prudes, but of course, somebody in the media complained about using a 14-year-old boy, but that complaint fell on deaf ears.

Dan waited backstage until the show was over. Johnny left somehow, immediately, and Dan figured when you did a show day in and day out for 30 years, you didn't hang around any longer than necessary. It was only 6:00 PM, as the show was pre-recorded, to play later that evening. He was to have a limo take him to the hotel, with a flight back to Atlanta in the morning. He figured an old pro like Billy Barty would "pull a Carson" and be gone by now, but suddenly, there he was.

"Hey, kid, nice job tonight. This one was really a hit and you're loosening up a bit. I know you're not flying back till the morning. How about if we get a meal. There's a great place nearby. We'll get a ride over. The restaurant was Bob's Big Boy, a local fixture, since 1949, and Dan recognized and appreciated the well-known Big Boy statue outside.

"Yeah, sure. That would be great," Dan replied.

Now it would seem that Dan couldn't fit in a car, but it depended on the car. At home, the family had a minivan which was slightly retrofitted so that the middle seats were removed. This allowed Dan to stretch his legs way across the van and could sit in relative comfort. Here in California, a stretch limo was ordered. That wasn't hard for Fred De Cordova, the Tonight Show producer, to figure out when the guest star was touted as "one of the world's tallest humans". At the hotel, the best they could do was a king-sized bed. Dan got used to his legs sticking way out. At home, his dad put together two large mattresses. They made it work. A custom mattress cost a fortune, and it was one thing Dan would do if he was ever rich and famous. The famous part he was already beginning to establish.

Billy jumped into the limo at the speed of a star. He wasn't an A-lister, but he had been around and at the time was probably the nation's best known little actor. Dan hunched way, way down and sort of slid in.

The limo would wait for the hour or so they expected to be at the diner. Just before they got out, Billy told Dan, "Now Dan, besides being a nice, polite young man, I'd like to get to know you a little and help you out. Call it an education, and it's gonna start before we even sit down. Will you trust me? Dan just nodded.

They got out and walked up a short set of stairs. Dan opened it and Billy walked in, Dan, as usual, hunched way down. He was nearly as tall as the ceiling and had dropped his head about a foot.

As Billy and almost anyone might expect, the entire diner went silent, and gazed their way, although Bob's had had its share of celebrities. There was even a famous "Beatles Booth", where the Fab Four had sat, and a ton of very cool artifacts from the world of fast food. It was like a museum, and Dan thought it was one of the coolest restaurants he had even been in. He wondered if Billy was thinking about that. Dan always imagined having a "man cave" of some sort, lining the walls with all kinds of memorabilia like this, as well as movies, TVs, and shows of all kinds. He loved this retro look.

Billy went into his act. "Hey folks, you didn't expect THIS duo to walk in, did you", with a giant grin on his face. The crowd laughed. "We just did The Tonight Show down the street. Be sure to catch this one if you can stay awake. I'm Billy Barty, and I hope to God a few of you recognize me or I'll have to talk to my agent." The crowd laughed and a couple of patrons shouted out "Hiya Billy!" "Now this young man is Dan Johnson from Atlanta. He's 14 and a star athlete. He's on the tall side". More laughter. "Now I know we make the strangest of bedfellows. That's why we were on Carson. We're just here to grab a bite to eat but we do have a couple of minutes when we're through, so just in case an entire mob wants my autograph, as I expect, it would be great if we could eat in peace, and then we'll be available." More laughter, with a couple of "Yeah, no problems".

Billy and Dan sat down. "Wow, Billy, that was pretty good., and this is such a cool restaurant!" "I thought you'd like it. You see kid, we're unusual, to say the least, and that's when we're not together. Together, we look like something, well, from a comedy sketch on a famous late-night show. Dan laughed. Now, most people will respect us and let us eat, though not always. You will get jerks, you know, nice, but stupid people. But the way I handle things, I am in control of the situation. That's what you're gonna need to do, kid.

Dan said "We'll, I've been getting a lot of that since I was practically born. How many 1st graders are six feet three. "I know, kid. I figured that. It's only going to get worse. You've been on The Tonight Show. Twice! Just wait.

Kid, you're very unusual. I learned things tonight I didn't know. A national champion in judo and wrestling, with the entire world begging you to do nothing but play basketball? Maybe the Olympics in two years, and in three sports? Has that even been done?" "No, I don't think so", Dan replied honestly.

"So, your favorite sport is a tie between wrestling and judo. As big as you are, you don't seem mean enough to hurt anyone."

Dan said "We'll, that's just it. I don't really hurt anybody. I may throw guys around on a mat, but there are rules, and there's a lot more strategy than people know." "Yeah, seems a little boring to me kid, but I can see, obviously, why every basketball team wants you." "Well, I like basketball, and I'll be training hard to be a good player. Coach has had a good strategy for me as a big man. It's complicated but it's designed for me to both shoot and pass where the percentages are highest, and to practice free throws a lot, because everybody fouls me."

"Yeah, yeah, that's fine kid", Billy said, with a look of disinterest. "Look, I have a lifetime of experience in the limelight. I'm not just a little person, I've also been acting since I was three.

Let me ask you, kid, what do you want for your life?" Dan looked confused. "Look, I know you're only fourteen, but with your size and athleticism, I heard you're very good as well as being 20 feet tall. What do you want in your life?"

"Well, I do want to make the Olympics in two years, in Barcelona. I have a great chance in Judo and Wrestling.

I've pinned the current NCAA champ twice. Boy, he was angry, and I haven't lost to anybody in Judo since I started competing in tournaments last year. I would like to play basketball in the Olympics, and they're already talking about me. I should be a lot better when I'm 17. But they have never let a high school kid play, although I'll be graduating then. I get it, Mr. Barty, the real money is in pro basketball, and some people say I could play in the NBA right now, but I want to go to college, then play in the NBA. After that, I don't know."

"Ok, kid, fair enough. First, call me Billy. Now I was made an actor at three, and I've loved it, but you have to find your passion in life. But you're only fourteen. Being so incredibly tall, hell, kid, large as a mountain, there's something to be said for playing to your strengths, and I'd be the last guy to tell you that money doesn't matter. If you like basketball, go hone your skills and make some money for a while. There will be life for you after basketball. And kid, speaking of honing your skills, here's one of the most important things I can tell you. Be as good as you can be. Don't ever let 'em say you were just a freak of nature planted in front of a basket. Cause they'll say it anyway (Dan didn't realize at the time that he would come to quote this comment by Billy again and again, in the future). I may be a little person but I'm not just a dwarf put on stage for a laugh. I'm a comic, an impersonator, and a singer. I have talent. Oh sure, I'll take a role when a little person is needed. I gotta eat and I'm realistic, but I live life on my terms, and you'll need to learn that, too. Just the way I addressed this diner crowd. You gotta expect people to stare. By now, you know that. Do what you can to have them respect you. I get respect. I can't stop the occasional jerk, but kid, that's life. You must play the cards you're dealt, but you CAN change your outcome in many ways. Be good natured but stand your ground, with a smile as often as you can. Especially you, because if you're aggressive, you'll scare everyone off. See, I can't do that. I'll have the small man complex. You lose your temper and you're on the 6:00 news, or in your case, MISSION SPORTS. Then you'll be laughed at, and I won't be able to make even a small difference." Dan glanced back. "Geez, kid, we've gotta get you a sense of humor, and maybe a personality.

Am I getting through to you?"

"Oh sure, Mr....Billy."

"Look, how many fourteen-year-olds know what they're gonna be doing the rest of their life? I have a feeling, and don't let this go to your head, that you may be the most influential basketball player to ever play the game, and they'll want you to play forever, kid. And some will look for a reason to criticize you out of jealousy. You'd be nothing if you weren't so tall."

"I hear it now, at Wheeler, sometimes."

"Well, kid if you're ready, let's go. But first, let's work the room." Billy, true to his promise, signed a couple of autographs and some couldn't resist a photo of the two extreme men together. Billy said, "I'd get his autograph. When he's more famous than Muhammad Ali, you'll be glad you did."

Billy and Dan motioned for the limo. It stopped back at NBC at a sports car. "That's yours?" Dan gawked. "Sure kid, I have a life, you know. Just a few modifications and off I go. Look, here's my number and let's stay in touch. Carson's gonna want us again at some point. One day, you'll be famous and won't return my calls." "Oh, no that would never happen" Dan said. "Well, that's good to hear, kid, and Johnny will want us back, because he told me so."

# The Wheeler Years

Dan might have been able to compete well before his freshman year at Wheeler. Some high schools in the area began in the 8th grade, and it looked a little strange seeing these little children, these 8th graders, walking the halls of a high school, but that had largely been done away with in favor of middle schools, by around 1990 or so.

Judo wasn't a sport practiced in Georgia, in public or private schools, or most anywhere else, but wrestling and basketball was, even if football was the religion in the south. It is easy to encapsulate Dan's Wheeler years for those reasons.

Dan had been practicing wrestling for a year with the team before ever having a high school match, not only at Wheeler, but at some other schools that had interest, where the coach was friendly with their coach. Coach Glasser continued to be helpful. Chuck Johnson rarely got involved, but he would talk to coaches and ask "Is Dan being taught how to effectively use his size? Is he being taught defensive techniques? Coach, how would you attack Dan?" That was Chuck, the engineer. But for a year, that's exactly what Dan learned. How to use his hands best, the brutal arm drag, the "bear hug" (for lack of a better word), hip throws, single leg takedown, shrug to a single leg, stand ups, arm bars, 3/4 Nelson's, cradles.

Dan COULD be taken down. In theory. It was deliberately proven in practice. It was demanded. In every practice, a teammate had the unenviable position of picking up that long, massive leg that Dan had to freely supply, and then trying to finish the job. All Dan usually was taught to do was to "step into it" with those 380 pounds of lean muscle mass, and the leg came down. Maybe a whizzer, which is a move where two wrestlers locked arms, but Dan dislocated an opponent's shoulder, and the parents got involved. So, Dan was constantly holding back. Never putting 100% into practice. It got so ridiculous that his coach had to tell him, "Now son, you're allowed to give it 100% in a real match. Not only that, but we also all expect nothing less." And then his coach would silently pray that Dan didn't kill an opponent while giving 100%.

Dan went on to win four state titles in wrestling. He never lost a match. He broke the ribs of three wrestlers over four years, dislocated two shoulders, hurt several shoulders without dislocating them just from arm drags to the point of the wrestlers forfeiting. Sprained several necks from shrugs, when he tied up and yanked necks down, and one time, a wrestler shook Dan's hand and then simply walked off, too frightened to go on, but that only happened once. Wrestlers are a tough lot. Dan later said that he never "went 100%". He said he was scared himself of what he could do.

In basketball, Dan had already been to "big man camp" as an 8th grader. His father drilled him for two years. Maybe from a book, but Dan, the engineer, did it by the book, literally. For a big man, Dan could dribble remarkably well. He passed constantly; chest pass, bounce pass, overhead pass, wrap-around pass. Dan would stand under the basket and Chuck would move around the perimeter of the court.

In the corner, top of the key, other corner, down court. Dan did it five days a week, for an hour before or after wrestling or judo practice, repeatedly. Free throw after free throw. Fade-away shots, 30 in a row, every practice. It was regimental and 45 minutes, to the second. Then a snack because Dan had to eat almost constantly, and then on to another practice. Homework from 9:00-11:00 and whenever possible, an hour in the afternoon. Chuck and Cathy wished Dan could get some more sleep, but when he hit the pillows, he was out.

Dan got to Wheeler in the 9th grade with better basketball fundamentals than any other player. The coaches feared they might be getting just a massive, clumsy kid to stick under the basket, all thumbs. They hated that his father kept him out of middle school ball and leagues for kids, but Dan had judo and then wrestling to deal with, and on an international level. Nobody in the Wheeler universe had to deal with anything like that, or any other high school in the area.

Wheeler already had a winning program. With Dan in place, the Johnson dynasty began. A ticket to a Wildcats game was the hottest ticket in town. Some games were played down at the Alexander Memorial Coliseum, on the Georgia Tech campus.

All sellouts. Coaches from every college you can think of.

Wheeler won four straight championships, by an average margin of 38 points. Dan and his parents had to shut their phone down if they wanted any peace.

Little time for girls, though Dan loved them, and Mr. Shy Guy even went to the prom with his 5'3" date. That was a sight. He was lonely, he later recalled, but so busy all the time that he hardly noticed it.

His parents said "Dan, is this what you want? At any time, you can walk away. We insist you keep your studies up, but sports are up to you. We don't care what everyone expects of you. The pressure. We love you and will support anything you want". But Dan wanted this. He wanted to win. He wanted to make his mark, somehow, because the words were so hard to come by. One day, he'll find his place and purpose. Right now, being admired wasn't so terrible.

# The Lion is Unleashed

To qualify for the Junior Judo Nationals, a judoka must place in a qualifying "pre national" competition. Georgia was part of the "Shufu" group, comprising most of the east coast states. By the time Dan arrived, not yet fourteen, the relatively small Judo community not only knew him, but he had traveled around and practiced against some of them here, but mostly, he practiced against top players in their 20s and even 30s. It was practice, but he was beating top players for the past year and a half.

Dan was now 7' 5" and 365 pounds. He wasn't fat and he wasn't the kind of thin people were used to seeing playing basketball. He was simply enormous. But it was more than that. He had practiced hard. His uchi mata and harai goshi were like a rocket taking off. If he wanted to, he could take you down and choke you out. He couldn't be stopped, and he was still thirteen.

He had six fights in the 16-year-old open division and won them all by ippon. "It was sort of anti-climactic" one player said. One player got out in a choke hold and simply tapped out without resisting. It was simply too dangerous.

There was no feeling "bad" for an opposing player. In fact, they all hung around after the tournament. In a way, Dan felt worse than they did.

The Jr. Nationals took place one month later, and the results were just the same. If a player stood up to Dan and tried to get a grip to throw, Dan just grabbed his belt from behind and threw him. He couldn't sweep and he couldn't

throw because he couldn't get a grip. It was evident that
most players had "something" up their sleeve from
watching the little bit of tape they may have had, or
instruction on "how to defeat a seven foot five" opponent.
The truth is, in Judo, there is always a way, but Dan's sensei
worried day and night about that and practices were
constantly about ways an opponent might win. His practice
partners would always be instructed to "try this on Dan",
"try that on Dan". Practices were designed for Dan to lose,
get swept, get thrown by a fast, low throw. Get beat in
practice so you don't get beat in competition. And they
tried everything. His sensei put a fear into him that he had
the world's biggest target on his back. If a player could
establish a grip, they would attempt a throw within a
second. But getting a grip at all was so difficult because of
his height. And once a player reached up, they were toast.
Dan was quick. He wasn't just big. He unleashed almost
five years of practice on opponents, without the benefit of
a single real competition. They would go low. What choice
did they have? Over Dan would go. Dan would get beat by
a Waza-ari or a yuko, partial points. Dan would get thrown
20 times during practice, but even simulating a throw
against him in practice was tough. Nothing ever seemed to
surprise Dan during tournaments because they had gone
over it during practice. Dan put an opponent in an arm bar
and in a few seconds, he tapped out. Dan could be heard
quietly saying something. Later, the opponent told a friend
"He said, PLEASE tap out! I don't want to break your arm.
Please!" The other player asked, "In an arrogant way?"
No", the player said. "In a pleading way. I have a feeling he

could have snapped my arm in three seconds. I believed him".

Once again, Dan won the most outstanding award and was a Junior National Champion, but it seemed so expected that there wasn't a big celebration. Dan and his dad simply went home. Most fights were over in a minute.

In 1988, the Summer Olympics were in Seoul, South Korea. Nobody seemed anxious for Dan to try and qualify as a 14-year-old. It just made no sense. The Olympics would be in Barcelona in 1992, when Dan was seventeen. He would be seen as young, but it was not unprecedented. Everyone was happy to see him develop more for the next four years, although that was a scary thought. Judo purists loved the idea of an exhibition between Johnson and Hiro Nukiyama, the two-time defending champion, but it never happened.

# Routine

In 2000, as a fifteen-year-old, Dan could compete in any Judo tournament he desired, but he was also wrestling and playing basketball. He and his dad talked ad nauseam about scheduling, also remembering that school came first.

He had three judo practices a week, two of them following basketball or wrestling practices. His Wheeler coaches staggered practice so that basketball was only 15 minutes after the end of school, at 2:15, and wrestling was 4:15-6:00. A few wrestling parents complained, but it fell on deaf ears. The answer was always the same, "The staggered practices were for the benefit of any athlete who wished to compete in both sports, but there was only one athlete who did so. Somebody mumbled "Prima donna" behind Dan's back, but the kid worked extremely hard, and the basketball players had nothing to complain about. Dan never missed a practice OR a game. He was unselfish and passed a lot. Kids had more open shots.

Dan did miss a couple of wrestling matches when schedules couldn't avoid it. Wheeler might make accommodations within their own walls, but competing schools weren't about to do it. Imagine thinking you're about to face Dan Johnson and then you win by forfeit, standing on the mat alone. Yet, for many, it was a great moment in their lives, like pitching against Babe Ruth or Barry Bonds, but even those players struck out sometimes. Dan Johnson did not.

The thought was, was that wrestling was not a team sport in the way that basketball was. Dan was not involved in his teammates' wrestling matches. He couldn't help them, but in basketball, it meant a lot more. The players seemed to understand. He was still playing for Wheeler, and the basketball team was always good.

Dan won the Senior Nationals in Judo, the wrestling state championship, and Wheeler won the basketball championship. Dan had been playing basketball for only a year, but it was a matter of outstanding coaching. Chuck was very smart, and Dan could dribble, pass, and post up. It seemed like an old story; Dan could overwhelm an opponent but first tried other methods. He could spin and dunk any time he wanted to, but before that, nobody passed the ball around more than the Wheeler Wildcats. Dan had his soft fadeaway, his spin moves, and his baby hook. Occasionally, somebody wound get a hand on the ball and the opposing crowd would go crazy. But all it usually did was take the score from 82-17 to 82-19, if even that.

One of the best instruction Dan has been at the "Big Man Camp", and he attended twice before he was even played in a real game. Dan learned how to play as a center. How to post up, pass fast to the open man. Use speed to get past another big man, rebounding techniques, and moving the ball up-court. Dan met 11 other players, all of whom were over 6'5 feet except for a female player who was 6'2". He had so much fun at these camps that he went every year and was offered free participation in his last two years, but he always paid. The head coach, a former center himself, had nighttime movie and campfire nights, which the players loved. Dan was not allowed to drink, and half the players were in college, so there was no drinking allowed, except for the three NBA players, who all seemed to have a flask of something or another. The owner of the camp said, "Look, no alcohol, so don't let me catch you, ok?" They all talked about the struggles of being so tall, and of course, nobody had it tougher than Dan.

Dan was 14, and the best college players couldn't stop him. Yes, it was because of his size, but size alone wouldn't do it. As one player said "Dude is 14 years old. I should be kicking that young white boy's ass, you know? Mopping it all OVER the floor. But here's the problem. I'm 6'10" and he towers over me. I can't move him because he's stronger than me, and I mean a lot stronger. I can't grab a rebound unless it takes a lucky bounce because he can jump higher than me. Hell, I'm a JUMPER man, but he has a two-foot head start. He's got a sweet fadeaway. No way God himself can block the damn ball because of the fade. If I push on him too hard, you know, you know, leaning on him forward, and he motions a pushing action with his hand. If I do that, he'll do this spin move and he even says he practices that all the time. He's right by me and slams it home. If I don't push and I lay back, he has a baby hook or just shoots from two feet out, or just passes off. He's constantly passing, and he finds the open man. Another guy on the team says they put music on, like Motown, and pass it all around, like the Harlem Globetrotters. If you foul him, which is hard to do, I mean you can try to shove him or step on a foot, he's a decent foul shooter and then you foul out. I'm not elbowing this guy in the ribs. Have you looked at him? Guy does martial arts on top of everything else. You gotta be crazy."

By now, there wasn't a network that hadn't done a story on him, or a university that wasn't paying attention. Dan began to get phone calls, mostly for basketball, but a few resourceful schools with solid basketball and wrestling programs figured it out very quickly.

# Wrestling for Wheeler

Dan walked into the Wheeler gym and then across the way to a small office where Glenn Cline, the wrestling coach sat. Dan's dad came because, to be fair to Dan, he wasn't a 9th grader trying out for the team. He was a 7th grader in middle school. Coach Cline was more straight forward than Coach Glasser at Lovett.

"Gentlemen, Dan here is in 7th grade. You cannot compete yet, but some schools do have 8th graders as paper of the makeup. So next year, you can compete. If you sign a waiver, which you'd have to do anyway, you can practice this fall with the team, but I need to make sure you're serious about learning the sport."

Most coaches would be salivating over Dan. Maybe Coach Cline was holding back on purpose. "Let me also get right to the point about something. Everybody knows about a seven foot thirteen-year-old. The entire state. Other states. By now, you've probably been written up by the Savannah Morning News to the Sacramento Bee. They also want to know why you're not doing what your average seven-footer does, and that's play basketball."

Chuck gritted his teeth but also smiled. "Coach, until now, that has been the elephant in the room. We have a plan for the next several years. It's Dan's plan. He wants to attend Wheeler. We live here. He knows the neighborhood kids here. If we tell you, could you keep it quiet?" "Sure, said the Coach". "Okay, Dan, you talk to the Coach."

"Well, Coach. My parents didn't want to put me out there as an athlete, not until I was older. But I learned about Judo, and I really like it. I have practiced hard for four years and they haven't let me compete. But this year, I can. I like combat sports. Grappling and throwing. I think I could do well wrestling, but it's very frustrating to sit around, go to practice and not compete. If you let me wrestle, I'll work as hard as anyone. I hate losing and my dad and others told me that I can't just rely on my size, even if I win. I need to put in the same effort as everyone else. Even more effort. I work my butt off in Judo. I would do the same here."

"But what about basketball. That takes place the same day and time as wrestling."

Dan continued, yes, sir. My parents said that basketball would be my way to scholarships and a good income, and that also had to be considered. We are shooting around at home, passing, learning about posting up and a handful of shots. Next summer we hope to find a "Big Man's Camp" I can go to, and then play basketball in the 9th grade."

"And then, you quit wrestling?" Coach Cline asked, with a bit of an attitude. "No sir, I want to do both, but I am more interested in wrestling."

"Well, Mr. Johnson", speaking to Dan, you can't always have your cake and eat it too. Do you know that expression." "Yes, sir, Dan said. My parents taught it to me. We don't want special privileges." "No, and we don't give them here at Wheeler." Dan looked down and simply said quietly, "No, sir."

"Well,", Coach Cline finally ended with "practice begins in six weeks. You are officially invited to be part of the Wildcat Wrestling team. As a 7th grader, you cannot compete, but beginning in 8th grade, you can. Let's see what happens. In the meantime, here's a little secret. We WILL be running. Endurance is important. Maybe do some light jogging but then come over to the football field early evening and start some sprints. Then maybe you won't be throwing up on the first day, like most of the kids who were eating at Krispy Kreme during the off-season."

Dan and Chuck shook Coach Buckley's hand and left.

"Dad, I liked Coach Glasser better." "Well, son", everybody is different. I promise you, Coach Cline is interested, but you look like Mr. Basketball to the world. I've tried to be honest about that. He doesn't want to get his hopes up high. Do you still want to wrestle AND keep going to Judo? Remember how far you have come in Judo, and the Jr. Nationals are in two months in Virginia. Your sensei will be making the randori harder, and on spring break, you're going up to NJ to practice against some national players."

"Dad, I can't wait for that tournament. But I want both Judo AND wrestling. And dad, I'm tired of practice and I'm tired of holding back. I could kill these guys I've been practicing against. Even the national champions. I'm tired of going 50% and they all think I'm trying my hardest." Dan said, I understand, son, and you'll get your chance.

What Chuck wouldn't tell Dan, but what he and his Sensei and others were afraid of, is that Dan Johnson was bigger, stronger, faster, and quicker than all these athletes. He had been running sprints for two years, and as far as that Lovett weightlifting session went, Chuck heard about it, and Dan was benching 460 as a 13-year-old. That number would go up. Chuck was excited but also afraid that one day Chuck would be the best in the world at Judo, maybe wrestling and basketball, who knows. Oh, screw it, Chuck knew, because he knew Dan. Dan was already shooting fifty free throws a day. He would go to big man camp. He would shoot and pass and pass and pass. He would jump and post up and beat down any opposing player. Only, Chuck couldn't say anything yet. Yes, he believed Dan would be the best these sports had ever seen if he didn't kill someone in the process.

# The Lesson

Kurt Messing was a senior heavyweight wrestler at Pope High School, just a little to the east of Wheeler. He moved with his family in the summer following his sophomore year at Philipsburg High School. His Dad worked for Delta at Newark Airport and every morning at 6:00 AM, he filled up his thermos with coffee and made the hour or longer drive east on I-78, from Philipsburg to Newark. It wasn't easy, but the family loved the town of Philipsburg, NJ, right on the border of PA and across the Delaware River from Easton. Kurt played football for the Stateliners, but his real love was wrestling. He started as a ten-year-old, winning tournaments throughout the area, and, as a sophomore, at 188 pounds, placed 4th at the state meet in Princeton, in 1988. A tenth grader placing this high put Messing in excellent company, but his family didn't celebrate "near wins", even when he was just in the 10th grade. He expected nothing less than a championship the following year, even after deciding to bulk up for 11th grade. He was very disappointed and even worried when he was told that his family was moving to Georgia, a place he only read about and saw in movies, and his initial reaction was anything but positive. He would miss the intense wrestling practices under Coach Rick Thompson, a legend in New Jersey, even the "wrestle backs", a demanding up and down style of sprints, and he'd miss hearing, "Goodnight, Irene", coming from the coach, from time to time, as he was about to pin an opponent.

Kurt's father had been given a big promotion with Delta, moving the family to Georgia. He wasn't too worried about the talent and coaching of the football team, not in Georgia. Not from everything he heard, but he was concerned about the wrestling team. Anything you look at it, he thought, it would not be like 'liners.

Kurt was surprised to see his neighborhood, in what was called "East Cobb" by the Atlanta area, to be a new and attractive place to live. Pope High School was only two years old, as compared to Philipsburg H.S., which was founded in 1871, and was one of the oldest schools in the state. It would be approximately 25 years until a new Philipsburg High School would be built.

Kurt considered his wrestling instruction to be inferior to what he had in New Jersey, but he was able to join a local "takedown" club, which allowed him to wrestle with "fresh blood", something every wrestler needs in order to get better. He also was able to sneak in a week at Jackson Valley Wrestling camp in central Jersey before heading down to Atlanta. After a not-so-good football season with the 2-year-old school, he was ready for wrestling. His plan was to win two state championships and then attend a college in Pennsylvania and wrestle there.

It didn't take long for Kurt to hear about "the 7-foot middle schooler". After all, he was the only kid to be on "The Tonight Show" with Johnny Carson. He said he was a judo player, and so Kurt just casually thought he could be a helluva wrestler, but this kid was in the 7th grade as Kurt arrived for his Junior year at Pope, so there wasn't anything to think about.

Nobody worked harder than Kurt, who at 6'4" and 275 pounds, was a beast in almost anybody's book. He was an inside linebacker and sometimes, a tight end in football. As a wrestler, he was tall, quick, and strong, and he had years of wrestling practice, so he had mastered a lot of moves. He was ready to go at Pope in that fall of 1988. He was more than ready. Kurt Messing was 34-0 and a state champ, with twenty-eight of his wins coming by pin during his junior year.

He expected no less from his senior year, but even before the season began, the buzz started. Dan Johnson, who had wrestled for a year, was entering the 8th grade and was going to be allowed to wrestle. He was 7'5" as a 14-year-old and 331 pounds, but he told a local newspaper that his goal was to bulk up to 365. He had only been lifting weights for a year and hoped to be able to put on more muscle.

A quote in the paper went as follows: "I've been wrestling for a year after five years in Judo. It's a different sport, but Judo has helped, I think, to make learning wrestling easier. I wasn't allowed to wrestle at the high school level until now and my dad just decided to keep me out of competition, but I have practiced at a lot of high schools, and even at colleges up in Ohio, where my dad is from, and at Purdue where he went to college. My aunt lives in Lebanon, Indiana, and during Christmas break I spent ten days wrestling with the Boilermakers team. That was awesome and really helped me." The reporter said, "How have you kept busy knowing you had to wait a year before wrestling." Dan continued, "Well, my coach and I have drilled, like thousands of times, different moves. We've worked at taking advantage of my natural height advantages and spent probably even more time on defensive strategies. My coach said opposing wrestlers were going to work extremely hard at ways to beat me, so we've had a lot of scenarios where the lighter, smaller wrestlers try certain moves on me that Coach feels could make me vulnerable, and I've learned to counter them." "Aren't all the wrestlers smaller?" the reporter asked. "Ha, ha", Dan said. Everybody is smaller." "And do you like that, Dan" the reporter asked? "Well, no, I hate it sometimes. I've been teased a lot, but mostly when I was younger. Now it's more of a nuisance, bending down, finding big cars to ride in." "So," the reporter asked, I guess your size and maybe a little maturity, have kept kids from teasing you. "Yes, I guess so, and when they saw I could lift a lot of weight, they began to leave me alone". "Holy, shit", thought Kurt. But Kurt could bench 320 himself. He was curious more than afraid. But still, a 14-year-old? He was already being asked about a state tournament faceoff. Pope did not meet Wheeler during the season, but post season, he likely would, unless one of them lost. Kurt did not expect to lose. The state of Georgia wrestling community was wondering what would happen with Dan, those that cared about wrestling, of course. Many were angry that Dan wasn't playing football, but he never had an interest.

Dan had wrestled for a year, so calling his first matches, "new" wasn't really accurate. Dan had wrestled a Big Ten champion at a scrimmage. He had wrestled top wrestlers that came by the Pope building, and he had wrestled at some neighboring high schools, including Lovett, with Coach Glasser. Still, he had not wrestled in an official match. He was "overripe" for a dual.

The arm drag that Dan learned at Lovett became his favorite move on his feet. He practiced it in front of a mirror. It was one of those moves that allowed for that. The arm came up like a karate chop, the wrist of the hand striking, quickly, on the same side as your opponent. Then, in a sweeping motion, you would bring the arm down with your opponent's, like a windmill, grabbing the opponent's triceps muscle as the arm went by. This gave you control of the arm. In an ideal situation, after the arm was "dragged" out of the way, you could step around your opponent, get in back, lift and take them down, but the arm drag was so versatile. Once the arm was out of the way, the legs were exposed. This allowed the offensive wrestler to perform a single of even double leg. The beauty of the arm drag was that even if your opponent resisted, you only needed a split second to expose the legs. The way to counter an arm drag was to keep your elbows in and palms up, and that was taught to all beginning wrestlers, but of course, wrestlers forget, get tired and lazy, or they're just not very good wrestlers. Dan practiced the arm drag until he could do it not only quickly, but forcefully. Opponents in practice were scared shitless of it, because it was violent, at least the way Dan did it. It put them on the defensive right away. Dan also liked to tie up and simply underhook on both sides, where he could throw his opponent down in any number of ways, with a bear hug, a move where he applied pressure on the rib cage (very painful according to practice foes), or just a leg sweep or "tai o tosh", a judo move where he throws his opponent over his leg. Once on top, Dan loved a ¾ half nelson and a far side cradle. In most cases, he couldn't be stopped, even if his opponent knew the move was coming. A few times, when an opponent just curled up. Dan simply got on top and lifted him up. His coach told him not to rely on that because he'd still go up against 300-pound wrestlers. Dan also likes arm bars, which he could slide in easily, and perform what he called a "modified" running arm bar. He had so much leverage and power from his legs, that once an arm bar was in, and the other wrist was grabbed, it was over. If his opponent curled his wrist in, he simply held it in place and rolled his opponent over. There simply was nowhere to hide. It was nearly 400 pounds. Dan's maximum height would be 8'11" during college, and 480 pounds.

All at 14 years old.

Dan finished his season at 26-0, and Kurt Messing at 28-0. Dan pinned everyone except one wrestler whose ribs Dan broke doing a bear hug. "I'm sorry, coach. I squeezed too hard." During an arm drag in his fourth match, Dan told a teammate that he wanted to lift an opponent. "Do it, man. Then slam him down". Both wrestlers laughed, but Dan meant it. He felt confident enough. Every wrestler wanted to try some kind of strategy, but so far, nothing came to close to working. This wrestler tried to tie-up, reaching well over two feet up. Exposing his torso like that, Dan could have just broken some more ribs, but instead, he pushed away, stepped back, and walked forward again. As his opponent reached out, Dan hit a brutal arm drag. The opponent, about 260, tried to fight it, but his legs were exposed, and Dan shot in, head up, and grabbed the opponent's legs from behind the knees, just as he was taught, because the legs are weaker there. Dan lifted him up like a sack of potatoes, and the guy kicked. But he was going nowhere. The crowd screamed while Dan was taking his time, planning to get an arm between his legs and gently lay him down for a pin. With dumb cries of "stop him", and "no", the even dumber ref blew his whistle and stopped the match. Dan's coach ran out to the mat. "REF, what the hell?" The other coach walked out but said nothing. He already understood. The ref, at first said nothing, then grasping for words, finally said "POTENTIALLY DANGEROUS". "What are you talking about?" Dan's coach yelled. He wasn't hurting him in any way. The other coach, whom Dan's coach had known for a few years, still said nothing. The ref said, "COACH, dangerous situation. That was a slam in progress." The coach motioned for Dan to come to the center, which was usually not done. "Dan, were you going to slam your opponent?" Dan answered, "No, coach, A slam is lifting and returning an opponent to the mat with unnecessary force. A slam is illegal, and I can't get him in a good pinning position that way, anyway, so I was going to lower him very slowly. The way I've done it practice about a hundred times." Both the referee and coaches were far more surprised at Dan's articulation. The opposing coach said, "Rich, this kid's 14?" "Alright the ref said, regardless, it was potentially dangerous. Back to the match." It hardly mattered, because Dan pinned his opponent 35 seconds later, and without a slam.

Kurt and his Pope coach discussed ways to beat Dan Johnson, like any wrestler that didn't simply resign himself to losing. They watched videos. Dan was coached well. You couldn't tie up because Dan was too tall. Anybody dumb enough to try would be down and pinned in 30 seconds or less. He kept his long arms in, elbows tucked, palms up, as if it was drilled into him over and over and over again. It was. If you shot on his legs, his hands where there before you got close, and he loved a ¾ nelson, which was a miserable thing to get caught in. Dan's coach discovered that an ankle pick could be a great strategy against a very tall man, so they practiced against it...a lot. Or a low ankle single leg, but way, Dan was taught to use his arms if an opponent shot. Since all were well over 200 lbs., they rarely did that anyway. Most were used to tying up at that weight, and they could even get to Dan's neck. In some ways, it would be better to weigh 175 pounds than a heavyweight. Dan, on the other hand, was trim and fast, and even at 14, 100 pounds heavier and stronger than anybody he wrestled in high school.

One night, Kurt's coach was putting his two-year-old daughter to sleep, and on top of the small bed, was a pinwheel he bought at the dollar store a few weeks earlier. His little girl was asleep, and his coach blew on the pinwheel, it circled around, the ends and their pretty colors circling around. But then he noticed something else. The very center didn't move much at all.

The next day, the coach had a talk with Kurt. They stood on the mat. "Kurt, you've played a lot of football. A lot of it at linebacker. How did you, to use wrestling terms, take them down?" Kurt looked a little confused, then he said, "You mean, I tackled them, coach?" "Did you always tackle them by the legs? Wasn't there some other way you tackled them?" "Well, Kurt said, "Sometimes I got them by the midsection because they were pumping their legs pretty hard." "This guy, Johnson, he's got long arms, long legs, you can't get to them, but nobody has tried to tackle him, and that's what I'm gonna call it. Tackle him 100% around his stomach. Get your arms around him, grab your forearm, and to drive him down, you're going to get one leg behind one of his legs, because you're not going to get both legs. Not on this guy. Does this make sense to you? You probably have one shot. He's a smart kid. I've watched him a bunch of times, now. So have you."

So, Kurt practiced. He had three weeks. His strategy was to take two or three steps forward, grab Dan's arms then yank them down. That will do nothing except throw Dan "off the scent". Take a step forward and then "bamm" like a freight train shoot to the mid-section. If Dan was aware, he would have his arms right there, but there was one chance."

As expected, both wrestlers easily qualified for the state tournament. Dan pinned everybody along the way, except for one wrestler who defaulted. Dan wasn't even sure what was wrong with him. Kurt pinned three opponents and then won his final 14-4, a major decision.

It was time for Dan and Kurt to wrestle, in the 285 class, the final match of the state tournament, and there was a big crowd from Pope. Bigger than Wheeler. In fact, there was a big crowd, period. The curiosity was tremendous, and there was an overflow crowd at the Macon Coliseum.

Both wrestlers lined up. The ref blew his whistle and Dan took a step forward. So did Kurt. Kurt put his arms up, and Dan was a second from powering him down in a bear hug, but then suddenly, Kurt moved back, and from this move it made him look frightened, but that was the plan. Suddenly, Kurt lunged at Dan and grabbed him around his midsection. His midsection couldn't push back, couldn't sprawl. Dan fell straight backward onto his back. The crowd noise was just deafening. People were wondering aloud if Dan Johnson would be scored on, if he decided to wrestle for four years, but here he was, on his back! However, getting Dan Johnson to a pinning position was an entirely different story. Despite the shock, Dan was an excellent student. One of the first things he learned was, if you were taken down, "get onto your stomach", "get onto your base." Yes, Kurt scored two points, but Dan stood up, just as he had learned, hands on Kurt's wrists, pushing down, his hips out. Frankly, it was more like a simple stand up. Dan stood up and got a point unopposed.

"DAN!" his coach said. "Get angry." Dan was surprised, and this moment of weakness would soon be dealt with. In fact, Kurt Messing had just given Dan a gift, a valuable lesson in eliminating, forever, a possible way to beat him. Dan WAS angry, and embarrassed. There was no shame in a 14-year-old giving up two points to an 18-year-old defending state champ, but Dan was, nevertheless.

Dan approached Kurt, underhooked his arms and pulled him down, and then a "pancake" move, onto Kurt's back. It wasn't so much a move as it was a simple, brutal, "yank". Kurt went down and was pinned in ten seconds, and the match was over. It was like slapping a grizzly bear across the face. You might get away with it once, but then you were gonna die.

Dan won his first Georgia State Wrestling tournament. Kurt would normally be so upset that he had been known to cry, except that he hadn't lost since he was in New Jersey. He shook his head as if to say, "Well, what can you do." The opposing coach smiled for the same reason.

After the tournament was over and the mats were being rolled up, Kurt came up to Dan and said, "Dan, we thought all season on ways I could beat you. I got that one move in and now nobody will ever be able to do it to you again. You are something else, and you're not just big, you're a damn good wrestler. Look, I'm graduating and I'm going to Slippery Rock up in Western Pennsylvania, to wrestle. I'd like to work out with you. I can still help you and I know you can help me. I can't be too upset losing to you." "Sure," said Dan. I was worried about you, too, all season. You're the state champ." "Well, said, Kurt, I was".

So, Kurt and Dan worked out all summer, when Dan wasn't practicing both Judo three times a week and shooting around the driveway. He would be going to "Big Man Camp" for basketball for a week, and visiting his aunt in Indiana, and Dan and Kurt got friendly enough so that he went to Indiana, too, and they worked out with a bunch of college wrestlers, both in West Lafayette and around the Indianapolis area. Nobody, it seemed, wanted to wrestle Dan in a dual meet, but everybody, it also seemed, wanted to practice with him. That was the place to try new things.

Kurt and Dan stayed friends for a long time, but never wrestled with each other again. By the time Dan was a high school senior and already on the world stage, Kurt was finishing his degree at Slippery Rock, where he eventually became an accountant. He had a respectable college career, qualifying for the NCAA tournament twice and being the Pennsylvania State Athletic Conference runner-up his senior year.

# The Final Skit

Ever since Johnny Carson announced that May 1992 would be his final month, after thirty amazing years on the airs, every celebrity wanted to get on the show, so Dan was surprised when he got a call from Johnny himself (instead of his producer).

"Well, hi, Dan, it's Johnny Carson". Dan couldn't believe it. It had been over a year since his second skit with Johnny, Billy, and Betty White. "Hi, Mr. Carson, how are you?" "Well, Dan, very busy. You know, the show is wrapping up in May, and we're trying to really go out on a high note. Say, we loved having you in those skits. You know, you were just meant to be a nice, interesting human nature story, but Billy loves you and we were talking recently, and he came up with a really good idea. You're young, but you know back in the days of vaudeville and some of the old movies, there were some well-known pie fights." "Oh, sure," Dan said. "Laurel and Hardy, Our Gang." "That's right, that's right", Johnny said. "You really are an interesting young man." He gave out his well-known chuckle that comedians would often try to copy. "Well, we've got an idea for an epic pie fight, on a smaller scale, of course, but we need you for it." "Well, of course," Dan said. That would be a blast." "We're still working on the cast. It could really be something special. My producer will call you in about a week when we've got the details and dates figured out. I think we'll want you out a day in advance for some rehearsal. This one will be a little more complex, but you'll do just fine. You'll be with pros."

Dan was excited and got his call about a week and a half later. The show would take place in April, about a month before Johnny's last taping, on May 22, 1992.

Dan went through an hour-long rehearsal and couldn't believe his eyes when he saw who showed up. He was nervous, but, as in the first two skits, he had the smallest line, but this time, he had some "stunts' to do. During the rehearsal, there were sponges used as "pies" with whipped cream on top, because the actors had to get used to wiping the cream from their eyes. There was expectation, especially with the surprise characters, that a bit of improvisation would occur.

Dan was so excited before he reached Burbank that he told his Principal at Wheeler, who announced it during home room. All the kids tried unsuccessfully to get the story from him, and even the Atlanta Journal Constitution put it on the front page of the "Living" section. "Marietta's own Mountain Man, Dan Johnson, to help Johnny Carson say farewell."

The show began with Johnny discussing news of the day, which included that month's conviction of Manuel Noriega, and then sat down with Ed. Johnny talked about the last show coming May 22, with all the surprises, "and that includes tonight. You'll all remember the great fun we've had with the Mighty Carson Art Players, with Billy Barty, and into skits now, our very tall high school friend, Dan Johnson. Well, right after these messages, we will perform for you our final installment of the Mighty Carson Art Players, with Billy, Dan, and some other surprise cast members. Don't go away, we'll be right back. Doc, take us out."

The show returned from the commercial break, and as usual, Ed would be all alone on the couch, announcing the skit. "And now, for the last time, please give a hand for the Mighty Carson Art Players". The crowd went crazy. Some brief music started and

107

there was Johnny in his used car salesman suit and corny fake mustache. "Honest Sam Sanderson here for Sam's Used but Not Abused Cars." The audience was already laughing and applauding. "We're back again to remind you that you'll always get a very big deal here at Sam's, and to prove it, I've again invited my nephew from Topeka" Dan's first line was one word. "Omaha". "Does it matter, kid?" was Johnny's response.

Well 20 seconds later, an angry Billy Barty walked out, pie in hand. "Hey, kid, I'm tired of you taking away my livelihood." Behind the camera, a man with a cue card was shaking it at Dan, but he handled it like a pro. "Well, I'm ready for you time, too." Dan rolls out a dessert loaded with cream pies. "Well, I brought my three brothers to make this fair." Our walked Robin Williams, Tim Conway, and Jonathan Winters, and the crowd went crazy and stood up. All three took turns, mostly improv, and all three were on their knees, down to Billy's size. Eventually, everybody was covered in cream pies. To end the skit, a bikini-clad Betty white, also in the last skit, walked out, holding a script, yelling. "Hey! I'm not even written into this skit like I was told I would be." On cue, everybody throws a pie at Betty, and Doc cued the closing music. It was a big hit, and the audience stood, to show their appreciation of having six legends on the stage all together (Dan wasn't one of those six).

The show over, and the skit a huge success, Dan and Billy went out to dinner, to the famous Canter's Deli on Fairfax, because both Billy and Dan liked pastrami sandwiches. As usual, Dan and Billy got into an interesting discussion about competing in the world as "unique" people.

Billy started, "Be confident but not cocky. You and are oddities, like it or not, good, or bad. It is your job to make the public see past your size. It isn't easy but you're young and you can establish this from the start. Of course, your young age will bring naysayers, but that's normal. What's not normal is you and me, kid, and especially you.

"Well, I don't understand how I'm supposed to be that way, Billy". "I know, but it'll come to you if you practice." "How do I start?" Dan asked. "Well, kill 'em with kindness, kid. Smile, be polite but stand tall. Can ya stand tall, kid?" "Yeah, that's the only part I've got down.

Well, he'll, kid, you're still 16, but you're gonna grow up fast. You've got a big future if you play your cards right and frankly, it'll be hard for you to avoid. But smile, and hey, shake my hand" "What?" Dan asked. "Yeah, I'll explain." Billy retracted his hand like it was hit with a bolt of electricity. Oh, no, Billy said. That's what we call a wet fish handshake." "But I don't want to hurt anyone," Dan explained." "I hear you can bench press hundreds of pounds already," Billy said. "Yeah, a few hundred or so," Dan said, nonchalantly. "Well, you'll get stronger. Gonna be scary kid, but that's not what a handshake is all about." "It's not?" "No" Dan explained. "It's about self-assurance. Too strong, you're a jerk, but too weak, you're weak of mind. I want you to give me a firm handshake. One anybody can handle but firm. And I mean a firm handshake to women, too. I knew a gal who would form her entire opinion of you, for life, if you have a wet fish handshake.

"What happened to her?" "I married her! Just kidding, she was too tall for me, so I had to let her down gently," Billy joked. "Really?" "Honestly, kid, I know you're only 16, but you're gonna have to get a little more worldly."

"Well, kid, It's all show biz. It's my trade, and one way or another, I have a feeling it's gonna be part of your world, too, and you're gonna have to be tough enough to survive that.

You see kid, I'm a dwarf. No kidding. The world knows that, but now what do I have? You see what I'm saying, Dan? Dan realized Billy was getting serious because he was usually referred to as "kid". I decided early on two things. One, I was a dwarf. I like to say little person. You know that. Not a damn thing in the world I can do to change that. Just like you. I realized that I could make a living I, just maybe, as an actor, and I was going to be placed in dwarf role. Wasn't any way I would be standing next to Lauren Bacall.

Now, I could go off in the corner and cry. See how far that'll get you in life, or I could live life on my terms. I'm not a funny dwarf. I'm a funny man who just happens to be a dwarf. Let that sink in. Are you going to be a super tall basketball player, or a talented player who is even better because they're tall? I honed my craft. I studied, and that's what you need to continue to do. I have in you, kid."

Dan always felt better talking to Billy. All that confidence in that little body.

# Moving Along

High School years for Dan were a blur, but about as exciting for a school as can be.

After big man camp, where the coaches predicted that Dan would be "unstoppable", he started practicing with the Wheeler team. The coach put together what would be the classic post-up strategy that Dan would use for the rest of his basketball career. Post-up, pass to the open man, get the ball back, and if it was there, take the shot, if not, and you needed to, take it anyway. When all else failed, or when you wanted to, take it to the rim.

Dan couldn't be stopped, and by the time was in the 10th grade, Dan was 7'5" and 365 pounds, but what made him special was that he was fast, he was strong, and he had a great shot. He didn't need to slam any home, but occasionally, he did it to prove a point. Maybe he was grabbed, elbowed, or stepped on. It almost never stopped him and often resulted in a 3-point play.

In wrestling it was worse, or better, depending on whether you were talking about Dan or his opponent. He wrestled in the 285-pound class, so 90% of the wrestlers had a similar build, like a refrigerator. Some were surprisingly strong and the ones that reached the state tournament, stronger, quicker, more skillful, but at the high school level, Dan was much better than all of them, even without his height. Dan had been going to camps up north, practicing his moves, and always, always looking for ways an opponent might trick him, fool him, take him down. His opponents were too short to tie-up. If they would shoot, which few this size could do well, Dan had his amazingly long arms ready to sprawl, or usually, just stop them in their tracks, and he would usually do a "shrug and spin" move to get behind and score two points, and then it was almost always over in seconds, because Dan could turn anybody over. Dan went 127-0, over four years, and the only reason he wasn't the most valuable wrestler his senior season was, the coaches that voted for it surmised, is that it was a foregone conclusion that Dan would win, so the award went to a lighter wrestler that didn't even wrestle varsity until his junior year and made continuous improvement.

No matter how hard Dan practiced, to improve, he had detractors that saw him as a huge body that others simply could not handle. His spin moves, his shooting, his cradles and arm drags, many simply saw him as a freak of nature and not good for any of the sports he participated in. It was no challenge for him, and too difficult even for the most seasoned, successful wrestlers. Just look at Kurt Messing. A big kid at 6'4", but for 285 pounds, not that unusual. A kid from New Jersey who had wrestled in leagues since he was little, most of his young life. A winner up north and in the south, college material, but against Dan Johnson, helpless.

In Judo, a sport never even discussed at his school, and only among the "judo community", Dan was no less successful. At thirteen, he began competition and won the Jr. Nationals in the 16-year-old age group. Then again, at 14. He was so dominant that even though he could have continued to compete as a Junior, up to age 16, he was "asked" to no longer compete in Jr. competitions, so it was on to the men. When Dan was ages 15-17, he won the men's national titles at the Senior Nationals.

The Barcelona Olympics took place in 1992, and Dan won gold in both judo and wrestling. He didn't seem to have much trouble transitioning from folkstyle to freestyle. He loved to underhook and throw. He incorporated a gut wrench into his routine to gain points, which he could do repeatedly, and when he started on the bottom, if he hadn't already pinned his opponent, he would spread out his body and nobody could turn him, and then the ref put them back on their feet. Even in the gold medal match, against an Iranian, his opponent said through an interpreter, "he toyed with me, I could do nothing." That was the comment heard repeatedly. Dan wasn't only big; he was skillful and knew how to use his size to punish his opponent.

He continued to worry about judo, with the importance on speed and balance, but like the other sports, Dan worked on potential problems and had a defense strategy. Still, he was so feared for his harai-goshi, choke holds or arm bars, that opponents were the ones on defense. His main hip throw, his harai goshi, he used often in combination with an osoto gari or with a Russian grip. He had an explosive uchi mata, which was an inner thigh through. When done well, he could often throw his opponent high above him, and it was spectacular. He was so tall that he could easily grab his opponents' belt in the back.

Hiro Nukiyama was the current world champion, two years running. He had studied Dan extensively and was large and explosive. But with Dan, he overextended himself, reaching up quickly for a grip, and Dan anticipated his move. Instead of reaching onto Nukiyama's back from up high, when Nukiyama reached up, Dan reached down, to his waist, and in a second, threw Nukiyama for an ippon, ending the match and giving Dan the gold. Just a brief interview on tv, the match shown at 2:00 in the morning, and he was done.

As a seventeen-year-old, Dan had won a wrestling and judo gold medal, but it did not create many waves. He was in the 11th grade, and it wasn't that he was an unknown, but the public was awaiting his college decision already, almost a year away.

# The Decision

"Good afternoon, everybody, this is a special edition of Basketball Tonight with Ed Simmons, and as always, the Phantom from Fayetteville, the Bud Walton Wonder, Mr. Hog, Marvin, "Double M" Middleton."

"Okay, first of all, man, I don't like 'Mr. Hog'. I led my team in assists my junior year." "Well obviously, then, you don't understand the reference," joked Ed. "No, I get it, man."

"Anyway, we are here for an extraordinary event, the first time our show has been coming to you from a high school gym, where Dan Johnson, the 'Wildcat Wonder from Wheeler' is about to announce his college choice, from a packed house here in the Atlanta suburb of Marietta."

"That's right, and speculation is running high, as Johnson has his choice of any program in America but has remained relatively silent on his leanings." That's right, Double M, but we do have this short video from 1991, from station WXIA here in Atlanta."

"So, Dan, you're getting calls from colleges all over the country, and you're still just a sophomore. Where are you leaning", said the local reporter.

"Well," Dan said. There are a few factors. Of course, we want a strong academic environment", Dan said. "Also, and hopefully, a school with both a strong basketball as well as a strong wrestling program. People forget about that. I think I also want to expand my horizons a little and live in another area of the country. My mom is from Alabama and my dad, from Ohio."

That got all the reporters, players, fans, and prognosticators betting. A great deal said that the Big Ten was where Dan would land. Many strong programs all around. It was hard to pin down Johnson, because he visited Purdue (his dad's alma mater), Ohio State, Michigan, Michigan State, Iowa, Iowa State, and Indiana. He visited Arizona State because he had such high regard for Bobby Douglas, who then switched to Iowa State, so many people were guessing that Dan would pick the Cyclones. It was good enough for Dan Gable. But aside from the "Big Man Camp", it went almost unnoticed that in the tenth grade, Dan went to the University of Michigan basketball camp for a week. Still, Purdue was a sentimental favorite and as solid an academic institution as you can get. Some dark horses included Kentucky and Duke, great basketball schools, but the southeast did not have a strong wrestling presence.

The chants started "Dan, Dan, Dan, Dan". He really had no nickname. Not yet. He sat at a microphone, wishing he could be anywhere else. At exactly 7:30 PM, he was instructed to speak into the mic. God, he hated this.

"Umm, thank you everybody. First, I just wanna say how great it has been to be a Wheeler Wildcat." Cheers erupted from the stands. Four state titles in a row are pretty cool." More cheers. "Thanks to my coaches and fellow players." "C'mon, Dan! Somebody shouted, and the crowd laughed. "Go Dawgs," and they laughed again, only because this was Georgia, but Dan already said he wanted to try playing in another part of the country, and wrestle, so another UGA basketball prospect was lost.

Dan hated speaking, so the anticipation didn't last long. "I just want to say that there are so many great colleges and coaches, and I want to thank them all for their interest in me", Dan read from a prepared document, "but after careful consideration and discussions with my parents, I have decided to attend the University of Michigan", Dan finally said, and then added, "Go Blue", Dan reached into a bag and put on the familiar blue cap with large maize "M". The crowd cheered, mainly because the decision had been made. Basketball loyalties in the crowd were mixed, so there was not really a great feeling of excitement or disappointment. It wasn't a football decision because that could have caused a near riot, and as for wrestling, many would have thought, "what is that?"

So, just as quickly as the fans and lights went up, they came down and dispersed.

The scene in Atlanta was relatively philosophical. The scene in Ann Arbor was anything but.

The huge headline on the cover of the Michigan Daily summed up the feelings of Wolverine Fans:

**"DAN CHOOSES MICHIGAN!!!!**

The Johnson era begins".

# PART TWO

# Ann Arbor and The Wolverines

# The Name

Dan arrived on campus, and it was a circus atmosphere from the start, even though the campus was getting ready for football season. First things, first. Saturdays at "The Big House" were something to see.

Dan couldn't go anywhere without stares, even though he got nothing but good wishes, as he "setup shop", aka his dorm area on South Quad, take in the beautiful campus in the fall, and stumble into popular places like Blimpy Burger and Pinball Pete's. Still, he was concerned about living up to the hype, and began to lose some sleep thinking about it. His parents told him to stay in shape, as working up a good sweat was always good for that, and to trust in his abilities. "Work hard, and everything will fall into place. Oh, and don't forget to pick up a book occasionally." He got lots of stares and smiles from the girls, but it really didn't differ than the guys. People didn't seem to know what to do with him. He was an oddity of sorts, and while we went out for a beer or burger with some guys from the dorm, he kept pretty much to himself. Life wasn't much different in Ann Arbor than it had been in Marietta. Dan just didn't fit in. He felt he would be liked if he performed. That would be the determining factor. What about the fact that he knew virtually every line from "Blazing Saddles", tons of movie lines, and jazz. Wasn't every 18-year-old starting college in 1993 like that? Dan was a nice guy, and he couldn't grasp what a "cool" guy once told him in Marietta. "You're too nice. Girls don't want nice. They want bad boys. Treat a girl nicely and she'll dump all over you. Treat a girl like shit and she'll love you, forever." Dan just couldn't do it. He'd wait for the girl that wanted to be treated nicely. Was that such a strange concept?

Dan wanted to be Dean Martin. Dean would walk around the UM Campus, not caring if you gave a damn about him or not, and the women would be flocking around him. Dino Paul Crocetti, an Italian from Steubenville, Ohio, could play a cowboy and pull it off.

The football team had an up and down season, finishing 8-4. They beat the hated Ohio State Buckeyes, but lost to that other rival, the Spartans of Michigan State. Dan did make friends with quarterback Brian Griese, who, unlike Dan's big fanfare, was a walk-on, but he was the son of celebrated Miami Dolphins QB Brian Griese. Also, both of their dads attended Purdue, which gave them some things to talk about.

Eventually, practice began. They were brutal. Welcome to Big Ten basketball. The coach had a plan to use Dan in the best way possible. He still couldn't believe his good fortune. It was the first and probably only time that the wrestling team moved its practices to 7:00 PM so that the new guy could practice basketball from 4:00 to 6:00. If anyone minded, they bitched to themselves, because Dan made this, not any other "perk", a condition of his attendance at the school. It also would save any school the embarrassment of this headline:

"School walks away from certain championship seasons due to a scheduling conflict"

Dan would be used to his fullest capacity, but it really wasn't anything new. The truth is that in the paint, Dan was unstoppable. He spent hundreds of hours practicing, and went to "big man" camp, a short turnaround jumper, a spin move, a baby hook, though none of it was really necessary. Dan could retrieve any high pass, out of reach for anyone else, and slam it home, every time. Again, every time.

But he and the coach wanted unity on the team. On a team like Michigan, every player was good. Every player had been a star in high school, "Mr. Basketball" in some instances, and it would be a very unpleasant place indeed if Dan just took it home on every possession. That wasn't necessary at all.

During his recruitment season, a circus in itself, Dan had mini strategy sessions with coaches. At Michigan, the message was simple enough. "Dan, you'll make every player on the team better. Yes, we will center the offense around you, but you'll be double and even triple teamed. We will practice over and over having you locate the open man. Everyone will get open shots and see their averages and field goal percentages go up. If we need a quick basket, we'll go to you. If we're up comfortably, you'll rest, backups will get their minutes. We'll have "with Dan" plays and "without Dan" plays, and we'll win. That's what it's about Dan. Winning. Come to Ann Arbor and we'll execute the plan. And Dan, it's a big school. The wrestling team, well you know about them. We also have a drama club and other things. There's more to life than basketball, Dan. You can find other things here, and we, the team, coaches, and students, will support. But of course, you'll work your ass off for me. There's no way around that. You're going to have the world's biggest target on your back and many in the basketball world will want to see you fail. You're not exactly an underdog, if you haven't heard.

It was the first official practice. A lot of running, stretching, passing drills. Not much shooting. The coach's speech, which didn't mention Dan by name, but the evidence was clear.

"Gentlemen, this is Michigan basketball. We have a winning tradition, and we have high standards. We stand for excellence, and I'm not just talking about what happens here at Crisler (the UM arena) but in many areas, especially in academics. I don't care if you think you'll be an NBA all-star, when you step onto this campus and when you wear the Blue and Maize, you represent everybody ever associated with this school, today, yesterday, and especially tomorrow. I expect you to work hard in the classroom as well as on the court. I don't care if you're 5'11" or 8'11", it applies to all of you, equally." At that point, a few eyes looked over to Dan and some smiles appeared.

Some more running, drills, and finally, a shoot around, and then the assistant said "alright gentlemen, hit the showers and be back here, center court, dressed and ready to go, at 4:00, and that doesn't mean 4:01, unless you enjoy running stairs after practice. And, as a throwaway, decided to add, "even for you wrestlers". There was, no doubt, a little cynicism. It wasn't lost on Dan. He would have to earn respect all over again. After all, he hadn't done anything for the Michigan Wolverines except sow jealousy among their rivals and build up expectations to ridiculous amounts. This was not The Tonight Show, or the friendly confines of the Wheeler gym. No doubt, they were beyond excited to have Dan in Ann Arbor, but the basketball world expected nothing less than three straight championships. Nobody in their right mind expected him there for a fourth.

The young men hit the showers, and Charles Winfield, from Detroit's Cass Tech, started up.

"Dan Johnson. Shiiit. Hey man, let me see that Johnson". Everybody laughed out. Doesn't look so special to me. Looks kind of pale. Like one of them long vanilla pops the "Tasty Freeze Man" would have in his truck. Of course, the extra-large one. The guys started howling. Man, what kind of name is Dan Johnson? You need a nickname. "I have one," said Dan. "The big man" Again, everybody laughed. "Hell, said Markel Smith" another freshman, a big man needs a big name. Markel had just come off a state title with Detroit St. Martin dePorres, a powerhouse. "How about Mountain Man". Everybody booed. "Hell no," said Charles. My uncle went to the Grand Canyon. He said he never saw anything so big, so mighty, so special. Hey big man, from now on "you the Canyon". Everybody laughed again, but then another player yelled out. "THE CANYON. The C Man". It took off, the screams echoing in the showers. "Then C Man, the C Man". Dan said out loud "C for Championships". It got silent, then loud again. "The C Man. championships." No longer in unison, but all over the place. "Hey C Man, you gonna deliver for us". Dan

123

uncharacteristically yelled "Damn right!!" And everybody yelled in satisfaction and agreement.

The C Man was born.

Anyone will tell you that some of the best bonding moments in sports comes in the shower room. So, we're told.

It briefly crossed Dan's mind, that "Mountain" indeed, was different than a canyon. A canyon was a large, deep crevice formed by perhaps millions of years of water breaking down a mountain until what remained was a deep cut of land, and usually a body of water. It could indeed be spectacular, as Markel's uncle discovered. Except you didn't scale a canyon. You went far down. Is that what Dan would be? Would he be a majestic mountain, soaring to great heights, or a huge canyon, a spectacular failure? The players would never come to this minor yet cerebral distinction, but it made Dan think. The world was expected of him. At 18, he was a two-time Olympic champion, but not in basketball. This, he felt, was a step-up. Michigan basketball. He was already being hailed, but in East Lansing and Columbus, Bloomington, Westwood, Lexington, Lawrence, Durham, and Chapel Hill, they couldn't wait to see him fall. Into a deep canyon.

Billy was right. Being tall would never be enough. What was inside of him? He may have proved that on the mat in Barcelona, but now there's was a challenge, and the expectations were big.

# Showtime

It was the first game, and while it wasn't a conference game that was three weeks away, it was one of the biggest games in school history, and everyone knew why.

Practices were closed from the beginning, with everyone from the networks to student media crews frustrated at not getting some inside scoop on how they were going, and most importantly, whether Dan Johnson was the real deal. Everyone had seen the high school footage, with Dan Johnson, a man against young boys. As monstrous as he was, he was nimble, he was strong, with arms reported to be 21" in size, yet he seemed, if not slim, then just the right size. His height made his arms and torso seem just slightly longer than average. Certainly, there were football players who had arms that seemed larger, yet by taking a tape measure to them, the numbers everywhere would astound. It was no wonder that Dan needed a limo or perhaps a bus anywhere he went. His height was so shocking that perhaps only his competitors realized that he was massive all over.

The only thing that escaped the press was the nickname credited to guard Charles Winfield, and that name was "Canyon". That was about to change.

"Hi, this is Kelly Hoffman with the Michigan Daily, and we're outside the men's basketball locker room speaking with Sophomore Guard Charles Winfield. Charles how are your practices coming so far, and what can you tell us about Dan Johnson's acclimation. How is he coming along?" "Well, Coach says we can't make any comments on the team. That's all I can say" Hoffman, doing what any aspiring journalist would do, wasn't going to take "no" so easily. "Well, Charles, is Dan as dominant as he was in High School in Georgia? Do you anticipate him starting at center next week?" Charles smiled in his east-going way. "Ha, ha! You tryin' to get me benched? I can't say nothing about the team, nothing about who's going to start and nothing about the C, or any other player." Charles immediately realized that he probably shouldn't have let even that slip, although Coach wouldn't care about that, maybe.

"C"? Charles, what or who is C?"
Charles pumped out his chest now. The cat was now out of the bag, never, ever to return. "Oh, well that's Dan's nickname, and it came from me. I coined it. History needs to remember that. It came from Charles Winfield." "But C? Why C?" "Well, no, not "C", Charles explained. C is short for CANYON. My Uncle Louis? He went to the Grand Canyon and came back saying that it was enormous and the most amazing thing he had ever seen, so we, no I decided that from now on, Dan Johnson would be the Canyon, the C Man!" "Wow!" Lisa said. Well, Wolverine fans, you heard it here. Let's get the Crisler Center pumped up for the CANYON and this much-anticipated 1993-94 Wolverine team. Something tells me we're going to hear this word, is it Canyon, C Man, C or all three, a lot for the foreseeable future. With that kind of endorsement, gag order or not, the confidence must be running very, very high in the Wolverine's locker room and on the court. This is Lisa Hoffman, talking Michigan basketball and the Canyon, the C Man, for the Daily Michigan. Go Blue!"

"Oh, shit", thought Charles Winfield, slipping away.

126

Charles Winfield reported into Coach Bill Cummings' office. "Charles, what did I say about not speaking with reporters?" "Now coach, I told that girl, those were my exact words, that you told us not to say anything." "I saw it, but do you see how things can happen? In another moment you'd be handing her the play book." Cummings smiled because the only thing Charles did was divulge Dan Johnson's new nickname, which was the team's doing anyway. The Coach remembered what a pretty girl could do to a young man, or an older one, for that matter. Besides, if the school thought they were fooling anyone, that Dan Johnson would sit on the bench for the season, that the entire world hasn't been watching him develop for the last four years, and his talent, then Michigan wasn't a great academic institution after all. And they were.

"Charles, it's going to be a crazy season and I'm glad you're here. Just be careful. I'm telling everybody that. Now get out of here," he said with a half-smile. Charles wasn't in trouble after all, because Bill Cummings knew that the circus was coming to Ann Arbor, fast.

Michigan was playing Cleveland State, who had a fine 22-6 record the prior year in the Mid-Continent Conference. With or without an appearance by Dan Johnson, Michigan was favored by a comfortable margin, a 16-point favorite, but these first games can result in some upsets, as the restless teams move from daily scrimmages to real competition. Cleveland State would be no pushover.

Two days before the game, Cummings sat in the office of Athletic Director Frank Furris. Furris was the man at the helm of a large, demanding Big 10 University, accustomed to winning teams across the board. Basketball was only second to football in terms of exposure, and winning teams translated into larger enrollment and just as important, larger alumni financial support. Furris knew that it was the careful, yet steady relationship Bill Cummings developed with Dan Johnson and his Wheeler coach that resulted in Johnson being in a Michigan uniform.

"Well, Bill? Surviving", Furris asked, with a definite smile on his face. The anticipation and pressure were enormous, on both men, on the players, on the school, naturally, on Dan Johnson, and even on the state of Georgia. There was even a WSB special recently called "Can Dan Johnson put Georgia Basketball on the map? Of course, it was referring to the state, not the University of Georgia, though Vern Fleming was a very fine NBA player still in the league and a former Bulldog, and Bobby Cremins of the GA Tech Yellow Jackets took the team to the Sweet 16 during the prior year. Regardless, neither team was expected to be in the hunt for Dan. For one thing, he wanted to play out of state, and his relationships, from visits to Wheeler Games, and especially to the many camps Johnson attended, plus the recruiting reputations of certain coaches, and just through interviews and speculation, pointed to a short list of traditional powerhouses, and Michigan never left that list. At times, speculation and rumors had him at Kentucky, Duke, North Carolina, and UCLA, but the Maize and Blue won the Dan Johnson sweepstakes, and they were now about to see if it would be anything like the skeptics said. It seemed that several people in Ann Arbor were walking around with Tums in their pockets.

128

"Frank, it's like I told you last week. It's almost too good to be true. We always said that this kid's attitude was good. Some of that was for the media, of course, but we underestimated this kid. Great parents, humble, amazing work ethic, willing to learn, great coaching, an amazing grasp of the fundamentals, six weeks at the Big Man camp. He's even got the other players, kids from tough neighborhoods, calling me, and the other coaches, sir. I'm pinching myself but I'm also scared shitless."

Frank smiled, "Hey, I hear ya." The Board of Trustees is spending money they don't have yet. Enrollment is supposed to jump to a record level next year because of a basketball player. At least that's the theory. " Furris asked, eagerly. "The play. How's the play?"

Bill said, "Look, it's no secret of how our offense is gonna run. But you know, everybody knew Nolan Ryan was going to throw a fastball, and he threw it anyway, with a whole lot of success." The ball gets fed to Dan in the post, and that son of a gun would rather pass than shoot. My biggest challenge has been to get him to shoot when the shot's there, same problem his coaches had at Wheeler, but hell, Frank, the shot is ALWAYS there. He's unstoppable, but we pass, and we pass, back to Dan, to the corner, to the perimeter. The guy's quick like a cat. He gets open but he can just as easily go right over the top. High percentage shots. Also, we know what's coming, and I've got him taking free throws for 30 minutes every practice. He's up around 84%, and he likes to run our run backs." "What's a runback, Coach?" Frank wanted to know. "Well, Cummings says, we lie the players down under one basket, on their backs. Then we blow a whistle, they must get up and sprint to the other basket and lie down on the line. They get about a second until we blow the whistle again, and they must get up and sprint back to the other side, and lie down again, and back and forth it goes. It's rough on your stamina and rougher on your legs. They just burn like hell, and this kid seems to like it. NOBODY likes run backs, Frank. I said to him. Johnson, you look like you're enjoying this, and he says, no coach, I hate it but 'no pain, no gain.'"

"What about on defense?" Furris asked. "He's disruptive", Cummings said. He'll block shots without fouling. He doesn't have to leave his feet, so it's all ball. We've been doing "recovery drills" all based on retrieving a blocked ball and getting a man down court. We've put a lot of time into it. The guy's moan about it, we do it so often, but a blocked shot means an errant ball, and we want it in our hands, not in the other guy, for an easy layup. So, we practice. Furthest guy back blasts across court and we send it flying down there." "How's it coming", Furris asked? "Well, it's not the sure thing of a set play, but we've been practicing."

Furris frowned, "What if he's out, he gets hurt, or you take him out." Bill said, "Well the team is built around Dan Johnson. We've got a one-of-a-kind player here. But we scrimmage every practice and every player leaves the game, sits out. We rotate, and that includes the big man. We altered the plan somewhat, but not entirely. We've got a pick and roll, some cuts, a Princeton offensive scheme, and a few others, but the pinwheel is what I'd say we use with Johnson. We're more than capable if the unmentionable happens and we lose Johnson. But I won't lie, we're playing the hand dealt to us, and shit, Frank, I've learned not to count my chickens and all that baloney, but we may be looking at a royal flush here."

130

Any little twitch and Coach Cummings got nervous. Just the week before, Dan said that he landed a little funny and his back was tight. Nothing serious. A little tight. Well, nothing was minor when it came to the health of Dan Johnson, and before the first came. He went to the Kaplan Chiropractic Clinic in nearby South Lyon, for three trips, with Dan feeling right back to normal when it was done. The man knows what he's doing.

"Well, Bill" Frank said. That's how I feel, but we've got to keep a lid on our excitement. One game at a time, okay? You're a seasoned guy, Bill. You run a tight ship, a winning program, and I leave you alone. Hell, Bill you know that. We're lucky to have you. Just stay calm. Stay humble. Keep that team humble and remind them that the media is a double-edged sword. I wouldn't give you this darned lecture if this thing was so extraordinary. I'm your friend here as well as a boss. It may be bigger than any one man can handle, so I'd like to see you back here every couple of weeks, just you and me. We know what might happen, but we don't know what WILL happen."

"I got it, Frank. We're prepared."

"So, you gonna start him?" Furris asked, truly wondering himself. "No, I don't think so. He's still a freshman." "Get ready for a shitload of boos!" "Well, let them boo for a while." Furris then added, "but he'll go in before too long, right?" Cummings continued, "I mean, NBC is broadcasting the game, and the entire school is being watched? I'm not an idiot. Let it play out."

The Cleveland State Vikings showed up in their forest green and white uniforms, looking sharp, maybe a little tight. Their coach was interviewed for this very unusual nationally televised game, which it would never be if #05 for the Michigan Wolverines wasn't making his first appearance.

Both coaches were interviewed briefly at mid court by an NBC reporter. "Coach, you've played Michigan and other top teams before. This game, with the addition of the highly recruited Dan Johnson, has not seen the kind of excitement and anticipation very often in the college game. How have your Vikings prepared? "We've prepared just like we would for any other game. Michigan always has a good team, and they recruit well. We welcome the opportunity. We're aware of Johnson, this young man, of course, and we'll bring our best game to the court and play our game, which is always to win." Pretty standard coach spoke, and it was no different in style when Bill Cummings came next.

"Coach Cummings, the nation has perhaps never seen the anticipation, the excitement, over a freshman basketball player like the eight-foot nine Dan Johnson, undefeated in high school and already praised by experts as having one of the most disciplined, complete game ever for an incoming freshman. First question, Coach, will you be starting Dan Johnson?" "No, Dan will not be starting the game for us." The reporter said, "When do you expect to put him in?" "We'll make that decision as the game progresses, but I do expect him to see some game time." "Final question, Coach", what's your prediction on the team's success for this year (an empty question the reporter knew would be answered only one way). Bill

Cummings said, right on cue, "The team has practiced hard. We've got a tough conference schedule, and anything can happen. If we play as a unit, play with discipline, we hope to do well. We'll take it one game at a time, and tonight our only thought is on competing against a fine Cleveland State team." "Thank you, coach." "Thank you, Go Blue" came from the lips of Bill Cummings, as it always did.

Around Crisler Center, as the teams continued to warm up, was an unexpected and amazing thing. It took about 12 hours for Charles Winfield's "CANYON" comment to go viral, if such a thing could have happened in the late fall of 1992. It spread quickly. Call it phone calls, radio, TV all through the state and especially in eastern Michigan, the word was out. This new, massive player, the player that came to Ann Arbor for every Maize and Blue fan, was CANYON, or the C Man, and it took off like wildfire. In fact, the name Dan Johnson might not ever be used again in this environment. Wherever Dan Johnson went, at Blimpy Burger, Gandy Dancer, the Cube, the Rock, the shouts would be heard, whether loud or in time, as his acceptance as a student and his sightings became a regular affair, more subtle, it would be "Hey Canyon, how's it going!" "Hey C Man, what's up?" Dan would spend all day, politely answering all, with "Hey, man, how's it going, or Hi, good seeing you, Hey, take it easy, oh hey, thank you, appreciate it." Always accepting a handshake but with time constraints, not an autograph, but in return, he would be seen, 50 times a day, patting a student lightly on the shoulders, and that seemed to work. "I'm sorry, I'm running late", but then extending a handshake. Everybody came to know, even as his legend grew, that any Michigan student, faculty, or employee, who were no less enamored, could approach him without fear, and he would engage them. The students loved Dan, even if he went through four years of school with barely a person he could call a friend, except possibly for his teammate and partner in crime, "Charles Winfield."

There were banners all over Crisler, showing "Crush 'em Canyon", "Welcome C Man", "Go Blue, Go Canyon." After this first, nationally televised game, the nation would know, then soon, the world, that Dan Johnson was, take your pick, the CANYON and the C Man.

And the announcers didn't miss a beat. First it was "Dan Johnson", then "look at these banners welcoming Dan Johnson, nicknamed by his teammates and embraced by the fans as the Canyon, or C Man. "Which is it," one of the announcers asked, to no one, or to everyone. "Well, a player with this much hype anticipation needs two."

Meanwhile, Chuck and Cathy Johnson sat at Manuel's Tavern on North Highland in Atlanta, complete unknowns. They had decided to go to the Atlanta Fish Market in Buckhead, and then to Manuel's to watch the game. They would be in Ann Arbor for the first conference game. Chuck wore a Michigan cap and Carole wore a Michigan windbreaker, though it was an 80-degree day in Atlanta. No reporters, no onlookers, a few other Michigan fans but certainly none from Cleveland State. Another couple asked if they went to the school, and Dan simply said, "no, but our son is up there". "Hey, did you know that Dan Johnson played up in Marietta?" Chuck answers, "Yeah, but I thought it was Roswell", "Nope, said the proud, more knowledgeable fan. Wheeler High School in Marietta."

Chuck and Cathy would not be disturbed for the rest of the game."

The teams came out for the tip-off, with the wild student section, later to be named the Maize Rage, but no less wild on this historic day, going crazy, but within seconds, it was clear that the Canyon was on the sidelines. The ball was controlled by the Wolverines, who took the ball up-court. Bennie Watkins passed to Miles Patterson, then to Noah Thomas, who was wide open near the foul line, and took a shot that hit the rim and then into the hands of a Viking player, who dribbled and then quickly passed to half court. The Vikings player passed to another player near the foul line, and Watkins tried to jump in front for a steal, but his timing was just off, and the Cleveland State player turned and laid it in, unopposed. 2-0, Vikings. Now the booing intensified. The Wolverines took it up-court, passed four times, with Thomas taking a shot from about eight feet out. It looked perfect but rolled around the rim and fell out. Again, Cleveland State was there and lobbed a long pass to their guard, passed it to a forward in the corner. Swish, 4-0 Vikings, and the booing got stronger. Michigan moved the ball up the court and executed a perfect pick and roll to Winfield, who laid it in. 4-2, Cleveland State, but not to be outdone, the Vikings moved the ball around, and an off-balanced shot went on, and a foul was called. The free throw was good, and it was suddenly 7-2 in favor of Cleveland State. A huge roar of "Canyon, Canyon, Canyon" could be heard. Michigan called time-out. This was not the start Cummings wanted, Dan Johnson or no Dan Johnson. He was hoping to put Dan in at the start of the 2nd quarter, with the team having a small lead. It was not at all unusual for an underdog to start out fast in games like this, even to keep it close later in the game. But that wasn't the problem, and Cummings knew it, but the players stayed silent. Coach Cummings ran this team, but he had no choice now.

"Ok, Dan, you're going in. This is what we've practiced for weeks. You've all busted your asses. Don't rush, work the pinwheel like we practiced. Pass when you need and look for the open man. And Dan if you've got an easy bucket, dammit, take it." Winfield added, even though he wasn't supposed to, "C Man you're gonna crush these guys, take some shots, man."

In went the Canyon and the crowd roared. It was 7-2 and extremely early in the game. The announcers at NBC said "Folks, this is what a lot of people have been waiting for, in some cases, for years. Dan Johnson, now known as the Canyon, is entering the game.

Watkins took the ball out and advanced it to Winfield. Dan was already up court. Patterson got the ball, and the choreography began. It went to the Canyon, simply towering over his opponent, who seemed helpless, but he was at least there, so Dan whipped it back to Winfield, who dribbled and was covered, back to Patterson, who shot the ball for a score. It was now 7-4. Nothing exciting yet, but the system was working.

The Vikings got the ball and passed it around. Their center had it and tried a fadeaway. Suddenly, "bamm", the ball was knocked away, and not only that, Dan got the ball. Instinctively, Bennie Watkins realized "furthest man out, furthest man out". Dan lobbed it over everyone, and it landed at half court. Watkins took it on one bounce and with nobody there, laid it in. 7-6, Vikings.

Cleveland State took the ball up-court. Dan was already there. The ball never got to the center, and a shot went in and out and into the hands of the Canyon. A yell and hand motion from the sidelines, and the play slowed. Dan bounced the ball to the point guard Winfield, and ran up the court, into position. A pass to Patterson, to Winfield, then to Thomas in the corner. The Cleveland State center took two steps toward Thomas. It was two steps too many, and Cleveland State was the first team that would fall into the trap for the next four seasons. Thomas lobbed it over to Johnson, and the crowd noise rose instantly to a roar, with nothing between Dan and the basket. Now, Dan didn't need to dunk. He didn't have to jump on offense except perhaps for a rebound, but the excitement of the night was too much, and this was what the fans had been waiting for. He slammed it through, and the crowd went bonkers. 8-7, Michigan, and the Wolverines would never trail again.

But it was worse than that for the Vikings. It was a clinic. The Wolverines passed, then passed some more, and when he wanted to, he just turned and scored. Soon, the score was 34-11 in favor of Michigan, then it was 54-17 at halftime.

In the locker room, Coach Cummings seemed to be relieved, but he was still nervous. Even though it was Cleveland State, a good team, it was a statement game. There was no doubt about that. It wasn't the hated MSU Spartans or Ohio State, or Indiana, and every one of those programs were watching this game, taking notes, planning, and the score, in Cummings mind, wasn't enough of a beating, but there was another half, and he wouldn't make the same mistake twice. Johnson was starting the 2nd half, and whether or not he ever came out would all depend on whether or not the Michigan coach felt that the team had made their statement. There would be no bragging, no boasting, only humility after the first game against a good but inferior program. The game was won already, but the statement had yet to be made.

"Gentlemen, I liked what I saw. A bit of a slow start but that was my fault. You worked your plays well. Our system is working but I want to see some crisper passes, some better shooting and some better decisions. Hell, he had to criticize something. The players understood and they couldn't wait to ramp things up.

"Hey C Man, Bennie said in front of the entire team. You're a generous guy. A lot of people are watching. Take over this game, man. Make your point. We're behind you. We'll get our shots all season. Be a little greedy for this one half, man." "Yo, C Man, for real", Noah Thomas answered. "This is important. We know you." "Dan said. "Guys, you really want it that way?" Winfield answered. "You've GOT to, man. This is the time. We'll get into a groove but for the next 20 minutes, tonight, lift your play man, just like at practice. I named you, C Man. I'm making you famous. We're all telling you, do it."

Everybody laughed and they got into a circle. Dan had to bend down to join it. "Okay, Dan said. I know what to do. It'll be fun. Winfield said loudly 1-2-3 and the team said, "Go Blue!"

"Well, after one half, what's your assessment of Dan "the Canyon" Johnson. The other announcer, the former ball

138

player, said, "Well, nothing is very surprising. It's the first game, a warmup for this Michigan team, already favored to win an always tough Big Ten Conference. The play of the Canyon was somewhat predictable, and to be honest, I think Coach Bill Cummings is holding him back a little. Plenty of passing, conservative plays, and a huge lead but really, nobody seems shocked and if anything, I think a lot of people in Ann Arbor are relieved."

Back at Manuel's Tavern in Atlanta, a satisfied but curious Cathy Johnson said to her husband, "Honey, what do you think?"

Chuck Johnson, the methodical engineer who held his son back at every sport he went out for until he was wound up like a steel coil said, "That coach is holding him back, he can crush this team and I hope that Coach lets him loose." Cathy had never heard her husband refer to Cummings, at one time the family's "best friend" during the recruiting process, as "that coach." It was just that Chuck knew what Dan could do, and so did Dan. But now, Dan has his teammates blessing to do his thing. It was more than that, they demanded it. They were fans, too.

With a 37-point deficit, Cleveland State took the ball out, took it up the court, passed to their forward who shot a high arching shot that went in from just in front of the 3-point line. 34-13, Michigan.

Winfield took the ball, dribbled past half court, passed it to Noah Thomas who faked a shot, then bounced it to Johnson, who spun like a tornado, something he had practiced in the dark on his driveway and for years. He slammed it home and the crowd actually gasped at his quickness. His Cleveland State opponent was left grasping at air.

Cleveland State got the ball, and it was blocked. The Wolverines, on the very next possession, passed it to the Canyon in the post. This time, there was no finesse, no spin. He turned and with his opponent in his face, or rather, his chest, slammed it right over him. "Oh, my" the television host said. "That was just brutal. Who is ever going to be able to stop that, on any team?" Dan was also fouled and made his free shot.

The fans were losing their minds now. Not because it was Cleveland State, but because in their minds, it was going to be the result against any team in the country.

The Canyon scored every which way one could imagine, except for shooting the ball from outside. He dunked at will. He tried the entire portfolio, and it was obvious he had practiced them all for this night. Baby hooks, fadeaways, more spins. Three times he missed a shot and got his own rebound to lay it in. On defense, he was equally insane. The Vikings couldn't get the ball inside the entire half, making them a one-dimensional team. The Wolverines' other players were all among the top in the nation. They were up in the faces of the Vikings on every possession. At one point, they were 1 for 23. Nothing could go right. The Cleveland State Vikings were the sacrificial lambs for this Michigan team, and as bad as they would feel, they would be in very good company. The Vikings would finish 20-8 and win their conference. This was a good team, but it didn't matter.

With two minutes to go in the game, the score was 127-40. Cummings did not want the Wolverines to go up by 100 points. Johnson came out. Point made by the Michigan Wolverines. The Canyon could play.

Dan Johnson finished with 71 points, 80% field goal average and 7 out of 11 from the free throw line, at 63%, and something he'd have to work on, but that was the only thing.

The team must make some adjustments. They could play better, and they WOULD play better, and that had to be a frightening thought by every team in basketball, from East Lansing, to Bloomington, to Lexington and Lawrence.

Chuck Johnson turned to his wife Cathy and said, "The 2nd half was better, but he needs to get back to practice and get on the free throw line. The engineer was precisely right, but he wasn't exactly disappointed, either.

Bill Cummings and Frank Furris, within minutes of each other and on other sides of the court, stared straight ahead and simply said "holy shit."

# Little Logo Annie

Ann Karlsson was a sophomore art major at the Penny W. Stamps School of Art & Design at the University of Michigan. Both sets of grandparents originated from Sweden, and Ann grew up in the Minneapolis suburb of Plymouth, attending Wayzata High School.

Ann seemed born to draw. She was known to even walk around with a sketch book to draw any kind of scenery she found interesting. Sketch drawing. Still-life, the many lakes she could find in Minnesota, like Brophy, Nokomos, and Winona.

She dreamed of one day having an art gallery and perhaps two, one in New York and one in Los Angeles or Chicago.

Ann had an idea, one she dreamed would change her life. We're all entitled to daydream. What would life be without the excitement of a good daydream? But it was time to act. In no way was Ann Karlson a stalker, but she had that idea, and she had to find a certain Dan Johnson, the Canyon, so one day she saw him walking on campus, creating a stir wherever he walked.

Everybody knew the C Man's dorm on South Quad, so one day, she followed Dan to the dining complex there. The C Man drew the usual and constant "C Man!" Dan was a sophomore and opted to stay in the same dorm for his sophomore year when he could have gotten an apartment, but that was an added cost. One day the cost would hardly matter.

It was interesting how these students treated Dan, by far the biggest man on campus, and by guiding the Wolverines to the NCAA championship in such dominating fashion the year before, some students just stared in awe but respected the Canyon's privacy. Some would extend a hand, with Dan always reciprocating, a high five, a hand slap. Sometimes they wanted to talk but Dan's steady walking usually kept that down. Rarely, there was an autograph request. but Dan would counter by saying "sorry, man, but I'm running a little late, and by sharing their hand usually helped get him through the situation.

He ate this dinner alone, as he usually did, with gawkers, but at a distance. By now, he, and others, had their routines, and many were used to seeing him. Some would later state in stories interviews, you know, the "I knew Dan Johnson back when", that they saw him nearly every day and left him alone.

Ann had her tray, a little Asian, a little Italian, from the many cuisine stations fixated around the dining hall. You had to be one picky eater not to find something here. She felt, absolutely, like she was in a pickup bar, but the tables were turned. She was a very cute young woman, ironically, just five foot one, with short-cropped blond hair, looking every bit the girl with the Nordic DNA.

She nervously approached the Canyon's table and could actually feel her heart race a little quicker and her palms getting sweaty, but she had to do it. "You know, you're missing something important," she said with a slight smile. Dan was mid-chew and held up a single finger, the gesture for "one second while I finish swallowing." Ann felt so embarrassed. "Dammit, I got him mid-chew."

Dan finished and turned with a smile. Now it was his turn for a quick heart-skipping. He found Ann to be adorable. She was short, shoulder-length brunette hair, and wearing slightly over-sized round glasses that made her look studious "I'm missing something. What am I missing." "Look, can I talk to you for a second? Once I explain, you'll understand." "Dan said, well, ok, but I hope you're being truthful. I don't let anybody pick me up while I'm eating." "No", said Ann. "I'll explain."

143

Ann sat right across from Dan and had to look high up to meet face, even as he was sitting down. "I draw. I'm in art school and I've been drawing all my life. I want to do it for a living. One day, you know, have a gallery." Dan liked her. He said, "Oh, you want to draw me. Well, you know, you're the third art major that has asked about that in the past week. Do you pay me, or do I pay you? And let's get one thing out of the way. I don't do the nude modeling thing." "Okay, Ann," she told herself. He likes you. I TOLD you he would! "It's because everybody wants to see if all your body parts are in proportion", Ann said with a giggle. "Are you blushing", Dan said mischievously.

"No! Ann said with a smile. "I'll get right to the point". "I wish you would," Dan said. She ignored him. "You need a logo." "A what?" She pressed on. "This is it, Ann." "You're already famous. You'll get more famous still. All the students here will be able to tell their grandchildren that they saw you all the time. You're going to play professional basketball and become very rich." "Well, I don't know," Dan said. "Yeah, right." Ann said, rolling her eyes. "It's a sure thing. SO, here's the deal. You're going to get endorsements. You're going to play internationally. Some people, I've heard, said you could have played in the '92 Olympics. In HIGH SCHOOL. But in'96, you will. Then you'll really be famous. Then you'll play in the NBA. Like I said", Ann repeated herself with anticipation. "You're going to be a brand, and it's the CANYON brand. Everybody I know here, and I mean everyone, calls you The Canyon or the C Man. Nobody calls you Dan." "I prefer, Dan," he said. "You can call me Dan." Ann smiled. Was the Canyon a little smitten with her? Fine, whatever it takes. She just needs him to listen. "Okay, look." She opens a folder and there is a piece of paper. "Do NOT commit this to memory. It's mine." Dan could finally see that she was serious and maybe even a little annoyed. "Ok, let's see, now that my food is cold." She looked from side to side, as if the continued stares were from onlookers hoping to see her piece of paper."

She pointed to the drawing, now turned the other way, so Dan could see it properly. "What do you see?" Ann asked. "Dan, still in flirting mode, said, "Umm, two triangles and a basketball." "NO! Ann said, look again." "Oh, wait", Dan exclaimed. The triangles only have two lines. They have no line at the bottom." Exasperated, Ann finally let it all spill out. Finally. "No! This is a canyon, two mountains with a deep gorge in the middle. I have seen similar icons, which is what this is. An icon, a symbol, and instead of a sun, it's a basketball. This can be YOUR logo if you own the trademark." People would have to pay you to use it. Remember, not everybody knows English, and when you get that big endorsement, you can use the logo. It's coming, so you need a logo."

"So", Dan said, "What's in it for you?" Ann said "Money, what else? And enough fame to draw and paint for the rest of my life. Have my own gallery someday." "But what's stopping me from just copying it and trade marking it?" "Well, Ann said, maybe I already have it. I own it but I want you to use it." "I like it, but where do we go from here." "We go see a lawyer, together. Become my partner. You'll be rich either way, but you want to have my logo, the real Canyon logo, and you'll wish that you did, because it's cool. It's simple and it's cool."

Dan got Ann's number and said he'd think about it. Did Dan really need his own logo?

Throughout their professional relationship, which is what it settled into, Dan would call her Annie. Nobody else could. She didn't like it.

Weeks later. Ann called Dan and they went to see a lawyer together. Ann paid the lawyer's fee. They discussed an arrangement. They would share the rights to any revenue generated by the logo. Dan was a thinker but, in this situation, he just didn't seem to have the vision that Ann did. Ann could see it clearly. The logo would be seen worldwide. They couldn't profit from it everywhere, not from the millions of fans. Not the little boy who sketched it in his notebook, dreaming of fame someday, but from companies that made apparel, and others, who would have to pay a licensing fee. Ann had the vision, an art gallery in Ann Arbor and on West 43rd Street in midtown Manhattan. "The Ann Karlsson Gallery."

# Burgers and Brainstorming

Coming off the 168-92 walloping of Villanova in Dallas, Dan returned to his dorm in Michigan, and while lounging around, heard the phone.

"Hey kid, 74 points, not bad! Helluva game, but after going 34-0, I think the writing was on the wall. You'd never be able to hide if you lost." "Hey, thanks, Billy. Coach told me that this wasn't the game to worry about my over-passing tendencies, and to score when I could." "But you could have scored all of 'em, am I right." "Well," said Dan. "Most of 'em".

Billy didn't gush over Dan's success. He knew it would come and he knew Dan when he was still a bumbling skyscraper with "only" gold medals in Judo and wrestling. "Hey kid, you won't believe it, but I've got a three-night gig at the Senate Theater in Detroit in two weeks. Why don't I swing over to Ann Arbor and take you to lunch. You find a place.

So, Dan chose what else for this trip, The Brown Jug, as he had something to show Billy. Of course, he liked Blimpy Burger and the Fleetwood Diner, which was open 24 hours. And of course, he loved Good Time Charley's at S. University. No shortage of great places.

On that appointed Monday, Dan walked in, and everybody swarmed him, not because they hadn't seen him 20 times before, but because the first of what the entire world expected for the next three years had begun. Provided Dan dominated, he determined he would be loved.

A black sedan pulled up, and a man helped Billy out of the back seat. He didn't need the help, but this was simply Billy's situation, and long ago brushed off this gesture, with an "I got it". Sometimes people just mean well, even if they aren't thinking. Billy ascertained that this was a situation evident in all walks of life, and he was bound to help this raw, naive 9-footer (almost) learn the ropes.

Billy entered, and the entire restaurant noticed a man, in a tailor-made suit, enter on his own. Again, Billy was used to the stairs, and it wasn't because he was famous. A few might recognize him from "somewhere", but he didn't have the Canyon's fame, and certainly, not in Ann Arbor. This was Dan's town.

Billy hopped up on the booth's seat. Literally, a hop. He could reach the table just fine, though barely. So, could Dan. People sometimes thought that Dan wouldn't be able to fit anywhere, and yes, he could not sit in a normal car. As a bus or train passenger, he had to duck way down, but once seated, he towered way up over the table, but had no problem leaning down. People forgot that half his body length was under the table. His head, even sitting, might go three quarters of the way to the ceiling, but he could do it.

"So, this place good?" "Oh yeah, Billy, I'm here a lot and they leave me alone. Well, mostly. Dan's face lit up while he opened up a menu. "Billy, read the menu under 'burgers'". Billy scanned the page, and there it was. The Canyon Burger.

"Sweet Jesus. No wonder you like it here. They idolize you." The Canyon burger consisted of four patties, American cheese, bacon, lettuce, tomato, onion straws, pickles, and hickory smoked BBQ sauce."

"Kid, I think this was the cardiac burger before you arrived." "No Billy, it's new. It's for me." Billy rolled his eyes. If only Dan saw the things Billy did in Hollywood, but then again, he won't even reach his 19th birthday until October. He has two gold medals and an NCAA basketball title, and he was just getting started. Good lord. The only thing that could destroy Dan was having bad people around him, and Billy wanted to help him avoid that, because he was a sweet kid about to face a cesspool world.

For the record, Dan had two cardiac burgers, one fewer than normal, because he didn't want Billy to think he was some kind of slob. Billy got a chicken salad sandwich and a cup of tomato soup.

"So Kid, what's next?" "Well, Billy, I've decided to become a finance major. My friends told me that I could have chosen something much easier, and just concentrate on basketball, but I like math, and maybe it'll help me to understand what's going on when I play in the NBA."

"Are you staying out of trouble?" Bill asked, perhaps as a concerned Uncle-type, or perhaps to reminisce about college. Billy attended school in L.A. "So, listen to this," Dan said. The guys wanted me to run with them in something called "The Naked Mile". "Is it what it sounds like?" Billy smirked. "Oh, yeah, exactly, but I'm not doing it, and I'll tell you why." Billy laughed and said, "I wouldn't think I'd need a reason why you wouldn't want to run naked in the streets of Ann Arbor." "Oh, no, it sounds like a blast, but somebody will take my picture, and I've heard enough of 'let us see your Johnson' that I'll regret it." "Good decision", said Billy, but I've been around. Heck, I was in movies, pre-code Hollywood, when almost anything would go. We probably could have put this Naked Mile in a movie." Dan smiled, "Well, I probably shouldn't take the chance.

"What else have you been doing for fun. You know, with your clothes on?" "Ha, ha, well" Dan said. It snowed a couple of weeks ago, and we took trays from the dining hall and went sledding down the hill. I couldn't sit on a tray and like five guys put me on three trays and pushed me. That was kind a fun." "Wild stuff", Billy said. "Now that would have been perfect for a guy like me." Dan continued, "I've played a few pickup games at the CCRB, which is fun for meeting people, and they got a kick that I would play with them. I'm not supposed to, in case some guy steps on my foot, but I sneak it in because the guys appreciate it. I hang out at a place called Pinball Pete's and sometimes, the Blind Pig. Lots of grunge-type kids around. They're a little off the beaten path, like me. I like this place. There's a bunch of coffee places and occasionally, somebody might put on some jazz. Oh, and I met Bob Seger at a game. Turns out he's from Ann Arbor. That's pretty cool." "So, he came to see you." Billy didn't ask, but stated. "Oh, no." Dan insisted. "He's from here. You know the song "Main Street"? It's about a street here in Ann Arbor." "Sorry, kid, don't know it. I'm an old man but get used to meeting celebrities. You're one yourself."

"How's your studies? Doing anything to get smarter?" Billy decided to ask. "So far, so good. A lot of basic classes so far. I'm told in April there's an annual event called The Hash Bash, where there's speeches and political things." Billy laughed and said, "Hey, I love hash, especially with scrambled eggs." They both laughed and Dan said, "Yeah, that's PROBABLY not the kind of hash they're talking about."

The restaurant refused to take his money, but Billy handed the student waitress a $20, winked, and said "Here ya are sweetheart". She smiled and took the money.

# Scott Destin

Scott Destin was a local Ann Arbor kid who was 19 and loved basketball. Scott also had Down's Syndrome, and he lived with his parents, who both worked for the University. One introduction led to another, and one conversation led to another, and Scott was such a pleasant, eager young man, that when Dan arrived on campus, Scott Destin was asked to be a Wolverine team manager.

Scott had several roles, including getting equipment, setting up the scoreboard, helping in drills and filming the practices so the team could watch it back later. People were constantly amazed at how Scott had such an upbeat, pleasant personality all the time.

From the moment Dan met Scott, it just made him feel good about life. Every day was a new day for Scott. He wasn't a machine. He could get upset, but it was far less common for him, and he took his job seriously. Some people could find a way to complain about everything, but that wasn't Scott. He had equipment setup and everything he was supposed to do, he did it, and usually did it well. Dan would invite Scott to talk about the game because it gave Scott such pleasure. Scott loved stats and he loved calling Dan "C" just like the players. Dan would see Scott and say, "The D Man", and Scott would answer "The C Man", and they'd would give each other a high five, a low five, a "5" of some sort. Some days, Dan would say it quietly, like they were in some secret society, "The D Man" and other times, "THE D MAAANNN!!!", making Scott laugh and if course he had to respond in mind, "The C

Maannn!!!". For Scott, it was the greatest feeling of acceptance. For Dan, it was an honest and sincere friendship, the very few he would have. Scott would mention a stat or two the day after a game "C Man, 10 for 12 from the line", and Dan would answer, "I had it working yesterday, D Man. They were falling." The D man might answer, "Yes they were, C Man." Dan, in his own creative mind, sometimes in Scott, he had this secret relationship going on. He might have said "D Man, operation X5 is a go", and the D Man might have answered, "See ya in Brussels on the 18th, D Man."

Dan realized that he couldn't let his conversations with the D Man get too complicated, but the D Man would still surprise him now and again. Dan would even say it to him. "D Man, you surprise me with your knowledge!" Scott loved it, and it would encourage Scott to go home and try to learn something on a topic, to share with Dan. Anything at all. It was a special game they shared.

With all the hype surrounding Dan, he loved these special relationships. One day, with permission from the coach, Dan took Scott in front of the camera during a press conference of a key conference game. Of course, as always, the Wolverines were victorious. Dan said "Umm, before we get started, sitting here with me is Scott Destin, our equipment manager and much more." Behind the scenes folks like Scott don't get recognized nearly enough, so I asked him to sit in tonight, because he's an important member of the team." The press understood.

Scott's friendship with Dan was pure. Best friends can argue, go through turbulent times, struggle, rise and fall.

Scott couldn't be a best friend, but Scott didn't want attention, or money, or fame. The complexities of a friendship with Dan weren't of importance to Scott. He only wanted friendship.

Years later, Scott was gone, and Dan was talking to Melanie in bed, in a pensive mood, for one reason or another. "You know, Mel, when you get right down to it, I've had six friends in my entire life, You, Billy, Tony, Charles, and Scott Destin, our equipment manager. And little Wendy from the hospital. He conveniently left out Ann Karlson, his logo creator, as she was more of a crush and now a business associate. Dan wasn't stupid. I've had 1,000 good relationships, nice acquaintances. I've met multiple Presidents, a ton of celebrities, world and business leaders, but I probably have had five friends."

"So", Melanie said, sheepishly. "That's all I am? A friend?" "A friend with benefits," Dan said, smiling. "Well,", Melanie said, "I got a benefit for you," and shut off the lights.

# The Canyon System

The music and studio lights went on, and the familiar logo on the back. The volume went down, and the familiar voice of Ed Simmons went live.

"Good evening basketball fans, and welcome to another night of information and insight on basketball tonight. With me as always, the Fayetteville Phantom, the Bud Walton Wizard, Double M, the freak of the Final Four, Marvin Middleton.

"Whoa. I get a new nickname every show from you, Ed Simmons," Double M responded with a laugh. "So, what should we call you? Ed said. "YOU can call me, Mr. Middleton", Marvin said. "We'll stick with double M," Ed said with a smile.

"Ok, well Double M, it's March Madness, and the question on everybody's mind is, can anybody dethrone the magical Michigan Wolverines and the Canyon, the C Man, the Magician of Marietta (Dan cuts in, 'now no M nicknames, that's my domain, man!'), ok, can anyone knock of Michigan, the 3-time defending champs, on the most dominating 3-year undefeated tear in college basketball history. Can it be done?"

Marvin answered, "Well baby, that's why they call it March Madness. Hey, that's another double M. Take that monicker away from this tournament!" "Too late for that", Ed said with a smile. "We'll return with a prediction, and with a detailed breakdown of the Wolverines magic strategy, when we return."

After several commercials, including a commercial for "The Fresh Maker", Menthos Mints, the show returned. "Hey, we're back with Basketball Tonight, but before we dive into the Michigan formula for success, you know one our sponsors, Double M, is "Grey Poupon, so Double M", Middleton cut him off, just like they rehearsed, "Hey, you ain't getting none of my Grey Poupon, man." "Okay, that went well, so now let's talk basketball strategy out of Ann Arbor. Double M, break down some of the strategy of this Wolverine Championship team. This dynasty."

Double M got ready. "Well, Ed, there's absolutely no secret that the success of this Michigan team begins and ends with that 8-foot eleven-inch center, Dan Johnson. With great coaching and support players, the Wolverines have developed an unstoppable system with what appears to be no weakness. If they have one, those coaches have identified and worked around it before we have."

Double M, far more serious than he usually was, spent the next 12 minutes showing clip after clip of the Wolverines destroying the completion. "This Michigan team makes use of the big man as well as any team can, and NBA scouts and the league in general is watching and learning.

Michigan had a well-oiled machine, but the fact is, even if it wasn't well oiled, the C Man can score at will. Just keep that in mind. Once he posts up, he can turn around and dunk on any player on the planet. Oh, you can try to rip his face off, which probably won't stop him. Remember this; he's an inch from being nine feet tall. Let that sink in, and unlike some other very tall players, he's built like Wilt Chamberlain. Bigger. That's 480 pounds of height, speed, and skill. This is a man who can run with the fastest players, out jump any player, out rebound, spin.

He has the baby hook, the fade-away. Now who's going to block that? Nobody, that's who, the spin and dunk, the spin and layup.

And even if you stop him, which you must foul the crap out of him to do, he's got a mid-80% free throw percentage, not the highest but better than a lot of other players. We all saw the video of Robert Benson who almost got his arm ripped off, and when he was the one attempting a flagrant foul on the C Man. It's like trying to knock down the Empire State Building by running full speed into it on the street. Now who's gonna win THAT battle? So, opposing players, centers but others, too, are fouling out all over the place, trying to stop him. You CAN'T stop him, that's the problem.

This is a man that was once interviewed, a rare interview I admit, but he said. "Ever since I decided I would play basketball, what everybody begged me to do even as a little kid, I decided I wasn't going to be just a really tall guy they stuck on the floor. I would practice like crazy. My dad had me do drills, dribbling, ball-handling, passing, taking shot after shot from the foul line. We found that if we turned our picnic table on its side, under the hoop, it would bounce the ball back to me, so I could practice alone for hours, into the night. My dad installed lights. Then I went to big man camp in the 9th grade and played against college and even a couple of NBA players. My dad wanted me to possess all the fundamentals, especially passing. I wanted that, too. He knew I would be scrutinized.

"So, this kid, this man since he was about eight, is a basketball machine, and I'm just getting started."

"Ok, laughed Ed," We'll get to part two of the review of Dan Johnson's game from Double M, right after these messages.

After a "Got Milk", Miss Cleo, and a Taco Bell Commercial featuring a hungry Chihuahua, "Basketball Tonight Returned". Ed Simmons got back to the story, "Welcome back to Basketball Tonight, along with our basketball expert, the Phantom from Fayetteville, the Outlaw of Arkansas, the Man to See from the SEC, the Unstoppable force, that man, of course....is "Double M", the incomparable Marvin Middleton." Marvin finally chimes in, "Man, you're stretching the boundaries of good taste there, but speaking of unstoppable force, let's get back to our special profile on another man with a long list of iconic nicknames, the Canyon, the C Man, soon to be the very rich man, Dan "I'm nine feet tall and the world is small" Johnson.

Double M began again, "Well, right you are, Ed "Prince of Pepperdine" Simmons, the Canyon is soon to become a very rich man, indeed, because he's the championship ticket these lottery teams are begging for. Now before the break, we were talking about the Canyon's skills, his work ethic, and what he can do with the ball all alone, but that is NOT how that Michigan team functioned, and it is NOT how the Canyon's next team is going to function, either, believe me, so let's talk about the way the offense has been built up in Ann Arbor, and soon to be in New York, Atlanta, Portland, well, we'll have to see what happens next week.

The Wolverines used what one might call a Pinwheel or Hub and Spoke offense, with one Mr. Dan Johnson as the main cog, but far from the only talent. Let's watch some video.

Now watch, point guard Bennie Watkins, from Chicago, takes the ball up court. Watch him. Excellent ball control, switching hands. Defenders swarm him in the backcourt because they know what's going to happen once the C Man posts up. He can pass off to another guard like Charles Winfield, the best high school player in Michigan two years ago out of Detroit's Cass Tech, like he just did. Another great ball handler, so you see, give the C Man lots of credit, but this Michigan team didn't just win four straight championships with just one man.

So okay, the ball goes to the C Man who posts up. Look how he makes the other players small. That #32 in this video, Richard Teal, he's 6' 10" but looks like a little child trying to guard the 8' 11" C Man. Let that sink in. But he is guarding him, so watch what comes. It's a thing of beauty. He kicks it back to Watkins, part of that double W famous backcourt, Watkins is covered, so back to Johnson. Now Johnson already knows he's passing it to Miles Patterson, to Winfield in the corner. Now watch this mistake by Teal, who moves two feet to try and get a hand on a possible shot by Winfield, BAMMMM! Winfield passes it to

Johnson, now unguarded, for the easy slam. Child's play, Wolverine style."

"Incredible, Simmons said."

Double M confined. "That's just one scenario of many. They can't cover the Canyon, but they pass the ball around. No, they whip it around, until that split second where somebody has the best shot. It could be the C Man inside, or another Michigan player on the perimeter. And then when they take that shot and miss, who's there most of the time for the rebound? Do I have to tell you? Watch these four scenes in a row showing the Canyon getting a rebound and just slamming it home. Up and over defenders. He's already massive but he can jump. Think of yourself trying to climb Mount Everest, man, nearly impossible the way that it is. Now think of it rising the whole time you're trying to climb it. This is what college teams have had to face against this mighty Michigan team."

Well, things played out that first year about as well as every Michigan fan dreamed that it could. The Wolverines, with the CANYON averaging 42 points a game, went undefeated and won the NCAA championship. Dan cut down the net and waved it around in the air inside of the Louisiana Superdome. That photo would be voted twenty years later as the greatest Wolverine moment in the school's history, and second in the world of sports, all-time, to the photo of the young Cassius Clay standing over the body of Sonny Liston, to win his first heavy championship. And number three? An aging, shaking

Muhammad Ali lighting the Olympic Cauldron in Atlanta, in 1996.

It was just the beginning.

# Word on the Street

While b-ball news made the headlines on TV, and Dan was shining, he was even more dominant in wrestling, even if some of the wrestlers were a little jealous of Dan for missing some of the practices that coincided with basketball. It was part of the deal for Dan going to Michigan, and Dan was doing his part by winning. In fact, he hadn't lost a match yet, won the Big Ten Tournament by pinning his way to the finals, and had made his first NCAA wrestling finals as a freshman. It was no surprise because he had been destroying most of the collegiate wrestlers are he made his way to tournaments while still in high school.

A Conversation took place between a current place-winner in the NCAA Tournament, and a writer for a wrestling publication, Mike Franklin, as they were sitting in a lobby area.

"Hey, off the record, can I ask you some questions about Dan Johnson? What's your take on this guy? I mean, how do you really feel?"

The kid was a little tentative, then shrugged his shoulders. "First of all, his size gives him some incredible advantages, so that the match is practically over before it begins. All he needs is the skill set of an average high school wrestler to become an NCAA champion."

Franklin: "Do you really believe that?"

Wrestler: "No. Alright, anyway you look at it, he must be good. I'm not going on record saying a big guy can't get his ass kicked but his size gives him advantages that nobody has ever had, because he knows how to use it".

Franklin: "So he didn't put in the effort like other wrestlers?"

Wrestler: "I didn't say that. No, I hear he works his ass off. Guys have seen him at camps, at different practices. He's all business. Sometimes he acts like he doesn't even want to be there. Hardly talks to anybody. Goes and does Judo AND basketball. This is a hobby. This isn't a damn hobby to me.

Franklin: "So, you resent him"

Wrestler: "You're not going to print this? I don't need that."

Franklin: "No, I'll never mention your name. I hope I can interview him, and this will help me with questions."

Wrestler: "Yeah, I resent it. He approaches it all like it's a science project. He has great endurance. He runs and runs. Then he practices moves and situations hundreds of times. Hell, thousands of times, and he uses the moves that helps his size against smaller opponents."

Franklin: "And everybody is a smaller opponent."

Wrestler: "Much smaller. You've seen these guys in the NBA every so often, you know they're 7'5". Total string beans, 240. Weak. The Canyon, man is 8'11" and 480 pounds, all muscle. Can you understand that? He benches

820 pounds. I mean, man, can you <u>understand that</u>? You wanna go up against that?"

Franklin: "No."

Wrestler: "But then he knows what he's doing. He was coached well. He dislocated a guy's shoulder with an arm drag man! That's not supposed to happen. You can't shoot on him but heavyweights aren't gonna do that, anyway. Not often, anyway. They're too slow. The Canyon is quick and fast. He arm drags and gets behind you and just forces you down. Two on one, with the wrists. You're down and you're not getting up. He turns everyone over. Technique, strength, and leverage. He turns over world champions. I'm not saying he wouldn't be a good 6-foot wrestler, but he uses his advantage so well. Most of his opponents are 6 feet to 6'4". 250-325. Normally, that would be huge. Monstrous. And most all carry some weight up front, even the ones in shape. The Canyon is trim. He's cut, you know?" He takes full advantage of his size.

Franklin: "Can you blame him."

Wrestler: "I guess not, but I don't know that he's good for the sport."

Franklin: "Why not?"

Wrestler: "Because it's not fair. It's like a boxer with three arms. You ask around and see if somebody says something different."

# Atlanta My Town, Atlanta, Your Town

It was two years later, and the Wolverines had just won their 3rd NCAA championship in a row. So far, Dan and the Wolverines were undefeated.

Dan was thrilled to be chosen to be on the 1996 Olympic Team in basketball. He had already earned the right to compete in Judo and Wrestling from the recent trials, just as he had as a seventeen-year-old. With all the talk of professional basketball, he knew that this would be his last hurrah in those sports. In fact, that had been the plan in his mind, and then later, his parents. There would be money at stake, maybe a great deal of money once he was chosen in the NBA lottery. He just finished his junior year at Michigan and would be playing another year. He was so tired of hearing that he should leave. Others were doing it. At the end of the day, it was about the money. He asked his parents, and they told him what they always did. Don't be afraid to listen to advice on all sides of a question. Get as many of the facts as you can and try to find people who have gone through your situation, and then make your decision. Make it yours.

Dan felt that there were few things in life more prestigious than a degree from the University of Michigan. His stock after the Olympics (if they won) would go up if that was even possible. He had every right to stay for four years. That's the way it used to be done, and after all, the students wouldn't complain, so that's what he was doing.

In the meantime, he was the only collegiate player chosen for the Olympic Team. Some say he could have played as a seventeen-year-old, but the politics even this year could be seen. Dan plays, an NBA player is left out, but the European and South American teams were getting stronger, and there was no taking chances. They wanted Dan and maybe they needed him.

One of the networks asked months ago if Dan could help host a special on Atlanta, helping viewers learn about the sites. Dan was excited about that, but with a non-stop practice schedule, it would be difficult. The Judo and Wrestling associations were particularly uneasy about Dan missing many practices since the new "dream team" had to practice so much. With any other player, he would have been dismissed, but he was the stronger player by far.

In the meantime, Hiro Nukiyama had only Judo on his mind for the last four years, practicing, watching film, consulting with coaches. How could Dan Johnson be beaten?

During one Hiro Nukiyama practice session, the sweat pouring off his face, Dan was at the Varsity Restaurant with a New York-based reporter, getting chili dogs. Dan, ever so familiar with the Varsity's interesting lingo, was enjoying the workers shout "What'll ya have?" Dan said "Five dogs all the way, rings, jumbo F.O." Dan spent some high school days practicing at the Georgia Tech SAC (student athletic complex) with other wrestlers, right off North Avenue, just like the Varsity. Dan drank his F.O., or frosted orange drink and ate his hot dogs and onion rings. He walked inside the fabulous Fox Theater, took a walk along a portion of the Chattahoochee, viewed Stone Mountain, and had a drink atop the Peachtree Plaza Hotel's Sun Dial. The producers made it look like he was a co-host, but he was rushed in and out of these locales, said a few lines, and rushed to another, before heading back to a practice in another city. When it aired, they pieced it together nicely.

Dan marched in the Olympic opening ceremony, as he did in Barcelona, and watched in awe as Muhammed Ali lit the Olympic Flame, hands shaking and all. Dan wished he had the charisma of that great man, but did anybody? What the "Greatest" Ali had done for the world, could Dan help others, at least in his own way?

Dan insisted on staying at the Olympic Village, another "feather in his cap", as he was the big celebrity, even though the NBA players stayed in private homes, and it would have been more comfortable and certainly quieter to do the same. These were world-class athletes, so at least he had no door knocking in the middle of the night. That had happened to him elsewhere, where sometimes it was a very nice surprise, and other times, not.

The big social event was five days before the Olympics, where Dan had a night off from everything, and called a former Wheeler friend now at the University of Georgia, 75 miles away. Dan and four basketball teammates went barhopping up there, and had a crowd following them wherever they went, and that was fun.

On July 27th, Dan and three basketball friends decided to take a limo over to the Centennial Olympic Park, where bands were playing, and of course, they were swarmed by fans, but they only stayed from about 8:30-10:30, listened to some music, and went back to the village. His friends then stayed in the limo to go to a home they rented somewhere. It was only the next morning when Dan heard about the bombing in the park. That changed the tone of the Olympics until the end and was something nobody ever forgot.

# Atlanta Preview

The men all stood out. They looked like athletes. Blazers, a couple in warm-up suits.

"Wow, what a crowd!" The crowd went crazy. "This is Fred Peters with Sports Radio, MISSION SPORTS, and we're at the very lively Centennial Olympic Park in downtown Atlanta, with only a week four days to go before opening ceremonies, and we've got a very special show for you tonight. We're dedicating this hour to the one and only, world's tallest man, the Wolverine Machine, the C Man, the CANYON, Dan Johnson. Nobody has seen an athlete with the combination of size and skill that Dan Johnson brings to the table, in three distinct sports, and many feel he could excel at many more if he chooses to. Tonight, we have athletes that excel in these sports, and we're going to deconstruct the CANYON and see just why he appears nearly unbeatable.

After several commercials, the host returned. "Alright, we are back from the Atlanta Olympic Centennial Park. Can everyone hear me?" A huge eruption came from the crowd, trading pins, drinking, and milling about. "Okay, let's get right to it. I've got a 1988 Olympic Judoka, or Judo player, from the Uptown Dojo in Chicago, Bill Channing, twice a senior National Champion and graduate from San Jose State, a school considered to have the top-rated Judo program among the college ranks. How are you tonight, Bill?" Channing said, "Well, it's an exciting place to be. Atlanta is the center of the sports universe for the next two weeks, and the Judo competition begins on just the

2<sup>nd</sup> day." "So, Bill, we've got a lot to go over in an hour from our experienced group here. Everybody knows how tall the CANYON is, but what else makes him so strong as a Judo player?" "Well, Dan", Channing continued. "Dan Johnson loves Judo, it was the first sport he started taking seriously, and he actually practiced for five years before he was even allowed to compete, because the governing body couldn't figure out how to *let* him compete. He was 6-foot four and around 290 pounds as a nine-year-old." The entire group laughed and shook their heads. "I've practiced with him. He practices very hard. Throw after show. Lots and lots of randori, or free play. That's like a scrimmage. It's not a competition but it's treated like a live fight. He went years doing that, and he was invited to practice around the county and in Japan. He had good coaching and his throws of choice, uchi-mata, harai-goshi, ippon seonagi, are ideal throws for the taller man. I know you don't know what in the world I just said." Fred answered, "Not a clue", and they both laughed, but Channing continued, "Well, they're Judo throws, and those are throws that are ideal for a tall man. Anyway, he has excellent balance, great speed, and incredible strength. His opponents have an extremely difficult time getting a grip, but he doesn't. He almost always controls the fight, no, correction, he ALWAYS controls the fight, and his opponent is on the defense constantly, just trying to stay alive. Plus, he's not opposed to choking you out or taking you out with an armbar if he can't throw you right away, and that is very hard to break free from. Quite frankly, an arm bar from Dan is frightening. He got me in one during a practice session and simply let it go because he had it and I thanked him for not destroying my career. Actually, he's a real decent guy and there's no doubt in my mind that he could kill people."

Let's move on to former Montclair State Wrestler Don Snelling. Don, what makes Dan such a formidable force on the wrestling mat. "Well, Snelling said." First of all, my response wouldn't be very different than why he's so strong in judo. He's massive, far bigger than the largest wrestlers he will meet, but he's a good tactician. He knows the best moves for his size and he's almost impossible to stop, even when you know what's coming. His opponents are large and much slower than he is. He's over 400 pounds but he's still trim. So, he's very fast. He can get around his opponents, and when that happens, he can easily take them down. He has an excellent grasp of pinning combinations, but he doesn't usually waste them, not when we can just throw an over on this back.

Ok, finally, a sport's particulars that are a little better known, former All-American Basketball player for the Louisville Cardinals, 6'11 Center Mike Chandler. Mike, you're a big man, obviously. Why is the C Man so hard to stop? "Wow", Chandler said, "Where do I begin?" Once he posts up, and you can't stop him from doing that, he's a well-oiled machine, and even more dangerous, so is his team. You'll be going to see The CANYON constantly passing around the court. If he's double-teamed, he finds the open man, if he's not, or if his man gets out of position, he scores, and he can score at will. Spin and slam, fadeaway, that little baby hook he's got. If he were only 8'11", he'd be a big problem. But he's very, very good. He might be out there if he was only six feet tall. The knock on him is that he's all size, but that's a bunch of baloney. He uses his size, and so far, he's been unstoppable. These Olympics will be nothing than a clinic and autograph session for the opposing teams, and he doesn't even give autographs."

"Ok, Fred Peters back here at the Centennial Olympic Park, where's there going to be a concert every night that the Olympics are in session, so if you're here for the games, be sure to come on down. Admission is free.

We're in what organizers call the 'Olympic Ring', the downtown area where a great many of the main events will be held, including basketball, track and field, gymnastics, swimming, and a host of others. Georgia Tech, host of the swimming competition, is within about a mile away, and so are the stadiums, and wow, I've never seen so many t-shirt vendors before, so come down if you're in the area.

We're taking you now to the International Broadcast Center. It's going to be a very exciting Olympics, with the CANYON and so many other amazing athletes from the USA and the 196 other participating countries."

# The Judo Streak Ends

Dan breezed through the first judokas, many trying anything to throw Dan off his match. Quick grasps and attempts to throw, with virtually no power behind them. At one point, Dan simply yanked a player down and choked him out. With his amazingly long arms and legs, it was a wonder he didn't do this every time. When asked why he never put an arm bar on an opponent, Dan said, in complete sincerity. "I would break their arm before they'd have a chance to tap out. "

Just like in Barcelona, Dan scored ippons on every opponent. If they stood, he threw them with a hairi goshi. One opponent fought off the throw admirably, only to have Dan turn pivot forward and slam him so hard with an osoto gari, or large outer reap, one of the most basic of Judo throws, that his opponent seemed seriously injured. However, he simply had the wind knocked out of him. It was a scary scene as the player gasped for air.

Hiro Nukiyama was next, the former world champion. Hiro stepped forward and pushed Dan back. No grip attempt. All it really did was force Dan about a half step. Dan was trying to figure out his strategy. They moved forward. Dan grabbed him. Grabbed his belt in back, usually a death sentence for the other player. Hiro wrapped his legs around Dan's legs from behind. When Dan turned to throw him to the mat, Hiro jumped up and back. An interesting but strictly defensive move. No offense could come from this. Dan would eventually pin him or choke him out if he refused to stay on his feet.

Suddenly, Hiro trapped a lapel and pulled Dan forward. It only took Dan to step forward an inch. It was that split second, with Dan's ever so slightly lifted off the mat, that Hiro Nukiyama hit him with a foot sweep and turned Dan in a clockwise position.

Dan went down, falling barely on his slide, and half on his butt. The referee called a yuko, and the crowd went crazy. In a sport where one full point ended the bout, as in a knock-out, a yuko would be enough of an advantage to win the bout.

Now Dan felt a little rushed, which turned into desperation with only thirty seconds to go. Hiro, too, this massive, skilled predator, hung on for dear life, making his body as heavy and lifeless as can be.

Dan grabbed Hiro near the edge of the mat, and with a giant kaia, threw Hiro with a thunderous harai goshi that sent Hiro what some say was twelve feet in the air and over eight feet high. Hiro's and Dan's bodies flew beyond the mat, and onto a hard wooden floor normally used for basketball. Eight hundred combined pounds of mass landing with a slap on the wood. The crowd gasped in horror as the bodies landed, and in spite of the brutality, their training kicked in, and the most pain Hiro later said he felt was in his hand. As a matter of fact, while the crowd expected two corpses, they both got right up, with three seconds left to go in the match.

The match ended. If Hiro Nukiyama was excited, you would not know it. If Dan Johnson was crushed, it was not to be shown. They bowed and shook hands and walked off.

Mike Swain, coach of the men's team and former world champion himself, gave Dan a conciliatory tap on the backside, and Dan walked off.

Hiro Nukiyama was the Olympic Gold medalist and American Dan Johnson, the silver medalist. In spite of Nukiyama being a tremendous, former world champion, it was called the greatest upset in the history of the sport.

A month later, Dan accepted an invitation to be on a Japanese talk show called Saikō no nyūsu or "The Best News". On the show the hero of Japan, Hiro Nukiyama, wearing a beautifully tailored suit. Dan wore a sport jacket and a dress shirt.

Asked for his assessment of the fight, with the translation to Dan being "We want your honesty." Dan said "Here is my honest opinion. Hiro Nukiyama is a great champion. He was a world champion before I competed internationally, and he is a champion again. Hiro did what all great champions do. They find a way to win. I believe Hiro studied my fights and found a weakness. Then he practiced that strategy for weeks, perhaps for months, for his one chance. It worked, and he deservedly won. I congratulate him for such a bold and clever strategy".

The audience applauded and Hiro shook his hand. It was his turn. "We looked for a weakness for the last two years and could find none. We then came up with the ideas of a distraction technique. We believed we had one chance for it to work and we were very, very lucky."

"Could you win with it again, asked the host" "No, of course not" said Hiro. It was our only chance."

"And then you had twenty seconds left and Dan threw you very viciously, but you landed out of bounds. How did you feel then?" "I was scared for my life." Hiro said to laughter.

"Mr. Dan, what will you be doing now? Will you seek a rematch with Hiro Nukiyama".

Dan said, "No, with great regret, I am retiring from Judo competition to focus on my basketball career." The crowd sighed but it was no secret. Riches awaited Dan as a pro basketball player.

"Any last words on your Judo career, Dan" asked the host. Dan said, "Judo is a great sport and I thank Dr. Kano and the Japanese people for bringing such a wonderful gift to the world (Dr. Jigoro Kano having been the found of Judo in 1882). Now I am off to a studio in downtown Tokyo to make a scotch commercial." The crowd smiled and applauded and laughed while Hiro, a usually serious person, clasped his hands in approval.

Dan's judo career was over, with one Olympic gold medal, one silver medal, two world championships, and six national titles, at the age of 21.

# The Lottery

A representative from Earnst & Young sealed the final envelope and brought them all down to the CNN studios in New York, where it was decided that the 1997 NBA lottery would take place during the third week of May. So high were the expectations and possibility of drafting Dan Johnson that teams were accused of deliberately losing games, but that happened every year and could never be proven. Still, in the history of the lottery system, which began in 1985, there was never so much at stake, and experts practically guaranteed a championship season to the team that had the Canyon as their center. Some, simply to hedge their bets, brought up other "can't miss" draft picks, not only in basketball, but in other major sports. It was a good opportunity to show footage and add stories about the "Biggest Bust" by league and team. Whether anybody really believed the Canyon, center behind the 4-time champion Michigan Wolverines, undefeated in four seasons, with Dan Johnson was totally unstoppable on the court, remains to be seen.

The lottery system involved a random drawing of an envelope from a hopper. Inside each of the envelopes was the name of a non-playoff team. The team whose envelope was drawn first would get the first pick. The process was then repeated until the rest of the lottery picks were determined. In this system, each non-playoff team had an equal chance to obtain the first pick. The rest of the first-round picks were determined in reverse order of the win–loss record.  In later years, a more sophisticated, weighted system using 14 ping pong balls would be established.

Giant TV screens were tuned into the event in New York, Atlanta, Boston, Portland, Washington, Milwaukee, and other cities, in bars, even up on the jumbotron in Times Square.

Dan Johnson, diploma in hand, was coaxed out of his apartment and into the center of the Regents Field Sports Bar, along with about 200 of his closest friends, CNN, WXYZ, the Detroit ABC affiliate, local reporters, and others. Everyone was awaiting to see who would win the lottery, because that was the team that the C Man would play for. It was a sure thing. Nothing could be surer, and in fact, the Sun had a better chance of never showing up the next morning than the lottery winner not choosing Dan.

Dan received many calls. Agents, realtors, wedding proposals, you name it. Requests for money, hard-luck stories, even though Dan had about as much money as the average college student. That was about to change in a way that would shock, well, probably no one. Dan's dominance on the court was such that there wasn't a basketball analyst or personality around that didn't feel he would get the most lucrative contract ever awarded in sports. The fact that he hadn't accomplished anything yet in the NBA didn't matter at all. He had spent four years on the court with boys, and again, the experts predicted more competition but probably the same results as in college.

The fact is, that no college or professional player had been analyzed or scrutinized more than Dan Johnson. Many credited his father, who kept him off every court except the home driveway, for six months, training him from a book on the basics, then three trips to the much-respected Pete Newell Big Man camp, where he was the only high school player, practicing against college and even NBA players. Many credited him for helping the big man avoid the bad habits that can grab hold in any sport. As a matter of fact, Dan seemed to benefit from that in all three sports.

In wrestling, for example, he learned from the beginning never to dip his head, let his arms down or reach out, where an arm-drag, fireman's carry, or duck-under was just waiting to happen. The only problem was that Dan had the advantage of size and that helped him cover up, or recover, from mistakes like that. The thing was, however, was that he made very few mistakes, because he learned from very good coaches, and he was smart to begin with.  In the history of the game, many experts already felt like few could play center like Dan Johnson. The combined, amazing height, size, and basketball skills were just overwhelming. It wasn't that the Canyon overwhelmed his opponents physically, which he could easily do, but there was seemingly not a possession in four years where Dan didn't post up, hit the open man, again and again and again, and shoot whenever he wanted to. The NCAA record for field goal percentage before Dan's arrival was 74%. When the C Man played his final game at Michigan, his percentage was 91%. His free throw percentage was a respectable 86.25%. The fact is that Dan could have scored every time he got the ball, but his unselfish play raised the level of the entire Wolverine team, and the only fault his coaches had was that he had easy put-ins only to pass the ball back out. More than four times each season, the Wolverines had to turn over the ball when the Canyon let the 30-second clock expire, passing the ball off one too many times. The individual scoring record in Division I was 72 points. Dan Johnson scored more than 72 points 16 times, with a high game of 97 points. In almost every occasion, he was pulled out as Dan once said in an interview, one of the few he ever gave, was that he never wanted to score 100 points in a game. He felt it was unnecessary and disrespectful to the opponent as well as to his teammates. He was usually pulled in the 4th quarter, so even though Dan was the highest Michigan scorer for the last four years, he was 4th in minutes played over the same span.

Few players took the abuse that Dan Johnson had to deal with, saying at one time that every rib had been bruised, bruised hips, black and blue knees, and two broken toes. And yet, the worst retaliation seemed from him was when he would push an opponent that had elbowed him, with some great video footage of players flying into seats or onto them behind on the playing floor. He was made to shoot free throws since the 8th grade, saying he had probably, over a nine-year stretch, taken about 250,000 free throws, the equivalent of about 75 a day, every day.

At the end of the process, the New York Knicks won the lottery, and the chance to choose Dan Johnson as the first NBA pick on June 25th, in Charlotte. The news ran in Times Square, on the electronic news ticker, and on television stations in the USA and even in other countries. New York celebrated as if it had already won the NBA Title.

Dan would be on his way to New York, just 30 days after receiving his bachelor's degree in finance from Michigan Ross, the school's college of business. He stuck it out when others in his position would have left for the money and the glory.

This time, Dan believed deep down that those things would come soon enough.

# PART THREE

# New York, NY, West Orange, NJ and The Knicks

# The Contract

Dan sat down with his new agent two days after the big Lottery. The Knicks were anxious. His agent, Mike Vance, told Dan "Let them wait". Truth was, Dan was trying to move his belongings out of his Ann Arbor apartment. He was still almost broke, but that was to be expected from a college kid. But was also expected was that that he was pegged to become a very wealthy man in short order.

Mike Vance was a lawyer and had negotiated contracts before. He knew that the Knicks were desperate. They had to have the C Man. He would caution Dan to be patient, to wait, stay in shape, be positive, but act as if "if it happens, it happens." Don't blink. Mike wouldn't have to work very hard. Dan Johnson took his college team to four straight national titles. Only UCLA did more.

"Dan" Mike said. This is the biggest moment of your life. How this negotiation turns out will define your life. And no bullshit here, Dan, the more you make, the more I make. To that end, I want to ask you how you would feel if I brought another attorney into this. Blake Jennings is the best negotiator in professional sports. They all know him in the NBA. They respect him. There's no clause he hasn't seen. Nothing will take him off his game. "So," Dan said, "You want me to fire you and hire him?" "No, Dan, you know that isn't what I meant. We'll get you more money if we can work together." Then Dan did something that surprised Mike. He got up and walked out. "Mike, I appreciate everything you're doing. I'm tired. I had tough finals. The NCAA finals weren't long ago. All this stress with the lottery and draft." "Dan, everybody wants this contract signed quickly. You want to get it out of the way, find a place to live, make financial plans, and most importantly, show up on that first day of practice."

"Mike. I'm going home to my parents' house in Atlanta tomorrow morning. I'm staying there for a week, and then I'll call you." "You won't do anything until we speak?" "Mike, I don't plan to."

And out the door Dan went. Mike felt a wave of nausea.

"Dad, I did what you told me to. I walked out." "Good, son. Nobody is going to walk away from you. We'll get the newspaper over here tomorrow night."

Dan and his SUV, one of the few cars Dan could drive, took off down the New Jersey Turnpike, down to Petersburg, VA, where he would then get onto I-85 South to Atlanta.

He stopped at a Marriott in Petersburg, for one night. The hotel apologized for not having a customized super-king-sized bed. That was going to be Dan's first big purchase. A 12-foot bed, and he found a company to do it, along with a 12-foot mattress. All custom-made, for $16,000.

And one day, every bedroom will have that same bed, and people can roll around in it and be happy.

Dan got home and greeted his parents. It was so nice to be in Marietta. His Mom said that the phone was ringing off the hook.

# 77 West

Remi Garnier was the General Manager at 77 Central Park West, known, affectionately, or otherwise, as "77 West" She ran this property, along with several other buildings owned by her billionaire father, Claude Garnier. Doormen came and went, but she had been in charge for 14 years. Her job was to be sure that residents had a place of refuge, a real home, away from the paparazzi. A place to literally take your hair down, kick off your shoes, and recharge. Some residents, quite obviously, were wealthy but inconspicuous. A hedge Foundation manager, a plastic surgeon, a real estate tycoon, some who won the family lottery and did, relatively speaking, nothing to earn their fortunes, but there they were, and earned or inherited, money is respected, money speaks volumes.

Certainly, the least inconspicuous man on the planet was the C Man, the newest resident of 77. In fact, these "digs" not a term associated with this building very often, were recommended to the Knicks by Remi herself. It was said that at one time, Knicks legend Walt "Clyde"'Frazier, took up residence, his outstanding choice in clothing and cool, quiet demeanor, welcomed at 77 West, a place that seems to love being famous, but not in the limelight.

Located next to the Museum of Natural History, it was built in 1926 and held only 64 units, several that were 2-story, with high ceilings, so it was a cinch that Remy Garnier would be giving the Knicks a call, especially since one of the largest and most expensive units was up for sale.

Rod Dorfman, the 41-year-old GM of the Knicks, walked into the lobby to meet with Remy, who told him that the Knicks could stop worrying about where their prized catch would live.

Remy had been married twice, and even at 52, was very attractive, except for the occasional cigarette in her mouth, which she wouldn't take out even in the no-smoking buildings that she herself ruled with an iron fist. But, then again, the rules never seemed to apply to her. She was known to sometimes yell and embarrass her staff in front of others, giving her the moniker of "Princess of Mean", similar but less horrific as the original "Queen of Mean", Leona Helmsley.

"Rod Dorfman, how are you are, and how is that lovely wife of yours, Nan." "Remy, we've been divorced for over a year now." "Oh, yes." Remy said, and she was shallow enough to have forgotten. She thought, "well, at least she isn't dead." "Oh, yes, oh Rod, I am sorry. Next time you come to one of my parties, and we will get you back on track." "Ok, Remy, tell me about this unit." "Yes, Rod, this is perfect for your big new Knickerbocker, Dan Johnson. Two floors, 14-foot ceilings, unparalleled beauty." "Sounds nice, but I was thinking of checking out the Dakota, Rod said." "Well, said Remy, the Dakota is very nice, but also very famous. Your draft pick is shy. I read the papers, too, Rod. And besides, they have nothing right now. Plus, I want you to come look at the unit with me now. The tenants are out for two more hours. I have a surprise for you." For a second, Rod couldn't help thinking about another one of Remy's reputations, and that's her "bad girl" side, and doing whatever it took to make a sale. The story he heard, Remy found under a restaurant table, "selling" to a prospective buyer, had been circulating for a few years, but never proven, and only seemed to elevate Remy in her circle, not hurt her, and Remy never went on record of admitting or denying the story. Let people wonder. Since his divorce, Rod hadn't been out much. But then again, it wouldn't be worth the risk. The deal falls through and just maybe, he's out of a job. It used to be so much easier to get laid.

There was no doubt that the 5200 square foot apartment was luxurious. Two stories, four bedrooms, a beautiful, modern kitchen, and formal dining room and causal family room, and library. Beautiful views of the Central Park Reservoir. There was a knock on the door and a middle-aged man wearing work pants and a tool belt, walked in. "Hello, Ms. Garnier, and Mr. Dorfman. I am Charles Hembry, the superintendent of the building." "Rod, darling, the reason I asked Charles here is because there isn't a soul on this planet that doesn't know that Mr. Dan Johnson stands close to nine-feet tall." She turns to Charles and whispers (but in a mocking way that anybody within six feet would have heard, "My God." He probably hasn't had a decent shower in 15 years. Charles, please tell Mr. Dorfman what you can do. "Well, the shower for the main bedroom is located on the top floor. We cannot go up; we can actually lower the floor and make the shower height 12 feet instead of the eight feet it is now. It's a lot of work but it can be done. It should take about five days. It will look very nice although there will be a rectangular box evident from the bottom floor, but it will be in the kitchen and will look just fine." "You see, Rod," said Remy, that's a big advantage. He'll have quiet, and the unit will be empty in 17 days."

"Remy, we don't have a contract yet with Dan, and sometimes, these things can take several weeks or even months, so until we have a contract, there's nothing I can do, but I can certainly recommend that he look at the unit. He'll like the shower. Smart-thinking, Remy. It's hard to underestimate you." "Rod, darling, I live to please. You know that, and The CANYON will be pleased to call 77 West home. It is the best and only real choice. You tell me what I can do to close this deal. Remember, you tell me."

After Rod left, Remi had another task, and that was, to talk to all the doormen, beginning with the two on duty, Tony Minnelli and Nick Rivers. Nick was a quiet, unassuming guy from Lynn, MA, who was a Red Sox and Celtics fan, but wasn't about to say much about that, not even to Tony.

Tony came from money, yet it could be hard to know it, sometimes. His great-grandfather came to the U.S, from Sicily in 1917, embracing America, but with less than $50 to his name. There's no other way than to say he worked his ass off as a bricklayer, and then modest owner of a masonry business. He kept his nose to the grindstone, ignoring the dark side that so often lured young immigrants in New York, and establishing a thriving business. He was always in demand and his long hours and insistence that there was never, ever, to be cutting corners, helped to give his wife and children a good home, and family meant everything.

Tony's older brother, Paul, had bigger plans. He learned the business at an early age, then Penn State and MBA at Rutgers, Newark. Work was simply expected. His family wasn't doctors or accountants, not that they couldn't be, but they put their smarts into building things. Now that Paul was older, he put all he had into the company. He wasn't exactly the life of the party, but then again, Jimmy liked that. Even more serious was the middle child, Gina. A Penn and Wharton graduate, Gina was all business. Even Paul knew to go to the frat houses and join a club or two, but not Gina. But Gina had Jimmy's trust more than any human on the planet, and Gina knew it.

But back to Tony. Always an underachiever, Tony had the world at his feet, but his dad, of all people, would give him nothing that wasn't earned. He decided on Lehigh. Out of state but close enough to drive home. After all, screwups or not, family was family, especially in the Minnelli family. There would be lectures, you'd better believe, there would be laughs and there would be tears. There would even be the occasional smack across the head, but family was family. You had a home, a place. You wouldn't manage $80 million in real estate holdings. Gina, who developed a passion for commercial properties, would do that, and grow it, but you couldn't be "disowned", forgotten. And you might, with enough time, trust, and love, find yourself in the Minnelli family, and there would prove to be no better place to be. A lifelong reward.

In 1981, when Tony was six, his dad, Jimmy, decided that they were to move to nearby Short Hills. Yes, just a few miles away, but far more affluent.

"We don't need to wave our money around" said his wife, Carole. "What's wrong with a new home?" Jimmy said. "I want the best for my family". "It's not about that. I like where I am. A nice middle-class town with plenty of Italians. What are you running from?" Arguments were never seen as a catastrophe in the Minnelli household. They were expected. It didn't result in separations or "cold shoulders". This is life. This was normal and an almost daily occurrence.

"I run from nothing. You can't be Italian and live in Short Hills?" "That's not the point, said Carole". This went on for a while, but ultimately, Short Hills never happened. She wasn't the loudest, she didn't say a lot, and she wasn't a man, but one thing was certain in the family; One way or another, Carole usually won.

Jimmy's dad, Dominick, longed to be an American. English had to be spoken and spoken well at home. Dominick himself and his wife Luccia, may have struggled, being immigrants, but his children wouldn't. Paul, Gina, and Anthony, the youngest, couldn't speak any Italian.

# The Minnelli Clan

Dominick Minnelli was born in the northeast of Naples, in the town of Calabritto, in 1914.

It was a tumultuous time, as World War One began throughout Europe. Italy, originally a member of the Triple Alliance, with German and Austria-Hungry. However, a strong sentiment existed within the general population and political factions to go to war against Austria-Hungary, Italy's historical enemy.

Capturing land along the two countries' borders, stretching from the Trentino region in the Alps eastward to Trieste at the northern end of the Adriatic Sea was a primary goal and would "liberate" Italian speaking populations from the Austro-Hungarian Empire, while uniting them with their cultural homeland. During the immediate pre-war years, Italy started aligning itself closer to the Entente powers, France, and Great Britain, for military and economic support.

By April of the following year, Italy signed the secret Pact of London by which Great Britain and France promised to support Italy in capturing Italian-speaking land, in return for entering the war on the Entente side. On May 3, Italy resigned from the Triple Alliance and later declared war against Austria-Hungary at midnight on May 23.

At the beginning of the war, the Italian army had less than 300,000 men, but the Armed forces grew to more than 5 million by the war's end in November 1918. Over 450,000 men were killed and nearly a million were wounded during the war.

Dominick Minnelli's father, Antonio, fought and was killed at the Battle of Selz, along the Italian/Austro-Hungarian frontier in northeastern Italy during the 2nd Isonzo Offensive.

When the fighting ended in November 1918 Italy, despite being on the winning side, found itself with an impoverished population. Then, in 1922, Dominick's mother died from consumption, or tuberculosis, leaving him, at eight years of age, an orphan. His mother's brother, Alphonso, his wife, and two children, decided to travel to America, taking young Dominick with them.

They boarded the Citta di Milano out of Napoli in May 1923, and arrived in the port of New York 16 days later. Skipping the more well-known lower east side of Manhattan, the Chichelo family, along with young Dominick Minnelli, the family would take a ferry over to Newark, NJ, and settle in the First Ward area, along with several other Italian immigrants.

Not unlike so many immigrant families, everybody, especially the male members, had to work, and after the 8th grade, Dominick dropped out of a school and began to learn the brick and masonry business. He continued with this work for many years, becoming highly trained, and supervising others.

In 1938, when he was 24 years old, Dominick married Luccia Calogero, living in a small apartment in Newark. He continued with the masonry business until December 8th, 1941, when he and millions of other men, enraged by the Japanese attack on Pearl Harbor, volunteered for the military.

Army Private, then later Sergeant Dominick Minnelli, despite his pleas to see action, never left New Jersey, instead serving at Camp Kilmer in Edison until his discharge in 1946. He was told many times that he was good at "moving men in and out", that he was irreplaceable at the Camp. He was allowed to take the short, 23-mile trip home most weekends, so he was very fortunate in this manner, though he always carried some guilt.

Sergeant Minnelli was discharged November 16, 1946, and immediately formed the Minnelli Masonry Company, forming important partnerships with builders that were putting new homes up throughout the NJ area. Before long, Minnelli had crews stationed just outside Philadelphia, to central and northern NJ, to Westchester County, NY, and to Nassau County in Long Island. He had contracts all over and was part of the home-boom welcoming returning servicemen. Before long, he had 16 crews and was earning large sums of money.

In the fall of 1946, James Antonio Minnelli was born in Newark, and in 1952, the family purchased a two-family home in West Orange, about six miles away, on Cherry Street. They rented the upstairs to friends from the old neighborhood. Newark's "Little Italy" was not how it once was by the mid-1950s.

Jimmy Minnelli was the oldest of three children, including two younger girls. He graduated from West Orange Mountain High School, class of 1964, and by then, his parents bought a new home far on the other side of West Orange, off Mount Pleasant Avenue, on Nance Road, right before the town of Livingston. They kept the house on Cherry Street and rented out the entire home.

Joe worked in his father's business as long as he could remember. Even when he was six, there was always some small work he could do to learn something. Mostly, his father wanted him to learn the concept of hard work, how it didn't have to be a curse, but a blessing. When Jimmy did some work, he was paid. That was an important lesson, too. Work and reward. Jimmy played football and baseball for the Mountain High School Rams but worked for his father not only off and on during weekends, but all summer long. He told his father that he wanted to take over the business one day. His father said that that was a worthwhile goal, but he had to have a four-year college degree. "Work, get your degree, then come back and I will have a management job for you because you have already worked on a crew. Maybe you will manage a crew for a while, then become a regional manager for over ten crews. We will see."

With 65 crews and over 550 employees, Minnelli Masonry was pulling in over $40 million per year, and after all expenses, including administrative, advertising, and investment in the business, Dominic Minnelli was bringing home over $5 million per year.

Dominick had become an American success story.

# The Plan

For two weeks, Tony Minnelli watched the Canyon come and go, head slightly down, this massive presence stepping out of a limo with a backpack in his massive hands. Returning from practice out in Purchase. Ordering delivered food. Back out again. Each time, Tony would do just as he was ordered. "Good morning, Mr. Johnson. Have a good day." "Welcome home, Mr. Johnson. You have yourself a nice evening." He let slip out, "Anything I can do for you, you just call downstairs, ok?"

Part of Dan's contract, a masterful document thanks to Mike Vance, was the use of a limo day or night. Vance argued to the Knick's lawyers that "You do not want your meal ticket roaming these streets or crashing his car into pedestrians in this crazy city. Protect his ass because it'll be YOUR ass if he is hurt and can't play. Don't get cheap now." "Dan, that limo will save you about $35,000 a year, trust me. Get a car if you want and park it. Save it for drives into the country with your girlfriend, and if you want, you'll have plenty of 'em." The limo was a perk that Dan found indispensable. Dan handed a business card to Mike and spoke. "I liked the guy with this company." Mike answered. "Let me have that card. You just got that driver a raise." So, Pete became Dan's semi-permanent driver, whenever he was on duty.

Sometimes Dan just wanted to get out. Joyride? Perfect for a limo. Tinted windows. People gawked at an almost nine-foot man, not a stretch limo, not in New York.

Tony was sitting at home, and he still lived at home, college degree and all, and the family didn't rush him to leave. He was two months shy of his 23rd birthday. He got his degree from Lehigh; people were a little surprised. Not because he wasn't smart enough. That was just it. In a family of smart people, Tony could compete. He just seemed to be missing that spark that Paul and Gina had. That his dad, Jimmy had. Nothing excited him. He could achieve whatever he wanted. If he wanted.

"So, I tell ya, this Canyon guy says nothing. Head down. The whole world was wondering about him. What's he like? "What IS he like?" Paul added. "Well, like I said, he doesn't talk, and I'm only allowed to greet him a certain way. 'Good morning, Mr. Johnson. Have a good evening, Mr. Johnson." "Well,", Paul said. "Add an extra sentence tomorrow. Ask him how he's liking the city." "That boy, he's a lonesome." Grandma Luccia added. He's alone. His a mama and daddy are far away." She gives Tony a playful slap on the shoulder. "Why you no invite this man over to our house for a nice dinner. This a mountain man." "They call him Canyon, Grandma." "Whatever his a name is, he needs a home cooked meal." "Grandma, he's got access to the best restaurants in the city. Any of them would prepare him something to take home." "No, no, you bring him here. We make him feel welcome."

"Would he come, Tony?", Jimmy, finally with some interest, perked up. He had mentioned that his son, HIS son Tony personally greeted the Canyon, the hottest commodity New York has ever seen. Bigger than the Babe, the Mick, and the Beatles, rolled into one. Literally." So now Tony had marching orders from the family. Engage this lonely man, eager for friendship, and bring him to the home across the river in West Orange. Grandma and Carole would bring home extra everything for this big man. Gina had her head in a book but looked up occasionally.

The next day, like clockwork, came the Canyon. The fall weather made for a nice day. About 68 degrees in the morning. There he was head down. But the limo wasn't there, forcing the C Man to nervously stand outside, one passerby already yelling his name. "Good morning, Mr. Johnson." This time, without the ability to walk past and duck his massive frame into the car, he felt the pressure to answer. "Good morning". "No limo today, sir." "Should be pulling up in a minute. He told me he was five minutes late." Wow, the Canyon can talk. "Well, sir, how are your practices coming, sir. The Knicks looking good?" Now Dan was engaged, like it or not. "Yeah, we look good, I think. Getting our plays together." This was a Dan Johnson speech! Okay, Tony was going for all the marbles. "Look, Mr. Johnson, if you don't mind me saying this. You're 22. I'm 22. I got friends, family. Be happy to have a beer with you anytime. There's a place right over there on 8th Avenue. It's actually called Danny's Pub, and it's been called that for years, way before you were drafted." Finally, Dan turned and smiled a little bit, but was embarrassed as well. "Oh yeah? Well thanks, maybe someday." The limo pulled up and just before he disappeared, he turned to Tony and said, "Look, I know your name is Tony. From that name tag that says Tony. Why don't you call me Dan". "Tony smiled. A breakthrough. "Alight, Dan. Not Canyon?"

"No, a crazy guy from Michigan came up with that. People that know me call me Dan because that's my name. Dan."

Dan disappeared and Tony had a swagger in his step like he'd just been kissed by a pretty girl.

"So, any luck with the Mountain Man", Gina said, a week later, with her usual cynical tone. "Luck? Try skill. Guy talks to no one. Camera crews outside. But every day he says a little bit more. To me." By the way, his favorite food is Italian. "Have you two gone all the way, yet", said Gina, with a smirk. Carole looked at Gina. "Gina, you stop that". Grandma, never missing a chance to be a smart aleck, moves in close to Tony and half whispers in Tony's ear, but loud enough for the family to hear, "He's a you boyfriend now? He snuggle up to you?" Everybody had a big laugh. Gina smiled because she never laughed. Carole thought it was hilarious. Even Tony laughed. "Good one, Grandma, good one."

# Zapped

In the meantime, Dan had a date with Kelly Tate, a girl that, ironically, had just moved to New York after getting her degree at The University of Georgia. Dan knew several students from Wheeler that attended UGA, which has grown in stature as a good academic school to match its reputation as having a good social scene and, as always, a strong school spirit, cheering on its beloved Bulldogs. During the 1997 football season, Georgia finished a 10-2 record, defeating Wisconsin in the Outback Bowl.

As a senior, Dan, a curiosity wherever he went, as well as an up-and-coming celebrity that most everybody knew was destined for stardom, was seen strolling down Milledge Avenue, home to many of the fraternities and sororities, to downtown restaurants and bars, and twice, "between the hedges" at a couple of basketball games. He even travelled to Jacksonville, FL with two friends when the Georgia Bulldogs played the Florida Gators in what was called "the world's largest cocktail party."

Dan never seriously considered UGA as a school, and everybody knew it. What kept in the good graces with the locals was that Dan made it clear that he wanted to wrestle in college, and Georgia no longer had a team, and secondly, he was primarily a basketball player in the minds of Georgia people. Had that talent been in football, there would have been pressure.

Of course, the Wolverines had supreme bragging rights now, completing a perfect 12-0 record and being crowned national champs, and in basketball as well.

Nobody seemed to ask about Georgia basketball, but the fact of the matter was, the Dawgs completed a fine 24-9 record.

Kelly attended North Cobb High School in Acworth, and the family Golden Retriever, Dooley, was a regular patient at Dr. Cathy's Acworth Veterinary Hospital. One word led to another during Dooley's checkup, and Cathy and Dooley's human Mom, Pam, and the date was made. Whether or not Dan and Kelly had a say in the matter, well, who knows.

Cathy told Dan that Kelly was waiting for a call, and Dan took about a month to do it, leading Kelly to complain to her mom, "Well, Mom, I TOLD you not to do that. He's a celebrity and he's too tall. And do NOT 'check in', as you say. He's obviously not interested.

Dan looked at the paper with Kelly's name on it. It was mid-November, and the Knicks were off to a great start, but Dan's love life, not so much. He got a lot of smiles from women who seemed to have interest. He was obviously well-known and now, well-paid. But Dan was shy and was his own worst enemy. In time, he'd get better. In Michigan, he left it up to more aggressive, adventurous women that simply took what they wanted, and that included Dan, and he didn't mind that. It was a lot of work to change your persona for the sake of a date.

Dan hoped what everybody else hoped, that he'd find somebody that liked him for himself. You want a big sports star? The rich guy on Central Park West? Not waiting for tables and getting tickets to the best concerts? Well, then, you'd had better know a line from a Woody Allen movie. If a date doesn't know what "the sheriff is near," means, well, then, Dan has already crossed you off in his mind. That doesn't mean you can't stay the night. After all, a Johnson has needs.

So, Dan called Kelly, said nothing about waiting a month. After all, he's the CANYON. They talked about where and when, and Kelly said that she had to be in Chelsea Saturday afternoon. Dan suggested she come up to the apartment at 77 West, they have a drink at Dan's (not named for him), a block away, and they could go to a nice steak place nearby.

At about 6:50, Dan came outside, a doorman, James, not Tony, was on duty. Good evening, Dan, how are you tonight? Is your limo coming?" James had the ok to call him Dan but kept it formal. After all, not everyone was Tony. "Hey, James. I have a date that should be here any minute. I thought I'd walk with her in the park for a few minutes. She's never been to Central Park. She just moved here from Atlanta. My mom treats the family dog, ha ha, we'll see what happens. We're going to go to Dan's bar for a drink, unless we decide just to go to Luther's for dinner." "All within walking distance." James spoke. "Say, I know you can take care of yourself, big guy, but call the building if you need anything." "Will do." The two young men talked about, well, not much, until two minutes later, when a cab pulled up in front, and a cute brunette got out.

200

Nobody ever must ask Dan if he is Dan. He's famous and there's never another 8-foot eleven guy standing around. Kelly says, "Hey, Dan", "Hey being the preferred greeting in Georgia that Dan used himself." Dan helped her out of the cab, and she proceeded to do what everybody does when they first met Dan. She looked up in disbelief. "Oh, my." "Yes," Dan said, "I hear that every day". "Oh, sorry", said Kelly. "No, I'm used to it", Dan said." "Every day of my life."

Dan introduced Kelly to James. He then turned away toward Central Park and said, "Well, there it is. Wanna take a walk?" "Sure", Kelly said. "It looks beautiful. What a great place to live. A little nicer than Brooklyn." James said, "Remember, Dan, call if you need anything."

Dan asked Kelly about living in New York, the differences from Atlanta, her new job. A little bit about music. What she liked to eat and not to worry, Luther's had great steaks, chicken, and fish. She was nervous being in New York the last two months. She missed Athens and Atlanta. Already, Dan wasn't feeling it. Not "love at first sight", which he didn't believe in anyway, but some attraction is important. She was attractive, to be sure, but nervous, uncertain. No "sassiness" that he liked. At the same time, who was Dan Johnson? A wet sock if you ask some women. From strictly a personality standpoint, some men thought the same thing. Dan knew he had a "quirky" personality. Jazz, the obscure movie quotes. I mean, what young lady sees "Love and Death?" How many can share his dry sense of humor? Imagine, a nerd that bench presses 800 pounds. Oh, yeah, and just a tad under nine feet tall. Sure, you see them every day.

Still, a nice girl, a nice night, a Georgia girl. Jeez, Dan, give her a chance. Suddenly, a guy walks toward them. Seemed about forty, medium height and build. "Hey, CANYON. I saw you walk out, and I know you live over there. Fancy place. Glad somebody's making the big bucks, and for playing a game." Dan was suddenly on alert. Scanning the man's hands. Control the wrists, control the man. He said something to Kelly, who was visibly shaking. "Keep walking, ahead of me, ok?" She gave a feeble, ok." He kept walking but he knew it probably wouldn't be that easy. He never took his eyes off the man's hands. The hands, that's the key. The eyes? That's for Bruce Lee movies. Dan expected the worst but hoped for the best. The best never came. "Hey man, I'm talking to you." Oh shit, not those words. This would not end well. Be ready, Dan. Dan stopped and faced the man, but deliberately took a step back. He said to Kelly. "Kelly, walk across the street, away from this guy, then back to my building and go get James."

Dan said. "I don't know what you want. The best thing you can do is walk away and I'll do the same. Nobody gets hurt. Nothing happens. All is good. He saw Kelly getting to James. "Give me an autograph for my kids. You owe me that." That irked Dan. He didn't need this. "I don't give autographs. Not to you, not to anyone. So, goodbye." The man reached in his pocket. Dan watched. "Don't be a gun", he thought. His hand came out of his pocket. Dan saw James running toward them in the background. Out came a black cartridge of some kind. He moved toward Dan and lunged. Dan moved to the side and the guy missed. He saw a bunch of sparks. A large "crackle" sound could be heard. He bent over slightly, and stood up, and took another step toward Dan.

202

Dan had a vision. The basement, in Marietta, GA. A speed bag, a heavy bag. Chuck never wanted his son to be a boxer, but even at eight, he was down in the basement. "Son, when you hit the heavy bag, it's not just your fist. It's not just your arms or shoulders. It's your entire body. Your legs, your butt, and your hips. Your torso. It's torque and it's a straight arm. Put everything you have into the punch. One day, you may need it, and that's how it's done." Boxing in a ring, no, thought Chuck. Boxing for exercise and self-defense, damn right.

Just as this thug turned to face Dan, Dan pivoted, arm back, and twisting his body, reared into the man's face with a 16" fist.

Dan's fist met the man's face just as he turned, and he never knew what hit him. James was standing about ten feet away, watching, mouth wide open, the fist completely encircled the man's right eye and two thirds of his nose. A loud crack could be heard. The man went down, unconscious, and quite frankly, appeared dead. Motionless. Nothing in the eye socket except a mass of blood.

"Holy shit". Said James. "I had no choice," said Dan. "He came at me. I tried to deescalate the whole thing. He was crazy." Dan went over to him and the first thing he did was kick away whatever that black cartridge thing was. James checked his pulse and watched his stomach. Dan thought. "Everything is over for me." "He's breathing", said James. "Your date called the cops."

Dan explained to James what happened, but James broke in. "Hey, man, I saw the whole thing. He came at you. You had no choice." Dan stood over him. "But he has no eye left and look at his nose."

The police siren could be heard, and in a moment six police officers arrived. It could be standard procedure, or it could be the voice of a hysterical female saying, "Help, Dan Johnson, the basketball player, is being attacked in Central Park, across from 77 West."

The police, and an ambulance arrived, followed in ten minutes by a tv film crew. The man was examined by paramedics and taken away. Dan and Kelly explained the entire thing, along with James. Dan was alone but insisted that he tried to deescalate the situation. Ultimately, it didn't matter. There was a witness, a history of mental illness, and possession of a weapon, a 50,000-volt stun gun, that was illegal in the state of New York.

When the dust cleared, the problem wasn't whether Dan Johnson was guilty or innocent. Dan called his NY lawyer, Paul Reynolds, who, for the money Dan paid him, also came over to 77 West, talked to all three involved, and made an official comment to the press.

"Dan Johnson was walking in Central Park, less than a block from his building, when he was confronted by a mentally disturbed gentleman, who knew where my client lived and immediately made threatening remarks. My client tried to deescalate the situation, but the perpetrator lunged at him with a deadly weapon, and my client had no choice but to protect himself."

My Reynolds, what was this deadly weapon? Was it a gun."
"No," Paul Reynolds said. It was a 50,000-volt stun gun, illegal in the state of New York, and my client was unharmed."

But, Mr. Reynolds, you say Mr. Johnson was unharmed. Lennox Hill says that this man, a Mr. Eugene Steubins, has severe eye injuries and a broken nose. Doctors say it looks like it was the result of numerous attacks of blunt force. Wasn't this excessive and possibly a criminal act on behalf of your client."

"Madam, an increasingly angered Paul Reynolds said, we have a witness that said it was the result of one man throwing a single punch because he was being attacked with a deadly weapon. Mr. Johnson performed an act of self-defense and showed amazing restraint."

The NY Daily News made the point clearer.

"CANYON single punch decimates attacker."

The hospital public relations representative announced the following day that Steubins "suffered fractures of the orbital floor and the medial orbital wall or a "blowout fracture" of the right eye, a zygoma arch fracture, and a nasal fracture, otherwise known as a broken nose. He has blurry vision in his right eye, which is a common occurrence of blunt force trauma, but could, in time, correct itself."

The NY Times featured an editorial that perhaps the state should prosecute Mr. Johnson simply because he was excessively large. "If a gun can strike and kill a human being, and it is illegal in the state of New York, then shouldn't the use of similar force be against the law, even if it is a man's fist?" Of course, the views of that person did not necessarily reflect the views of the newspaper.

In the following days, a couple of doctors explained the damage a 480-pound-man, who could bench press 820 pounds, could inflict on a flesh and bones face, provided he had the knowledge of how to deliver a punch with sufficient force. "Dan Johnson has the strength and ability to kill a human being with his bare hands, with a single punch, so I wouldn't go out of my way to anger him."

Sitting at home with two of his buddies, watching the report, Nets forward Jacob Mitchell told his teammate, 6' 11" Center Sammy Park, "Hey Sammy, maybe you should hold off some of those rough fouls on the CANYON."

"No shit", said Sammy.

Six months later, Dan found out that Kelly was homesick and tired of New York. He never saw her again, but one relationship held together. Dooley still went to see Dr. Cathy at the Acworth Animal Hospital.

In the following days, the planet could not stop talking about the "punch heard around the world." People found it fascinating. The CANYON would be considered strong by anyone's estimation, but there were those who believed he lacked the disposition, the will, to hit anybody with the strength he possessed.

The attack in Central Park changed everything.

A student at MIT did a paper that analyzed the likely power behind the punch, several factors.

Lin Huang, a third-year physics student at MIT, stood with his Professor in Boston in front of building 6C in Cambridge, MA.

"Good morning, my name is Lin Huang, a Junior Physics Major here at MIT. I have calculated the force and impact of the punch from Dan Johnson to the face of assailant Eugene Steubbins last week in New York."

"Several factors were used to derive at an approximate force, measured, naturally in "N" units. "Just then, his professor whispered something in his ear, where then Huang could be picked up saying, "but everybody knows that!" Looking impatient, Huang returned to the mic and said, "That stands for Newton Units". The professor pointed to a paper down in front of the mic. The student sighed, and continued, "The newton is the unit of force in the International System of Units. It is defined as 1 kg·m/s$^2$, the force which gives a mass of 1 kilogram an acceleration of 1 meter per second per second."

"In any event, I've calculated several variables in determining the N unit force applied to the face of the perpetrator. This includes the area of Dan Johnson's fist, his overall height, leg, hip, back dimensions, plus an estimate of both men's speeds. It uses his documented bench press of 819 pounds taken three years ago, and even calculates wind speed as established for Manhattan at that time by the national weather service. It then compares this N force to the average skin elasticity and bone density of a 43-year-old, 213-pound Caucasian man, with Dutch, English, German, and Swedish ancestry." A hand went up and a reporter asked with a straight face. "Why is the background of this perpetrator given equal weight." Huang nodded his head rapidly and spoke. "Yes, exactly, but we don't yet have DNA results back. That will be another week but is not expected to deviate more than the standard deviants for elasticity and bone density by region, especially given the regional similarities for Western Europe.

Anybody who had wondered what an angry, determined, or desperate Dan Johnson was capable of doing, now had their answer.

# NBA Action

The Knicks' first exhibition games took on the air of a playoff game, because of curiosity. The fans were curious, the competition was curious, the media, and the Knicks themselves. Even Dan himself was curious, but much to the disappointment of the fans, the first games were like so many exhibition games in professional sports. The players moved in and out. The starters didn't play much. In the first game against the Mavericks, Dan didn't go in until the $2^{nd}$ quarter, with the Knicks down by four. He immediately fed the ball for a fade away and hit it. The opposing player, a veteran and one-time all-star standing 6'10", could do nothing, just like in college.

When Dan was in the game, he did what he wanted. One time he went up and a player shoved him, and the sold-out Garden crowd (sold out for an exhibition?), booed loudly. Dan had no reaction. Not yet. If there was anything he'd be warned and coached about, it was that opposing players would see just how much abuse Dan Johnson was going to get. Nobody had the guts to take him on, physically, but they would push, shove, smack talk, whatever they felt they could get away with, and they were looking to see if they could rattle him. It was doubtful that anyone could hurt this man, but if they could rattle him, they could, maybe take him off his game, hurt his free throw percentage, maybe get him into foul trouble, to where he couldn't assert himself as easily.

Dan scored 17 points by the middle of the $3^{rd}$ quarter, with the Knicks up eleven. He had some interesting moments, like four slams, a good spin move, and three easy fadeaways, barely contested. He passed a lot, but the players moved in and out a lot, just as the Knicks planned.

The Knicks won by five, and nobody seemed to care. Announcers, the seasoned ones, stressed repeatedly that the Canyon was used sparingly, just like all the players. The Knicks knew what they had with him and were more interested in getting everybody into the game.

In the locker room, players on both teams also took a conservative view of things. One Maverick player, when asked about Johnson said. "Well, obviously he's a huge talent. We've all seen him in college, but the NBA is a lot different. He's massive and he's quick. The Knicks used him sparingly, which is about what we thought. We really won't know what he can do until we're closer to the start of the season, but obviously, he's going to be a major force. I mean, I don't believe he could be a bust."

A Knicks player said much the same thing. "Look, these games help the coaches and players ease into our gameplan. Man, the Canyon can take over a game but that's not the purpose here. He'll step up and do what the coaches ask of him. We all will. We'll be fine and there's no way you can take much from this game." The Daily News had a different take: "YAWNFEST". Knicks hold back the C Man. The newspaper exists to sell newspapers, so they ignored common sense. "Is this what the hype was all about? Yes, it's an exhibition game, but is this what the Knicks spent millions on? Surely, the fans, after a disappointing 1997, should want to put Dan Johnson on display, not hold him back.

But the Knicks knew what they were doing.

There were only 5 preseason games. Game two against the Warriors was much the same. Dan started and scored 14 points in the first quarter. No opposing players could really stop him. He rebounded, and the Knicks started to put on the passing show like the Wolverines. When Dan was double-teamed, he passed to an open man. On one occasion, he simply powered the basketball up and over a 6'9" opponent, who could do nothing, but it was another rookie. Dan sat out the entire 2nd half and the Knicks lost by two. Nobody seemed to care.

Dan played even fewer minutes in game three, and the Knicks won by seven. Another yawner. Coach Masters said that this was the purpose of exhibition games. No, they had no concerns about Dan, and did not put much stock into these games. Perhaps, no stock at all.

 The Knicks had one more exhibition game against the Heat. Dan started. He posted up, passed, took a pass and slammed it through. The Knicks played hard on defense and kept feeding the ball to the C Man, as if to say, "We can do what we want". Dan hit several fade aways, baby hooks, passed around the court like the Globetrotters. It was a clinic. The Knicks were up 67-24 at halftime. The Canyon sat out the entire 2nd half after scoring 32 points, and the Knicks cruised. 109-70.

The Daily News headline was, "Knicks let the Canyon out of the bag."

Things only opened up more as the season started. No more fooling around. The Knicks passed the ball around freely, and whenever Dan wanted to score, he did. When the shot was there, he took it, otherwise, he found the open man, players who, uncontested, hit a majority of their shots. The Knicks were suddenly 21-0 and fans across the basketball universe were beginning to ask if the Knicks might go undefeated.

The biggest problem that opposing teams faced wasn't so much that Dan Johnson was a good player. Of course, size or no size, Dan almost never missed those short 3-foot soft fadeaways, or baby hook shots. Nobody could get their hands on it, ever. The problem is that Dan had to be double-teamed to slow him down even a little bit, and then Dan, after eight years of high school and the game on a collegiate level, whipped the ball to the open man. One on one, Dan had to be fouled to stop, and in most cases, players could commit fouls, but couldn't stop him, resulting in a lot of 3-point plays. And Dan's foul shooting percentage was up to 84%.

Players, as expected, were getting frustrated. One player, already noted for his dirty play, figured out if he couldn't reach Dan's head or shoulders, he could most definitely find his feet. One way or another, this player's feet found their way onto Dan's. In other words, he stomped on his feet. It wasn't always easy to see, either. Dan did nothing, at first. Finally, Dan leaned down and said something to the player. The fans never saw it, but a Knicks player recalled it in the locker room. "Man, that dirty player. We're sick of that guy. He can't stop the C Man one bit, so he kept accidentally stepping on his feet, you know. Finally, the C Man, and I was standing right there, says to him.

212

"You stomp on my feet again, I'll stomp back and you're gonna get hurt." When asked what the opposing player said, the Knick player said, "Oh, he looked at Dan and shrugged his shoulders, like, "Who me?"

Dan would establish his power more and more. He had to suck it up and take regular shoves and even the occasional elbow. During one exchange, he said to a player. "Keep it up if you want that right back." The opposing player, very matter-of-factly, said "Look, CANYON, you're a beast and you're gonna get hit. What do you expect. If I can throw you off your game, I have to do it."

Even in the locker room, when asked about the fouls, Dan was philosophical. "I always knew it was coming. The coaches have gotten me ready. I have a lot of size and the opposing players try to slow me down. There's a certain amount of physical play I have to accept." "And what happens when an opponent goes too far?" "Well", Dan said. "I'm more than capable of standing up for myself against anyone in this league, and when I need to, I'll do that, but we're here to keep our composure and win games."

At the halfway point, the Knicks had a 39-2 record, top in the league by a long shot. In the only two games the Knicks lost, the Canyon was stepped on or ill, and taken out by halftime.

Dan was the starting center for the East during the NBA All-Star game and scored 26 points during the first half in the East's 142-121 victory and was voted the MVP for being the high scorer, even though he sat out the entire second half.

The second half of the season saw Dan Johnson take more control of games, scoring nearly at will, and averaging 46 points per game. The Knicks were 36-5 during the 2nd half and were the #1 seed in the playoffs with a 75-7 record.

The playoffs took on an aura perhaps never seen before in New York. Ticket prices for the games soared to record heights. Celebrities were seen in the arena like it was a major heavyweight boxing match. The Knicks made easy prey of their first two opponents, then played the Celtics in the Eastern Conference Championship.

One of the local TV stations took to the streets around New York, asking the crazed fans their prediction. "Man, I'm telling you, the C Man has been cruising. Wait until this series. He's just playin' with these guys. He's gonna blast those Boston Butt-Holes." Another fan said, "Hey remember the captain? Will Reed walking onto the court for game 7 against the Lakers? It's gonna be bigger than that except there won't be no game 7. Get the brooms out, baby. Sweep city!"

The hype was outrageous, and the Celtic fans had their regular field day with their "who can insult the CANYON worse". Signs with "freak" were plentiful, but much more creative than that, and crude. The Celtics came out ready for blood, Smacking the ball, smacking limbs, three technical, but the more they did that, the more the ball was fed to Dan, and at time he was even triple-teamed, and for one of the few times, Dan showed what he was capable of, power not displayed at Michigan or anywhere else. The man was 8'11" and 480 pounds. He simply powered his way over any Celtic player, and it was obvious that the Knicks went off their gameplan to show the Celtics that if they wanted to, they could beat and bloody them. At halftime, the score was 71-29, and Dan was kept in for the entire game, and though it seemed impossible, he stepped it up in the 2nd half. Dan scored 92 points and the Knicks won, 153-87, in the most lopsided playoff game in NBA history, and it would have been worse had the Celtics not caught fire in the last eight minutes and gone 6-8 in three-point attempts.

The Knicks swept the Celtics and went on to beat the Lakers just as badly. During the press conference, a newspaper reporter said, "Dan, it seems like you can simply do anything you want on the basketball court, that you're playing with your opponents like they're little children. Dan had no reason to boast. "No, I don't believe that at all. We've played tough opponents all year, but had a good gameplan, and that plan worked out, and I'm grateful for my teammates, coaches, and of course, the best fans in the world, here in New York."

Dan was voted the MVP of the finals, as well as the All-Star game and for the entire season. Another good reason for winning the finals was the clause in Dan's contract, paying him $10 million for winning the finals. He accepted his $15 million salary, which some thought of as low considering his potential, and instead put himself on the line to win a championship, and now he was the 2nd highest earner in the league.

The next day, the Daily News headline said, "C Man delivers, Knicks World Champs! Naturally, some of the celebrations got out of hand, including overturned cars. Dan stayed out late, and then got his limo back to his apartment on the upper west side. It was a Thursday, and a parade down, fittingly, the "CANYON of hero's" from Battery to City Hall. Dan had already called the owner of the Star Tavern and said, "let's have a local party". The owner loved it, and it was open to the public. Dan said he'd give the servers the best tips they've ever had, so they were excited. Dan only asked for one large table in the middle, and once inside, he told the crowd that all food and drink was on the house. Considering he just got a windful of $10 million, the $5,000 or so the night at the Star Tavern cost him was like a cup of coffee for almost anyone else.

Dan knew exactly what to say when the Star Tavern attendees yelled out "speech, speech." Dan was never one for words, but there was great relief, a great lift off his shoulders. He said, "Let me tell you, I am so excited to help bring the Knicks a World Championship." Shouts of "You did it, C Man, it's because of you!" Dan continued, "Hey, I'm glad to be part of it, and if I helped a little bit (putting his fingers together as if to say 'a little') then I'm happy. But of all the places I could be, where I want to be is in Jersey, in West Orange, (somebody yelled "this is Orange", which it was, by a couple of blocks.)" Dan laughed and said, "Okay, the Oranges, and what kind of name is that in Jersey?" You people in this state are so anxious to move down to Florida. People laughed, and then Dan went for the coup de grace, "It's a GREAT fucking name, that's what it is, and I don't want to be anywhere else tonight"). Dan got hugs all around, from the women, from the men. Billy always told him "Know your audience", and Dan, tonight, did.

Total happiness is a rare and amazing thing to be a part of.

# Downtime

Dan sat back with his feet in a bucket of cold water. He envisioned himself smoking a cigar and drinking a beer. He tried the cigar once, with his teammates, and turned gray while they laughed, but he did like his beer.

He then got up and put on a Dean Martin record. The front said, "The Reprise Years". His dad loved good albums and got him hooked on the "Rat Pack" and he wished he was half as cool as Dean. Nothing bothered him. He was carefree and happy, hanging out with Frank, Sammy, Joey Bishop and Peter Lawford. Nobody was more talented than Sammy, had more charisma than Frank, was funnier than Joey, and was, well, more European and Kennedy-esque than Lawford. But nobody was cooler than Dean. The music started to play.

*Somewhere there's a someone for everyone*
*Somewhere there's a someone for me*
*Though I may be lonely now*
*I'll see it through somehow*
*To someone's heart I know I hold the key*

*Somewhere there's a someone for everyone*
*Somewhere there's a someone for me*
*And I'll search my whole life through*
*Until I find a love that's true*
*For I know somewhere there's a someone for me*

As the music played, Dan put the beer bottle down, leaned his head back, and closed his eyes, slowly putting his enormous feet on a small table covered by a towel. The vision of his feet from across the room would be a sight to see for anyone. Meanwhile, the New York streets teemed with traffic.

# A New Deal

Dan's agent was at game four, in the locker room, and part of the festivities. At one point, one moment of sobriety, he whispered in Dan's ear. "Dan, the time to strike is now. Today is Thursday. Come to my office Monday." "I get it, Dan said", and on Monday, tired but exuberant, he stepped into Mike's office.

"Okay, Dan, the Knicks got a taste of winning the big one. They couldn't have done it without you. We can be modest in public, but this isn't the time to be modest." Dan liked being modest, but he agreed. There was a time and a place.

Your salary was $15 million when it could have been $25, but of course, you're getting that $10 million. Now, you've proven your case. Now we ask for $28 million straight out, for the next four years. "No incentives?" Dan asked. "Why, you've earned the right to ask for more, to be rewarded." You're still #2 in the league, and that's fair.

"Now, I've got better news. A shoe company, you remember who they are, want to make a shoe called The CANYON. They want to use the logo you've copyrighted. Dan, you're the top athlete in the world right now. They will market the hell out of CANYON, all over the world. The Chinese love you, Europe, Australia. They are predicting 20 million pairs in the first year. You'll get 5%. Dan, that's $75 million, and you'll hand over about three and a half million of that to me. It'll dwarf your NBA salary." Dan was silent. "Jesus. What do I say?" They want to fly here on Friday, in four days. They'll tell you how the shoes will be made. Get your artist friend over here. I know she owns half the copyright, but Dan, you're getting paid for you. Part of the deal is that you star in ads, so we have to talk about the timeline for that. They already have scripts. They know you're not exactly Cary Grant or Tom Cruise. "You have about five words." My advice is that you take 5% and ask for 1% for your friend.

"Let me call Ann Karlsson".

Jimmy Minnelli: "First comes the family."

*Gina & Grandma Luccia – Food is love.*

The Phantom of Fayetteville, Double M, Marvin Middleton of Basketball Tonight

Anne Karlsson at her New York Gallery

THE CANYON ON THE MAT

# Japanese artistic depiction of CANYON San

CANYONVILLE II
The REAL Mancave

# The Net Comes Down

**Painting by Anne Karlsson-1993**

Hail to the victors. The best 4 years.

People and Places Through the Years

## The Del Coronado Hotel, site of Dan's and Melanie's Wedding

**Two Friends
By Ann Karlsson 2026**

# CANYONVILLE

**CANYONVILLE** – Flowery Branch, GA
at Lake Lanier

# Vickers Stands for Victory

In 1759, William Abbott Vickers was a poor cobbler who learned his trade from his father in Northamptonshire, England, which would grow to become the shoemaking capital of Europe.

Vickers settled in Norfolk, Virginia, where he continued to make a meager living from the manufacture and repair of shoes. An early lithograph hanging in the Towson, MD offices shows an image of a small shop with a sign that simply says Vickers, Cobbler.

Vickers continued making and repairing shoes, some with fabric and buckles, which were common for the more well-to-do colonists, as well as more ordinary shoes, to inexpensive sandals with straps. William and his wife had a son named Thomas, who worked alongside his father.

A chance meeting with Patrick Henry, at the time a member of the Virginia House of Burgess, in 1773, led to a business proposition that would forever change the course of what would soon be called the Vickers Shoe Corporation. Henry, in Norfolk from Williamsburg, stopped at the Vickers shop to have a small repair done to his shoes. They struck up a conversation, an interest in horticulture, as well as American Independence, and Henry promised to visit again in the future. That visit later took place when Richard Henry Lee, Virginia delegate to the

First Continental Congress, and other delegates, in 1775, had to deal with the inadequate provisions to the Continental Army under Virginia native and former delegate, General George Washington. Henry, remembering his congenial encounter with William Vickers, penned this urgent letter, which now hangs in the Vickers Shoe Museum at the corner of W. 43rd Street and Eighth Avenue in New York City:

"1775

Dear Sir,

I send you greetings and salutations. You may recall our chance meeting at your shop approximately eight months ago. I had expressed a desire to communicate with you at some future point, and that brings me to an urgent proposition related to the welfare of our Continental Army, under the leadership of our Virginia comrade, General George Washington.

Sir, it is most obvious that a militia cannot function without proper footwear, and General Washington's troops are in dire need of, among many types of provisions and arms, ankle boots.

Your immediate cooperation in assisting with this need, and of expanding your facilities, and meeting the needs of our militia, will be greatly appreciated, and help to secure your business objectives.

Please respond back by courier, so that we may deliver a purchase agreement to you at once.

I am, Dear Sir, Your most obedient and most humble Servant.

P. Henry

Within a few short months, William Abbott Vickers had established the space, materials, manpower, and orders for thousands of pairs of boots, backed by the fragile yet earnest power of the new American government treasury.

The modern-day Vickers Shoe Corporation was born and has never looked back.

During the Civil War, the company moved, amongst growing tension between the northern and southern states, and settled just north of Baltimore, in the village of Towson.

Vickers continued to make boots for the military, as well as shoes of various types, and this continued into the 20th century.

It also remained a family-owned business.

George Vickers was the great grandson of Thomas Vickers, the founder's son, and he was born in 1872. George became a baseball fan and noticed how George Herman "Babe" Ruth had begun to transform the game. Ruth himself had humble Baltimore beginnings. Vickers was also a big believer in advertising, but his father felt it to be largely a waste of money, since most of their revenue still came from government contracts.

In April of 1923, Yankee Stadium, "the House that Ruth Built" went up in the Bronx, in New York, and Ruth as a sensation, a personality that the sport had never seen.

It was then that Vickers began to test the making of cleats, hardly a new sensation, but they hired Ruth to advertise them. The first as was simply an illustration of Ruth hitting one of his massive homers, which the caption, "Vickers baseball shoes keeps me rounding the bases." The company shelled out a lot of money to Ruth, but the shoe quickly became a top seller. Other well-known baseball players were signed up to represent the brand.

The concept of advertising started even before the early baseball years, with some inserts in newspapers to publicize the company's continued production of boots for the military. One such ad had the headline "They're over there. So are we."

"All our boys wear Vickers boots." This was, of course, a take on the hugely popular "Over There" tune written in 1917 by George M. Cohan. This was the first time the "Vickers stands for victory" slogan appeared, but not like it would be during the Second World War.

During World War Two, the Vickers Corporation established itself as one of the most iconic advertisers that the nation had ever seen. Under the leadership of young 35-year-old, Walter, "Walt" Vickers (1907-1986), George's son, the company put out a steady stream of award-winning ads that came from an illustrator that the company lured from Disney.

Some of the illustrations were so iconic that they became revered by collectors, could fill a museum's halls, which they did just two blocks from Times Square.

Some of the great headlines included.

- Let's March to Berlin with Vickers
- Shoes make the man. Vickers makes the shoes.
- Stepping all over the Fuhrer

It wasn't so much clever headlines, but the artwork; the fighters, the bombers, the ship, the ads that pulled all your heartstrings, like the famous, "They fought for freedom", and "Leave a present for them under the tree".

Some ads used stereotype drawings that would be considered insensitive today, it but was a sign of the times.

Of course, at the bottom was the company slogan, "Vickers stands for victory!" The "V" in Vickers transformed in to now-famous victory sign flashed so often by Winston Churchill. Churchill himself bought a pair and wore them to a session of Parliament, reminding everyone that the company was "British inspired", conveniently leaving out that the company was formed largely to help defeat the British.

After the war, the "the Good War", as coined later, the military began a major downsizing, and that included the number of boots and other military footwear. It wasn't unexpected, but Walt Vickers didn't at all plan well. Much of the company downsized, and within twenty years, moved much of their production overseas. It was a common move, and so was the ugly commentary, threats of a boycott, and even violence, as when a car, owned by a disgruntled former worker, ran through part of a building, killing three employees, and the driver as well.

This began a dark period for Vickers, and the weak leadership of Walt's son Danley only made matters worse. Even with experience in using athletes as spokespersons, the company was slow to move production overseas. Margins shrunk, and competitors from Converse to Nike took control. Vickers has a famous name but not as much among the Generation X Group and even less among the Millennials. It was time to move aggressively or put a final nail in the coffin of what once was an iconic American company.

Enter Lisa Vickers Sawyer.

Lisa Vickers Sawyer was a smart-alecky kid who nobody ever said "no" to. She was given material possessions instead of tough love, and it showed. Problems in school and troublesome boyfriends were her tools for grabbing attention. Then suddenly, just like that, she seemed to turn the corner. Two years at a community college, one of the only schools that would take her, led to a transfer to Boston University and a 4.0 GPA over two years, and then across the river to Harvard Business School, where she graduated third in her class. Not bad for a kid that only eight years earlier was a lost cause.

Lisa Sawyer was made CEO at the shockingly young age of 32, after a rapid six-year career at the company, straight out of Harvard, though it was a company tradition to get a

Vickers in charge, and good ole dad, Dan, at 58, was ready to retire to the family homestead in the Hamptons.

Lisa had a fresh attitude along with a thinly veiled, wild streak from her earlier days. She married Todd Sawyer of Sawyer Industries, when she turned thirty, in a move many considered more of a merger than a marriage, but Lisa had a survival instinct, and she was going to put Vickers back on top if she had to kill somebody to do it.

Lisa Vickers could have a wicked streak of humor, so people that knew her joked that "she might stab you in the back, but you'd die laughing". To the surprise of some, she hired Stephon Williamson as Director of Marketing. Stephon came from a tough upbringing in Camden, NJ. His Dad left the family when Stephon, aka Stevie, was two, and he and his mom and older brother fought to survive every day. Stevie was a bright, precocious kid, and everybody knew it, including his teachers, many who had just given up. A school system that didn't care, students that had lost hope and felt abandoned, parents that wanted to care, but had to figure out how to get something to eat on the table and make sure a stray bullet didn't take out one of their kids during the night. It wasn't a neighborhood on the way down. It was a neighborhood anchored to the bottom.

Stevie dreamed of traveling to other worlds, being on Star Trek, and playing Saxophone in a famous jazz band. Somehow or another, Stevie became that one-in-million. He fought off the taunts of "Uncle Tom" and beatings, to ace his classes and get a full academic scholarship to Drexel, and then another scholarship to Wharton. All within a few miles of Camden. And then, he caught the attention of Lisa Vickers herself, who needed a fresh vision. It was July 1998, and the Knicks had just won an NBA Championship with Dan Johnson at center.

Stephon Williamson laid it all out. Vickers had the name, but needed to dive into the world of sports like it did in the military world, and do it largely in the inner city, the basketball world. It had to appeal to the African American crowd the right way. Teach them the history of Vickers. Reach across and narrow the generational gap. Find a savior. That savior was going to be one Dan "The CANYON" Johnson.

While it was true that Johnson was white, he played the Black Man's Game, had been around young black men since high school. Most of all, he was "the man". A champion. Dominant and strong. This would appeal to all young men. Even non-players and certainly white, Latino, and Asian young men wouldn't want to be left behind. Yes, Dan Johnson transcended race, and even sports. Stephon presented "The CANYON Basketball Shoe".

Stephon told Lisa Vickers. "Close your eyes". Vickers responded with "Remember, we have an anti-sexual harassment policy here."

Stephon was in the zone so that lame joke went without a response.

"Close your eyes, the commercial starts with military music but quickly changes to a hip-hop beat. Vickers Shoes supplied the nation with shoes made for war, and now a new battle on the court, sleek, powerful, taking your game to its highest level. Named for the biggest force in the game. THE CANYON BASKETBALL SHOE." The background will show Dan Johnson posting up and slamming the ball through. He grabs a rebound, turns to the camera, and says coldly, "ELEVATE YOUR GAME."

"I love it. Call his agent. Figure out the details and expand the plan. I want to see it all laid out, timetable, budget, and most important, 3-year revenue projections."

That night, Lisa had dinner and drinks with her gal pal, Sue Buckley, in the city, who she confided in on just about everything. "This is how we bring the company back, and I'm the leader. I'll get the credit." "So, what do you think of that huge guy, The CANYON". "Oh, c'mon, Lisa laughed, a dirty laugh." A nine-foot man? He's hot." Sue smiled and said what they were both thinking. "Can you just imagine?" "I'd ride that Johnson into the next county. Yippee Ki-Yay." Sue spit out a little bit of her drink. It was just between close friends. Girls just wanna have fun.

# The First Meeting

Stephon requested a meeting at Mike's offices with Mike and Dan. It was a Saturday morning, a little unusual, but Stephon and Mike were anxious to get the obvious going. This deal is worth a great deal of money. For Mike, it was the money. Only the money. Mike loved going to Yankees games with his kids and having nobody notice him. He didn't want the life of the CANYON. Screw that. It wasn't just the notoriety. It was the demand that the public thought you owed them. Dan tried to get away, but how can you? Do you owe the public more? Humphrey Bogart once said, "All you owe the public is a good performance." Wasn't a world championship enough? No, Mike was more than happy with the money and anonymity. Lots of money.

For Dan, well, he had money now. Any more would be nice but he figured out a way to Foundation something more important, like a charity or something outside of sports.

For Stephon, it wasn't the money. Oh, he'll take it. Think of how much it could help his mama and brother. No, it was about redemption. Maybe he could talk his boss, Lisa Vickers, whom he trusted as far as he could spit, into a nice bonus, but most likely, it would be a great addition to his resume so he could get the hell out of there. After all, his name wasn't Vickers. Just think of William Abbott Vickers watching a Black man as CEO of his company. Stephon laughed. No, snicker would be more like it.

No, Stephon Williamson wanted redemption. For all the years he walked terrified in his own neighborhood. For all the times his mother was pushed around by men, for all the times his classmates called him "Little Uncle Tom". "Quit, you're acting like a little while boy. You ain't never going anywhere."

Stephon, who had to take a bus to Marlton to learn calculus. Stephon, who was the Boys' State Delegate for his school, which was held at Rider College, just seven miles away, in Lawrenceville, but where he met other boys like him. Eager, hopeful for the future. Boys who told him. You can get out. You can make it. Only listen to positive people. Boys that in another year would not be walking the streets at night, but walking campuses in Princeton, New Brunswick, Annapolis, and University Park.

"Stephon, please come in," Mike said. "Coffee?" No thanks. "Good drive from Baltimore?" "Not bad", Stephon said. "I actually drove up here last night and stayed in Secaucus for the night." "Do you go by Steve, or Steven?" "No", he said. It's Stephon."

"Well,", Larry said. Is it okay to dive right into it? You want to start? I guess that's the proper thing."

"Yes," Stephon said. "Look, this is a big thing. I don't want to make it any other way, but it doesn't have to be complicated. We want to make a great basketball shoe and name it 'The CANYON Basketball Shoe.' Named after you,

Mr. Johnson. Advertised by you. A bold, aggressive, expensive campaign aimed at capturing the imagination of our target market, people who aspire to be like you. People who will pay a lot of money to acquire these shoes, and then buy another pair every year. We want to make annual editions, maybe a kid's version, maybe a woman's version. We want CANYON to be the #1 brand and for that, we are willing to pay you a great deal of money."

"Well, Stephon", Mike said. We love the idea. We want to do it, but the devil is in the details. The manufacture, the materials. We want to bring in our own Footwear Design Engineer experts. We want tensile strength tests from independent labs against the competition, the ad vehicles, is Dan in all of them? We want to see the scripts, we want to see storyboards, we want to know where ads will be placed, what kind of shoes. We want to know in what details outlets the shows will be.

Then, of course, is the financial structure. How is Dan to be paid? We prefer a percentage of the business with a guaranteed annual minimum and no cap. We want a lifetime contract. Dan just finished his first year and will play several more years."

Stephon kept a straight face. "Did you forget anything?" Honestly, probably, but let's talk again.

"You write up your demands and send it". Next time, we will meet in Baltimore to finalize this. We'd like this wrapped up in two weeks. Please send over your list in three days if you don't mind".

"Great," said Mike. Have a great trip back home.

Dan said nothing the entire time. "Went well, Mike said. "I couldn't tell," said Dan. He looked a little pissed. "Oh, hell no. For Vickers, it's now or never. This is their last grasp. Maybe 'gasp' is a better word. Maybe you haven't studied everything about them, but I have. You don't need them. They need you. This is negotiation, and the best part of my job."

# Turning up the Heat

Dan dropped by Mike's office on Monday, two days later.

"Dan, there's another big athlete getting a 5% commission on gross sales, and a lifetime contract. I've also put in some language on when commissions will be paid, beginning 90 days after the start of the first month product is shipped, and then a monthly check. You and I will add an additional amendment."

"Mike", Dan said, "that's fine. You're my agent, just like many athletes have agents and lawyers. I do want you to negotiate on my behalf, and you'll always get the money we agree upon, in writing, but I do have the authority to speak up when I'd like to." "Of course, Dan", Mike said. You're the client. You own the business transaction. This is all about you, and I am your advocate. I am here to see that get the best possible deal that you can." "Thanks, Mike" Dan said. "I appreciate that. I'd like to tell you a few things I know today that I didn't know two days ago.

"I followed Stephon out the door on Saturday and bought him a beer at that place you told me about around the corner. You know the one with the little spinning wheel in the urinal. I wanted to learn a little more about him. Why he's so serious. He's had a hard life, and he is a warrior. He never should be where he is. He's one in a million. Came up on the streets. No father, and when I think everything, my dad did to guide me, and even today, other men in my life that have guided me, and he and his mother did it alone. I find it both terrible and amazing that Stephon went through that. Terrible for the loneliness and peer pressure to give up, and amazing that he DIDN'T give up. This kid hid in libraries so he wouldn't get beaten up after school. His mother kept saying, "Baby, don't give up, don't give up, because you're smart enough to make it, and you will make it. Those other boys don't want you to succeed. You want to get back at them? You keep studying, baby, and you'll go far. If you get top grades, we'll find a way to get you to college. So, Stephon got an academic scholarship to Drexel University and was Vice President of his Junior and Class and President of his Senior Class. He was a big brother in a program they had, and a member of the Alpha Phi Alpha fraternity for three years. Then, graduating magna cum laude, he received a scholarship to study at Penn's Wharton School of Business. This guy is an overachiever, and the CANYON Basketball shoe was his idea from the very beginning."

"That's commendable, Dan, but", "I'm not done, Mike." Dan continued.

I've also read about Vickers. I knew about their ads because studying about World War Two is a hobby of mine. They've got cool, vintage ads. I didn't know about the museum here in the city, so yesterday, I went. Vickers is an iconic company, Larry, formed during colonial times. The founder was personally asked by Patrick Henry and

George Washington to make boots for the Continental Army, and in World War Two they reached their peak. Since then, they've been hurting. They've slipped. Lisa Vickers Sawyer, I've read, is a tough cookie, and she's not going to pay this guy Stephon any more than she must. This is his time, and we can make it happen while getting rich ourselves."

"But Dan", this is a good time to teach you that you can't be responsible for other people all the time. Whatever financial agreement Stephon makes with Lisa Vickers, or the Vickers company, is none of our business. You've worked hard, too, and this is the deal that will make you a very rich man for the rest of your life." "Yes", said Dan, but I think we may be Stephon's only chance. He will NEVER run that company. A Vickers has always run it, and that's fine, but let's give Stephon a piece of this deal. Let him wet his beak." "His what?". "Oh c'mon, Mike", I don't know if I can do business with someone who doesn't know the best quotes from the Godfather." "But I saw that movie and I don't remember that line." "It's from Godfather 2, and some people think the sequel was better than the original." "Not to get off-topic, which you always do, but which did you like the best?" "Oh, the original, I'm a purist, but the 2nd one was damn good. We'll talk about it some time."

"Anyway," Dan said. I've got some ideas, and I may take over. It's my deal and I may have few things to say, and from my vantage point, you know, that's high up, Mike, we're holding the cards, not a 2nd rate shoe company that might be on its last breath. I respect their history, mind you, but our little business is on the upswing. They can jump on it or get run over." "Wow," said Mike. "I don't know if I like this 'new you' or not." "Well said Dan, "Once in a while, it's gonna come out to play."

"Well, you do what you gotta do", said Mike. "Isn't that a Godfather quote?" "You know, Mike," Dan said, smiling, "you got me there. Maybe the Don to Sollozzo. Of course, now I've got to watch it for the 65th time. But, Mike, fair notice. There's a very good chance I stand up and walk out down in Baltimore. You know better than anyone what the Knicks pay me and what other offers I have. Funny how $30 or $40 million gives you confidence."

# Forgiveness

It was June 15th, 1998, when Cathy and Dan had just returned from New York, where there was a tickertape parade for the Knicks first championship in twenty-five years.

They've seen Dan stand atop a podium at the Olympics several times, and they couldn't keep up with all the national championships in Judo, in Wrestling, and perhaps even crazier and more delirious than everything else, combined were the final fours and celebrations in Ann Arbor. College kids are crazier than ever, and Dan and Cathy, as the C Man's parents, were the toast of the town everywhere they went around Ann Arbor and New York. Certainly, they were celebrated everywhere they went around Marietta and Atlanta. Kids in Ann Arbor literally bowed down to them, as a cute, ceremoniously symbolic "thank you" for getting together to make this boy. But the parade down New York's "Canyon of Heroes", the name not being lost on the public or the newspaper headlines ("City Honors the CANYON and the Knicks with glorious parade down the Canyon").

It was a great weekend. It wasn't the first time that Dan and Cathy met the Minnelli's, as they came to visit Dan last Christmas, but the Minnelli's attended the parade, with great seats, and the entire group went out to dinner in New York's Little Italy and hung out at a bar in the neighborhood until after midnight. Grandma Luccia even joked that she took an extra-long nap that day so that she could keep up with everybody. Dan put everybody up at an extremely nice hotel in midtown. Nobody was going back to New Jersey after this night of celebrating.

As the years went by, the city seemed to expect a championship from Dan, and they got it, seven more years in a row, and by the fourth year, the parade was cancelled due to "costs". That drew the ire of many fans and even the media, who criticized the city for feeling entitled. "The day will come, and maybe faster than you think, when the Knicks and city won't have the CANYON to lean on anymore." It spoke to his roots in Georgia and his cozy if not amazing lake house. "This man, this man named, for some reason, CANYON, will be tired of the expectations. The expectations that simply by lacing up his shoes, shoes named after him and will, at some point, make him a billionaire more than playing the game now, that he will continue to take the Knicks to the glory land. He told the public that we would retire after five years, and the response to that was 'nonsense, a 27-year-old doesn't quit the game when they're so young and on top.' It would be no surprise then, that after seeing the city downplay the accomplishments of any one championship, that it was simply another year with the CANYON, that the large man himself will pick up and leave the west side and sit back with a cold one on the shores of Lake Lanier in North Georgia. After all, many New Yorkers dismiss the fact that this young man has competed at the highest levels since he was a young teen, in not one, but three sports.

One day, and that day may come soon, the CANYON will decide that he has had enough, take his trophies and go home, and New York won't have to worry about the cost of confetti and police protection.

But this wasn't the third or fourth year, it was the first in twenty-five-years, since the days of Walt "Clyde" Frazier, Earl the Pearl, DeBusschere, Bill Danley, future coaching legend Phil Jackson, and Captain Willis Reed. The city was awash with excitement, and the Johnsons, all of them, were the stars. It was bigger than any of Dan's many awards before. This was the world's most exciting city, rolling out the red carpet, and it was an amazing thing.

Cathy and Chuck had a brief, quiet moment in the mayhem, clinking champagne glasses, and wondering if they really thought a day like this would happen. Chuck said, "I always dreamed about it. I mean, despite the classical music we played, the insistence that he take AP courses in high school, the sheer odds of it all, yes, I always dreamed about world championships for Dan. I saw past his size, which I've had mixed feelings about, and I saw the determination in his eyes, even in our driveway, when he would throw me, chest passes over and over again. School all day, then practice, then more practice, then homework until 11:00 PM, then bed, and then the next day, do it all again. I'm tired now just thinking about it." Cathy smiled and said, "Well, I always hated it. I wondered why he couldn't be a normal size. I hated the "snickers" around Marietta, the looks, and I wondered what people were saying to us, but mostly, what they were saying about little Danny." Cathy stopped to realize her use of the word "little". "Ha, ha, little. But that's how I've always seen him. Little Danny. A little boy with a big imagination, a sweet disposition. I'm just a country girl at heart from Baldwin County, Alabama. I didn't want our family to be thrust into this limelight, especially Dan, but God chose this path for all of us. But Danny will do more than this. I just feel it. But I still worry about his health. The stress on his body, and I want him to retire at a young age and go enjoy life in some other way. "

The next morning, at the Minnelli's insistence, everybody took a limo over the Hudson to the West Orange home in Llewellyn Park. There was cooking to be done, and Dan, much to the shock of his parents, sang the Italian Song Al Di La, somewhat decently, anyway, that Grandma Luccia had taught him. At some point, Tony ushered everybody into cars, and they went up to Eagle Rock Reservation. Tony opened a cooler, but instead of Pabst Blue Ribbon, there were three bottles of champagne, and in a bag, cheap plastic cups, and with the New York skyline in the background, even though some haze, still visible, they toasted the Knicks championship, and toasted to family and friendship. Tony said, "Hey everyone, championships come and go, and they're great, but friends and family are forever, and they're better." Dan joked, "Tony, that is really good, and it was clean, too." Tony laughed and said, "A time and a place for everything, my tall friend."

Cathy and Dan spent another night in the city, this time, alone, and caught up on some sleep, and the next morning, took a commercial flight out of LaGuardia, to Atlanta. They went unnoticed, fortunately.

It was a Monday evening, Dan and Cathy back at work. They didn't get a break, not yet. At about 9:00 that night, the phone rang. A little late for their liking, but not what most would consider a "scary hour to get a phone call." Cathy answered the phone in a halting voice. "Um, yes, Cathy?" Cathy answered a little suspiciously, "Yes?" The voice continued, and Cathy could hear a shakiness to it that made her a little nervous. "Cathy, you probably don't remember me, but my name is Lisa Chambers. We had little boys around the same time, and we even had them in a little play group for a short time." Well, she could have stopped at Lisa Chambers, because Cathy remembered. It was more than a remembrance. It was a burning hole in her chest, even after all these years. Well, maybe not a burning hole, but it was tucked away and every so often, Cathy pulled it out, and it got her angry all over again. "Yes, Lisa, I remember you, and I remember why Dan and I left that little playgroup. What can I do for you?" "Well," Lisa said nervously, I know it seems so silly. It was such a long time ago, and Dan is now so famous and all, but I have never forgiven myself for the way we treated you that day." "Well," Cathy said, "What was said didn't come from you. I remember it like it was yesterday." "No," Lisa said, "No, it didn't." "It was Ginger", said Cathy. "Well, yes. Well, again, I know how silly and stupid this all is, and how I know it seems like I just want to get a burden off my shoulders,

257

which I do, but I laughed at her comment, and I have always felt very guilty about it. I have carried a lot of remorse, but I suppose I have been too embarrassed to call after all these years, but I am doing it now to say that I am sorry." Cathy could hear Lisa crying softly on the phone. Cathy felt a little foolish now herself. "Well, it has been a very long time. I haven't forgotten but you didn't say it. Yes, it was wrong. More than that, I was hurt and angry, but Danny didn't understand anything and to this day, has never been told, so I forgive you, especially considering that you didn't say it. Of course, you shouldn't have laughed. It was hurtful, but I can forgive you, especially now. If I were you, I would strike it from my memory, because I'm not so small that I can't forgive someone after an apology. Besides, it should be Ginger calling instead.

Well, how is your son doing? I'm sorry, but I've forgotten every little boy's name from that group. It didn't last more than three of four times." Cathy could hear more crying from over the phone and immediately had a feeling of dread. "Well, Joey, he grew up to be such a cute, little boy, always curious about everything, but then as a teenager, he got caught up in the wrong crowd. Lenny and I tried to do whatever we could to help him, but nothing seemed to work. There were small victories but always followed with a setback. Anyway, a little more than three years ago, we lost Joey to a drug overdose. I realize that I'm just feeling sorry for myself, and I suppose I'm jealous, too. You know, Cathy, we didn't need a basketball champion, or other sports Dan is so great at. We told Joey we love him. We tried everything to help him, but he wouldn't help himself."

Cathy was speechless, so she said the only thing she could think of. "I'm terribly sorry for your loss. I'm sure you did all that you could do. I wish there was more I could say to ease your pain." "There's not," Lisa said. "You know, we watched Dan succeed all these years. Joe wasn't at Wheeler, but we all watched him. In Michigan, during the Olympics. In a way, and despite my terrible actions, we took Danny on as a sort of second son. I know it sounds weird, but I do want to tell you that we always rooted him on. You and your husband have done such a great job, obviously, as parents, and then, more crying started. Cathy felt remorse now at her prior anger but had to end the call.

"Lisa, I'm sorry, but I must leave now. Please accept my sincere condolences. I do forgive you and God Bless you and your family. Goodbye."

Naturally, Chuck could sense the strain of the call, even from just Cathy's voice, and they had a conversation about it. "How do you feel", asked Chuck. "I have a lot of emotions swirling right now, most of them sad, but some of them grateful. Does that make any sense, Chuck? "Yes", he said. "Especially the grateful part".

# Oh Say, can you See?

It was the 1998-1999 season, the 2$^{nd}$ in the great C Man's storied career. The Eastern Conference Finals. The Knicks got off their bus just outside the Boston Garden for their 4$^{th}$ game against the Celtics, leading 2-0. The Celtics had put up about as tough a fight as any team could do, with the best-known strategy to keep the Canyon busy and less effective, if that's ever possible. That included a lot of passing and interference trying to keep the ball away from his mammoth wingspan, by going around and under his reach. The problem on offense with the C Man isn't much different than being on defense. Even though you can somewhat preoccupy Dan Johnson, the other players on the team were more than adequate in compensating. The Knicks took games one and two in New York, winning 128-72 and 141-90. As in the regular season, the Canyon gave the Knicks just too many options to score, seemingly at will. The Celtics could never establish an inside game and had to rely on outside shooting, the dilemma of every team facing the Knicks this season. On defense, the Knicks moved the ball around the court, finding the open man or letting the Canyon put the ball into the hoop, usually by an easy fade-away, or spin move that allowed him to just lay the ball in as easy as about any athletic man standing nearly nine feet tall. It has become a broken record of sorts, with the Knicks once again taking care of business. With the extremely capable Lamar Pennington taking over the Canyon's role throughout the game and most of the 4<sup>th</sup> quarter, the Knicks simply built a cushion and have been able to at least sustain it.

On offense, Dan found the open man, except of course, when the team simply needed a quick score, and it was fed into Dan, which was always done, anyway. Dan could find any opening for a quick finger-roll, dunk, turn-around, or baby-hook. Nobody could reach the ball with the arch Dan put on it, the result of thousands of hours in the gym, repeating moves, and repeating them again. Ultimately, the opposing team needed to foul, and it took a monstrous foul to stop Dan. You couldn't slap his arms when they were nine feet in the air. You couldn't push a 520 lbs. man out of the way very easily. You could work the lower body a lot easier, the needs, the feet, but even then, it took a serious blow to disrupt him, and by then, the entire arena saw the frustration that every team and every opponent had to deal with, every possession, every game, and every season. And it didn't end there. Too many fouls and you were out. Every team in the league broke records for the number of fouls, forcing players either out of the game with a quarter to go, or having to let The Canyon go to the basket, which in almost every case, he was going to do whether the opponent liked it or not. And then, when he did shoot, the C Man had an 86% free throw percentage, good for 36<sup>th</sup> in the league. That was often the best choice when paying Dan Johnson. The decisions went from "bad" to "worse". The Knicks practiced a scenario of situations where a defense would practice a way to stop the C Man. When something new was tried, the Knicks simply put hours of time adapting to it, countering it. Making it just as exasperating as all the other moves. The problem came down to this. Dan Johnson was not only incredibly tall in a tall man's game, but he was also one of the best players in the league, regardless of height, and the Knicks took every opportunity to exploit their prize. In addition, his teammates had some of the best years. Field goals percentages went up since Dan was usually double and even triple-teamed, allowing for wide-open shots given to some of the best shooters in the world. When the team was up by over 15 points, Dan rested, and the back-up, Lamar Pennington, the first-team, ACC player from Duke, got in the game and often played an entire half, keeping him happy as a most valuable 6$^{th}$ man. This was done as much for team harmony than strategy, as Lamar could start for most any other NBA team, and he often contemplated leaving for a team he could call his own. He didn't leave, because he liked winning championships, and he didn't like the thought of playing against the C Man. The solution was to give him quality minutes against the top centers in the league, and there were times when Lamar started the game. Dan would often tell the press, "LaMarr is one of the world's top players. It's amazing that we have him on the team. He's a better shooter and I'd say, better player than me. Together, we're a tough combination to beat and I hope I can play with him for my entire career here in New York." Once, Lamar told Dan, "Well, it's so comforting how the team babies me, tries to keep me happy as a backup, where I would start almost anywhere else." Dan answered the only way he could, sincerely. "Lamar, you really are one of the world's best players. I would never blame you if you left but I would be among the most upset, because in addition to making us so tough, you're a good friend. I'll support you and love you no matter what you do." It was hard to answer that when you already had two rings on your hand, and a fat paycheck. Lamar stayed.

As the Knicks walked through a covered area just before the opening to the building, with a series of reporters wearing "official credentials" badges, Knick and Celtics representatives, wives and families, and assorted arena personnel, somebody yelled "Hey Canyon", and Dan looked to feel a clear liquid squirt into his eyes. They burned tremendously, and he knelt way down with his hands over his face. Somebody from the team yelled, "Get that guy", and somebody else, "C, what is it? Despite the burning, Dan said, "He squirted something in my eyes, and I can't see. Shrieks of horror filled the area. The worse fears of the team were coming true. Of course, how many cared for Dan the person vs Dan the player will never be known, but for the moment everybody wanted to help, or kill the SOB, who was already being held down on the ground. "Somebody get water, a lot of water. Somebody from the arena ran inside. "Dan, keep your eyes shut. We're going to flush your eyes out with water. Hurry up, damn it, where's the water. The team trainer and traveling physician, who was an orthopedic surgeon, knelt before him. Out came a resource worker who grabbed a bucket and filled it with water. "Okay, Dan, it's Dr. Gleason. We're going to pour water into each eye slowly. It's gonna burn, but we gotta get that out." Dan lied down and one of the attendants said to a third "hold his legs". They leaned on his side so the water and hopefully, whatever contaminant was in his eyes, were flushed out. They poured into one eye and then the other. Then they did it again. "Fill this up again and get a second bucket!" Within two minutes, they were alternating pouring water into both eyes, turning Dan's massive body to one side and then the other. Ten minutes of eye flushing. Finally, Dan said "It doesn't burn so much anymore." Dr. Ben Gleason, head physician for the Knicks told the trainer. "We're covering his eyes with gauze and getting him to a hospital. He's not playing today." Dr. Gleason himself called Massachusetts General Hospital and said, "This is Dr. Benjamin Gleason, head physician for the New York Knicks basketball team. An assailant has attacked Dan Johnson, one of our players, with an unknown chemical irritant of some kind. We are rushing him to the hospital. Please have your best ophthalmologist on-hand. Call him in. This is an emergency.

"Hey Doc, it stopped burning," Dan said. "Dan, I don't care. We don't know what we've got going on here. We're going to find out." "Doc, we've also got a conference playoff game." "Dan, you're not playing tonight, period."

"This is Byron Clarke with NBC Sports, and we've been told that Dan Johnson has been injured while walking into the Boston Garden, and that something was thrown in his eyes. He has already left the area and is being transported to a local hospital for observation." "Byron, this is Kathryn Reynolds back at NBC Studios in New York. Do we have any idea what kind of substance was thrown into Dan Johnson's eyes?" "No Kathryn, we have no further information, but we do have a witness we're about to speak with. Let's take it to our courtside analyst, Steve Danley. Steve?"

"Byron, this is Steve Danley just outside the Boston Garden where a terrible incident involving Dan Johnson, the Canyon. We have a witness, Joey Richardson, who was on his way into the arena as a concession worker. Joey, what did you see?" "Yeah, so I'm walking into the Garden and get my stuff, see? Traffic sucked, you know, with the game in town, and even though I wasn't supposed to use the players and media entrance, I had my pass and all, so I thought, 'fuck it'", just get inside, you know? I see the Knicks walking in a single file from a bus. No mistake, you know, bunch of giant guys about to lose to my beloved Celtics, right?" Steve was getting impatient, "Please, sir then what happened", "So yeah, like I was saying, these wicked tall guys pass me, and I see the Canyon. Can't exactly miss the guy. Holy shit is he tall. Minding his own business, you know, when suddenly this dude with, like a plastic bottle, acts like he knows where he's going, to look inconspicuous, right? Then he walks right past the Canyon and yells something like 'Hey Canyon'. The Canyon is so freakin' tall, right, so this asshole squirts some liquid up in the air, and most of it, maybe not all of it, but most of it goes right into his face. It was like a clear squeeze bottle, you know." Steve looked like he was trying to pull teeth. "Well then what happened, did he scream out in pain, and please, sir, watch your language, we're live on tv." "Oh, shit, sorry about that. Well, that's the thing, he didn't make any noise at all. He covered his eyes and got down on one knee, like to get his balance because his eyes were closed. He didn't yell or make any noise. Then, all hell broke loose, and a bunch of guys pushed me out of the way. Then they talked to the Canyon, and he lied down."

Steve went on, "and what about the assailant?" "Oh, the guy who did it? He got about ten feet, and he was knocked down to the ground. I saw at least one of the players knock him down and then about ten guys landed on him. I shit you not." Steve was unable to control this guy. "Well, yes, okay, so he was detained. Then what?" "Well, the police came and cuffed the guy. When I looked back at the Canyon, they were pouring just a shitload of water into his eyes. Like bucket fulls, and I mean freakin bucket fulls. Some guy with an arena badge, you know, like I'm wearing. You see, you can't do shit without one of these badges on." Steve was exasperated, "Yes, we know. What happened next." Joey, the concession worker went on. "Yeah, so the Canyon is on his side, see, and he's very calm. He was talking to a couple of guys; I think they were from the Knicks. Then an ambulance came, and they put him in, and they left. Oh, they wrapped a bandage around both his eyes, covered them up, you know, and put him on stretcher but it was a freakin joke because it went as far as his ass and then the rest of him was hanging out. You'd think an ambulance already at the Boston Garden for an NBA game would figure out to have longer stretchers, you know? I was thinking, "Holy shit, who's in charge of this? So anyway, he goes in. I was afraid the guy would stick out. Maybe they moved the front seat way up, and they got him in somehow, and they drove off. And that was it. I tell ya, I love my boys in green, but I wanted to kick that asshole terrorist in the face, you know what I mean? I mean talk about poor sportsmanship. Fuckin' people in this world." A blast came from the NY studio, "Cut this damn guy off, already." Steve quickly said, "Ok, that's an eyewitness report from just outside the Boston Garden".

Byron Clarke recapped, "If you're just tuning in, superstar center Dan "The Canyon" Johnson was attacked just as the New York Knicks exited their bus to walk into the locker room at the Boston Garden, soon to play game three of the seven-game series, with the Knicks leading two games to zero.

Ultimately, physicians at Mass General determined that the irritant was simply hydrogen peroxide, likely straight from a bottle of contact lens solution. The trainers and physician with the Knicks were credited for minimizing potential long-term damage by performing a thorough flushing of the C Man's eyes.

Dan did not play, and the Celtics won the game by five points. The uproar and demands that the Celtics forfeit the game was tremendous, but that never happened, and things calmed down somewhat when Dan played the next two games, and the Knicks dominated, winning the series 3-1. It didn't put an end to the arguments about security.

Wanting to show his appreciation without "going crazy", Dan sent the Knick's physician the top set of golf clubs by Taylor Made. He never lifted a club, but Rod Dorfman, the Knick's GM, played all the time, and helped him out. The Knick's trainer, not on the same pay scale as the Orthopedic surgeon, must want something, Dan thought. One way or another, Dan discovered that his trainer, Jim Beckley, had a girlfriend just dying to go on a cruise, so Dan called a travel agent he knew in the city, and asked her to get on the case, for a premium, of course, and "make it happen." The next time he was in the building, after the series, Ralph was all hugs, deliriously happy that he and his girlfriend were going on a 7-day cruise to the Greek Isles, all expenses paid, plus a very sizable "account" for all the extras. For what Dan was worth, insurance or not, it was a small "thanks" for potentially saving his sight.

# The Gift

Aurelio Pugliese was one of Italy's most prominent artists. His paintings hung from the Vatican, royal palaces and even in the White House. An original Pugliese was a difficult find, said to be worth $100,000 or more.

When the Knicks were to play an exhibition in Rome, in August of 1999, Dan asked the hotel and guests how to find the best portrait painter in Italy, the question bounced around until somebody thought of calling the Borghese Gallery, famous for both statues and paintings. The word got back to the hotel and then to Dan. "Mr. Johnson, we are told that perhaps the greatest living artist today is Aurelio Pugliese." "Thank you", Dan said. I would like to get in touch with him about a painting.

After the Knicks played around with the Italian National Team, and Dan sitting out the entire 2nd half, he got a phone call from the hotel. "Sir, this is Angelo from the Concierge Desk. When you arrive, a car is going to take you to see Senor Pugliese. He lives in Rome.

The limo stopped in Trastevere, an affluent area in the historic center of the city, housing many young professionals. A man was already waiting outside of a stately home. He appeared around sixty, graying hair, about five feet eight inches tall.

"Hello, The Canyon, yes, I know you. My God, you really are bigger than life. You come inside. You want tea, coffee?" "Oh, thank you sir. Coffee would be nice. Moments later, Aurelio hands Dan a shot of espresso. His English was flawless. "So, I am told, you like my paintings. Thank you. I like your basketball playing. You are an artist. I am an artist." "Yes, sir. Well, I try my best." "Please", you call me Aurelio. So, let's talk about business. That is why you are here."

# Christmas 1999

Christmas was a festive time when many people took time to celebrate, unwind, and reflect. Not in the NBA, and the Knicks, 3-time defending champions, had a Christmas Day game at Indiana. But the Minnelli's went all-out the entire month of Christmas, all month long. Dan had the day off Thursday. Tony knew, Jimmy knew it. The ladies, including Grandma, Carole, and Gina, didn't know it because they didn't care, not so much about basketball, but they did care about Dan, and he was coming over Thursday, where he didn't have to leave until the next morning for Indianapolis. It was a drab, rainy night. As usual, Pete was in the limo, but as usual again, he was invited in. He couldn't drink on the job, but there was a "virgin" egg nogg for him as well as coffee and of course, all kinds of pastries and snacks. Ever since the first time Dan landed on the porch of the Minnelli's West Orange home, with Pete waiting outside, and Grandma found out, she insisted that Pete come inside.

Jimmy's sister, Rosa, and her son, Vince also came up from Freehold, a little over an hour away around central Jersey. Vince was twenty-two, just two years younger than Tony, and was going to school at Monmouth University in Long Branch. This enabled him to stay at home and work. Rosa and her husband had divorced, and finances were tight, and while Jimmy quietly offered to help with tuition, Vince wouldn't accept it, and was right now a Junior, as he would take off half the year to work. He expected to have his degree before he turned twenty-four, and he would be doing it on his own. He was a former high school wrestler, and a good one, though not on the same level as Dan. But he was fascinated with Tony being friends with Dan. Imagine, this guy who plays for the Knicks, a gold medalist in wrestling. For Vince, it was like meeting John Wayne, the Beatles, and Rachel Welch all on the same night. But Vince had met Dan three times before, at the West Orange house, so he had calmed down a little since then.

During his first visit, Dan had casually mentioned, "I don't drink much, but even if I did, my limo driver Pete is outside waiting". "What, you got a boy in this rain waiting outside?" Never allowing a chance to smack Tony to go by, she slapped his shoulder and say, "You go out and you bringa that boy inside right now." Pete would come inside while Grandma would say "Look at you, all cold, (or all-hot, or all wet, or even all-alone), that's a not a right. You come eat something, then you go back out if you want." She might add, and it became one of many Minnelli inside Grandma jokes, "You no wanna be around our family, that's okay, but you eat and then you back out. That's you job, we know." She would wink at somebody, making sure that Pete saw it, but it was a thinly veiled attempt at letting Pete know that the Minnelli's took caring for people at a premium. You might just have to roll with the punches while Grandma joked, even pretended to be upset, (when she was usually joking or half-joking), or Tony and Gina squaring off about something. Gina would mock anything she could about Tony, usually his lack of common sense, or his foul mouth, or his laziness, but do something to Tony when you weren't in the family, and Gina would come after you in a way that would blow away a lioness. There were rules.

The family decided to do something they never did before, all on behalf of Dan, who had now been coming to the house at Llewelyn Park for over two years, usually once a month or every other month. It took a year before he spent a night, the family insisting, when there was very rough weather outside. Pete was asked to stay quite firmly, but he also lived in Jersey and took the limo to Nutley, not far away. The Minnelli's just didn't have the emotional "pull" they had with Dan. In any event, the family would be opening presents that night, and Dan had an advanced warning. Pete was on the list, because how can you not do that? In the Minnelli home, it was about hospitality.

When Rosa and Vince arrived, Tony had a fun idea, using Dan. In the living room, Tony whispered to Dan. "Hey, help me pull a joke on Vince." "What is it?" Dan asked. "Ok, so we've got this meat here in Jersey. It's pork and it comes in a roll. You slice it and cook it with eggs or put it in a sandwich. Sort of like bacon. I know you Georgia guys never heard of it." "Nope", said Dan. "Okay, well, anyway, all you have to do while we're sitting down is say, 'Hey Tony, I really liked that Taylor Ham sandwich you made me." Dan looked puzzled, "Why is that such a big deal, I don't get it." "I'll explain, later, but can you remember that?" "I liked that Taylor Ham sandwich you made me," Tony said, "Perfect. Just give him a little while to settle in. When Tony went to the bathroom, Dan went up to Vince,

"Hey, Vince, I want to ask you something," "Sure thing, C Man" showing Vince's admiration for Dan, because no other Minnelli called him that. Maybe that was because Vince was a Rossi and not a Minnelli. "Tony is up to something. Let me ask you, what is Taylor Ham." "Vince rolled his eyes. Did Tony tell you something about that?" Dan said "Yeah, he told me to say to him tonight that he made me a good Taylor Ham sandwich." "Jesus", Vince said. "Okay, I'll explain because you're not from Jersey. It's not Taylor Ham. Oh, it was once for a couple of years, about 120 years ago, but the government made them change it because it really wasn't ham. It's pork. It's Taylor Pork Roll. If you saw the package, it says 'Taylor Pork Roll', and do you know why, Dan, the package says, 'Taylor Pork Roll?" Dan smiled and went along, "Uh, because that's the name?" "THAT'S RIGHT!" said Vince. That's the name. "So then why would Tony call it by the wrong name?" "Excellent question, Dan" Vince joked. "Because in parts of this fucked-up section called North Jersey, they keep that name alive, but it's wrong." "So", said Dan, "let's turn the tables." "I like it," said Vince.

So, a few minutes later, Dan motions to Tony, as if to say, "should I say it now?" Tony nods as if to say "Sure, do it." Dan says in front of both, "Hey Tony, thanks for making me that Taylor Pork Roll sandwich. It was good." Tony looks up, then looks at Vince, who's laughing already. Tony yelled at both, "You double-crosser!" Then, to Vince, "You turned him to your pathetic side." Dan was laughing but obviously did not understand the seriousness of this subject. "Hey, I haven't even eaten it, whatever it's called, so you guys fight over it. Leave me out of your crazy New Jersey feud!"

The family liked gag gifts and then of course, more serious gifts. Dan got an Italian cookbook, a book called "100 Best Movie Quotes" which he already owned but lied about that, and a special heel that you attached to your shoes to help you add up to 2" to your height. That was from Gina, who sat there stone-faced. She had a wicked, dry sense of humor if people would take the time to look. He got a copy of a gossip magazine that claimed to list all of Dan's girlfriends, from Tony, which thoroughly embarrassed Dan. "Oh, those magazines, they're so trashy, don't let those lies upset you." Only they weren't all lies and Tony, of all people, knew it. There was a quick glance, and Dan wanted to throw his ass down onto the ground for that one. But he just went with it. Jimmy looked at both young men with a smirk and said nothing. Not that Tony would break the vow of loyalty he made to Dan. Despite all Tony's shortcomings, he was loyal beyond any doubt. It was just that, well, Jimmy was a man.

Tony got a fake "Sporting Life" magazine that looked like it was from the '50s, but really contained a Playboy magazine inside. He loved it. Gina got chattering teeth that you wound up, there were gag gifts for the parents and family "How to Speak Southern" was a popular one. Then it was Grandma's turn. Dan, after months of calling Luccia "Mrs. Minnelli" had no choice but to begin calling her "Grandma" after she insisted about ten times. "No more a Mrs. Minnelli. That's a my mama's name and she no around anymore." With a hug, she would say, "The kids a call me Grandma. You like a kid now. You come around a lot, no? Yes, so now you family whether you like it or not, Mr. Big shot. You too good to call me Grandma?" Luccia knew when she had you and was not above a little embarrassment to get her view across, but it was also her way, obviously, of telling Dan that after all the months of his coming, they had taken a shine to him, and he was special." That first time, he looked at Tony, asking for help, and said "Tony?". "Oh no," Tony said with his hands up in a surrender pose. "I'm staying out of it, but I would advise you to listen." So many months ago, he began to call her grandma, but with an uncomfortable feeling every time." Still, it was a great honor. She knew how to get Dan every time. "Whaa, you too good to call me Grandma? Bigga basketball man. Too good to show respect." Dan was on to it but still he'd say "No, I don't mean disrespect!" The rest of the family loved it. Even Gina would smile slightly and shake her head at such nonsense. "Okay, you call me Grandma. It's settled. You a good boy. A BIG boy."

So finally, a medium-sized box that said "Grandma" was handed to Luccia. "Look", Jimmy said. Look at Dan, all smiling and giddy. This is from him. Inside was a mug with a photo of Judge Judy, Luccia's all-time favorite TV personality. The judge didn't look happy. Over her head was a "bubble" used in cartoons when quoting people, and it said, "Don't piss on my leg and tell me it's raining outside." Luccia knew it well and laughed out loud for several seconds. But Dan wasn't done. He pulled out a VHS tape, and he knew that the Minnelli's still had a player. Sure, DVD's had been available for two years, but the Minnelli's were never ones to jump to new technology right away, but Dan was so concerned that he had a portable VHS player with him in case the Minnelli's switched over during that month.

"Now, I've got another gift for Grandma. Now, everybody was curious. Carole said "Jimmy, put the tape in, put the tape in". The drinks were loosening everybody up, and even Gina perked up, a little bit. "Hey C Man", Tony said with a grin, I told you, give those special tapes to Grandma in private. You wanna embarrass her?" Grandma, faking outrage, said "Whatta you talking about, special tapes. You gotta dirty mind." The tape went in, and it was Judy Scheindlin, otherwise known as Judy. For just a second, it seemed like maybe Dan bought her a "best of" series, of some episodes, but that theory was dispelled in a second.

"Hello, Luccia Minnelli. Mrs. Minnelli, this is Judy Scheindlin." Grandma shrieked and almost dropped her egg nogg, which was not the virgin type. "My new friend, Dan Johnson asked me very nicely to make a short tape for you since I understand you're a fan of the show. Thank you for that. He'll sign some basketballs for me on his next road trip west, and we'll call it even. I want to wish you and all the members of the Minnelli and Rossi families a Merry Christmas. Now I must go." She moved into the camera for effect, raising her voice. "I'm a VERY busy woman, Mrs. Minnelli". Luccia and everyone just shrieked with laughter and joy. The fake scowl on Judy's face was replaced by a very nice smile. "I hear you have a wonderful family. That comes from some very good information. Thanks again for being a fan and enjoy the holiday season."

In the eyes of Grandma Luccia, Dan could never do wrong again, for Judge Judy was her hero. Even Tony had a good time with it. "You bastard. I'll never be able to upstage you now. Who do I know that's famous? Oh yeah, you. Hey

276

Grandma, I'll get the C Man to make you a video from me."
Luccia was barely paying attention, "Whatta talk about?
What video? Danny make a me this great Judge Judy video
already." Tony sighed and said, "Forget it, Grandma." Dan
laughed. He had been looking forward to this gift for three
weeks.

Jimmy stood up. "Dan, you've been coming here for more
than a year. You're like one of the family. We hope you feel
the same. You're a good friend to Tony even if you haven't
helped him get a real job. Tony looked dejected as hell. But
we understand because you get to see each other almost
every day. Remember the first time we convinced you to
stay here? You wound up on the floor?" Dan smiled and
shook his head affirmatively. Well, you created a bit of a
challenge, but where there's a will, there's a way."
Everybody was looking at each other in anticipation, but
Dan was clueless. "Okay, everyone, follow me."

They walked down the hallway of their six bedroom, 5500
sq foot home, into the guest bedroom. In there was a
massive bed, the same size that Dan paid over $20,000 for
back in the city. "We brought in guys from the Philly crew
that did metal fabrication and welding. They had to do it all
right here in the room. Grandma added "and it was a
noisy" And then Tony helped us find out where you got
your mattress custom made, and they made another one,
for your second home. Dan looked at Tony, "Is that why, a
few months ago, you had this sudden interest in beds? Hey
C Man, who made you that mattress? It's amazing." Tony
laughed and said "We'll, we figured, why reinvent the
wheel!"

Wow, this is great. Thank you. Dan was embarrassed. "Well,", Jimmy said, all our guests can play flag football on this, and now you can have a decent night's sleep.

"Thank you," said Dan. "You know I'm a little shy." "Don't a worry", Grandma said. "You a good a boy, AND a big a-boy."

This was Dan's second Christmas as he was able to go back to Atlanta last year, in just over 24 hours, as the Knicks were always playing that week. Dan had been preparing for this since his visit to Rome the year before, to play the Italian National Team as part of a Goodwill Tour. By then, Dan had been coming to the house for a year and wanted to do something very special, hence his meeting with Aurelio Pugliese back in March. Seven months later, a well-insured and well-protected large crate arrived at 77 West. In a few minutes the contents of that box would make its way into the Minnelli's house.

Dan had a big bag when he arrived, and the contents of that bag were scattered along with other presents under an enormous tree. Playing were traditional Christmas tunes. At that very moment, Bing Crosby was singing "Mele Kalika Maka that's the thing to say on a bright, Hawaiian Christmas Day".

But of course, Dan wasn't done.

Next to him was a box. Somehow, it went unnoticed. It said nothing on it. Dan had removed the shipping labels and so forth. He said, "Is it okay if I start the real presents first, because I can't wait." Gina looked curiously at the box. "Dan, my God, what's in there?"

Dan looked so proud and excited. "Well, everybody, I told you that about six months ago, the Knicks were in Italy to play the Italian National Team and some other teams that came in." "Yeah," Tony said, "and did you invite us to Italy?" More ball-busting. "Well, anyway, somebody open this because it will be a lot easier to explain."

Gina said, "I'll do it." She went to get the scissors which were already out since it was, after all, present time. The box was opened, slowly. Even Dan said, "Good idea, do it slowly." First foam, then a lot of plastic. "What's in there?" Tony asked, "the Mona Lisa?" "Oh, jeez, Tony", Dan said. "You're a lot closer than you think."

"Gina, take it out." Gina said, Oh my God, it's a painting. What is it?" Everybody, the most famous living artist in Italy is Aurelio Pugliese, and this is his present to you and only you. It's a one-of-kind painting and he calls it "Maria in Pace", or "Mary at Peace."

The family was silent. Even Tony. Finally, Jimmy said. "Gina, hold it up, hold it." "But Dad, I want to see it." Carole said innocently, "Dan, you're tall, hold it up", soliciting a laugh. Gina, of all people, was totally moved. "Dan, oh my God. Aurelio Pugliese? He has paintings in the Vatican. In the Louvre. In the Met." "And now", Dan proudly said, "At the Minnelli's." Jimmy said, "Dan, I don't know what to say. It's magnificent." Gina chimed in, "Dad, it's a Pugliese, do you know what that means." Tony said, "It means we have a museum now." Carole talked, "But Dan, how?" "Well," said Dan, now laughing. I don't mean this to sound arrogant, because look at this man's work, but it turns out, I'm more famous than Aurelio Pugliese. I met him in Rome and commissioned an original." "Dan", said, Gina. "Do you understand that this man's work will be known, will be museums, in 1,000 years. This is an original Pugliese. How were you able to do such a thing?" Tony said, "Aha, you finally gave somebody an autograph." "Nope", said Dan, it was a business proposition. A job. A commission." Carole, always thinking of the money, said what other people were now thinking. "Oh, Dan, the cost of something like this." "Well, I don't want to brag, but I had a good year." Of course, there was some laughter, and Tony said, once again showing a lack of tact, "Do you know what this guy here made last year from his shoe deal, alone?" "Hey", said Jimmy. "We don't talk money here. Dan, it's beautiful. We will put it right over the mantle. It will be a source of pride and of love for the Virgin Mary, for years and years. There is no way we can thank you."

The entire time, Grandma just stared in wonder. Dan took it as a good sign.

Jimmy put on a record. He looked at Carole, who smiled sheepishly, and said, "Oh no, you don't." Jimmy, probably with the help of some wine, smiled back and motioned for Carole to meet him on the dance floor, otherwise known as the family room floor. She persisted, but not really. This is what the holidays were for, what marriage was for, when you weren't fighting all the problems of life, the kids and their problems, the money, the gossip, aging parents, medical problems, problematic neighbors. This is what couples thought they'd be doing every day, for a lifetime, on their wedding day, what they hoped and dreamed for. Where do all those dreams go? Jimmy wondered, Carole and Luccia. The kids had just started. Maybe their journey would have fewer bumps along the way. That was always the hope of parents.

The beautiful voice of Connie Francis began singing the enchanting "Al Di La" (Beyond), while the middle-aged couple danced away, family smiling or simply preoccupied with something else. It wasn't their first dance, after all.

> Al di la, del bene piu prezioso, ci sei tu
> Al di la, del sogno piu ambizoso, ci sei tu
> Al di la, delle cose piu belle
> Al di la, delle stelle, ci sei tu
>
> Al di la, ci sei tu per me, per me, soltanto per me
> Al di la, del mare piu profondo, ci sei tu
> Al di la, del limiti del mondo, ci sei tu
> Al di la, della volta infinita, al di la della vita
>
> Ci sei tu, al di la, ci sei tu per me
> Al di la

"Beyond the most precious asset, there is you."

What surprised everyone, was Dan approaching Luccia. C'Mon, grandma, pretty ladies don't stand in the corner. Luccia blushed and laughed and gave Dan a playful slap on his arm. "Oh, stop it. You're a young boy, leave me alone!" But she would have been crushed if he left her alone. It didn't take much coaxing, and the sight of Dan, head just below the ceiling, reaching way, way down to hold Luccia's hand was both humorous and touching. Even Jimmy and Carole stopped to watch. It was sweet.

"And to think", Tony told Vince, "I couldn't get that guy to say hello to me a couple of years ago." "This family", said

Vince, is good for him, even if some dumb family members can't read the package of freakin' PORK ROLL!" Tony just laughed, as they both watched.

When it was over, Grandma, of all people, shouted, "Hey, pick it up a little, huh", Jimmy had a record all ready to go, and within a few seconds, the bouncy beat of Spiral Staircase filled the room.

> I love you more today than yesterday
> But not as much as tomorrow
> I love you more today than yesterday
> But only half as much as tomorrow

# Vincent's Pond

Another game night on a very cold Friday night at the Minnelli's, followed by coffee and pastries. Carole, Gina, and Grandma Luccia got together at least once a month to bake. It was another family tradition. Canolis, and Bombolini's were lined up on a tray, along with coffee. Dan, by now, was beginning to loosen up and join another tradition, in the way Tony would describe it, but probably nobody else. Busting Balls.

"Wait, I really prefer Dunkin' Donuts," Dan said. A napkin went flying into his face, along with choruses of boos. Jimmy laughed and said "Ok, you, out of our house. That's blasphemous."

After the pastries and coffee, Gina had an idea. "Let's go up the hill to Degnan and go skating on Vincent's Pond". "Hey, I'll do it", Tony said. "Yeah, alright, Paul said". Jimmy and Carole agree that their winter Olympic days were well past them, and Grandma would stay in the warmth of the home, watching four episodes of Judge Judy that she taped. "That Judge Judy, she got what the Jews call Chutzpah". Yes, Grandma got around. Everybody laughed. Dan said "Grandma, (because that was the expectation made clearly to him, but Luccia herself, and was a tremendous honor), where did you learn that? Luccia laughed, "I don't a know. Maybe at the butcher shop up near Pleasantdale, where they got good cuts of meat. Funny man, the butcher there, and I like a the ladies, but you know, the Jews, they try, but they can't cook a like we do." "Oh my God, Grandma, you're awful!" "Whaaa, what I say?", Grandma's favorite response. Grandma ALWAYS knew exactly what she was saying, and Dan believed she had the most wicked sense of humor of all, and she played a brilliant card, old, forgetful, with less than a full command of the language, but everybody saw right through her. Luccia laughed and hugged Dan all the way up to his thighs. "Danny, you a good boy. A BIG boy!".

"Skating?" Dan said. "First of all, I can't skate. Never could, but it's also in my contract. I'm not allowed to skate, and will the place rent me a size 24?" "Uh, no, probably not" Tony said. Everybody laughed. "I hear they stop at 20, tough luck." "Well, Gina said, you come anywhere and walk around. Does you contract say you can't walk on ice or you can't skate?" "Skate", says Dan. "Well okay, then, you come and walk and watch the rest of us fall on our faces." "Not me, boy", Tony joked. I'm a regular Mark Messier." "Hey, I saw him once at the Garden", Dan said. "Did you ask him for an autograph?" Paul asked. "No, but he asked me for mine."

The family minus Grandma, rode up Eagle Rock Avenue, turned left on Pleasant Valley Way, past West Orange High School, and then into Degnan park, next to what everybody called "The Green House". This was the cinder block building that had cubby holes for your things and a snack bar. It was right next to the skating pond and a placed to walk inside and warm up, whenever the weather got frigid.

"Holy shit, it's Dan Johnson" said one person in the group of about 50 at the park. "C Man, it's the C Man!" Okay, Dan, do your best Billy Barty Diner impersonation. "Hey

Canyon, can we have you autograph". Dan did his best, "It's freezing out, man. Keeping my gloves on, but can I hang out with everyone here while my friends skate a little bit?" Oh, hell yeah, Canyon. You hang around West Orange all you want. "Hey" Dan said, "West Orange is one of my favorite places". "Alright, went the crowd". Dan added, "Hey, the media and crazy fans are driving me crazy, so I have friends in West Orange, and I know I can hang out with normal people". They ate this up. "Hey Dan, we won't bother you. Hang out with us!". Thank you, Billy.

Tony and Dan walked toward the frozen pond, next to an area where the ducks were kept, even in the winter. Tony said, "Right here, on this sidewalk, I kissed a girl for the first time. I think I was in the 5$^{th}$ grade. It wasn't much of a kiss, but it was a start. You never forget that kind of thing. We were both wearing thick coats, and I don't know if I was shaking from the cold or from getting up the nerve to kiss her. I thought she was the most beautiful girl in the world, and I was so nervous around here, I could barely talk. I have a lot of memories tied-up in this park. Kids played here, fought after-school here, made out in the bushes on the other side of the pond, played tennis, basketball, and softball, and I suppose they still do. I almost lost my virginity here, too, just a few feet, over there." "Almost?" laughed Dan. "What happened?" "Aww, she figured out what I was trying to do." They both laughed.

Thirty minutes later, Dan was inside the Green House, taking pictures, putting arms around astonished people like they were his best friends. "Oh my God, you're such a decent guy." "Hey thanks. I'm just a regular 8-foot 11 guy." Everybody laughed and Dan had to admit that he felt pretty good. "Hey Dan, how many more years are you gonna play for the Knicks." "Oh, I don't know," said Dan. At least a couple more, then I might retire and look for something else." "Ah man, don't retire. You can win when you're fifty!" It sounded like a joke, but in the minds of many a metro-New York fan, it was the truth. Dan might not ever get out, but today, he was in his element. Really, it wasn't bad.

They decided to go and rather than sneak out. Dan walked around and said "Hey, thanks for giving me a little fresh air to breathe, away from all the lights". "Oh, hell yes," said one skater. You come make West Orange your home." "Well, I feel like it is." Dan said to a loud, appreciative crowd.

Gina walked up to Dan and said, "Yeah, you're a real shy one, you are."

# Chase

Tony called Dan while he was walking out of 77 West, "Hey, Mr. Big Shot. Grandma says you haven't been to a game night or at least to the house for dinner in a month, and you don't love the family anymore." "Oh c'mon, she didn't say that," Dan said, still with concern. Upsetting Grandma Luccia would keep Dan up at night. "Well, that's what you think. The season is over. So are the big parties which we Minnelli's didn't get invited to. Where have you been." "Oh, just on a trip to a beach." "What's her name and what movie has she been with." "Nothing you're going to find out. But I can come next week. How is Tuesday?" Tony said, "We'll make it Tuesday. I'll drive with you Pete." "When do you NOT drive with me and Pete, Dan asked." "Well, you're going where I live. Doesn't it make sense?" "Yes, Dan said. It makes sense. Tell Grandma and the family not to disown me." "Well, family doesn't get disowned. Or you. Not our family, anyway. We bust your balls, but we never disown you." "Hey," said Dan. "That's what it would say if there was a New Jersey dictionary under the name 'Family. A group of people who constantly bust your balls but are always there for you." Dan laughed because he thought he was clever. Tony simply said, "Well, whatever. Just show up for game night."

It was late July with training camp opening mid-September, but Dan was given a training schedule that he was supposed to begin in two weeks, which lasted until training camp opened in early October.

"Dan and Pete took off on a Friday and 4:00 PM, with Tony climbing in, and they made their way to Llewellyn Park. Inside, the smells of food were amazing, with some Sinatra playing from some speaker. How could Dan have missed coming here for an entire month? He was greeted with a slap on the back from Jimmy, handshake from Paul, and hugs from Mrs. M., or Carole, and of course, the biggest hug from Grandma Luccia. "Why you no come around no more. Too good for us now? I saw you on Jay Leno after you win the championship. He's no Johnny Carson." "I know", Dan said. I'm sorry everyone. For the past month there have been a lot of commitments." Of course, nobody was anything but happy to see Dan. There weren't too many people more famous than Danny in the entire world, and deep inside, all of the Minnelli's knew it. Yet, they were attached to him now, as he was to them, and the expectation was, you are loyal to your friends and family, and you come visit. It was more than that. Dan was a friend to Tony, a good influence, his acceptance of the Minnelli's made them feel special. What Dan wanted from them you couldn't buy. It was friendship. No, it was acceptance. Basketball was hardly mentioned. That's what the rest of world talked about it. Grandma didn't even watch it. Instead, they played board games, they watched and compared movies, they listened to great music. Music none of the players or people he met could appreciate or understand, like Dean, Frank, and Sammy, Louie, Ellington, and Michel Petrucciani, who was introduced to the Minnelli's by Dan. They liked that Dan "got" Gina when, so few did. She was moody, cynical, unlike a Minnelli, but inside, she longed for camaraderie, liked to match wits

288

with people and Dan had that intelligence and most of all, he accepted Gina for whom she was. Dan understood those things. She wasn't impressed by Dan's size or success, at least not outwardly. Inwardly, she cared for him very much, lit up as much as could be determined when he arrived, and if perhaps not for the fact that Dan and Tony were friends, and not for the fact that Dan was famous and in the limelight, maybe there would be something between them….oh, that's just stupid. And now, he was like a brother.

Speaking of Gina, where was she? Paul said, "Oh, Gina's on a date with Chase." Tony said, "Well, Danny Boy, this is what happens when you don't come around for a month. Chase is Gina's boyfriend, the one she didn't even want to bring over to meet the family, which is a strict no-no, you know a family faux pas. "Yeah", Paul added. "Even Anthony here brought you over to meet us, once you decided you'd talk back to him, and you became a couple. We needed to meet you, size you up, and give Tony our approval before you guys got to 2$^{nd}$ base." Tony punched Paul in the arm. "Hey! I was just reluctant because he was so much taller than me." Jimmy stood, arms crossed, sometime clearly bothering him. "Anyway", Tony said. Gina met Chase at some real estate thing. He's a brainiac like her. Connecticut guy, old money, Yale grad, some kind of hedge Foundation manager, but too good to come see us until Dad put his foot down." Dan knew that there was nothing Jimmy could do about living Gina's life. She had her own place in Livingston, the next town over. Close to family twenty minutes away, but still, her own place. It's true that she had to work for her dad, and to some degree, get along with Paul, but more and more, Gina did her own thing, buying and selling commercial real estate for the family business, and understanding that side a lot more than Jimmy or Paul, and vastly increasing the company's revenue flow, that besides a guilt trip, there was not much Jimmy could do. However, nobody should ever underestimate the value and intimidation of a guilt trip. It was a mainstay in an Italian family just like it was in Jewish families and probably, other ethnic families.

"Dan", Paul added. You haven't been here for a month. We were just joking around with you. You had a lot going on with the Knicks and the league. Man, we couldn't be more excited, especially having those seats for two of the games. The fact is, Gina has been dating this guy Chase for almost four months. She didn't tell us because she said she, you know, it was coffee after the real estate seminar. Then, dinner a week later. Then some kind of concert a week after that. Another dinner. We couldn't even find her one night until late when she returned Mom's call and decided it was her right to act angry for us looking in on her. You know Gina by now, but even this, this was out of the ordinary. So finally, she says, 'Look, I'm seeing a guy I met from the real estate seminar. His name is Chase, he's in real estate and helps manage a financial Foundation, and he's very successful. I'm fine and really, there's nothing else to say.'" Dad told her that she should bring him over for dinner, and do you know what happened? They were late and then they walk in about ten feet, into the house. Gina brings Chase in, and I'll tell you, that guy, he had some kind of chip on his shoulder." Jimmy still stood in a defensive posture, arms folded. "Really?" Dan asked, realizing that the mood was no longer jovial. "Yeah, he uttered something about 'we aren't staying for dinner, we're meeting some of my friends." Gina looked down for a second, because she knew what we were all thinking about, but said. "Yeah, we got to go. Goodbye." Jimmy, at time this happened turned to Carole and said quietly, "Son of a bitch". Carole said "Well, they'll come back, maybe next week." Jimmy said, "That guy doesn't need to come back." "Oh", Carole said, now back in the present, "It's fine. He had some friends in town unexpectedly. It'll be okay." Jimmy looked at Dan and said, "Now you, you can have a drink." Dan, sensing a chance to help mend Jimmy's irritation said. "Why did it take you so long to ask me?" Jimmy smiled and the two of them walked to the bar. Dan knew the way. Grandma was asleep on the reclining chair, a common theme.

# Billy's Gone

It was Saturday, December 23, 2000. The Knicks were off but had games the next two nights. Dan was at a Christmas Party at his building, 77 West. It had been three years since Dan moved into this upscale residence, and yet he only knew a handful of residents. They all knew Dan, these celebrities or at very least, unassuming but wealthy corporate executives, real estate barons, or recipients of large inheritances. At first concerned with a newly wealthy professional athlete coming to 77 West, with their "drug-infused" parties, late-night shenanigans, bringing attention to their quiet lifestyles, Dan Johnson had turned out to be the perfect tenant. True, a few women had mysteriously knocked on his door, but that was hardly noticed, and certainly tolerated. After all, the doorman himself initiated it and it couldn't have been more discreet. Any noise taking place would be well confined enough within the walls of one Mr. Dan Johnson's private residence. Many residents would, under questioning, admit that they had never even seen Dan at the building. A quick ride, head bent down or sitting on the stool furnished expressly for his comfort, a quick duck under two lights and a door, and a final squat and duck into a large limousine. Limos were a far more common sight than Dan Johnson, the famous ball player, than the man himself.

The stool itself became an interesting, and sometimes funny conversation piece. Tony himself put it there, as a gift to Dan, and funny not, Dan appreciated it, because he could not stand in the elevator without ducking down.

Tony found it at a store for bar accessories called E&A Restaurant Supply in Plainfield, NJ. It was made with leather and sort of like a King's throne in miniature version. It was actually very attractive and "cushiony" and when Dan saw it, he laughed, but at the same time, he always sat down on it. The big joke, which was shared among the doormen, was that other people liked it, and the doormen would say, "Ugh, excuse me, ma'am, but that stool is reserved for Mr. Dan Johnson." Some of the residents laughed and sat anyway, knowing Dan couldn't get less and probably found that funny (which he did, for sure), but some said, angrily, "Well, he's not here!"

One of the other doormen said. "C Man, that stool will one day land in the Smithsonian Institution, which was always good for a laugh." But one day, it did.

At the party were about thirty people, and the apartment's owner, a multi-millionaire hedge Foundation owner, knocked on Dan's door himself and personally invited him. Dan had nothing else to do. He was at the Minnelli's just the night before for Christmas celebrations, singing, a dance or two with Grandma, and getting a reluctant but slightly inebriated Gina to dance with him.

The game of the evening was Trivial Pursuit.

Dan won. Fights broke out as they always do. Grandma was too slow; Tony was seen throwing out a card he didn't like. Paul was bragging, Gina wasn't paying attention. Dan won the last time and that wasn't fair. Maybe he was even cheating somehow (but that was a joke).

Back at Dan's building, everybody at the party wanted to meet and speak with him , from the hedge Foundation guy, for which Dan had had to twice say "my financial guy makes all of those decisions", from a slightly aging and more than slightly drunk divorcee who asked if Dan wanted to see her paintings, to a couple that were famous in their own right and gave Dan some space. "Did they really live there?" Dan wasn't even sure, but the last time he saw them was on TV, on the red carpet at the Oscars.

At about 11:00 PM, and within minutes of Dan's departure back downstairs, his phone rang. He was careful not to give his number out to too many people, although it did get out at times. This time, it was an unknown caller with a California area code. Dan picked it up.

"This is Dan." Dan would never refer to himself as the Canyon. That would sound appalling to him, but by now the world had accepted and embraced it, so Dan at least had to accept it. It wasn't growing anywhere, and the logo had made a certain Ann Karlsson very successful, and Dan was glad.

Hello, Dan. This is Mickey Rooney. Dan knew right away it was really him from his older yet distinctive voice. Also, he was one of Billy's friends, so somehow, Dan wasn't shocked. He had seen the Andy Hardy, Boys Town, and the other assorted movies with Judy Garland.

At the peak of his career between ages 15 and 25, he made 43 films, and Dan had probably seen 20 of them.

"Mickey Rooney? Yes, I can tell. I know your voice. How are you, sir?" Mickey said, "maybe you know me," "Oh,

294

seriously, Mr. Rooney, I've seen Boys Town ten times."
Ordinarily, Mickey Rooney, accustomed to accolades like
Dan, although not from the younger generation, would
bask a little in the attention. Not tonight.

"Well, Dan, I really appreciate all of that. Billy has told me
so much about you. Things you can't read from articles or
see on TV. He said you a very special young man, and he
cared deeply for you." It then struck Dan, and he felt a
wave of trepidation. "Is Billy alright?" Dan eagerly asked.
"Son," Mickey Rooney said gently. "Billy passed away early
this morning." There was a pause. Dan felt helpless,
confused. "What happened?" Dan asked, his voice
cracking. "It was his heart", Mickey said. "It was his time".

Mickey gave Dan information on when and where a
memorial service would take place. "I know he'd be happy
if you said a few words." What could Dan say? "I'll be
there, and ok, I'll say something."

Dan said his goodbyes at the party and went back to his
apartment. He sat down, numb. Slowly, tears began to run
down his face. He admired him so much. Billy seemed to
understand Dan better than anyone he knew. Yes, Billy was
a dwarf and was stared at, but accepted, in part, for his
celebrity. It was the same with Dan. Billy knew what he
would face, but also knew that Dan could become much
bigger than Billy could ever imagine for himself. Dan knew
this inevitable. He sat in his big chair, the one he liked and
where he sat to think, read, and listen to music. He wanted
to listen to something, for Billy, or maybe, for him, but
what? He decided on Thelonious Monk's version of "Round
Midnight'". For some reason, he didn't cry. He was sad,

though. Of course.  Crying was easy, Dan thought. It didn't take much thinking, and crying was fine. Crying had its place. Big men needed to cry simply because they weren't supposed to, and Dan never understood that. But tears shouldn't flow too easily. There was a time for them to pour freely, and a time to keep them back. Dan wanted to drink bourbon, sip it, listen to the music, and think about Billy. The song was titled "Round Midnight", and as Dan looked up, it was 11:50 PM. It just fit. He closed his eyes and thought about meeting Billy. What he really thought about he couldn't put into words, but he understood his thinking. The world had roughly 6 billion people in it. Few people really had character, had value. Oh, sure, everybody had value, but now Dan was alone, he didn't have to sound all noble for society. He didn't know how to explain that statement and was glad he didn't have to. It sounded irresponsible, but Billy had a special way about him. He rose about pettiness. Scoffed at his disability, which never became one for him, anyway. He had compassion, wit, and wisdom. Dan admired wit. It was different than being funny. A clown is funny. Wit was for the thinking man, and a pie in the face could be the result of wit. You see, Dan thought, that's what people, so many of them, failed to understand. Wit was humor, but humor wasn't always wit. "Oh, Dan, forget it, either it's there or it's not." Billy was funny, but Billy was also witty. Funny brings you a paycheck because a paycheck feeds you. Wit is for a special group, and if all you have it wit, you might starve. Billy was funny because he KNEW he had to eat, but Billy also had wit, and it was the wit that Dan loved about him.

It was hard for people to reach out to Dan because he was, quite simply, very difficult to reach. From the front door of 77 West, where a door man ran interference, to a limo, ten steps into the Garden and more security, and when the time came when he had to travel in crowds, he eventually acquiesced and used an armed bodyguard service. Usually, the same company that got to know him. He had a private number that few people knew. Family, about ten friends (some of which could hardly be classified), his agent, financial advisor, a couple of doctors, his attorney, and the Knicks organization.

Billy had his number, and that was a call he would always pick up.

Dan had called the Knicks to tell them that he would have to miss the Christmas game. The GM, perhaps in a bad mood himself, said, that the Christmas game was the "game of the week" on a major network, and a sellout Garden Crowd, and that the other players would love to take Christmas off, too. In a very uncharacteristic phone call, which sobered up the General Manager, Dan said, "My mentor and perhaps best friend died. If it wasn't for him, I don't even know if I would be playing basketball. You've had Prima donnas and troublemakers on your team before. I've never said this, and I hope never to say it again. I'm a dream for you guys. Never a day of trouble. I show up and do my job, and it's a damn good job I do, too. I'm set financially, so any more shit and I won't play ANY more games, and I'll tell the media the truth, that a dear friend died, our record is 38-2 with the two losses when I didn't play. We're two-time defending NBA champs. What little life I have outside of basketball I want to give to people I care about. So, you decide what you want to do, but I'm going to a funeral. I like playing for the Knicks, but I can stop at any time."

Dan was filled with remorse the moment he hung up. It was two years and maybe many more years, of pent-up frustration. Billy would have reprimanded him for being unprofessional. He has been a vehicle for a university and now a professional basketball team. It wasn't that he didn't love going to school in Ann Arbor, and as a matter of fact, the fans went out of their way to respect his privacy. They honestly seemed to like him as a human being. He was humble, he was a good teammate. Anybody could approach him, if they were respectful and at least get a handshake and usually, a picture. He wasn't a big autograph guy. Not on the spot while walking around. He hated people approaching him at restaurants. He was sometimes offered a private room, but he didn't think he was better. He just wanted to enjoy his meal without having somebody stick out a piece of paper, saying "Hey, sign this," like he was public domain. That didn't always happen, but yes, it DID happen. Dan liked the "80-20" rule with respect to people, and lot of things. Billy liked to use it, too. "Dan, remember, 80% of people are extremely decent. They work hard. They love their families. They like a good meal. They appreciate the opposite sex, which he sometimes altered, and said smiling, "Or the same sex, whatever. They want to feel important, feel wanted, feel loved. And then, even that 20% that remains, 15% of them have been hurt, fired from a job, tortured by the loss of a loved one, stepped over for a job promotion, depressed over why things haven't gone their way, why life is so unfair, and so, on any given day, you have all these people walking around with holes in their heart. Holes in their heart, Dan," Billy reemphasized. Dan looked hard at Billy. He had never really given this so much thought.

"Wow, Billy", Dan said. "That really gives me a lot to think about." "Well, kid, think of me as the wise old man, even if I take a lot of things from the movies." Dan looked surprised. "You took that from a movie?" Billy laughed and said, "Well, not that I know, but somewhere, there's probably a speech by someone that's similar". But you get the point.

Dan finally realized something and said to Billy. "Hey Billy, if 80% of people are good, and 15% of people aren't bad but have a hole in their heart, what about the last 5%?"

"Well," Billy said, with a smirk, in a way Dan had never heard him speak before. "They're just assholes."

Dan stepped off his limo at Teterboro, just steps from the corporate jet that would take him to Burbank Airport outside of Los Angeles. The pilot and co-pilots knew Dan and had flown him before. His seat and extra space were made available to him without disturbing the other six passengers this late morning. Dan sometimes had celebrity passengers with him. Sometimes not. Most left him alone and, like Dan, were to pay for added convenience, comfort, and mostly, peace and quiet. On this flight, Leonard Nimoy, the famous "Mr. Spock", had a seat next to Dan. They exchanged pleasantries and it one point, Nimoy said, "Thank God for these flights." One can only imagine the

"Trekkie" admirers staring at, and perhaps disturbing, him. He had not heard about Billy and offered his condolences. "My lord", Nimoy said, "he started out very young and worked a lot in the industry. Very talented."

A large sedan picked up Dan, and took him to a hotel in the area, at 3:00 PM, and Dan did not leave the room until the next morning, getting room service. The same sedan would pick him up and he would return tomorrow. The memorial service would start at 10:00 AM at the Church of Latter-Day-Saints not far from Glendale. By 2:00, he would be headed back to New York. Dan passed the time by reading "Why England Slept", by John F. Kennedy.

Dan was driven to the church, wearing one of twelve tailor-made suits made for him in Atlanta. Black, white shirt, black tie. It was Billy himself that told Dan, "Always have a nicely pressed suit, starched shirt and tie ready to go at a moment's notice." He laughed and then added "Why do people say, 'at a moment's notice'? Better to say, "without any notice." How ironic for Dan to remember that today.

There was a small group of about thirty people. There was no media frenzy. Billy was 76 years old and was always a popular "working actor." Sure, when the script called for a little person, there were other choices. When they wanted someone with talent, and if they could afford him, they asked for Billy. For nineteen years, Billy had a star on the Walk of Fame just a few miles away. Mickey Rooney had four.

In the room were family members, actor Donald O'Connor, the great dancer, actor, and comedian from one of Dan's favorite movies, "Singing in the Rain", was there despite not being in the best of health. Dan wanted to tell him how much he always loved "Make 'em laugh." He noticed five or six little people among the group of about two and half dozen people. They nearly all looked at Dan with great surprise. "What is he doing here", was probably whispered, but you never know who a funeral might bring for a final goodbye.

There was a religious component to the service, and then several speakers. Mickey was as close to a "master of ceremonies" as you might describe for a memorial service, making sure things moved along. Mickey told stories about Billy's enthusiasm and joy for life, and how they had a camaraderie and great friendship since the old vaudeville and the "Mickey McGuire" series. Mickey kept a positive attitude about life and helped many others, and Dan was to find out about some of that.

A Director from LPA, the Little People of America, talked about all the legislative work Billy had done to make everyday life easier for little people. Dan learned that Billy helped design size-appropriate furniture.

He met little people, one was a longtime camera man, who admitted that he couldn't act. Billy told him "First, you have to eat", and urged him to find a way to work behind the scenes. He couldn't properly reach the camera controls. It was adapted so he could.

He met a successful lawyer who was a little person, and a few others, but it was a small group.

And then, toward the end, Mickey got up to the front and spoke. "Many of you are surprised by the appearance of a very famous athlete. An Olympic Champion, a collegiate NBA champion. Maybe shocked is a better word. "And to you, Dan "The Canyon", Johnson, Billy considered you a special person in his life. I was one of the few who even knew that you were friends. He said to me after one of your many championships and awards, "I'm proud of that kid. I knew him when he was only seven feet, seven inches tall. There was a little laughter. An introverted high school kid. And now look at him, an introverted eight-foot eleven-inch NBA champion, on top of the world. Why don't you say a few words, Mr. Dan."

Everybody seemed interested in what Dan might have to say. He didn't want to go up for that very reason. But there was no turning back.

He got to the front and nervously unfolded a piece of paper. Then, he folded it back up. "I prepared a few words to say about Billy, but I'm not going to use it." I didn't realize how much Billy did to help others. That's because he never spoke about himself to me. He asked me questions and helped guide me. We met doing a skit for Johnny Carson, and he went out of his way to speak with me, and that was the start of a correspondence and friendship for the last ten years. It wasn't all the time. A few times a year. We had dinner when he was in my town, or I was out here. It was always about me, and now I feel embarrassed about that. To me, Billy, along with my parents, were my mentors in life. He had wisdom, not me. Even as I made a name for myself, I treasured his words, I appreciated his humor and positive outlook. I loved Billy but more importantly, I liked him. I will try to be a better person as I live the rest of my life, and give back, as he has. Thank you for allowing me to be here today." And then, Billy went back out into the audience.

# A Little Comedy

After Billy's funeral, Dan went to see the Knick's GM to apologize. Rod Dorfman apologized in turn to Dan. He said the Knicks were the luckiest team on the planet, of any sports organization, not only to have a man of Dan's immense, almost supernatural talent, but Dan, the man, was somebody every Knick, past, present, and future, aspire to be like. A great, unselfish teammate. The players all understood, and while Dan wasn't sure he liked it, he found out that the Knick's quickly pulled together about a minute's worth of "best of" clips from Billy's career and splashed it up on the scoreboard, while the announcer explained why Dan was absent.

"Well, the Rod said, we still won by three points." "Yes, I heard". The GM said, "We were wrong, and your teammates all understand. You've got a night off, and then we'll see you tomorrow."

Tony spoke with Dan, and could tell that Dan was down in the dumps, so he called the Manager of the Rascals Comedy Club, right in West Orange, and arranged a "mini roast" of Dan. Not a real comedy roast, but to let that night's lineup know he'd be there, and if they could put him in a joke or two.

Tony and the family had been to the Rascals location since it was a pizzeria called Durkin's, and he'd go out with some of his West Orange High friends from the area, even though Tony went to Seton Hall Prep. The pizza was good. Not Star Tavern, but still good. On January 23rd, 1992, when Tony was only seventeen, he saw Sam Kinison at Rascal's, and never laughed harder in his life. Kinison died only two months later in a traffic accident. There were scores of not only "up and coming" comics, but big-time comedians trying out new material, because West Orange was so close to the city.

Tony invited his brother Paul and four other couples, all with instructions to "make the C Man feel at home."

They all met at the Minnelli's West Orange house and had a couple of drinks. Only one couple had met Tony, so there was degree of "stardom" that they had to get over, but Tony told all of them that he had "broken in Tony" with three years of good ole' Jersey humor and profanity, so he begged everybody to "be yourselves, because Dan will pick up on it if you're not being yourselves."

Naturally, having the CANYON at the club was a big deal for the club, the patrons, and the comedians, all came armed with a joke or two about this 8-foot Knick's star.

Tony recalled some of the jokes the next night by a handful of comics:

> Every time Dan Johnson got an erection, he fainted

> You know he's a big judo player, right? Former Olympic champion. The first time he visited Japan, they shot missiles at him said, "Godzilla is back."

> But he's lucky, when he stubs his toe, his brain doesn't know about it for ten minutes.

> His last girlfriend was in a wheelchair, and everybody said she fell and was all banged up. Well, they got half of it right.

> But this guy's tough. He's so tough that Chuck Norris goes around telling Dan Johnson jokes.

> Three man-made-objects can be seen from space, the Great Wall of China, the Pyramid at Giza, and the top of

Dan Johnson's head

> And this guy's got an appetite. When the "all you can eat" Chinese buffet sees him coming, they close for the night. One time, Dan ordered $2000 worth of food from a Chinese restaurant, and an hour later, he returned for more.

# September 11, 2001

*(This is a true accounting of the events of September 11, 2001, as explained to the author by Thomas King, retired Essex County NJ Detective, and proud native of West Orange, NJ).*

Thomas King was a tough, hard-nosed police officer for the Essex County Sherriff's BON, Bureau of Narcotics, born right in Orange, and raised in West Orange, right on Eagle Rock Avenue. He was sent to Our Lady of Lourdes Catholic School, and then eventually, Redwood Elementary, Lincoln, Jr. High, and West Orange Mountain High School, all grouped together near Pleasant Valley Way, Conforti Avenue, and Eagle Rock Avenue.

At one time, he was a Court Officer, that was before he was involved in an altercation that killed another police officer, one critically injured, and sent shrapnel into Officer King's head, and shattered his ear drum. He helped capture the killer, and after being awarded a medal of honor for his heroism, found his hard work and dedication recognized with a promotion to Detective.

But Tom King was no stranger to hardship. Not in the least. His family was torn apart from one tragedy after another, beginning when he was just a young child. His father was exposed to radiation from a special project and passed away when Tom was two. Both his brothers passed away at a very young age, one at 28, and one at 38, less than a year apart, and then his mother, suffering through the weight of losses that no human should have to bear, succumbed only a year after 9-11, from a heart attack, hospitalized that very September day from the stress of not being able to reach Tom. With limited phone service, she went the entire day not knowing if Tom was dead or alive.

Tom King had seen as much personal tragedy as one person should be allowed to see, but he was a survivor, and persevered for the sake of himself and his family. His family loved him and would want him to live a good life, for as long as he could.

After several rainy days, the New York City area was experiencing a nice, clear day on the morning of Tuesday, September 11th. Detective King, just a few minutes after 9:00 AM, was driving East on Route 280, passing the cliffs produced many years earlier when the mountain was blasted to make way for the highway. Up ahead lay Prospect Street, with the Essex Green Shopping Center just down the road, and Crystal Lake and Pal's Cabin Restaurant going the other way. Tom was listening to Joe Walsh on Dover station WDHA, "the Rock of New Jersey" 105.5 on the dial. Maybe it was Rocky Mountain Way, or maybe Life's Been Good. That detail was lost on him in the following minutes, but you really couldn't go wrong with either song. In another minute, he'd pass the exit for Jimmy Buff's, and he hadn't had a double Italian Hot Dog for a long time, but it was early, and he had to get to work. Funny how it's the simple things, sometimes.

Just as he reached the crest of the mountain on 280, he saw the smoke, and nearly at the same time, he heard the music end on DHA, and the news break in about what appeared to be an "accidental" plane crash of a small commuter plane into the World Trade Center's North Tower. It was just around 8:55 AM. Tom already had a terrible thought that how could a plane not avoid that iconic tower. It must have been deliberate. On February 26, 1993, a van bomb detonated below the streets, under the North Tower. Maybe this was simply random.

Detective King continued to his office in Orange, where by then, all doubts of an accident were erased as a second plane struck, this time, to the South Tower, which they heard on the Statewide Police Emergency Network (SPEN). Several men changed from plain clothes into their uniforms and headed to the Holland Tunnel in a police-issued Caprice Classic.

By the time several officers came out of the Holland Tunnel, from NJ and into lower Manhattan, both towers had collapsed, and first responders were lined up on the West Side Highway as far as they could see. Just then, building number seven collapsed due to fires caused by falling debris, while the officers ran for cover.

The bravery by fire fighters was astounding, from running upstairs against every human urge to run away, to their inevitable deaths, to teachers, carrying two infants at a time at a nursery, to safe quarters, to ordinary citizens, taking off their shirts to shield young children from falling debris, to first responders, working around the clock. Some Salvation Army volunteers flew to New York and served 10,000 meals per day, around the clock. People came together as Tom King and others had never seen them do before. That was more of a cliché, as the men and woman in the area regularly went above and beyond, but today was indeed, something never witnessed before.

For the next ten hours, Tom King, and many like him, provided medical supplies and anything else that could be done. Eventually, like those who made it out in time, they were so badly covered with a dust from the building that you couldn't tell black from white, or Latino, or Asian. Everybody looked the same, and King realized that they were covered with pulverized human remains.

From this experience, Detective King would eventually become a fire fighter, to honor those who perished, and where he would serve for the next fifteen years.

Dan Johnson woke up in his apartment, and like millions of others, was glued to the TV during the ordeal, shocked, feeling sick and unable to help. He offered any kind of services he could, just to hang out, talk to people, and he did some of that. He came to Shea Stadium ten days later, when the Mets played the Braves, and he wasn't too upset this time when Mike Piazza hit a 7th inning home run to put the Mets on top of his hometown Braves, 2-1.

It was one time in Dan Johnson's life, in and out of New York, where he was reminded that basketball and other sports were just that. Sports. It was the everyday people, the people who go through their lives facing challenges and hardship, some not to make it, sadly, and others, like Thomas King, getting back up again and again, and never quitting.

# Chase's Dilemma

Dan suddenly looked at the clock. 4:09 AM. Lying in bed, he heard a very faint line of music. An accordion, trumpet? "Dumpta, dumpta, dumpta, dum, dumpta dumpta dumpta dum.

The door opened and the music got louder. Somebody walked through the door. Was it Gina's boyfriend? Chase Pennington? Yeah, Jesus. It was Chase, just strolling in like he owned the place. Holding a drink, obviously drunk. He shut the door behind him, and the music got a little softer, but it was on the other side, in Dan's living room.

It was still playing, over and over like the introduction of a song. Like Deano would be starting at any time. Now THAT would be a fantastic dream. This one was just weird.

"Chase, what the hell. I just saw you a few hours ago, not that you were in a holiday mood. How'd you get up here, and who are those musicians and people in my living room?"

"Now first of all, Canyon boy, or whatever the world of sports calls you." "Just Canyon, but I prefer Dan." "Yeah, well ask me if I give a shit," Chase replied.

"This is the crap I'm dealing with. You marry a girl and you've got to marry her entire family." "Marry? exclaimed Dan." "Not yet, but Gina is perfect for me. Smart, sticks to business, not crazy over the top like other women I meet. Whatever the opposite of emotional is." "Uh, 'unemotional'? Dan answered. "Right. Oh, I forgot, a

Michigan man. Just remember, it's still not Yale." "It's Yale with a better basketball team" an annoyed Dan answered. Why are you here, and tell me fast, because you see that window, in a minute, I'm throwing you out of it."

"Now hang on," Chase said. I thought you'd be different. It seemed so at first. I thought you understood me, and Gina. We're a great couple and I love her. Her family is different and even she wants to get away from them. I don't need them, and I don't want them. You saw tonight at that Christmas thing, and by the way, it's not Christmas."

Dan was getting more irritated. "They 'did it' as you say, because I'm leaving for a game later today, if I can get any sleep. I have a game on Christmas Day. That's life in the NBA. The Minnelli's knew I had a Christmas Day game, and they went out of their way for me, like they always do. Hey, you don't think I know about being different? How many real friends do you think I have? You think I believe anything said to me in the name of friendship? You know how many former friends who never WERE friends want things from me now? Suddenly, they're all my friends. Hey, I know this family can be a little over the top, but they don't need me OR you. They don't need my money. They reached out to me. You love Gina but the entire family is smart, sophisticated when they want to be. They just love life and they're not afraid to show it. Paul sits in a boardroom making deals and then he goes to the Star Tavern and drinks beers with his buddies. It's called being balanced. Jimmy put his company on the map, so what if he prefers polo shirts and khakis over 3-piece suits? They dragged me into that family circle, and I didn't want to go, but now I'm there and it has changed my life."

"Hey, were we even talking about you?" Chase, Mr. Tact, decided to say. "You think I decided I bust into your sub conscious in the middle of the night to hear YOUR sob story?" "Well then what the hell do you want, Dan said, exhaustion showing in his face."

"Just listen to what I'm up against", Chase, and he slowly opened the door. "Alright, come in and give the Canyon Boy his dream."

In walked a band that looked like they had just come off the boat. But then Jimmy, Paul, Carol, and Tony walked in, dressed like they were at the party just that past night. There were also three people dressed like the band, clapping their hands along with the little group of musicians.

Finally, the music went into a verse and Paul stood out in front:

"I told my sister time and again.

Go ahead and climb the corporate ladder.

Be yourself but don't forget.

That in the end, your family matters."

He stepped back, and Chase turned to Dan and said "Wait, it gets worse."

Carol walked forward,

"I try to keep house, the maid, the baker.

313

Always calm, the official peace maker.

I don't want my daughter to break my heart.

Please Mr. Chase don't pull my family apart."

Chase pretended to play the violin for Dan.

Up walked Jimmy.

"I know Gina's different; she has her own voice.

An Italian man might not be her first choice.

But what's this guy got, he's spoiled and rich,

Our family don't need this son of a bitch."

Chase yells in Jimmy's direction. "That's right, Mr. M. Don't hold back."

Tony walked forward. Chase looked at Dan and said "Oh, great, the smart one's turn." "Hey, shut up" Dan said to Chase. Chase just shrugged his shoulders.

"Of all the guys walking on the map,

You fall in love with this piece of crap,

Italian guys can be smart as hell.

My good friend Lou owns a Taco Bell."

Tony expresses to the entire crowd "He owns six Taco Bell's and a Wendy's, but I couldn't make it rhyme."

Chase looked at Dan and said, "I swear, you can't make this stuff up."

Finally, Luccia stepped slowly forward, a scowl on her face. "Chase said, oh no. Just when you thought it couldn't get any worse."

Grandma said her peace and in an over the top, cartoonish Italian accent way beyond even how Grandma talked.

"You no comma here for the family to meet,

You no comma here for some dinner to eat.

You dress so fancy it's just for show,

So, I just say to you leccaculo."

"That's a curse word", Carol said quietly to Dan.

"I'm a-sorry, Danny" Luccia said, but this a boy, he makes a-my blood boil. Don't worry, you're a good boy." Dan said, to be kind "A good boy and a big…" "No, no Danny. I'm sorry. Today my blood is boiling."

"YEAH! You go Grandma!" Chase mocked. He turned to Dan. "You know, isn't it time for that Sicilian woman to go up to that big pizzeria in the sky".

That was it.

Dan grabbed Chase by the throat with one hand, three feet high, to the same level as Dan's face. "You asshole. All these great people, willing to give you the same chance they gave me, loving their daughter, trying to understand you, and you just stand here and mock them." "Now, now", Chase said, "don't throw that big paycheck away, and think about the endorsements. They tend not to sign with murderers." "I don't care," said Dan. "Gina can do better, and the world would be better without you." Dan opened the window in his bedroom, the street 10 stories below. The window opened. Dan literally held the panicking Chase in one hand, his mouth open with fear. "Suddenly, a calm but stern James Minnelli stood forward, just as Chuck Johnson would have done. He waved a finger at Dan and said harshly, "Dan! Put that man down. You have a career, friends, and family. You have your parents that love and you have us and well, we love you as well. Don't throw away your future. Put him down." Chase looked at Dan and said, "Listen to him and put me down. Besides, everybody knows that if you weren't so tall, you'd have nothing. Your height defines you. You're tall but you're weak."

Out the window Chase went. There was silence. Everybody stood with their mouths wide open. Suddenly, Jimmy said to nobody in particular. "Well, I tried to stop him." Paul said, "You did your best, dad".

Dan just kept looking out the window. Tony had his face in his hands and said sadly, "Oh, no. There go my Knicks season tickets."

# God and Fabulous Musicals

"Tony, do you think there's a God?" Dan just suddenly asked, like he'd been waiting to ask it just at this time, like it was planned for exactly this day and time. No emotion whatsoever.

"Ohhh!" Said Tony. "What the fuck?" said Tony. If not, I wasted a lot of time down at Our Lady of Lourdes, getting chewed out by the sisters. But I mean, don't talk like that."

"You see, you're religious and you say the f-word. I'm not religious, and I don't. Or rarely," Dan insisted. "Now what the f-word does that matter?" Tony said, partly joking, and struggling not to say the word that came out of him so easily. "That word, you must understand. I was born to say it. I learned it at home. It's just a natural expression. Others say, 'My goodness', I say fuck. "I'm not so sure you learned it at home," replied Dan. "Maybe on the streets. I've never heard your father, your mother, and certainly not your grandma say it. Paul, I don't remember. Gina, yes, but not like you. With her, it was like she built up to it, for one grand sentence of frustration for the night. For you, it's just a constant thing." "Hey, God understands", said Tony, "but to deny God, I don't know, that's a sin."

"Well," Dan said, I'm strictly philosophical about it. I mean no "sin" or "harm" as you put it. I'm split right down the middle, I suppose. I see the work of God all around me. The Universe, the stars, a baby's birth. That's the work of God. Violence, pain, suffering, war, then that's also the work of God?" No, Tony said. That's the work of the Devil."

"So, I've heard, said Dan. "Is God more powerful than the Devil?" "No", said Tony. "Don't be stupid." "Well," Dan said, "Then why doesn't God just destroy the Devil and we can have a perfect world?"

"Shit, I don't know", said Tony. "Free will," said Tony. "Anyway, Socrates," Tony asked, "What's your take? You're so smart." "No, that's just it," Dan said. "I'm not smarter than you. I just think about it." Dan continued. "Is God not all powerful? Or is he not all good?" "God's gonna get you, you dumb ass," was Tony's reply. "Well, that's a 'prophetic response."

"There's a saying I've heard," Dan said, "That God is either not all-powerful, or he's evil." Tony, in a rare moment of seriousness, said "Dan, you're always looking up at the stars, talking about light years and even down here on Earth, talking about matters so complicated, so amazing, so beautiful, and so beyond our ability to understand, that now, in a moment of duress, you feel you understand God?" "You're right," Dan said, and it hurts me even more because I want to understand, and my brain can't. Billy Barty should still be here. How can that man simply cease to exist? I was talking to him a few weeks ago. He had funny things to say, and observations about the people and the world, and you mean to tell me that he just doesn't exist anymore? Maybe he never did. I don't know what to think anymore. People like that can't simply vanish." "Well, I think you need to make peace with the fact that you're not meant to have all the answers. Maybe if you knew everything, you'd always win basketball championships. Oh wait, that's exactly what you've done all this time. Are you

318

God??". Dan laughed and then, so did Tony. "Look," Tony said. We don't have the answers. Read the Bible, my friend. A lot of the answers are there." Dan, not wanting to tread too hard on a recommendation from Tony he didn't buy into, simply said, "Well, maybe we weren't meant to know, 'cause I'll never understand why a man like Billy has to die, or a little girl has to get sick with her whole life in front of her."

"One more thing", Tony asked. "Can we talk about something else, like beer, or getting laid?" "Oh, so God wants us preoccupied about getting laid?" Dan laughed. "Listen, you, who understands more about getting laid than God?" Dan had no answer to that. "I have no answer to that," said Dan.

"No, really," said Dan. "Something else. Why does God always need so much damned money up there in Heaven?"

"Tony?" "For God's sake, WHAT?" said Tony. "I'm going to help kids get better and help people eat," and let God take care of the rest." "Good", said Tony. "I'm sure God will appreciate it," he said, cracking open another beer." "I know I will." Tony said.

"I won't be your door man anymore," Tony added. "I'm going to work for my dad. If you can't beat 'em, join 'em." "Yeah, that's great!", said Dan. "Where will your dad put you?" "At the bottom", said Tony. Like everyone else, but with extra credit for having a Lehigh diploma." "But" said Dan. "Doesn't that mean you start in management?" Tony replied. "How do I manage people when I don't know their job? That's the problem in this world. My dad's right." "But doesn't a college degree mean anything, anymore?" "Yeah", said Tony. "It means I'm willing to get my ass off and work toward something, and the fact that I had to take calculus one semester, and accounting, means that in time, maybe I CAN be in management. But at the same time, I know my dad. Family comes first but not at the expense of a job well done. I'm twenty-three. I do this, work hard, learn the business well, and I'll always have a job. I do my best and my dad will always be there for me, like his dad was for him. If I do more than my best, and achieve, I'll be promoted. Time for me to grow up." "Hey, I'm proud of you, man." "Guess we'll just have to meet here." "Here, my house, Star Tavern, Pal's Cabin. The family won't let you off that easy."

"So," Tony said. "I have a surprise." Dan said, "I don't like surprises." "Too bad. Get your things, we're taking a trip." Tony replied. "No, thanks, I'm about to get comfortable and not get up for a while." "No, I'm serious. We must go somewhere." "What are you talking about?" Tony said, "No, I mean it, we have to go to the Cabana Club Swim Club, right down the street." Cabana Club of one of several popular swim clubs in the norther NJ area, made popular from the '50s through the early 2000's. It carried names like "Cabana Club", "Mountain Crest", "Shadybrook, "Sun Valley", and "Skyline".

"Yeah, I've seen it, but I don't feel like swimming right now." "No," Tony said. "Why do you have to be such a wise ass all the time?" "ME? Dan replied. "You've got that distinction cornered." "No", Tony replied, "I'm serious. "I've been talking to this girl, Shelly Simon. Her family belongs to that club and she's directing some kind of teen musical, and she asked me to come watch, so we must go." Dan was now somewhat interested. "Okay, maybe

I'm interested." Tony said, "What's the musical?" "Interested or not, you have to go, it was part of the deal." "What DEAL?" Tony said. "That the famous CANYON would come." "So, wait, I'm going so you can make it with this girl?" Tony snarled, "Did anyone say, 'make it'? She's a nice young lady from a nice Jewish family that I'd like to get to know better." Tony saw an ideological opening. "What does the Jewish part have to do with anything? Why do you all label everything around here." Tony said, "Look Sister Teresa, I say hello to more Jewish people on any given day than you've ever seen in that cow-town of Marietta, GA in your entire life, so don't label me as anything." "You know nothing about that cow-town. My dad is helping design the next generation of stealth fighters there, while this town makes mushroom soup and hot dogs." Even Tony had to laugh at that one. "Yeah, but as mushroom soup and hot dogs go, they're the best!" The ball-busting was in fine form tonight. "You should know," Tony said, that both my grandfather and my dad, knew Arthur Goldman very well, and Minnelli Masonry did all kinds of work around his hotel over on Pleasant Valley Way, and West Orange was once considered "country", where New Yorkers would come out to visit for vacation." "Balderdash", said Dan. Tony said, "How long have you been waiting to use that word somewhere?" Tony laughed. "Way too long," Dan said. "Well," Tony said, "You should have waited longer."

"Anyway, about labels" Tony continued, "that's the way we talk around here", Tony said, "An Italian guy, an Irish family, a Jewish girl. It doesn't mean anything. It helps us identify people. People can call me 'that Italian guy' all they want. I'm proud to be Italian." Dan asked, "Would you marry a Jewish girl?" Now it was Tony's turn to have fun. "Oh, hell no. Marry one, no, the family wouldn't like that." "You see, said Dan!" "I'm kidding, I'm kidding, said Tony." "You are NOT kidding," said Dan. "Fess up." "Okay", said Tony. "There's still that 'old country' stuff, marry in the family, the faith, but there are enough examples of that going away. We live in a melting pot." "Eh, you don't convince me," said Dan. "Well, who knows," said Tony. "I guess it matters with some and for others, it doesn't. Besides, there's a quick fix to marrying outside your faith, race, and so forth, and that's grandchildren. A lot of it seems to be forgotten when that happens. Suddenly, they are the most beautiful mix of backgrounds God ever intended to put on the Earth.

"Well, anyway," Dan said. "You never told me the name of the show." Tony, said, "Hell, I don't know. Flower Song, or something." Dan perked up, "Flower Drum Song?" "Yeah, yeah, 'Flower Drum Song', that's it." "Well why didn't you SAY so?" asked Dan. "Suddenly, Dan stands up, his large frame stretching upward, and he sings in a mocking way,

> *When men say I'm sweet as candy*
> *As around in a dance we whirl*
> *It goes to my head like brandy*
> *I enjoy being a girl*

"You are one fucked-up individual," Tony said. "C'mon", Dan said, "I hate being late for shows."

From this night on, a new, inside joke was born. Anytime Tony called Dan for things, he'd say, "Hey come down to the house this Saturday, the family's putting on 'Flower Drum Song', or "let's go to a Yankee game, they're singing a song from "Flower Drum Song" during the 7th inning stretch. He became relentless, more so than usual.

So, the show went great. Lots of proud parents and grandparents. It scored points for Tony, while they stood way in the back, where Dan always had to stand. He heard one or two "Oy, veys" referring to Dan's height. A couple made it obvious. Tony whispered, "sorry, people are jerks everywhere." "Well," Dan said. Somebody's 'oy vey' is another person's 'marone'" "Yeah," Tony said, "Ain't it the truth. Well, you DO get noticed."

After the show, Tony and Dan accompanied Shelly and the teens to Gary's Restaurant on Eagle Rock Avenue, where the swim club day campers and teens often went after dances and shows. Scores of ice cream sundaes and "California Burgers" arrived. It was no "CANYON Burger", but then again, what is?"

# Kaufman Homes

Kaufman Homes is the largest builder of residential homes in the United States. Founded in 1946 by Martin Kaufman, it was largely responsible for the "boom" in baby boomer, the influx of affordable housing from coast to coast, serving all Americans, but especially those returning after World War Two. Its simple, mass produced method of prefabricated materials cut down expenses and allowed millions of Americans to realize the American dream. It closed a record 220,000 closings alone in 1948, a number not surpassed to this day, and has averaged more than 75,000 closings a year, as it celebrated its 60th anniversary in 2008. Its headquarters were in the Long Island hamlet of Purchase, NY.

The founder, Martin Kaufman joined the Navy at the relatively old age of 34, due largely to his fluency in German, taught to him by his grandmother on the lower East Side of Manhattan, long before both World Wars, along with a healthy dose of Yiddish. Living in a crowded Orchard Street Tenement, Isidor and Sarah Kaufman, Sarah's mother, Ruth, and their three-year-old son, Martin, moved from Frankfurt to America, the reasons not entirely known to this day, but they arrived with few possessions and big dreams.

From the start, Isidore and Sarah insisted on learning English and speaking it exclusively in the home. However, Ruth, the bubbie, or grandmother, and primary caregiver to Martin, struggled to learn English, and eventually, Martin's parents shrugged their shoulders and gave up. Ruth would speak German and Yiddish. Yiddish was originally a German dialect with words from Hebrew and several modern languages and is today spoken mainly in the US, Israel, and Russia. Isidore and Sarah came to realize that Martin would learn English soon enough, at home, in the streets, and in school, and he did. But Ruth lived to be 94 and Martin spent all of his younger years in her presence and having a knack for language typically reserved for girls at this age, Martin spoke German effortlessly, and that and Yiddish really weren't a problem using on a daily in the overcrowded, tenement-infested lower East Side of Manhattan.

Martin was an energic, affable, and likeable boy in an age where good health was indeed a premium. Martin was cherished, indeed, as most children are, but as an only child, he was protected and loved in a most extreme way. The family saw illness and death regularly, and Martin's parents clung to him.

Martin was urged to study hard, to reap the benefits of this great new country, but he struggled to find his passion except for one area. He loved to take apart things and build things. His father worked as a laborer in a machine shop, when he wasn't working at a meat plant or clothing factory, while his mother worked as a seamstress at another factory nearby. The family struggled in the most densely populated neighborhood in the country, and the parents prayed that Martin would find a way to educate himself and live a better life.

While he begged many times to quit school, like so many did, his parents continued to push. They had dreams of sending Martin, somehow, to college, and then from there, who knows. College. It was a wild dream, perhaps, although their families had always made learning a lifelong ambition. Every Friday, the family lit the Shabbot candles, while much of the neighborhood activity died down until sundown the following night. Martin was taught that nothing in the world was more important than respecting God and family, and that good, honest work was not only a blessing, but a commandment. "Six days shall you labor and do all your work and the seventh day is a sabbath to the Lord your God [on which] you shall not do any work."

New York was a playground, a flourishing petri dish of architecture. The downtown skyline teemed with new buildings from the Singer Building in 1908, which reached 612 feet, to Madison Square in 1909, the Metropolitan Life Insurance Tower at 701 feet. Soon after, the Woolworth Building went up, with a spire that soared to 792 feet. Martin grew to wonder at the New York skyline. Yes, indeed, Martin wanted to build things.

In March of 1911, when Martin was just four, there was a commotion in the Greenwich Village area, many blocks from Martin's home. A building was on fire, a building where garment workers, mostly women, were locked inside each floor, and unable to leave when a small fire grew until it enveloped three floors of the Triangle Waist Shirt Factory. Martin, cursed to be walking just a block away with his mother and father, couldn't look away, even with the police shooing them away. You really couldn't see too much at first. Fire fighters were going but virtually nobody was coming out, and then he saw something he would never forget for the rest of his life. He saw not one, but perhaps ten bodies flung out of the windows of the 8th, 9th, and 10th floors. Then, he saw several more and horrified, he had to turn away. For years, his parents told him he was too young to understand what had happened, but Martin saw those bodies falling, people, dying. He knew it and he never forgot it. It was many years later when he learned and could understand more of the details, including the youngest death of Kate Leone, just fourteen, and when he read about that in school several years later, it took him right back, whether he was four or not.

The city was aghast not just at the 123 deaths, mostly women, but the fact that many could have lived had there been adequate safety precautions, like unlocked doors and more exits. Martin would never forget this scene as grew up and became a builder himself. He swore to uphold standard of safety, while making homes affordable to many.

Isidore, at one time, became a masonry worker, when Martin was 14, and for one summer, Martin worked on the job, laying, and moving bricks, and doing whatever asked of him.

With many young men drafted during the Great War, Martin continued to work and study hard, being just 11 when the war ended. He attended the College of the City of New York, uptown, and studied business, even though he told his parents that he wanted to build homes. Well, this was part of it. He continued helping his father on construction sites, maybe the longest tenure his father had, where it wasn't uncommon to take on whatever job you could get your hands on.

After the war, many young soldiers needed homes. It was nothing like the influx after the 2nd World War, but there was plenty of work for Martin, who by now had moved to homesites in Brooklyn and even to Long Island. All through school, he worked as a general laborer, working every weekend, learning several tasks involved in the building of homes. The Sabbath had to take a back seat to carpentry work, putting up drywall, installing fixtures and appliances, and mixing concrete. He worked on floors, he painted, he worked on roofs. He spent the year as site supervisor. He was told that if he kept working hard and got his degree, he could rise high in the company. In time, he could be a superintendent, in charge of an entire project of multiple homes, and from there, who knows. This was it for Martin. He'd have a college degree and an outdoor job he loved. A blue-collar guy with a business degree. The best of both worlds.

The depression years were difficult, but there was still work to do. For a time, Martin had to leave his construction job and do some general accounting work. He got his CPA. Then, he met Beatrice Rosenberg at a dance in Brooklyn, and two years later, in 1931, Martin and Beatrice were married. They would go on to have three children, Robert, Michael, and Rachel. Life was better for the Kaufman's than most families, and they settled in the town of Garden City, which experienced a small boom of residential homes, and Martin moved out of the office and back on the construction site, eventually overseeing all new home quality and purchasing. His accounting abilities, something he once cursed, now helped him as he became in charge of buying all materials, learning how to negotiate and buy wisely. He took additional courses where he learned new styles of construction, architecture, and design. Martin and Sarah moved into a nice ranch-style home and Sarah raised their children. They couldn't join the local country club, but they weren't country club people. Martin somehow managed to keep a nice tan year-round, and his hands seemed permanently calloused from all the years working outside. Still, nearly every Sunday, he visited his family. Isidore died in 1927 from a fatal heart attack, and his mom and Bubbie moved to Brooklyn, which made it easier for Martin to see them, or have them come to Garden City. In 1938, his Grandma Ruth was 84 and while slowed, still vibrant enough to converse in German with Martin on every visit. Ruth would live to be 92, just after Martin started Kaufman Homes, in 1946.

First, though, there was the War. On December 7th, 1941, Martin Kaufman was 34 years, and eligible for the draft. He showed up at the local recruiting station the next morning joining a long line of men with a chip on their shoulder. The Japanese and Germans saw the Americans as inexperienced and weak. Inexperienced they were. The USA scaled down their military after the first World War, ranking 17th in the world, but thanks to the massive strength of U.S. industrial might, it didn't take long to become a military juggernaut.

As part of the normal induction process, a Sergeant asked Martin if he spoke any foreign languages. Martin said, "Yes, I speak fluent German, as well as mostly fluent in Yiddish". The Sergeant said, "What was that other language?" Martin didn't want to deal with it. He said "Oh, a German dialect my grandmother knows, but I speak German fluently." After taking a physical and providing contact information, he was told "That is all. You will be contacted via telegram if you are needed". If Martin thought? Well, maybe they didn't need me. but he wanted "in". It wasn't just the dastardly sneak attack on Pearl Harbor, it was the years of stories about the Nazi's and their treatment of the

Jews. Nobody knew at that time just how serious it was and how much worse it would get.

Four weeks passed and Martin wondered if he would serve at all. Then, he received a telegram, with instructions on meeting at Grand Central Terminal. Nothing else was said. Needless to say, the one person who was fine with a rejected 34-year-old husband was his wife. She was distraught, as everybody was. All he could tell his family, all he knew, was that the Army was sending him to Baltimore on a train with other recruits. He would call or write when he could. In Baltimore, recruits were bused to Hagerstown, on a commercial bus. From there, they were met by Army MP's who took them in another bus to their destination. Fort Ritchie, Maryland.

Martin wasn't very surprised to see and speak with many Jews in New York, on the same train, but as the approached Fort Ritchie, he noticed many of the same Jews arriving at the same place. "Hey, maybe they're forming an all-Jewish regiment to go stick a knife in Hitler's belly." As it turned out, he wasn't that far off.

Martin became part of an elite group of mostly German-speaking Americans called "The Ritchie Boys". He learned many kinds of interrogation techniques, and for the first three years, he never left the U.S. and was able to go home quite often. "Maybe you'll always just serve here", Bea said, but Martin knew better. The Allies would be invading Europe, sooner or later. When and where, nobody knew. Hitler was certain it would be at the Pas de Callais in France, but thanks to the most elaborate deception in history, the allies instead would land in Normandy, and then on the march to Paris and Germany.

Martin landed on D-Day later in the day and had been trained to perform several tasks related to intelligence. Lent to the British Army briefly, on April 15th, 1945, Martin and his British allies discovered the Bergen Belsen concentration camp. Thousands of bodies lay unburied around the camp and some 60,000 starving and mortally ill people were packed together without food, water, or basic sanitation. Many were suffering from typhus, dysentery, and starvation. The stench was unbearable. Martin's mind flashed back to the Triangle Shirtwaist Factory. As horrible and negligent as that day was, something he thought about regularly, this camp was other-worldly. Martin stepped off to the side and threw up, dropping to his knees, struggling to catch his breath, dry heaving as the stench of rotting human flesh and smoke filled his lungs. "C'mon mate" said a solider from the British 11th Armored Unit. "It's bloody tragic, but you've got work to do." The stories he heard from the German-speaking prisoners were unbelievable. Suffocating cattle cars, families torn from each other at the arrival gates, never to see each other again. Old men and women, sick, and children too young to work, marched away with minutes in a very efficient, orderly process. Heads shaved, numbers stitched into clothing (or at other camps, tattooed on arms). All forms of dignity stripped. Martin had never witnessed such terror. How could humans, even Nazi's, do this.

Within three days, Martin was part of a detail team that went through the town of Bergen near Celle and organized a forced march of citizens into the camps, with the bodies remaining unburied, to witness what they say they had "absolutely no idea of". Through the smell, the burning of human flesh, they simply didn't know. With shame on their faces, they marched, many holding handkerchiefs over their faces. Some crying.

With the war over in May 1945, the busiest part of Martin's work began. He was sent to Nuremberg in October, where he would become one of many German translators for Nazi's suspected of war crimes. He did not consider himself lucky when he had to translate into German and back into English, the testimony of one Hermann Goehring and other criminals and killers.

At the end of 1945, Martin was shipped back to the U.S., into New York, and eventually, discharged. It would be many years before he could speak to his family about the horrors he witnessed. It made him more eager to help his fellow man and get back to his passion. After one year of construction supervision, he set out to build his dream, Kaufman Homes. He spent the better part of the years speaking with architects on the best way to build a home of good quality, using mass production techniques, at an affordable price. The government was also going to provide a means for returning GIs to buy a home at a fraction of the regular price.

Along with pioneers like J.J. Levitt and sons, Martin established Kaufman Home and spent the next 50 years building affordable homes to help Americans of all backgrounds. The company grew fast, with locations up and down the east coast, into Pennsylvania and Ohio, then eventually, across the country. A separate division "KS Homes, short for 'Kaufman Select' was founded, featuring specialty and even customer homes, for premium prices, of course.

Martin was acquiring great wealth, and wanted to give back wherever he could. He liked the idea of helping children's hospitals and providing college scholarships for needy students. He started the Leone Scholarship, named for Kate Leone, a 14-year-old who lost her life in the Triangle Waist shirt fire. Martin spent much of his time, especially as he delegated the management of his company to his children and others, to recruiting other companies for the purpose of making the Leone Scholarship known and respected throughout the nation. Few knew where it came from, but the words "Why don't you go for a Leone scholarship" were heard by ordinary students, teachers, and parents from coast to coast. Martin would start every speech, when he gave one, on the subject with "What more can we do for the youth of America, and for the future of America, than provide for them a sound education? The Leone scholarship is an investment in America". He was a tireless Foundation raiser. The "Leone Sweepstakes" was an amazing vacation and black-tie dinner in Hawaii that several random winners received every year. After his family, it was the love of his life, now more important than building. He loved to build, but he saw it as a way to provide for others.

**December 2001:**

Robert Kaufman, the 43-year-old President of Kaufman Homes stood in front of his board of directors and his senior staff, including both his brother, Michael SVP of Marketing, and Rachel, Senior Vice President and General Counsel. Each child of Martin and Beatrice Kaufman got the best education possible, each with either MBA's or law degrees. Kaufman Homes, in all transparency, gave them the easiest road to prosperity and advancement, if you call working your ass off and dealing with your dad always looking over your shoulder. In all fairness, Martin was not an unreasonable boss, but he always liked to say. "Kids, Mom and I love you. We tried to bring you up right and give you the best education we can. You will never know the feeling of going hungry, being cold, or being without a home. But if you want to come work in the family business, you'll have to perform." Martin had a soft heart, as everyone knows. The kids were set if they did their best, and that they did. Each had a working knowledge of home building, and each, yes, Rachel, too, started at the bottom, learning how to paint, put up dry wall, and build a home, step by step. How else could they someday make big decisions for the company? Today, they were doing it.

"Good morning, everyone", Robert began. I'm going to get right to the point. Over the next decade experts believe that the economy, including the housing market, is going to slow. Our growth rate, which we have experienced in all but four of our fifty years, could be flat, or even in decline. This is unacceptable. We must find new ways to build our business. It's no secret that we've looked to compliment the home businesses for years now. As expected, while new home sales are expected to flatten or decline, the home improvement business is projected to grow strongly, as much as 15% per year, as people stay in their homes and instead do more projects. This can mean anything from building a fence or sidewalk, to home additions.

We've been looking at a few companies in the area, and one of them is very intriguing. That company is called Metro Holdings. This is a family-owned company that began in the 20's by Dominick Minnelli, and is a successful company, but it took the son to take it to new heights.

Sound familiar? Laughter broke out in the room. Rachel said "Hey, it took the children, big shot". More laughter. Robert smiled again. The smile stopped and he continued. Both his son and his daughter run much of the company now. What was once Minnelli Masonry grew into 22 states. You've probably seen their clever ads. For a long time now, they've been Metro Holdings. They have crews covering nearly half the country, doing all kinds of home repair. From a handyman to a room addition, Metro does it all. They also very wisely put their money into what is now a very attractive portfolio of commercial properties.

I have a good source that tells me that their majority owner, James Minnelli, is open to a sale. He's a family man, like Dad, and understands the value of his company today is at its peak. I don't know what his kids think, but James owns at least 51% of the company, with the rest split among his family.

I believe I can set up a meeting between myself and Mr. Minnelli. We'll have some of our staff and advisors come and toss around some terms.

This is the right time to make this move, ladies, and gentlemen, for the ensured growth of our company.

In the back of the room sat 91-year-old Martin Kaufman. A stubborn old codger, he ran the company until he was eighty, with just as much spunk and sharpness as he had ever had, and only an extra push from Bea and a kind but firm mention from Robert that his time was "now or never" to take over the day-to-day tasks as President. Even now, Martin would show up at the monthly meetings, shake a few hands, then go play nine holes of golf, not very well anymore, but he still did it. He spent more time going to meetings to support his favorite charity, the one he founded. The Leone Scholarship.

# Tunes

Once again, with training camp just a few days away, and Dan having run, lift, shot, and lost the eleven pounds the trainers estimated he should do, he called Tony, by now managing one of Metro's 65 crews, he called Tony and said, "Let's go drinking up on Pocahontas", his nickname for the Eagle Rock Reservation. Tony would sigh and say "It's not even funny. Just call it the reservation if you want to fit in". "Really, you think I'll ever fit in, anywhere?" Tony quickly said "No."

The discussions and bantering usually kicked in after the 2nd beer. Dan really never got drunk. Let's call it "relaxed". Tony was simply a more amplified version of himself, the volume up a little more, "f" bombs a little more frequent if that's possible. To Tony, saying "fuck" was no more than a very useful word to show emphasis, like a punctuation mark. In Tony's mind, it wasn't profanity at all, and strangely enough, as much as a NJ blue collar stereotype it might be, the rest of his family not only avoided profanity, but they also attacked it. Not a day would go by when any of them would say "Tony, enough of the cursing," but you could no more stop Tony from using that word than you could ask an Eagle not to flap its wings. It was part of his DNA. Take Tony with his f-bombs or don't take him at all.

"Springsteen's playing at Giants Stadium in two weeks. I'm taking a girl I know," Tony mentioned. "He doesn't do much for me," Dan said. "You know, Tony said, I've had to listen to your crap about up here too many times, and until now, I've put up with it; your Woody Allen quotes you somehow think I'm going to get, your double-entendre crap that go over my head, but now you've simply gone too far. It's time to go to the mattresses." Dan said, "Oh, now I know that quote. But it's just business, right? "Everybody knows that quote."

"Anyway, you and your Georgia cowboy music, you can have it", Tony said, taking another sip of whatever, the beer of the day was. "What? Dan said, amused. You don't know what you're talking about." "Yeah, yeah, you like that Italian piano player, Paisano something or another". "It's Petrucciani, and he was French, and he was brilliant." "Was?" Dan asked. "Yeah, he died in 1999, last year." "Yeah, well is he playing Giants Stadium?" Tony asked, sarcastically.

"Well,", said Dan matter-of-fairly, "not anymore." Then, he added, honestly, "but he never would. He was for discriminating tastes. What would you pick, your mom's cooking, or the all-you-can eat pizza-pasta place over in Parsippany?" "Hey," said Tony. There are some things you don't joke about, and that's one of them. "Yeah, but you and I went to that buffet. It wasn't bad". "First of all, Tony said", It was garbage, and never tell my mother or even my family that I went there I was starving, and it had to do." Dan laughed. "Oh, man. You take your cuisine so seriously." Tony responded, "Food is life, my brother. Italians take joy in their food, and nobody in the world does it better." Dan said, "the French might disagree." "Ah, Baicai il culo to the French." "I suppose I don't want to know what that means." Dan said. "No, not for your tender ears," Tony said. "Besides, you have nothing down south."

338

"You're crazy, Dan said. "We have fried chicken, chicken and waffles, Brunswick stew, hot Nashville Chicken, of course there's barbecue, shrimp and grits, peach cobbler, collards, and boiled peanuts." "You boil peanuts?" Tony asked, shocked. "Hell, yes. You find them on the side of the road, places like Jasper, outside of Dawsonville, Elijay, Blue Ridge, even way up in Clayton." "What do you mean you find them?" Tony was laughing, the beer finally kicking in. "On the ground? In trees? They boil and fall?" Now Dan was laughing, "No, people are sitting on the side of the road and boil them in cauldrons." "And you eat them just the way they are?" "Well, of course not," Dan emphasized. "They need a little salt, like grits". "I've seen what you call grits", Tony said, but we put sugar on it. It's called farina." "You're nuts, Dan laughed. That's wheat and grits is corn and salt goes on corn." "Alright, alright, but this collard stuff, you gotta admit, it looks like a clump of grass, and you eat that?" Dan was insistent. "Collard greens are delicious if you cook them right. My mom's family is from Alabama and make great collards. My dad's from Ohio and he's like you, but I love them. You put ham hocks in there, salt, chicken broth, some hot sauce and cook them just until they're tender." Tony said, "Our dog ate collard greens." Dan said "what?" "Yeah, except we just called it grass from the backyard lawn." "Funny, Dan said."

The discussion turned back to music, "Well, Tony said", you keep your jazz. Now my dad, he loves the Rat Pack stuff, and of course Jerry Vale, Julius LaRossa, but not jazz so much." "Well, I love those guys, especially Dean Martin, the coolest guy ever to walk the planet." "Alright, at last we find some common ground", Tony added, "but" Dan said, I like many styles of music, "I like the Allman Brothers, REM, Lynyrd Skynyrd, Atlanta Rhythm Section, you know, ARS."

Tony said, "Nope, never heard of them". "Of course, you have." Dan starter singing in a not half-bad voice:

> Doraville
> Touch of country in the city
> Doraville
> It ain't much, but it's home...

"Sorry, does nothing for me", Tony said.

"I have a surprise for you," Dan said. "You've been traded to the Celtics." Said Tony. "Naw, think I have a death wish?" Dan answered. "I bought six acres of land on Lake Lanier and I'm going to build a house." "Great, Tony added. With high ceilings, I hope. "Damn right, 15 feet high. And it'll have six bedrooms, and a boat ramp and jet skis, and an outside kitchen, and a pool." "When will this masterpiece be completed, "Tony asked. "Next year. I bought the land, and an architect is finishing the plans next week.

I want your family to break it in for me," Dan said. "Will you do that?" Tony responded, "A lake house with a dock, jet skis. It might be something I can talk the family into, Dan said." "Well, talk it over. I want it to open by next August. That's eleven months."

"I might even play a little Springsteen when you arrive", Dan said. "And Tony said, "And I guess I'll put up with a little 'Atlanta Drum Section" or whatever they're called.

# Lady Monarch

Melanie Jacobs was the best girls' basketball player to come out of California in 1995, and that said a lot. She averaged 17 points a game for the Escondido Cougars, but just as important, she controlled the tempo of most every game she played in. It was no surprise that her teammates called her "The General." She could have played anywhere, and it was not easy to say no to Coach Pat Summit of Tennessee. But knowing the history and great play of Lady Monarchs including Nancy Lieberman and Anne Donavan, its history, and its proximity to the beaches, Melanie felt right at home in Norfolk.

Melanie loved her time at Old Dominion, where she was a solid player, and one of the team leaders, even if she didn't quite have the star power of Nyree Roberts, Ticha Penicheiro, or Clarisse Machanguana. The highlight of her career, of course, was her eleven-point performance in the Lady Monarchs 1997 national championship game loss to, of all teams, the Tennessee Lady Volunteers, in Cincinnati, losing 68-59. After the game, Pat Summit found Melanie and whispered to her, "Melanie, you're having a fine career and should be proud of your season this year". She paused, and added, "You're still the General to me." Melanie told Dan that that was the greatest compliment ever said to her in her life, and she expected nothing ever to surpass it.

She graduated college in 1999 with a 3.5 GPA in biology, and she opted to retire from basketball, move to New York, and work for a pharmaceutical company. She had already had knee problems and wanted to protect the remaining cartilage so she could walk when she was old.

Melanie loved the city, and lived close enough by, in Brooklyn. She loved musicals and all kinds of movies, and was often seen watching Turner Classic Movies, where she could quote famous scenes like a pro. She was soft-spoken but had a soft confidence that was born and nurtured from leading players as "The General". She had a dry sense of humor and secretly looked a little bit down at most people who lacked her wit and sarcastic nature, though she never led on about it.

She never gave much thought to whether she was a "feminist". Like anyone, she wanted respect and had worked very hard for it. She wanted to get married someday and have a "partner" in life. They would laugh together, love together, and fight the battle of life together. If that meant that they both worked for an entire career, so be it. If it meant that they had children and Melanie stayed at home, or her husband did that, that's something they would decide together. She wasn't too caught up in what other people might think, including marrying a "shorter" man, although if she were to be completely honest, she did like the idea of marrying a man who was taller, and as she prepared to try out the "Tall Clubs International" or TCI, she had no idea what she was bargaining for.

# Restricted Club

Sometimes life changes for you when you least expect it. A couple of players convinced Dan of attending, of all thinks, a "Tall Clubs International" part in New York. Well, Dan certainly had no problem qualifying for that, but if anybody could easily find a date, it was the C Man. But a date isn't the same as a girlfriend, and the three players waltzed in and caused a near riot. Oh sure, a couple of 6'3 and 6'7 basketball players walking in the door didn't exactly turn heads, but one of the world's most famous man DID, all 8' 9" of him. What followed was part stampede and part "camera lovers convention". But Dan was accustomed to this. He'd be a nice guy, pose, sign some napkins, and head home. But then, he saw her. Pretty but unassuming. Tall, for a woman that is (she was a whopping 6'1". What attracted Dan to Melanie was that she wasn't even interested. Oh, she was plenty interested, but shy, and she had always promised herself and her parents that she'd never throw herself at a man. Her biggest problem was finding a man taller than her. Well, with Dan, that's never a problem for anybody.
Maybe Dan showed he was interested by his awkward approach. "Man, I don't know why I'm here. It's not like I have a problem getting a date." Melanie smiled and said "Well, I know you're famous, but not everybody's interested in a guy just because he's tall. Besides, your field goal percentage fell to 84.7% and who wants a guy who's in decline." "You've been waiting to use that line for a while", Dan joked. Melanie responded. "I suppose so, but aren't you supposed to be using lines on me? I'm the girl." So, Dan came back with. "Look, I don't date dwarfs, sorry." She laughed and Dan was hooked, but didn't let on.

Here's what hooked Dan.

"So, besides the obvious basketball game or two", Melanie asked, what do you do. Oh, and besides the Olympic medals in other sports. Do you have any hobbies?" I like to read, I like music, but more of the oldies stuff that I'm sure you wouldn't like." "How do you know I wouldn't like it?" Melanie asked. "Because nobody our age seems to except me." "Well," she said, then you're probably right" "Well", she said, "test me." "Okay, said Dan, you certainly know Dean Martin, right?" "Dean who?" Dan looked upset. "Oh, ok, I heard of him, and Frank Sinatra, too, although I can't say it's my style." "Ok", Dan said. "What are some of your hobbies?" Melanie smiled and said, "Well, I have some land. I keep it in my pocket." Dan perked up. Could she be taking this where I think she's taking it? "Well, maybe I'd like to buy your land," Dan said. Melanie answered. "This land is not for sale. Someday, I hope to build on it."

"Ok", Dan said. "You certainly passed my test." "EXCUSE ME?" Melanie asked. "Your test?" "Ha, ha," Dan laughed. "I am most certainly kidding, but I will never meet anybody again that drops a line from 'Love and Death' around, so we may as well get married." "Well", Melanie said, smiling, you'd better know a lot more movie quotes than that." "Movie quotes are my hobby." "Well", Melanie said, "That should give us something to talk about for a few days, and you won't know as much as me!" "Aha", Dan said, a challenge. I like that. Better than playing one-on-one." "Well," Melanie said, "How do you know that? I played for the NCAA Women's Title just three years ago." "Wow, that's awesome. Sorry I didn't know that. I was playing for Michigan that year." "Yeah", Melanie said, "like the entire world doesn't know that." "I hate the dating game", Dan

finally said. I'm that tall, awkward guy you've heard about."
"Well", Melanies said for about the tenth time, "As tall,
awkward guys so, you're kinda cute." Melanie dropped
another quote from Woody Allen's movie. Dan knew it,
and Melanie KNEW that Dan knew it.

"Let me at least buy you a drink", Dan finally said. "Oh, no",
Melanie answered. "You don't need to do that." "Oh,
please," Dan said in an indistinguishable foreign accent.
"Hurt feeling". "Okay, where is that from?" "I'll leave that
to you to figure out." "Hmm," Melanie said. "Ok, I like a
challenge. I'll figure it out."

They talked for the next 90 minutes, went out again two
nights later, and never looked back.

Dan told Billy the next day. "I met a nice girl. I already think
it could lead to something." "So", Tony said, no more
grabbing women off the street for you to sleep with." "No",
Dan said, "let's put that on the backburner for a while".
Maybe for good." "Well, big boy, don't rush things. Is she
over eight feet tall? You know, similar height is good."
"No", Dan said, in the same dry tone as Tony." She's five-
two but we'll figure something out." "You're shitting me",
Tony said. "trying to outwit me again?" asked Dan. "I didn't
ask her how tall she is, but I met her at a 'tall' club social,
and I figure she's six-one or six-two."

"That's better," said Dan. "At least you'll look freaky
together."

# Random Thoughts

Tony popped open another PBR. On the ground was a bag. Hs turned to Dan and said. Have a cannoli. Dan answered, "what's that?" Tony stands up, very seriously, and walks over to Dan. "Do NOT do that. Do NOT show that kind of incredible ignorance in my presence. Frankly, it's embarrassing." "All right", Dan finally said. "I've heard of a cannoli." He says "leave the gun, take the cannoli." "Is everything in your pathetic life from a movie?" Dan sat up and thought. "A lot, yeah. Anyway, I've definitely heard of a cannoli." Tony looked serious again. "Well, young man. I should hope so." There was a deliberate pause from Dan that Jack Benny himself would have been proud of. "But I never ate one." Dan said, and Tony finally said. "Are you FUCKING KIDDING ME! I knew you had a deprived life down in Hooterville but no cannoli in your life? That's like never having a woman." "What's that like?" Dan said to Tony.

"Shut up and eat a cannoli." "Can I still drink a beer?" Dan asked. "Do what you want, man." Dan takes the cannoli and eats about half of it, part of the ricotta oozing out. "Oh my God. That IS good." "Start of a new life for you", Tony said.

"So on the news, a reporter said scientists think they discovered a planet that humans might able to live on," Tony announced. "You gonna go?" Dan asked. " With our current technology, it'll take 20,000 years to get there." Dan said "Well, you'd better get going." "Funny".

"You think there's life on other planets?" Dan asked, staring straight up to where there were stars, invisible due to the city lights. "Man, I hate to think this planet is the best thing going." "It's statistically impossible for there not to be life, somewhere.", Dan theorized. Tony said, "I heard a guy interviewed on tv that said aliens brought him aboard their craft." Dan replied, "Don't

346

tell me, he got probed." Tony laughed, "Yeah, how'd you know?" "Because", Dan said. "They've only got one thing on their mind." Tony replied, "Then we're more alike than we think." Dan laid there, thinking of something to say. "Isn't that our job as humans, always probing, ever the inquisitive beasts, questioning, analyzing, reevaluating, trying to find our place in the universe. Our purpose. Our destiny." "All that?" Tony said. "I thought our job was to get laid." "That's part of it, Anthony. Sustaining and nurturing life. Creating. Nurturing and molding.

Dan reached over to eat the rest of the cannoli. Suddenly, two attractive woman walked by, just a few feet away. With Dan and Tony admiring them, Tony whispered something to Dan, who laughed so hard that the beer exploded out of his mouth, and he then held his hands over his mouth and nose. Tony watched and, feigning shock and disgust yelled out loudly, "You sick bastard! There's cannoli and beer coming out your nose!!!" "Oh my God", Dan yelled. Why did you say that? That image will never leave my mind, now. You're the sick bastard." "Not me," Tony said. "I call it like I see it."

"You're gonna ruin my love life", Dan shouted. "What love life?" Tony said. "You mean the ones I yank off the street for you?".

"Now that's a closely guarded secret." Dan announced. "And it was like what, five times?" "Five times, my ass." Tony said "And never question my loyalty. Isn't that the movie quote ?" Tony asked. "You mean, never take sides against the family ever again., Dan said.

# The Sale

Martin and Robert Kaufman had lunch after the meeting, which they did all the time. Martin took out a cigar at the Capitol Grill, a regular routine where there was no smoking. Over walked his "girlfriend", Cindy. "Okay, Rockefeller, put the cigar out." Martin looked over to Robert "I can't get away with anything anymore". Robert basically ignored it as it was only the 50th time he had seen the routine. Cindy truly like Martin. She liked solid tips, more.

"So, dad, you're not the boss anymore, but you're the founder and you're the name" and we've reached an important juncture. I sent you the background. Purely out of respect, of course."

Martin laughed. "It's your baby now, and it's in good hands. Time marches on. You think this is the right move?" Robert replied "I know it is, Dad. If it's not Metro, it'll be someone else. We're going to have a recession. We'll be laying off people and that's the last thing you ever want."

"Okay, well I know a little about Metro, Martin said. They're over in New Jersey. I've met Jimmy at a couple of functions but nothing more than a nod and a handshake. I read some background. So, here's what I propose. Let me go talk to Jimmy Minnelli. No figures, no proposals. Just let me meet him and get to know him for a few minutes." "Dad, this is a serious thing." Martin countered. "Robert, before there's a company, there's a dream. There's survival. There's family. The money is important but it's not what comes first. Show this man some respect. Don't just

348

wave a bunch of money in his face. Listen to me". "Dad, no numbers, no 'estimates'. You want to talk about family, the military, grandkids, fine. No money. I've got a team working on that part. Don't mess things up."

It was Sunday night, family night at the Minnelli's, and while this important tradition wasn't always kept up, now with the kids long out of the home and into their own places, tonight, it did. A few minutes into the meal, Jimmy spoke up.

"I got a phone call from Martin Kaufman." Everybody had heard rumors. "I thought Robert Kaufman was the President there", said Paul. "He is." Jimmy replied. "This was from his father." Paul went on, "The father? He's still alive? Why would he call you? What did he say". Jimmy replied, "He said, hello Jimmy, I'm Martin Kaufman from Kaufman Homes. The old man. My family thinks you have a great company and feels like maybe you'd have interest in selling to us. That's a pretty big thing to do. Would you like to talk about it? No numbers, no deals. That's for my son and his cronies. Just talk about a step like this and what it would mean to your family." "Dad, that's a typical move. The old man wants to soften you up. Don't do it. Money talks." "Well", Jimmy said "I don't know if it's typical or not, but I don't mind it. Generations have gone into this company and people must understand what that means." Gina added, "Dad, the outlook for our business is very good. New home sales are slowing. We would sell at a premium, and Kaufman had better be prepared to pay a hefty premium if they want us. And what would we do for the rest of our lives?" Jimmy said, "Well, it would mean security for generations, and you'd find something else to do. Start a family, for one." "Dad, don't go there", was

Gina's reply." Jimmy then said, "I'm meeting him tomorrow, at the Tic Toc Diner in Clifton, for breakfast."

It was Martin's idea to meet at the Tik Toc Diner in Clifton, right on the busy Route 46, just a few miles from the Lincoln Tunnel. While it could be looked at like a deliberate move to "dress down", Martin had been there many times. Both men had humble beginnings, Martin even more so than Jimmy, who's middle income father had a growing masonry business. Martin grew up on the lower east side, never to get out until he graduated from college. Besides, the food was good.

"Jimmy, nice to see you again. I like this place, hope you're okay with it." "Absolutely, I've been here a hundred times and would rather be comfortable." "We don't have to impress anybody anymore. I stopped trying to impress when I turned 85 a few years ago." Martin was remarkably lucid and fit at 91. In fact, nobody could ever believe his age.

"So", Martin said, "West Orange man, huh?" Martin asked. "Born and raised", was Jimmy's reply. "Well, born in Newark but moved to West Orange from Newark when I was little. I don't even remember the Newark place. We've moved around a few times in West Orange, though, but have stayed there. Our class was one of the first graduates of Mountain High School in 1964. Funny, all three of my kids went to Seton Hall Prep. on Northfield Avenue, which for decades was the original West Orange High School. Hard to follow, I guess and not important." "No, Martin said, your school years are very important. Everything seemed better, didn't it? Things made a lot more sense. You felt safe. Well, I did, but I guess we grow up to see that there were always good and bad things. Anyway, I was asking about West Orange because I had a second cousin, once removed, who lived there. Stan Block, maybe you know him." "No, sorry, don't know Stan." "Well, that's okay. Nice kid, good tennis player. Just passed away in late '98. I don't suppose the Blocks or even the Kaufman's have a long history together with the Minnelli's." It's just the way some things are." Jimmy smiled. "No, not too many in my circle but then again, in West Orange, you'd be surprised." "Well," said Martin. "That's good. People are people, when you get down to it."

"Jimmy, I'm a straight shooter, but as an old timer, I take a different approach than my kids, so this is it. Our company wants to grow, and it may be tough the next few years. I'm mostly out of the business, but I see the point the senior staff is making. Your company would be a great fit. There's very little overlap. It's worth a lot of money and we'd be prepared to pay a lot. You've spent a very long time growing your company. These things don't happen overnight. It's not just the money. It's the blood, sweat and tears. If you sell to us, great. If you're not interested, I understand, even if my kids don't. It's yours, your family's. Why don't you tell me a little bit about your family?" So, Jimmy did.

Jimmy talked about his dad, and how much he loved America. He wanted his kids to be American, to stand tall. He started with nothing and handed over a small masonry business to his son, who grew it to where they operated in 22 states. His daughter Gina began to strategically buy distressed commercial properties, which their own company fixed up and either sold or managed. They

351

changed their name to Metro Holdings. Paul is married with two sons, and one day, the company will go to them.

Martin said, "That's wonderful. We have things in common. I grew up very poor. I've seen a lot in my life. I've seen death up close, here in the U.S. and during the war. Terrible things. I wanted to give back to fellow G.I.'s, ordinary people, my family. What better way to do that than make for them a well-built home? Something they could afford, but something sturdy. Of quality. Something to build memories on. Maybe this sale will allow you to provide for your family for a very long time, if you want to do it. I haven't made any of the big decisions for 15 years. I've been semi-retired and work on charitable projects, including the one dearest to my heart, the Leone Scholarship."

"Hey, I've actually heard of the Leone scholarship", Jimmy said. "My daughter came home in high school with a brochure, and wanted to apply, but we told her we were over the income level", Jimmy said with a chuckle. "You started that?" "Yes", Martin said, started it from scratch. Bumbled my way through it, but then I went to other companies, and it has really grown. It has over a $1 billion endowment; can you believe it". "And named for an Italian?" Jimmy added? "How did that come to be?" Martin told Jimmy the story of the Triangle Waist shirt Factory Fire. "That little girl, Katie, was 14 years old. Trapped in a sweatshop. Burned to death. Or maybe she jumped out of a window. My parents said I was too young to remember, but it's not true. I saw bodies falling. I decided to try and keep the name of Katie Leone alive."

Martin never mentioned Bergen Belsen. It was just too hard.

A week later, Jimmy called Martin and said, "How's your family, Martin". "Just great Jimmy, good hearing from you. I'd like to take you up on fishing off the Jersey shore, but I'm afraid I'm too frail not to fall in!" "Ha, ha", "I understand", Jimmy said. "Martin, we've been speaking over the things you said. Like you said, it's not easy. It's a lifetime of working, building a reputation, something to put you name one, and just like that, it's gone, but they said we should get the principles together and throw around some specifics." "Good enough, Jimmy. I won't be there, but I hope to see you again soon."

The two companies spent over a month looking at figures, floating recommendations, negotiating, pushing back, discussing their employee's futures. In reality Kaufman did not have a crew to replace Metro's home crew, but they still signed a clause protecting them for one year against attrition, as long as no severe policies were broken.

At the end, Metro Holdings would become a wholly owned subsidiary of Kaufman Homes, and eventually, "Kaufman Home Renovation."  Gina Minnelli was offered and accepted a one-year minimum role of Senior Vice President, Real Estate. In other words, in addition to pocketing millions of dollars as an 18% stakeholder in Metro, she would be paid a higher salary, and become an equity holder in Kaufman, for doing just as she had been doing for several years. Running the real estate portion of the business.

There really was no place for Paul, but the millions proved a good salve for his wounds. He would travel, something he could afford with his wife, but never had the time. Almost 40, he and his wife would spend a year travelling the world. Foundations would be setup ensuring the future of the Minnelli family, and Anthony, the underachiever who finally came around, never reaching the status of his siblings, he was still family. He held a 13% stake and walked away with a few million bucks in his pocket. Now, he just had to hold onto it. He looked forward to doing more with the West Orange PAL group, or Police Athletic League, coaching the young Mustangs team and maybe even taking on a larger role.

# It's How They Pour It

All day, Dan just hadn't felt right. A little bit dizzy, but not in an overwhelming way. Sort of like "brain fog". Just off, a little. His stomach felt strange, but again, it wasn't overwhelming. It was 8:00 AM, and the Knicks had a short flight at 1:00 for a 7:30 game in Boston against the Celtics. That would get them to the Boston Garden at around 4:00 for a quick shoot-around, back in the locker room before 5:00, and the team meeting, and back out for warm-ups at 7:00. Normal routine. The Knicks were blowing away the league with a record of 65-4, on an absolute tear, with those two losses coming from the controversial 2-game suspension Dan received from throwing James Youngman three rows into the stands for elbowing him in the ribs for the fifth time since Dan got into the league.

Pete picked him up and took him to the hanger at Newark, where the Knicks boarded their private plane with extra wide, long seats. He still felt queasy but said nothing, and because he rarely spoke, the other players and coaches thought nothing about it. Just another night, even if the Celtics were fighting for a playoff spot and would be out for blood. It didn't seem to matter. The Knicks had a system, and the Celtics couldn't stop it. It wasn't arrogance. Dan was finally coming to grips that this was reality. He had this height and he worked very hard to be a good player, and sometimes, life's not fair, and you make the best of it. Well, if things went your way, don't take it for granted and be happy. Dan took nothing for granted. First at practice, last to leave, didn't party much. He was the regular Lou Gehrig of basketball. Quiet and boring. Sure, keep going with the boring jokes, guys. Even his teammates who were interviewed got on the band wagon. Late night jokes, too. One late night comedian had his little shtick that he could depend on Dan for. "Now I'm not saying that the C Man is boring, but ………." "Or Dan Johnson is so boring, (que the audience 'How boring IS he?'). But Dan had to take it. Mostly, because he WAS boring. Because he was the 2$^{nd}$ highest-paid player in the league and there was some resentment given to the rookie. But there were worse things. Was there a crazy Dan Johnson inside this 8-foot man waiting to get out?

The team dressed and shot around. Dan had the same Queasy feeling but nothing to the degree of being sick. He could play. Then, the team went inside and got the "talk", otherwise known as the team meeting:

"Okay guys, the Celtics need a win to stay in the playoff hunt, but they're not getting it from us. It's the same plan as always. We're gonna work our plan. We pass, we find the open man. When we HAVE the shot, we take it, right DAN?" Yes, same speech and comment for Dan not to overpass. No jokes. The players were ignoring it. They were a well-oiled machine at this point. Another day at the office. One of the players had headphones one. The coach pointed and said, "Do you think you could take those off and at least pretend to be listening.?" A slight chuckle from the players. He removed the speakers and said "Sorry, Coach." He continued, "Now you know these guys. They're aggressive. You know what I mean. They're not going to out hustle us, outrebound us, out defend us, but don't let them throw you off our game. I don't want any technicals or fouling out. Ok, play our game and we'll walk outta here with a W.

Ten minutes later, with the noise of the crowd in the background, the door swung open, and it was 7:20. Everybody got up except for Dan. Not a big deal. He sat there. The last man leaving besides Dan was the coach, unconcerned, who turned to Dan and said, "C'mon, Dan. Let's go." "Be right there, coach", Dan said, tying his shoes one more time, undoing and then redoing them, a nervous, superstitious habit that they coach was probably well-aware of.

Dan entered the Gardens' tunnel, the other players a few feet ahead in the distance. Suddenly, the dizziness got a little worse and felt a little shaking in his hands. It was almost a feeling Dan read about when somebody was having a stroke, but it was a new feeling for him. Suddenly, it just stopped. Dan walked out onto the court there was a capacity crowd.

It didn't happen at once but took about 15 seconds. After all, it was just a pre-game shoot around. People were getting their beer and popcorn, talking, looking the other way, but within seconds, there was an audible gasp from the crowd. Everybody turned and looked at Dan. Dan saw it and HE turned, too. What the hell was going on.

"Folks, this is Byron James getting back to you, and there's a commotion on the floor." James Bennett, the ever-colorful NBA veteran, was his partner in the booth. "James, what do you see down there." "Well Byron, it's hard to tell but that is not Dan Johnson in the Knicks #5 jersey. This is some kind of joke the Knicks are pulling but I'm not sure these fans are going to appreciate it. No, wait a minute, that IS Dan Johnson, and he looks noticeably smaller than normal." "That's not smaller," Byron said. That's a total transformation." And it was true, Dan Johnson looked to be about 6-feet tall. Maybe less than that, as the other players towered over him. The other players stared in disbelief, and everyone sat down on the bench, leaving Dan all alone on one side of the bench. The starting five stood up, including Dan, and the Coach looked from side to side, uncertain of what to.

"Johnson, stay on the bench. Lamar, you're at Center…. NOW!" "What's wrong, coach?" Dan said. "What's wrong with you? Are you sick?" "NO coach", Dan said. "Well, I WAS feeling a little rundown today, and" "NO, dammit" Coach Ramsey said. "You shrunk". "I what?" Dan asked.

Up in the bleachers, two 30-year-old friends, holding beers, were standing and cheering. "The guy shrunk! Holy shit! We're gonna kick their ass tonight, finally. I can feel it. His friend shouted, "Are you fucking crazy! People don't shrink!" "Well, what happened, then, genius?" "Hell, I don't know, but look at him. He looks BAD, and that's good for us!" "No, people DO shrink. My grandma, out in Worcester? I swear. She was like 5 foot five, you, know, before we moved her into that place intown. In Newton. Now she's like 4 foot 8. I swear, she shrunk."

The game started with Lamar at center, but the crowd was thunderous, and a Celtics forward hit a 3 pointer from the top of the key and the crowd noise simply went up.

Four minutes into the game and the Knicks could do nothing. It was 11-0 when Eric Danley hit a jumper from near the foul line, but then the Celtics went on another 7-0 run, and it was 18-2 when he called time out. He just didn't know what to do. "Coach, what happened to Johnson, man?" He shrunk or something. We gotta do something. We're gettin' blown out. Nothing's falling.

The coach was exasperated. He looked up at the scoreboard and then around the arena, tugging on his collar like Rodney Dangerfield might have done. Finally, he looks at Dan, who has his face in his hands, and he says "Johnson, get in the game." "But coach!" Dan cried out. What do I do?"

"You play basketball, that's what you do. What in the hell are we paying you for, Johnson. His teammates, each one, a portrait of pain and terror, looked at him. "Get in there, man. You better do something." One of the players, his own teammate could be heard saying. "You're the big man. You better fix this."

Oh, wait, Byron James told the vast TV audience. The Coach is sending in Johnson." "Oh man", James Bennett said through the mic. "I ain't feeling' good about this. No, keep him out, coach! This is not going to end well." Ed added. "Just listen to this raucous Boston Garden Crowd. More than half a season of watching total domination from their Eastern rivals, the Knicks."

The Knicks took out the ball, and up the court jogged Dan Johnson, appearing less than six feet tall, like a spell had been cast over him. The players looked at each other, their previously flawless game plan in doubt. Phillips passes it to Johnson in the post. He turns around and ohhhh! The Celtics Avery smashes it down, a clean block, and the Celtics have the ball. Avery turns to Johnson and laughs, "Where you NOW, big man? You a tiny man, now. You ain't shit."

The Celtics scored an easy layup. The Knicks Summit, taking out the ball and with nobody else available, passes it to the now diminutive Johnson, who dribbles toward half court, when suddenly challenged by Austin Cooper of the Celtics, the Stanford 6' 9" Forward and 6th man, nicknamed "Professor" for his articulate nature and over the top narrative. "Cooper steals the ball and slams it home! The crowd is delirious, the NBC announcer shouted. Clancy Phillips added, "This is monumental".

The Knicks called timeout and Cooper jogged over to Dan, yanking him to his body in a sign of disrespect he never would have considered before, and whispered into Dan's ear, "Oh, how the mighty have fallen."

Dan sat on the bench until halftime, and the teams walked toward their respective locker room, Dan behind the rest. Just as he was about to enter the tunnel, a fan yelled "Johnson, you suck!" and threw a nearly entire large cup of beer, with better accuracy than any of the Knicks had so far. The beer landed on Dan's head, with a large amount of foam just running down the back of his neck.

"Oh, wow, a fan just doused Dan Johnson with a beer, and his entire neck is covered in foam", said James. "Now you see", James Bennett, the analyst said, "you gotta tilt the cup, all that foam? It's how they pour it."

The lights and music went up in the studio, with the familiar backdrop, music, and words "Basketball Tonight" flashed onto the screen. "Good evening, everybody, Ed Simmons here with my cost-host, the Arkansas Avenger, Double M, the "Razorback and King of Smack", Martin Middleton, and tonight we have, simply, news that has rocked the very foundation of the NBA."

So, Marvin, what can be said about the development of Dan Johnson, the savior for the Knicks who out of nowhere, appears not only to have lost his tremendous height, but his basketball skills as well?" "Ed, Ed, Ed", Marvin said, pounding a table for emphasis. "This is what so many people have said from the beginning. Not everyone, but you know, I felt it from the beginning. You take away this man's dominating height, and he is just another player, and now we know, without that height, he's nothing."

"Well, Double M, right now, it is hard to dispute that claim, but how does a man shrink almost three feet, a 23-year-old, seemingly healthy man, within a matter of hours." "I don't know, Ed. Maybe that is a question for medical experts", the obvious Segway being apparent. "Well,", Ed announced, the medical community is also at a total loss to explain it as well, but we do have some experts here with some possible theories.

"We go to the Columbus Clinic in Ohio with Dr. John Sanderson, an expert in rheumatology. Dr. Sanderson, is there a medical explanation for what has happened to Dan Johnson?" "Without being able to examine Mr. Johnson, a blood analysis, possibly MRI and other tests, no I cannot provide an expert opinion." "But Doctor, do you have even a theory on this?" "Well, it would be an unprecedented spine retraction phenomenon, previously discussed only in theory by experts, but never proven, possibly the effect of such rapid growth earlier in his youth."

"Ok, thank you, Dr. Sanderson". Opinions are coming from far and wide, and from unlikely sources. Dr. Gretta Van Steuben" popular author and television host of the show "Psycho Babble", has joined us. Dr. Gretta, as she was popularly known, what is your analysis?" Answering in her well-known, heavily German accent, the 75-year-old Dr. Gretta said. "Zees is und very unpdezented

phenomenon. There is no prior hiz-story of such a development, so we can only theorize. Quite possibly, this is a manifestation of negative, regressive thoughts." "But Dr." Ed said. "Dan Johnson is perhaps the most accomplished athlete in the history of sports, and it isn't just in basketball. A world and Olympic Champion in such diverse and physically demanding sports of Judo and Wrestling. Four undefeated collegiate seasons and four NCAA championships. A record never approached by any man or woman. Even Jim Thorpe, "Bright Path", never accomplished what Dan Johnson has done, and Johnson is only 23 years old."

"Vell", Dr. Gretta continued. "I do not know this Bright Path" but there is a point where eggs-pectations outvway the reality" and like skin hives and zuch, mental stress will manifest into a phy-zical condition." "But Dr. Gretta, a body that shrinks 3 feet?" "Dr. Gretta chuckled like a little school girl. "Vell, it has not been seen before." Finally, because she always seemed to slip in sex, she said, "Also, but of course not proven" sexual frustration is always a pozzibility, but in this case, it is a stretch." Marvin added, "So you're saying, use it or lose it, Dr. Gretta?" Dr. Gretta giggled again, "Ha ha, oh no, Marvin.". Marvin added, "Dr. Gretta, I'm a half-inch taller this year than last. You come have some coffee with me." All three laughed while the career of Dan Johnson was crashing down.

"On a serious note," the Knicks front office is meeting today to discuss their options, including a thorough review of Dan Johnson's contract with their lawyers. Have we seen the last NBA game with Dan Johnson, just as the Knicks were on a record regular season pace? We'll be following this story closely, and that brings us to another close of 'Basketball Tonight'. We'd like to thank our guests, Dr. John Sanderson and Dr. Gretta Van Steuben", both of their faces still on the video screen. Before the show faded out, Marvin joked, "Dr. Gretta, you come see me. Remember, half an inch." Dr. Gretta laughed and waved her hand, and the screen went blank.

Dan walked into his bedroom, with clock reading 3:00 AM. It was the worst day of his life. Suddenly, five loud, staccato notes blared out from a trumpet, trombone, and saxophone, a funk band. "JAMES BROWN?" Dan yelled, incredulously. "HEYYYY" The singer, wearing a sequined cape yelled. "Hey baby. I'm Sheldon Terayne Goodman" leader and star of the 'James Brown Experience.' The number one James Brown tribute band in the world,

available for Weddings, Bar Mitzvahs, Proms, and corporate events all through the New York area. Hell, we'll even go to Philly. We did the Ginsberg Bar Mitzvah just last weekend at Richfield Caterers, baby. You know the Ginsbergs?" "Uh, no", Dan said wearily. "How did you get the name Sheldon Goodman?" Dan asked, because even in his defeated condition, he just had to know. "Hey baby, I'm the 'Black Jew with a clue". "The soulful Hebrew", the 'Prince of Irvington', baby. He then spoke to Dan quietly. "Actually, my mother is white and Jewish, and I took her maiden name, but don't spread that around, and I'm from East Hanover. But I'm a Jew, baby and what matters the most, I got the James Brown moves, I groove like James Brown grooves. I even wear the same shoes, baby."
"So why are you here, in my bedroom. Dan asked, at the point of not being surprised at anything anymore." "Okay," Sheldon said to his band, "start it back up."

The funk music started, and Sheldon Goodman started singing,

"The 'Great White Hope' is a great white dope. Been a bunch of smoke and baby, that ain't no joke. The Canyon's gone, he's a star no more. He'll never been seen on the basketball floor." He looked to the band, "Great white hope?" The band members answered, "just a joke". The singer again turned to the band, "Great White Hope?" The band members yelled, "bunch of smoke."

Suddenly, there was silence, and Dan's eyed just blasted open, but his body stayed perfectly still. It was a dream, more appropriately, a nightmare. The whole thing. The entire damn thing.

# Little Cazzie

Crisler Center, the home basketball arena of the Michigan Wolverines, was often referred to as "the house that Cazzie built" after Cazzie Russell, the Wolverines prolific scorer, who led the team to three Big Ten titles from 1964-1966. Russell's popularity is so great, that the Yost Fieldhouse was no longer adequate for the number of fans, including years later, the "Maize Rage" student section, giving the Wolverines a clear home-court advantage. Still, there was more excitement than ever for the four years that Dan Johnson wore the Maize and Blue for the Wolverines.

Eric Dudley, an all-start player living in the Detroit area, was an energic, athletic basketball player who was recruited the same year as Dan Johnson, and it was that reason he, and others that year, were virtually unknown in the press. Eric could have played almost anywhere and been productive. In fact, once he began playing, and seeing significant minutes his sophomore year, players and fans alike began calling him "Little Cazzie", for his ability to make a difficult shot from practically anywhere on the offensive side of the court. It was indeed high praise.

Eric enjoyed that much more success because he was part of the teams "Pinwheel Offense", not an original term, but one that served the Wolverines so well. The ball was fed into the Canyon, who practiced, it seemed, day and night, of passing to the open man, and Eric, "Little Cazzie" Dudley got a lot of those passes, because he was such a reliable shooter.

During his Junior year, Eric was injured jumping for a rebound and being knocked to the ground by an opposing player. What seemed to be a relatively harmless play was the beginning of the end of Little Cazzie's career. Continued back problems began to keep him out of games, and while he toughed it out and finished his four years, his production went down. His draft prospects were poor, and he went undrafted.

Dan was never friends with Eric off the court, because he wasn't friendly with any of the players off the court, except for Charles Winfield. He was Dan, the quiet guy who enjoyed watching Mel Brooks and Woody Allen movies, among others, and listening to jazz, and there wasn't a big audience for that among too many of the students, let alone athletes. So, Dan started playing for the Knicks and never heard from Eric again.

Four years into his career, with the Knicks, and trying to keep in touch with the UM community and perhaps missing his many opportunities to do more, Dan accepted an invitation from the school's President, to speak at a Foundation-raising event for several school building projects. All schools needed a constant flow of revenue and donations to keep the school moving in the right direction. For the past four years, Dan had to politely decline due to scheduling conflicts, and was already giving some thought to what he was going to do when he retired, in just a year. He had given the Knicks three straight NBA Titles and he'd be done in two more. He had said it before, whether anybody believed him or not.

He wanted a way to help some organizations beyond just writing a check, which he had done without fail, every year. His financial advisor made donations for him, and of course, he received many requests. Dan had always planned to support the school that supported him for four years, improved him as a player and a person, and made it possible for him to enjoy what he had today. He gave generously to the Alumni Association, including the Camp Michigania complex, which he wanted to visit someday. He figured he could use some rest and relaxation. Yet at the same time, he didn't always know how his money was spent at other, miscellaneous organizations that he sometimes told his advisor, "Fine, go ahead". He also deflected any requests for money, to his agent. They would agree on a budgeted amount and then divide it up as needed. "One day," Dan thought, I'll have my own foundation and really get involved on where the money is going, but he couldn't do that now.

UM did some promotion on the event that Dan was to attend in another week. He'd fly via private jet into Willow Run Airport. During World War II, almost 8,700 B-24 "Liberator" bombers were built at Willow Run. During its peak production, the plant employed 42,000 people including "Rosie the Riveter." Now, it was the perfect airport for Dan to fly to. It was the first time and wouldn't be the last.

Dan got a phone call from the front desk of 77 West three days before he was to leave for Ann Arbor. They said, "Good Evening, Dan, (Dan had long instructed the entire lobby team to call him Dan, as much as their boss told them not to), this is Henry down at the desk." "Yeah, Hi Henry. What's going on?" "Sir, there's a lady on the phone that says you played basketball with her husband, and it was an emergency that she speaks with you. She told me to say you played with Little Cazzie." Dan was surprised because that nickname was more of a team thing. It wasn't known throughout campus, or at least never caught, like "Canyon". Of course, Eric, "Little Cazzie" Dudley missed almost half of his games with that nagging back injury. But Dan knew this must have been real. Of course, Dan also knew that Eric Dudley passed away less than a year ago, it was said, from an unknown illness. There was no kind of memorial service, and it was barely listed anywhere. It was a sad situation, but off the court, Dan really didn't know Eric. "Yeah, Henry, I knew her husband, you can put her on."

"Hello, this is Dan Johnson." "Oh Dan, or do you I call you "C"? Eric said the team mostly called you C." Dan said, "Oh don't worry, Dan is just fine." This is Eric's wife? I'm so sorry about Eric's passing. I didn't even know for almost a week." "Yes, well I didn't want everybody to know." My name is Janet, and I read you were coming into Ann Arbor, for a school event. I live nearby. May I please see you for ten minutes. Please, I know you don't know me, we never met, but Eric really thought the world of you. He talked about you all the time. "He liked to call me 'That tall white boy'" "Oh no, I'm sorry. You know Eric used to have a great sense of humor. "Oh no!" Dan exclaimed. I loved it, it was funny.

Ok, Janet. There's a coffee shop in Ann Arbor called Akire. It's on Packard." "Yes, I know it. Well, I'll be there for a few minutes at around 3:00, about two hours before the event. I just have about ten minutes, and I'm sorry to say that, or I would visit longer. I don't want you to think I'm that way." "No, I understand. I guess I won't have any problem identifying you, Dan." "Nobody ever does." "Well, I'll be early and let you know I'm Janet, Cazzie's wife." "Alright", said Dan.

Human nature being the way that it is, Dan figured it was a request for money, and he usually sent people to his financial planner. "Little Cazzie" might have made it in the NBA if he didn't get hurt, so he could make an exception.

Dan landed at Willow at 3:10 on a Saturday. He would attend the Alumni Event, say a few words, beginning at 6:00, leave 9:00 and take-off at around 10:30, straight to Teterboro. There, he'd get a limo back to the apartment. Everybody that needed to know his itinerary, had it. There were a few things that having money was good for, and this was one of them. Dan would never wait in line to sit on an airplane, rent a car, or sit in a middle seat.

He had a stretch limo provided for him by the school, but billed Dan. It was a bit unusual for a stretch limo to pull up to Akire, on a Saturday afternoon or any other day. Heads turned, and of course, there was an audible "Oh my God." He gave no advance warning. He had been there as a student, and there was a poster with his signature on it. When he walked in, again, heads turned but to their credit, there was no wild scene. The manager came over and said "Dan Johnson, it's amazing that you're back in Ann Arbor.

Are you here for a certain reason or event?" "Yes, Dan said. "I'm here for a big alumni event but for the moment, I'm meeting somebody here." During this, a woman who appeared to be in her late 20's, waited her turn, then walked up to Dan. "Hi Dan, it's me. Janet." "Janet, nice to meet you. My limo is outside waiting." "Wow, a limo is nice." "Well,", Dan said. It's only because I can't fit in a lot of cars."

"Could I get you a coffee?" "No thanks", Dan said. "Not wanting to feel like he was just taking up room, and with no line presently, a lull in business at 3:00, Dan ordered a medium coffee and shook a few hands, causing him to now have to rush with Janet."

"Sorry, Janet. I'm not complaining but things like that slow me down. How can I help you?" Dan felt, for some reason, like he wasn't doing anything to make her feel any better. "Mr. Johnson, I know you're busy, and I'm sorry. I wish I wasn't here. Sometimes situations force you to make decisions in life you don't want to make. To swallow your pride, and I'm at my wits end or I wouldn't be here." "Go ahead, Janet, I'm listening." Janet continued, "Mr. Johnson, Eric was a good man, and he tried everything he could for his back pain. Everything. He got addicted to pain medication very badly, and then other drugs to deal with his problems. He got very sick, and he died a few months ago. Everybody knows it. You know it. We had no funeral. For one, we couldn't afford it. Secondly, I was ashamed, and I now have two small children, and soon, nowhere to live. I used to work but then who's going to watch the kids? I'm angry. Eric was a decent person and now his good

370

name has been dragged through the mud. Some terrible things were said about him, and people don't understand. Yes, yes, Mr. Johnson, I'm asking you for help. For money. Nobody's stupid sitting here. You knew why I was asking you here, and now I've said it. If you saw the looks of my two boys' faces, you see, they're my life. We're not bad people, we're not crooks, we're not drug dealers or bums. I just don't know what to do anymore." Dan tried to think quickly. Above all, he hated it when people felt like they lost their dignity. He had had enough talks about this with Billy. Dignity was the most important human emotion. Well, I suppose that isn't true. Survival is, and when somebody is desperate, especially for their children's sake, then dignity, perhaps, is a state of being that nobody deserves to have.

"Janet, what are your sons' names?" Janet wiped a tear. She said, "Lamaar and Andrew". "We got a Lamaar on the Knicks," realizing that Janet wasn't exactly going to jump up in the air."

"Janet, listen to me very carefully. I must leave in five minutes, but you and I, we're going to take care of this. We're going to make a deal, together. We're not going to share it with anybody. If I make your situation, as a former teammate of Eric's on four championship teams in which he contributed, if I make it so you walk out of here knowing that your boys are going to be okay, and that you can hold you head up high, restore your dignity, because you don't want to be doing what you're doing," Janet quickly shook her head in a "no" action, almost violently, shaking. "Well,", Dan continued, "If you agree to that, just us two working on this, no discussions with anyone else. You must promise that, then you'll walking out that door with your immediate situation improved." "Ok, Mr. Johnson". "First", Dan said. "You must call me Dan or the deal in done. My friends don't call me Mr. Johnson, and guess what, my friends don't call me Canyon, or C Man, either. I know we just met, but let me explain something and I will be as honest with you as the day is long, and that is also part of our solemn agreement to keep this between ourselves, ok?" She shook her head, said yes. "First of all, enough drama from me. I am giving you money, and I mean a good amount of it. Let me talk to my financial advisor on the way back from this evening. It's my money. I'm thinking somewhere between $100,000 and $150,000." Janet's lips started quivering. "You're telling me the truth? For real?" "Well, do you believe that I'm Dan Johnson? See any other nine-foot guys around here?" She smiled and more tears flowed, "No, sir. No Dan". "Do you have a bank account?" She said, "Yes". Okay, I've been giving thought lately to some ways I want to help people when I'm done playing. Coming up here has made me think about it more. To this event. I don't mind giving to large organizations. Some are great, but one day, I'll be more involved directly with helping people. I want to see people's faces. This isn't exactly what I have in mind, but it's a good start. My advisor does what I say. It's my money. You know, what if I had a back injury? What if my pain was so bad that only a dangerous pain medication relieved it? What then?" Janet whispered, "Thank you!". Look, I have this massive height and I've worked hard to make it work for me. That's good for me. I make a lot of money. I make more money working on a commercial for four hours than many people make in five or ten years. It's crazy, but I'll take it because now the money I just promised you isn't a whole lot of money for me. I don't do things this way. My advisor warned me against it, that I would have a line ten miles long, so again, that's part of our agreement." Janet, drying her tears, nodded her head. "But that's not all, first, we get you that money. Get yourself an apartment. Have them call my agent, not me, if you need somebody to guarantee your rent. I would pay for six months. And don't live in a slum. Find a nice area. Get out from under wherever you are. Your kids need to know they can sleep at night and walk out the door safely. Fill your refrigerator with good food. Then I am giving you my personal phone number. Don't share it. Don't make me have to get a new number. I tell that to anyone I give my number to, and that list is very short. Right now, this is our deal, but I want more from you. We're going to discuss your future. Let's get you a job and a way to support yourself, but maybe that's in six months. Until then, get settled at a new place. I'm doing this for Eric, for Little Cazzie. He was a good man and have a feeling you're a good person, and we'll be friends. You want to know a secret?" Janet said, "Ok". Dan continued, "I don't have a lot of friends. I've met Presidents, Kings, and Queens. Even they want something. Maybe it's just politics for some. So, I'm doing this for Eric and his family and the next time, if it's needed, and our goal will be that I won't need to, then maybe I'll be doing it for you." "I, don't know what to say," Janet said, her tears nearly gone. "Well, I told you", Dan said, "that you'd walk out of here in a better place, but remember our deal, and I don't care if you have to lie to anyone, that is, if you told anyone you were coming here." "No", she said. "I was too ashamed, and nobody would believe me". Dan got up and gave her a card with his phone number and the name of his financial advisor. Then, he gave her a hug. "Hey, I'm learning more about life all the time", he said. She said, "me, too".  There's a movie called Sergeant York, and I know you haven't seen it because nobody I know every sees the movies I've seen. Anyway, in the movie, the lead actor says, "The lord sure do work in mysterious ways." I've seen it, and now, so have you. "I must certainly have," said Janet.

I'll be in touch, he said, and he walked out the door. Somebody shouted out, "See ya, C Man! Go Blue", but Dan was out the door.

# Horror on Eagle Rock

The rain was falling steadily as the car left the Manor and turned right onto Prospect Avenue, then another right onto Eagle Rock Avenue, one of the main arteries in West Orange. It was a long road that went up and over hilly terrain, and one of the roads separating what the locals called "up the hill, from down the hill".

The three couples were in a joyful mood, and why not. All were headed to college soon. Two to Rutgers, one to nearby Montclair State, one to UMass, and the adventurous one, Brandy, to Arizona State. Good grades, smart kids with the world in front of them, and most of all, nice kids. They had had nothing to drink while at the Prom, but the night was young and they were headed to another friend's homes in Roseland, only about four miles away. Even that party, like the prom, would be attended by parents, but you couldn't blame kids for drinking a little at an after-prom party, but nothing had started yet, which was a very good thing given the rain.

As they were in a hurry to get to the party in Roseland, the car took on a little too much speed, worsened by the fact that Eagle Rock Avenue was now in a steep decline. "Hey Amy, slow down", was the last thing uttered as the car passed by Fitzrandolph Road and attempted to navigate a curve. The pavement, just now wet enough to bring out the fresh oils in the road, created a dangerous situation. Amy felt a slight bit of panic as the car sped up, a little out of her control, and overcompensated by turning just a little bit too hard. The car slid over the center line and right in the direction of traffic riding up the road, toward the intersection of Eagle Rock and Prospect Avenue.

In the blink of an eye, without even enough time to scream, the car of revelers from West Essex High School slammed head-on into an SUV headed up the hill, driven by Gina Minnelli. Gina, ever so careful, and driving a tad below the speed limit, due to the upward angle of the road, never knew what happened.

Gina was on her way to Pal's Cabin for a family celebration, a week after a more formal dinner to celebrate the sale of Metro Holdings to Kaufmann Homes. In fact, that dinner, attended by over 125 associates, was at the Mayfair Farms Banquet Hall, literally steps away from the accident, on Eagle Rock Avenue.

The family was there, Jimmy, Carol, Paul, Tony, and their Grandma Luccia. Dan was invited but was out of town. After several minutes, Tony said "C'mon, let's eat already. Gina's working late, as usual. It wasn't a lie, as Gina had resolved to bring the company's two businesses together and get off on the right foot. It was three months after the initial meeting, due to the complexity of the deal, though Gina had been working to move all the properties over the new organization, and the paperwork was exhausting. Riches or not, she wasn't going to slow down." "No, we wait. I spoke to Gina twenty-five minutes ago and she was on her way." "Well, at least let me get some mushroom soup while I wait", one of Pal's Cabin's many well-known delicacies. "Tony, we wait". "Suddenly there was the sound of an ambulance, and who didn't worry when they heard that?" Nobody said anything at first. Then Paul said "I'm sure she's fine, but that ambulance sounds close. Let me make sure she's not stuck in traffic behind it." "I just tried calling again and she didn't answer." "Oh, my God", Carol said. "Something happened. I know it. I know it, Jimmy." He said "Calm down, you hear ambulances all the time. It's raining out. Did you ever know Gina to take a hand off the wheel? Give her a few more minutes. She'd wait for us."

After ten more minutes, Paul said, "Look, let me just ride down the street. It's probably traffic. I'll let you know." Paul could have ridden in four directions, but he rode down Eagle Rock. He knew where Gina was coming from, so it was the most likely way. There was a huge traffic jam. In fact, nothing was moving. Paul got about two blocks and turned to park at the curb on Blackburne Terrace. He could see flashing lights. He walked two blocks and saw four police cars. The ambulances had left, but there were two cars smashed almost beyond recognition, except from behind one car was a small UPenn decal and an Audi insignia. He felt faint, like throwing up. It was Gina's car. There was no doubt.

Paul reentered Pal's Cabin ten minutes later. Wet, ashen. His family knew him. Something had happened to Gina. "Oh my God, where's my Gina?" shouted Carol. "Ma, Gina was hit by a car that mishandled the curve on Eagle Rock Avenue in the rain. Gina's at St. Barnabas Hospital." "Oh my God, how is she?" "Honestly, Mom, I don't know. They already took her. Let's go but let's not rush." "Like hell," Carol said. "Oh my God, my baby!"

Paul spent several frantic minutes early talking to the police. They all knew. They pulled Gina's lifeless body out of the Audi. She was gone, but none had the heart to tell that to Paul. Let him go to the hospital where they can make it official. But they knew, and Paul saw the car and the faces of the cops. Paul knew, but he was somewhat in shock and couldn't believe what he saw, what was happening. Not Gina. Gina was always in control. Always had the answer. She had way too much work in front of her, even if she had just pocketed close to $15 million on the Kaufman Sale and could kick back. Even Paul, at just 43, was contemplating retirement, or at least maybe a year off to travel through Europe, something he could have afforded to do before from a monetary standpoint, but not from the standpoint of time away from the office.

They drove west on Prospect to Northfield Avenue, and then turned right, passing the Turtle Back Zoo and South Mountain Arena and over Pleasant Valley Way. In five more minutes, they were entering the lobby of St. Barnabas Medical Center. Rushing to the front desk, Jimmy said, politely, but rushed. "Excuse me, our daughter, Gina Minnelli. She was in an accident and was brought here. Please, help us find her." The receptionist, not without concern, but at the same time, it wasn't an unusual situation for her, said, "Please give me a moment and I'll find out for you. Please have a seat." "Have a seat?" Carol asked, incredulously. Paul said, "Ma, she's just trying to help." "Oh my God, oh my God. Gina baby". Tears were streaming down her face. Two minutes felt like twenty. Finally, an emergency room doctor entered. "Hello, are you the relatives of Gina Minnelli?" "Yes, Jimmy said. I am her father, and this is her mother. I'm James Minnelli". "Well, I'm very sorry, Mr. Minnelli. Your daughter was in a motor vehicle accident and has passed away from her injuries. We believe it happened instantly, and she arrived here DOA. Again, I'm terribly sorry for your loss. The receptionist will speak with you about next steps." He began to walk away. "The next steps? That's what you have to say?" He grabbed the doctor by his shirtsleeve. My daughter is **DEAD**. My daughter is **DEAD**, and that's all you have to say?" "Please Mr. Minnelli, the doctor said. "I understand your loss and I am very, very sorry. I wish there was more I could do." "You understand? You understand?" Jimmy was beside himself. "You understand NOTHING. NOTHING, do you hear me? Did you know my Gina? This can't happen to her. I am her FATHER! I am her FATHER! I look after her. I am her FATHER! You understand nothing. This is our FAMILY, you bastard. Our family!" Jimmy then turned around, faced his family, and fell to his knees in total disbelief and a pain he never felt in all his life. His voice, finally, lowered to a soft cry, tears streaming down his face. "You don't understand. My Gina, no, not my Gina. Please, no."

"La mia piccola Gina".

# The Aftermath

A limousine stopped in front of Our Lady of Lourdes Church in West Orange, and Dan Johnson got out, alone, wearing a black suit, white shirt, and black tie. He had taken his regular limo that has become like a $2^{nd}$ car to Dan's SUV which he kept just a block from 77 West. He wasn't going to drive to the funeral in his own car and figure out where to park. His limo driver, Pete, would figure all of that out, discreetly and professionally. The playoffs had begun, this being Dan's $4^{th}$ season with the Knicks, but the Knicks, the top seed once again in the east, had a bye and Dan wouldn't play for at least three more days. It would be in New York no matter the outcome of the first round series between the 76'ers and the Charlotte Hornets. It wouldn't have mattered, anyway, Dan would be here to support his family, the Minnelli's, whether the Knicks had a game or not. But still, Dan was glad he didn't have to deal with the pressures of explaining that to the New York fans and media.

The service was a very solemn one. The prior evening, there was a Reception of the Body, or Prayer Virgil, where the immediate family could visit the deceased in private and pray. This morning, there would be funeral Mass, also known as a Requiem Mass, because it includes Holy Communion. It therefore has at its heart the commemoration of Christ's death and resurrection. Paul's wife read Psalm 23:

"The Lord is my shepherd; I shall not want. He maketh me to lie down in green pastures: he leadeth me beside the still waters.

He restoreth my soul: he leadeth me in the paths of righteousness for his name's sake.

Yea, though I walk through the valley of the shadow of death, I will fear no evil: for thou art with me; thy rod and thy staff they comfort me.

Thou preparest a table before me in the presence of mine enemies: thou anointest my head with oil; my cup runneth over.

Surely goodness and mercy shall follow me all the days of my life: and I will dwell in the house of the Lord forever."

Dan got back into his limo for the ride to the Cemetery. He thought of asking Tony to ride with him, as a show of support, but he didn't know if that would be considered rude, so he passed on it. There was consideration for the family and if Dan's limo was needed for anybody else, they would ask. Pete already knew about the cemetery. He had read a notice and did not need to bother Dan, even thought the two were normally quite talkative together. Today, they rode in silence. Pete did walk over to the cemetery, because Dan asked him to. At the end, Dan, hugged every family member. He didn't know what to say, so he went back to Billy, always to Bill, for advice. Billy once told Dan "If you don't know what to say, say nothing, or little. If you must say anything during a sad occasion, just say 'I'm sorry'. Use your best judgement. I can't be everywhere with you and believe me, kid, I won't be around someday. There's an old saying, and something tells me you've never heard it, "It is better to be silent and be thought a fool, than to speak and remove all doubt." At the time, Dan thought about it and said to Billy. "Wow, Billy, that is prolific." "Well", Billy said, "I didn't write it." Dan introduced Pete to Jimmy. "Jimmy, this is Pete, my limo driver. Tony knows him." Dan motioned to Tony, who walked over. "Hey Pete, you came? Thank you." "Well, Dan hired me, and he told me to stay in the car, but I wanted to come out." They all smiled. Dan thought "Upon every life, there will fall some rain, so use laughter, in precious amounts, to help all ease the pain."

There was going to be a small gathering back at the house in Llewellyn Farms, just down the street. A small gathering, but Tony said his family wanted Dan to come in, and now, Pete, too. They said, "of course". As they walked away, there stood Chase, Gina's boyfriend, and the man she would have married. Everybody knew it. Never truly accepted in the family, thought truthfully, Chase didn't try. Dan had even talked to him once at a Christmas Party. He said, "Chase, the Minnelli's are a special family, and they're different than you and me. My parents are quiet and stoic. My dad always wants to be in control. My Mom never wants to make a scene. They chuckle, they don't laugh out loud." Chase was as smart as they came. Dan knew it, and for better or worse, (usually worse), Chase knew it. "Dan, seriously, spare me. I get it. The emotional, joyful, close Italian family. They wear their hearts on their sleeves. Well, I'll marry Gina, the black sheep of the family. I don't want emotion. I like dull. I like to be in control. That's what makes me happy, and Gina is the same way. I joke that she's adopted." Dan replied, "Oh, no, Chase. Gina has strong feelings. She wants to be loved. She wants to laugh, to live. She's just afraid to. Maybe she needed somebody the opposite of you." "What's that, exactly, Dan? Somebody who breathes?" "No, Chase, just somebody to light her passions, so to speak, to give her confidence beyond making million-dollar real estate deals. Beyond her comfort zone." "Who", Chase, replied. "You?" Dan sighed, "No Chase, I'm a terrible match for Gina, but I'm not going to go into my personal thoughts with you and explain why." "Thanks, don't", Chase said. Dan told Tony at the same party, "Wow, Chase is hard to like", in which Tony laughed and said "Hey, you're finally figuring that out?"

The cemetery service was ending. It was about as quiet and solemn as a funeral could be. Chase stood on the other side from Jimmy. Chase's parents both came to the funeral, his father looking very much like the corporate executive he was. In fact, both parents looked wealthy and perfectly dressed for a funeral. Solemn, expensive, but black clothing. Straight from central casting. Jimmy walked past the Pennington's. Chase said, "Mr. Minnelli, my parents." Chase's father said all he could say. No handshake, not today. Not now. "Mr. Minnelli, my wife and I have no words we can say to you today. We are very, very sorry." Jimmy nodded. Not a smile, but recognition, because what CAN one say? Jimmy understood. He then looked at Chase. Chase's eyes were red. He loved Gina, and Jimmy knew it. Chase gave him a long look. Jimmy thought of walking away but made one final gesture. He put his hand on Chase's shoulder, looked at him, and then walked away. That one gesture if put to words, might have been. "I know you loved my daughter, and that was all we had in common, but that was a lot. There is nothing else to say."

The Pennington's did not go back to the Minnelli's house, and neither the Minnelli's nor Pennington's ever saw each other again.

# The Big Guy

After several phone calls and a harder-than-expected agreement, Dan was to visit a children's hospital in the New York area. The last thing he wanted was a circus, and yet, for many complicated reasons that had to do with fundraising efforts and money more than anything else, Dan had to agree to allow a New York television crew to follow him around. It was his fourth season in the NBA, and he had given plenty, millions, to a host of good charities, but he had not done anything personal. That would change today, as he thought through in his mind about forming his own foundation at about the time he retired. He almost said no to the whole thing. He was under no obligation to do this. He had been nothing if not fortunate in so many ways. Decent health and unlimited opportunities. His parents worried about his condition for years, but Dan was none the wiser and he grew, and grew, in perfect health. They supported everything he did, all the time. He was known and loved throughout the world, and even the people who were said not to like him couldn't help but soften that stance once they met him. Dan was, at worst, a little aloof, but that was due to shyness more than anything else. Still, he had come such a long way. He was more articulate and outgoing than he had ever been. Practice makes "better", if not "perfect".

Dan took his regular limo to the hospital, entering in the back, as requested, to a service entrance. The last thing Dan or anybody else wanted was the sight of a limousine at a children's hospital. As far as Dan was concerned, it could have been a flatbed truck. He just couldn't fit into a regular sedan, and people would have to understand, and Dan didn't have time to worry about that. He had to duck way down to get into the door, and then watch his head as it came close to scraping the top of the ceiling as he walked to the lobby. When he got there, at 10:02 AM, a group was already waiting, the hospital CEO, Director of the children's unit, a TV camera, and five reporters. It was nothing that Dan hadn't seen before, but it usually preceded stepping onto basketball court, not walking down hallways to say hello to children fighting for their lives, fighting cancer. It wasn't a show to them, and Dan already hated it. "One day," he thought. "One day", I'll run my own program. One day, we'll give money to fight this thing, and feed people, and it won't need be a 'dog and pony' show." But today, it would be. Dan was given some speech as the group walked, about the history of the hospital, their victories, and losses, how many beds they had. The need for more money and how expensive care and research was. Dan wasn't sure if it was about him giving more or using Dan to gain more exposure for the hospital, to raise Foundations. If it helped bring in more money that paid for bills, helped with research, and saved the lives of these horribly afflicted children, then perhaps it was a necessary evil. Dan said, as they approached one room (the doors were left open by "receptive" families and kept closed this morning for families that wanted privacy), "what do I even say?" The Director said, "We'll introduce you as basketball player Dan Johnson from the Knicks. First, Mr. Johnson, you're very famous. All the children and their parents will know you. Most appreciate that you're here, and understand the need to raise money, to help their kids as well as future generations. We wish we could tell you that we wouldn't need these facilities, and one day, maybe that will happen, but until it does, we're going to fight it. "Ok", Dan said. "I'll think of something to say."

The routine didn't vary too much. Dan was introduced. "Dan, this is Mike Palmer." "Well, hi, Mike, it's so nice to meet you. Tell me about yourself." Dan was instructed not to ask the young patients how they felt, and that was harder than it seemed." Mike told Dan that he was from Long Island, was in the 4$^{th}$ grade when we able to get to class, liked baseball. Dan would say, "So, are you a Yankees guy or a Mets guy." "I like the Yankees." Dan made sure he was aware of the records of both teams. "Well, the Yanks are just two games out of first. Think they will win it this year? Who's your favorite player? Well, Mike, I'm going to meet some of the other patients. I enjoyed meeting you and wish you the very best." With a few variations, boys' hobbies, girls' hobbies, Dan practiced, not saying anything too controversial, staying in the moment, not discussing a future event when some of these kids simply had no future. It wasn't fun and his heart went out to the parents, most who were in the room, with half-smiles and weak, tired handshakes. Sad, weary, frightened as can be, desperate. Almost, Dan thought, a look in their eyes, "can YOU help us?".

They reached the end of corridor, and then Dan would be done with this thing. It was a mixture of pleasantries and agony. Seemingly, such terrific kids. It could be ANY kid, and that was the frightening thing. Did any of these kids do something, anything, to deserve this fate? Of course not. They were innocent kids. They deserved to be anyway else. Anywhere but here.

Dan went into his 2$^{nd}$ to last room. Same speech by the Director. Cameras rolling. They needed about 30 seconds, total, for a broadcast that night, or some other time. Dan said hello.

"This is Ayana." Well, hello, Ayana. That's a pretty name." She answered with a straight face. "It's Swahili and it means beautiful flower." "Wow." said Dan. "That's really pretty." Ayana then said, "I don't really like it. I like Wendy and I've told my parents that for almost two years but take a look at the door and see what it says." Dan looked and reported back to this very precocious, headstrong nine-year old. "It says Ayana." She says, now crossing her arms which made Dan start to smile a bit. "There, see what I mean." "Well,", Dan said. "Let's see if we can do something about that. I'll say something. Looks like maybe I carry a little weight around here." "How much DO you weigh, actually", Ayana said with a straight face. "Oh, a little under 500 pounds." Ayana raised her eyebrows a little, to act surprised but not impressed. "Maybe you need to go on a diet or something." Dan laughed out loud and said, "Oh, the Knicks will tell me if I do. Right now, they seem to like me at this weight." Ayana didn't stop, as her mother walked in. "Well, you must break a lot of furniture." Again, Dan laughed a tiny amount and said, "Well, most furniture holds me okay. The problem is getting into the furniture to begin with. A lot of chairs are just too small." "I can tell". Ayana's mother said, "Wendy, be nice, and smiled at Dan."

Ayana's parents had had many month of badgering by their daughter, and when you include her illness, calling her the name she desired was the least of their concerns, even though her Mom had dreamed of a beautiful African name for so long, ever since she dreamed of having a little girl, a family, but what's the sense of worrying about that now? Doctors told her and her husband that she had a very aggressive form of leukemia, and her prospects were not good. Dan was not told of each patient's specific situation while he walked down to each available room.

Dan said goodbye and went into the last room for a moment, but he kept thinking about Wendy/Ayana. When it was over, they passed Wendy's room, and Dan turned to the Director and said, "Can you do me a favor? The little girl in here is named Ayana. She prefers Wendy. Could your staff change the name to Wendy?" "I'll see what I can do," said the Director. Dan placed his hand on his shoulder and said, "It may not seem like much, but it will matter to her."

Dan took another step, then went back toward the room. Standing outside was the mother, and another man, heavy-set, mustached, around 45 and looked like he could bowl you over in his high school or even college football days.

"Are you Wendy's parents?" The Mom said, "yes, we are." The father said nothing, and Dan knew the type, but he had no idea of the emotions running through the minds of these parents. That would be too hard. He didn't try to shake hands because they didn't offer them. Dan asked, "mind if I go back in and just say goodbye?" The mother said quietly, "that would be fine."

"I just wanted to let you know that I enjoyed meeting you, Wendy, and I said something about the door." "Hey, Mr. Dan, are you being nice to me because I'm sick", Wendy asked Dan, seriously. Dan said, "You are a mature young lady, so I'm going to be very honest with you, ok?" Wendy said "Fine", as if to say, "I can't to hear the baloney you're going to say."

"Wendy, I've been wanting to make a difference all my life. I was born and grew up to be incredibly tall. Things came easy to me, and I felt bad. Do you understand so far." Wendy said, "I understand, that's called guilt." Sadly, and surprised at her precociousness, Dan said "Yes. I felt guilty. So, I am trying to help people. To make me feel better. Yes, I suppose so, but if it helps people, then does it matter? But I just didn't want to give somebody money and walk away. I mean, I've been doing that while I've been playing. But soon, I won't be, and I want to control how my money helps people." Wendy said, "But just like all adults, you didn't answer my question." Dan smiled, "I'm visiting a lot of sick kids. Yes, because they are sick, and I am helping raise as much money as I can so that sick kids can get the best possible care, and maybe help scientists and doctors find cures and ways to help people live longer lives. But I like you, for you. Of all the kids I've seen, maybe I like you the best. You're smart and funny. I like your sense of humor. It's like mine. And I want you to know something else." Dan replied. Wendy said, "And what might that be, Mr. C Man." Dan laughed under his breath. This little girl is a trip. "I want to let you know that if it's okay with you, and your parents, I'd like to come back in a few days and check in with you. See how you're doing." "You do what you think you need to do," but there was the tiniest hint of a smile. Dan meant it. She didn't know that, but he did. He'd come back, as he passed the parents and caught up with the media group.

After a few minutes speaking to the media group again in the lobby, Dan said goodbye and began walking toward the entrance, where his limo was waiting for him. Just before the doors, he noticed the hospital cafeteria, and sitting there, drinking what was likely a cup of coffee, was Wendy's father, a continued scowl on his face. Dan walked in. "Hello, Mr. Butler." Dan said. The father, Cleon Butler, looked up at Dan, and said with an expressionless face. "Yes?" Dan said, "I just want you to know that I liked Wendy. I know she has another name, but she asked me to call her Wendy." Cleon Butler said, "Mr. Johnson, sit down here for a minute. It was as much a command as it was a request, and being the man's situation and that he was in his late 40's, Dan sat down. Not very comfortably, but he sat."

"Look, I get it. You're visiting hospitals. Must make you feel pretty good. Like something special. Well, let me tell you something. That's my daughter upstairs, and she has a very aggressive form of acute myeloid leukemia. In her case, her prognosis is poor. That little girl didn't ask for this and your visit isn't going to do jack shit in helping her live. You walk out that door, and she's out of your life forever, and you go back to your Park Avenue Apartment and look over your kingdom, or should I say, you "Canyon". Where DO you live, anyway, Mr. Johnson." "Park Avenue." Dan answered matter-of-factly. "Hmmm", Cleon Butler, smirked. "Well, I see your limo is out there. Must be only for the likes of you." Dan said, "Yep, that's my limo". "Got anything else you'd like to say to me before I go back upstairs to my daughter?" "Yes," said Dan. "I like your daughter. She's got a wicked sense of humor, and I'm coming back to see her this Saturday, around 11:00 AM, unless you prohibit it, which you can do, of course, but if you don't, I'll be here." Cleon Butler just stared at him, silently, with the same scowl, and Dan walked out.

Four days later, on Saturday, and just when Dan said he would, Dan came back. Of course, he was recognized at the reception area. He never failed to get a slight gasp, even from people who have seen him before. It was that much of a surprise. Dan said to the lobby receptionist. "Hi, I promised a young lady up in 526 that I would come back to visit her, right at 11:00." "Okay, sir," came the response, go on up." "Dan hit the elevator button and waited for a moment. It opened. No leather stool. Dan bent over and stepped in and remained in that stopped position until the elevator got to the 5$^{th}$ floor. When he got out, a doctor was waiting to get on." "Oh," a surprised look, but everybody knew Dan had been there the previous Tuesday. "How are you" and shook Dan's hand. "See," Dan thought.  A handshake. What's wrong about that, anyway? He made his way down the corridor, opening one door to a new hallway. He passed a nurses station where one nurse tugged on the sleeve of another. Dan saw this every day, all the time, wherever he walked. This was his life. "Oh, hi. Nice to see you again. Are you visiting?" "Yes", said, Dan. "Oh, ok, who are you seeing?" "I'm visiting Wendy Butler, in room 526." "The nurse looked and said, "I'm sorry, we don't have a Wendy Butler. We have an Ayana Butler in 526." "Yes, that's her. She hates the name Ayana and would prefer to be called Wendy, and her the door name was supposed to be changed." "Oh, I see", said the nurse at the station, without any commitment to change it.

Dan walked down to 526. The door was halfway open, and Dan knocked twice. Both parents were there, Cleon and Renee Butler. Cleon didn't look any happier, and if anything, seemed annoyed that Dan had the nerve to return. It didn't appear that many people went against advice dished out by this man. Either that, or he was simply too unpleasant or just too intimidating to be around. Dan wasn't intimidated, but neither did he feel warm and fuzzy about it, either. "Well, hello Wendy." "Well, well, well, it's Mr. Dan. You came back after all. I stand corrected." Dan chuckled, tickled by this little girl's choice of words. He looked at the parents and said, "who gave Wendy here her sense of humor? Nothing I like more than somebody with wit." Renee gave a half smile and said, "Oh, 'Wendy', emphasizing the name that her parents wished she NOT use, Wendy has always had that sense of humor. Take it or leave it." "Oh, I'll take it," said Dan. Keeps me on my feet." "Well, we're going to go get some coffee, and be back in a few minutes." "Sure", said Dan. If it's ok, I'll be up here for 20-30 minutes. "Stay all day if you want, Mr. Dan," said Cleon, sounding more annoyed than cheerful.

"Oh, don't mind my dad," said Wendy. He's pretty mad that I'm sick." "Well", Dan said. I would be upset, too, but everybody fighting for you, so you can get better." "I don't think I'm getting better." Dan said, "Of course you will, don't say that." "No, I've heard whispers, I've thought about it. I think I'm going to die. My parents don't talk about that with me." "Well," Dan said, "you like the truth, don't you? You can tell when somebody is being phony." "Yeah, so," said Wendy. "Well, I don't know how sick you are, but I don't know that a lot of people are cured of the disease you have and live a very long life." "And some don't" said Wendy. "Yes", Dan said. And some don't, but don't you think it's better to be positive about things like this? It may even help your body to fight the disease. "Oh, I don't know", said Renee. "Well, anyway, hey, I forgot to give you these." "Oh," said Wendy. "Flowers, hurray." Dan laughed. "What's wrong, you don't like flowers?" Wendy said, "Are we still playing that game when we tell the truth? Because a lot of people don't tell the truth in this place." "Yeah, absolutely" said Dan. "Tell the truth." "Ok", said Wendy. "I don't like flowers. I mean, what's the point? They die as fast as some of the patients around here. They don't excite me. Why am I supposed to like flowers? Where is it written? I get some everyday and my mother tells me to thank people for their thoughtfulness, but I don't like them. Want to help me out, get me a DVD with a decent movie. There's nothing on the TV, the food's not good. I'm bored." "Wow," said Dan. "Well," said Wendy, "you wanted the truth". "Well," Dan said, "no more flowers for you, no matter how much you beg." "I would appreciate it, Mr. Dan." Dan laughed, "Why do you call me Mr. Dan in that way." "Because," Wendy said, "it's my way. I like to be sarcastic. I know, you're the CANYON, the C Man. I hate those names. Doesn't even seen to make sense to me. Why doesn't anybody call you tall white boy?" Dan almost spit up his water. "Tall white boy. Hmm. You know, every once in a while, in college, the guys would call me white boy. Every player on the team was black except for two of us." "Did that bother you?" "No! I liked it. I tell you what, why don't you call me 'white boy'?" "For real?" Wendy asked. "It would be funny." she said. "My mom would yell at me." "What about your dad?" "I never know what he's going to say anymore. He'll probably say nothing. Just fold his arms.

Dan said, "Well, people have made fun of how tall I am. Of course, now that I'm a big star, they don't. Maybe behind my back. I have a great life, but did you know that basketball's not my favorite thing?" "No?" Then what is, Wendy asked. "Oh, lots of silly things, I guess. Music, but I like old music that people my age don't like." "My dad likes Motown, but I guess you don't like them because they're Black," Wendy said, looking for a reaction. "Now why would you say that?" "Umm, because you're white?" "Well, that's ridiculous, and I mean it. First of all, I love Motown. I mean, c'mon. Diana Ross, Smokey Robinson. Do you know who my favorite rock and roll star was?" "No", Wendy said, "but probably a white dude". "Hey", where do you get this?" Wendy started laughing. "Ha, ha, I don't really mean that. I just like messin' with peoples minds." "No", Dan said. "I think you DO mean it!" "A little bit", Wendy laughed. "Sista's got attitude," "Ha, ha!!" Dan laughed out loud, and so did Wendy.

"My favorite rock and roll singer, by the way, was Jackie Wilson." "Who," Wendy asked. "You see, it's not the color of an artist's skin. It's the kind of music and the time period, even though most artists I like were well before my time. Anymore, you lookup 'Lonely Teardrops', if you want to hear a great song, and he could dance great. Even Michael Jackson said he learned a lot from Jackie Wilson. I'll get you that song. Also, I like jazz, and if I were to tell you all the great jazz artists who just happened to be black, I'll in here for the next hour, and I'm leaving now, but I'll be back next week."

"Okay, white boy. Thanks for coming." "Hey, Wendy," Dan said. "I know you're sick and that's why I came here the first time, but now I come because I don't have a lot of friends. You have a great personality and I look forward to seeing you. I like you. You're my friend, now."

"Wendy gave him a brief smile, and looked down, with slight embarrassment, and some happiness, too."

On the way out, Dan saw Cleon, once again, in the coffee shop. Their eyes met, and then Dan left.

As promised, Dan returned a week later with a portable CD player and headphones. He also had two small speakers that could plus into the player, so Wendy could listen in private or with the headphones. He walked in the sound of "Hey, white boy!". Wendy's eyes lit up, and so did Dan's. "What you got there, White Boy." Renee was there, rolling her eyes. "I don't know Wendy, about this White Boy thing." "Oh, mama, Mr. Dan likes it." "I know, honey, but people might not understand." Dan just smiled.

Dan had the Jackie Wilson's greatest hits all ready, and put on "Lonely Teardrops." "Hey, not bad!" Wendy said. I got you some other CD's, too. The Temptations, and your favorite, according to your Mom, Alicia Keys." "Hey, thanks, Mr. Dan."

Dan and Wendy spoke for 30 minutes about food. They argued over fish. Dan liked it. Wendy said he was an old crazy man if he liked fish. Dan couldn't stop laughing. Movies. She didn't know any old movies except "The Wizard of Oz" and Dan did his not-so-famous impersonation of the Cowardly Lion, in that unusual voice, "Put 'em up, put 'em up", and they both laughed. "You know who the greatest American entertainer was, and it wasn't a white man". "Michael Jackson" said Wendy. "Well," said Dan, he's really great, it's true, but I say it was Sammy Davis, Jr." "Not to me," said Wendy.

Do you know he was once a standup comedian?" Wendy said to Dan. Dan was shocked, "There's no way. Not your Dad. Not that man. Oops, sorry, I didn't mean it that way." "That's okay," Wendy said. "I don't believe it, either. My Mom said he did it three times at an open mic night. I was too young. He's never been very funny as long as I can remember." "Why do you think that is?" Dan asked. "Well," Wendy said. "I asked my mom once. I said, 'Momma, how could Daddy have been a stand-up comedian when he never seems happy?" Dan wondered the same thing. "What did your mom say?" Dan was quite curious. "She said, 'honey, believe it or not, when I met your daddy, he was a different kind of man. He was funny, goofy, always looking on the positive side of things." "How come he's not that way now?" Wendy asked her. "What did she say?"

asked Dan. "Oh, I forget. I think she said 'life', but I didn't know what that meant."

Dan told Wendy that he had to go out of town for nine days, due to a business commitment. Wendy, by now, believed him. "Okay, Mr. Dan, and Mr. Dan? Please come back. Don't leave me."

Dan walked out with his eyes watery. He couldn't let Wendy see that.

Wendy saw Renee Butler in the hallway. She began to realize that Dan saw something special in her baby.

"Hello, Mrs. Butler" Dan said. "Oh, please, call me Renee." "Ok, Renee, if you call me Dan. You know, if you don't mind me asking, Wendy said that your husband tried some stand-up comedy once upon a time. "Oh, no", Renee said. "She's got the wrong impression. He went to an open mic thing three or four times." "But wanted to do it, the way I wished I were a singer like Dean Martin." "Oh, yes. A long time ago. He wanted that, but you know, things changed." "Renee, what changed? I'd like to know."

"Well, Dan, I suppose it was life. Too many disappointments. You know, you're all excited about something. You don't mind the hard work. In fact, you welcome it, you know it takes work, you've been taught that you can achieve anything in the world if you're willing to work hard enough for it, so you welcome the hard work with open arms. And then, you fail, but you're told about that To expect it, you know? You WILL fail. You will learn. You get back up and try even harder, use what you've learned. And then you fall. You try again. And you fall, so you try again, and then again. And then, one day, you realize that the wonderful story of getting up and trying and trying wasn't written for you. It was written for somebody that for some reason, God felt deserved to have their day of reckoning. Their day in the sun, but for you, it was simply a cruel joke, do you see? Something destined for many, or for some, or for a few, but never for you. You will struggle and be disappointed. So, try to understand my husband. He loves that little girl up there with all his heart, She's everything to him, and I think he knows that she made him a winner. He won after all. I said to him not long ago. 'Honey, Wendy is so unique and wonderful, that the way God looks at it, you used up all your luck having her as your baby girl, and when I said that, it was the first time in a long time that he paused and seemed to reflect upon that, because, he knows how lucky he is to be her daddy, and I'm so very lucky to be her Momma, and if all I am for the rest of her life is her Momma, then I will be the luckiest person in the world. God let him down all those times so he could have his Wendy, and now she's fighting for her life, and Cleon doesn't understand any of it, and sometimes, neither do I. Why does God hate us, Dan. Why?

"I don't know why", he said. "I'm going to go now". Dan had to go home and perhaps think about Cleon Butler for a little while. When he was a teenager, he first read the book "To Kill a Mockingbird," by Harper Lee, and then he saw the movie, with Gregory Peck. Dan's mom, Cathy, said that Harper Lee still lived in Monroeville, Alabama, about 100 miles north of Liliian and about halfway to Montgomery. Dan remembered the poignant quote by Atticus Finch, You never really understand a person until you consider things from his point of view... until you climb into his skin and walk around in it". Could Dan do that with Cleon Butler, a man who may just lose his only daughter, a delight like Wendy Butler? And what other disappointments has Cleon Butler had to live with? Dan will never know because Cleon Butler isn't going to tell him, and Dan Johnson isn't going to ask him. But it sure gave Dan something to think about. He remembered his classmates disregarding the quote, when the teacher tried to convince them that it had relevance in life. But, son of a gun, it really did.

Dan returned to New York as expected. In his room was a bouquet of flowers, sitting in a vase, with a note on it. "Dear Mr. Dan. I'm sick of flowers. It's your turn now, ha ha! You go kick some ass on the basketball court, don't go soft on me, and I'll be somewhere, I promise, cracking jokes and chasing my own dreams."

A half hour later, the phone rang. "Mr. Johnson, this is Cleon Butler. Wendy died this morning. She liked you very much and you made her final days better. I know I wasn't too nice to you, but I had my reasons, and I wanted to call you and tell you that, well, I'm sorry." The phone clicked and Dan sat in the corner of his living room. A tear fell on a rose petal from the vase he was holding in his hands.

# The Final Letter

It was three years later when a letter found its way to the C Man's residence. He opened it.

There was a handwritten note that said. "Dan, we were going through some things and found this. I'm sorry, but it only said 'Dan' so I had to read it, to know who it was really for, and to send it to the right place. Hell, who even calls you Dan, anymore?"

Dan opened the letter, it was handwritten and dated June 3, 2000. He could hear the letter being told in Billy's voice:

"Hiya Kid,

We haven't seen each other too often. I'm slowing down and you, well, what can I say? Not are you only the tallest man in the world, you're all the things that being tall alone can't give you; talent, drive, a calm inner strength, decency, things I hope our discussions helped with. I'd like to feel that I helped in some way shape the character of such a famous person. The nine-foot man that I can say I knew when he was only eight feet. I was able to "reach you" a little better back then. Today, you are your own man, and I'm proud to call you a friend.

You have worked hard to be more than the really tall guy that people wanted to see play basketball. You dedicated yourself to your craft. When you stood atop the Olympic podium in three sports (show off), I felt like I was there, too. I stood tall.

I'm writing this not to say goodbye, but I stole the idea from an actor who said he wanted to write a letter to a good friend before it was too late. Now, I've done that. One day, you'll read it.

You were always a big man but inside was a bigger man waiting to figure out life, like we all must do, but few have had your challenges. Yes, I say challenges, because when you are so unusual, as you my friend are, the world wants to make your decisions for you. There is nothing wrong with listening. Always listen, seek out advice. Occasionally, it will be sound. Even I would have been disappointed had you not been an NBA champion. You'll win about as many titles as you want, but always make sure you're doing it for yourself. You have more to give to yourself and maybe, to the world. You're just one man despite your size. You can't be all things to all people.

You'll make the right decisions. You have so far. I'm always here when you want to talk, and maybe there's one more gig left for us, but it's gonna cost them!

To the world, you're The Canyon. To me, you're Dan Johnson, that humble kid I met in Burbank several years ago. And remember, you're not alone. We all must find our way, and it's not always easy. A wise person, wiser than me, once said "Sometimes, the hardest thing in life to find, is yourself."

Your friend,

Billy

Dan held the letter, gazed out ahead and smiled, a single tear rolling down his face. He was so very lucky to have someone like Billy. Dan saw him as a father figure. He respected him immensely, the way he handled himself. He stood tall despite his dwarfism. He never let it deter him from making it big, finding his way.

Dan realized that his size and abilities were a great gift in one respect, and a curse in others. He would always be questioned as a man whose size made him nearly impossible to defeat, not his skill. Billy could do nothing about his size. Neither could Dan, but so much was expected of him, and nearly everyone judged his worth on his ability to win, and not on his ability to love.

But there was nothing personal in the ways of the world. Anyone else in the same predicament would face the same judgement. The same expectations. There was more fame, more money, and more adulation than anyone could ever receive. Complaining would surely fall on deaf ears.

Too many people in the world have enough disappointments and complaints in their lives to be interested in taking on yours. Dan realized that those words could have come right out of Billy's mouth.

# The World's Most Famous Arena

Dan Johnson's first game in the NBA was at Madison Square Garden, on October 24th, 1997, where he saw only limited action in the Knick's 102-93 win over the Cleveland Cavaliers. This did not mark Dan's first-ever visit to the Garden, because over the years, his parents had taken him three of four times to the Big Apple, always trying to tie-in kid-friendly events in the city.

Of course, just a few years earlier, Dan and Chuck had seen the USA vs. Soviet Judo exhibition under the main Arena, in what was at the time called the "Felt Forum", but other times Dan went to the Ringling Brothers Barnum and Baily Circus and to a Rangers Hockey Game.

Dan was just the kind of young kid would love Madison Square Garden history, but it turned out that he knew very little, and people in the Knick's organization, the Minnelli's, and by his own research, he eventually discovered the interesting history of the world's most famous arena and a place he would call "home" for eight years.

The original Madison Square Garden was built in 1871 in Manhattan.  In 1890 the second Madison Square Garden opened on the same site as the original, and yet a third Madison Square Garden opened in 1925.  Lastly, the current day Madison Square Garden opened in 1968.  Each subsequent arena had a big impact on the culture of New

York City, even though that they were not all on the same site.

The first Madison Square Garden had no roof and was used mostly for cycling. The 2$^{nd}$ was not at all profitable, but the third finally took off. It was the first Garden not built at the site of Madison Square Park, but on 8$^{th}$ Avenue between 49$^{th}$ and 50$^{th}$ Streets. It was later demolished in 1968 when the current Madison Square Garden Center was built between 8$^{th}$ and 9thAvenues and between 31$^{st}$ to 33$^{rd}$ streets.

The Garden had seen its share of famous events, including:

➤ The Knick's victory over the Lakers in game 7 of the NBA Championship, in 1970, when Knick's center Willis Reed, injured through much of the series, walked onto the court to provide inspiration to the team, even scoring the first two points.
➤ The Rangers 1994 Stanley Cup Championship
➤ The famous 1971 Ali-Frazier championship boxing fight

There were numerous, other well-attended events, even if they weren't as easily remembered. The NY Chiefs Roller Derby team won that year's world championship with a come-from-behind 5-point score as time expired, and in front of a delirious 18,881 fans. Bruno Sammartino helped sell out Madison Square Garden 187 times, as he went up against wrestlers that included Ivan Koloff, Waldo Von Erich, George "the Animal" Steele, Prof. Toru Tanaka, Nikolai Volkoff, and shared the festivities with the likes of Chief Jay Strongbow, Pedro Morales, Mil Mascaras (the man of 1,000 masks), Freddie Blassie, Gorilla Monsoon,

Ivan Putski, Sky Low Low, Captain Lou Albano, and so many other colorful characters.

At one time, Dan recalled how a wrestling executive shared a couple of beers with Dan and talked about how he could enter the ranks of pro wrestling, and the stories that could be drawn up, especially Dan as the "good guy turned heel". "Hey, you REALLY ARE a world champion wrestler, or former champion. What a story line. You'll come into the league waving the American flag and wearing your medal, and something, who knows, will trigger you, and you'll turn. You'd never be more hated, and we'd never fill so many seats. Dan absolutely loved the concept as they sat in a bar near the Garden one night, but joking around, and donning pro wrestling trunks were two entirely different things, but it was great fun thinking about it. It reminded Dan about how just a couple of years later, an NFL owner was in New York, and had the chance to have lunch with Dan, and floated the same idea for football. "Imagine," the wealthy owner said, "You as an interior lineman, or as, holy crap, a tight end. Hey, think about it. A challenge. Dan didn't give it much thought. Pro wrestling would be a lot more fun."

Dan had also heard that the Garden once had a bowling alley, but it closed in 1988. He was sorry to hear that, and wished the Knicks personnel could join him in a game. The thunder that Dan's balls made when hitting the pins were so loud that it frightened many of the nearby bowlers, and he was asked not to play anymore. This happened at the AMF Marietta Lanes as well as an alley in Saline, MI. Dan never thought he was throwing the ball hard, but it was like a sledgehammer. He didn't even bowl that well, maybe a 125 bowler the three times he went, but if he placed it between the one and three pins just so, it was a massive boom that stopped everybody's action, and Dan just loved it. He felt like Hercules, and there was nothing like the laughter of drunk college friends that were there to hear it.

By the time the C Man was done ruling the courts of Madison Square Garden, eight years later, nobody, perhaps not even Bruno Sammartino himself, could lay claim to being a bigger hero.

# Meeting Kyle

In the summer of 2004, Dan and Melanie read that Kyle Maynard was speaking at the Cobb Galleria. Kyle had followed him since he wrestled for nearby Collins Hill High School. He admired how Kyle could barely score any points on the mat for a long time, but eventually figured out how to use his advantages, yes, his advantages, to beat opponents. In a bizarre twist, Dan thought that he and Kyle shared some similarities. Maybe everyone else on the planet would think Dan was crazy, but this is simply the way he saw it.

Kyle Maynard was born with no hands and legs that ended at his knees. It was a congenital defect that nobody else in his family had suffered. Yet, Kyle's parents, instead of treating him with an overabundance of caution, treated him no differently than any of their other children. Kyle played football, hockey, and finally wrestling. Dan was amazed.

Dan learned in his very first lesson from Coach Glasser, that one of the keys of success on the mat was to control your opponents' wrists. You control their wrists, and they can't grab you, they can't take you down, they can't escape, and they can't pin you. Kyle couldn't grasp anybody's hands, but at the same time, that meant that "they couldn't grasp his". Dan was mesmerized and would sit down, coaching Kyle in his mind. What could Kyle do to totally frustrate his opponents, throw them off their game? Well, apparently, his coach was doing that. They didn't need Dan, and by then, Dan had retired from wrestling, in

1996, when Kyle was ten. As a two-time Olympic Gold wrestling champion, Dan thought that it would be fun to sit down with Kyle Maynard and devise ways for him to use advantages he had. Turn disadvantages into advantages, but some very good coach in Suwanee, GA, was already figuring that out.

Melanie did not know about Kyle, so Dan explained his incredible story, and then Dan and Melanie drove from the Lake House in Flowery Branch, down to northwest Atlanta.

As always, Dan got the attention of absolutely everyone within sight. He and Melanie walked into the lobby, and took a seat in the last row, where he was always forced to sit. With his back against the wall, he wasn't too much of an obstruction, but still, throughout the entire event, people kept looking back and even sneaking photos, when it was not about him. That never seemed to matter. Dan, being the theater lover, was hardly ever able to attend a Broadway show, despite being just a few minutes away from the Great White Way. When he did attend, everybody gawked and turned around. There were times when Dan wanted to scream, "Jesus, would you turn around and look at the damn stage! That's what we're here for."

What was it like for Kyle?

Dan estimated that there were about 300 people in the room, used as a convention center for small to medium-sized events. It was a very nice alternative to the Atlanta World Congress Center downtime, not only the main convention center in Atlanta, but the venue for both freestyle wrestling and Judo, where Dan had famously won a gold and silver medal at the 1996 Atlanta Olympics. The Galleria was in the Atlanta northwest suburbs, not far from Marietta and the highway, taking them back up on GA-400 and Lake Lanier. Easy Drive when the traffic cooperates.

The lights dimmed and there was an introductory video lasting about two minutes. Kyle wrestling, playing football, meeting Oprah Winfrey, collecting an ESPY award, and climbing a mountain. It was done well.

Kyle got up, dressed in a nice, custom shirt and vest (Dan knew a lot about customized clothing) and began to address the crowd. This guy could be on the cover of GQ, Dan thought. Handsome, self-assured, happy. Happy with who he was, his lot in life. At least, Dan thought so. How could Dan quietly have guilt about life, feel less than satisfied, when he was given so much while others were born with less? But this was just thing. In listening to this young man talk, who was only 18 and now a freshman at the University of Georgia, he didn't talk or act like a guy who had less. Why not? Was it fair that he didn't have hands or feet? Fair or not, Kyle talked about all the great things he DID have. He seemed to have few regrets, and he didn't like to make excuses for the challenges he had in life. Dan felt like he had challenges, too, but the more he thought about it, the more he felt a wave of remorse roll over him. He felt somewhat ashamed. What would Kyle Maynard do with hands and feet? He didn't seem to be unhappy at what he didn't have. He still scaled mountains. He still overcame obstacles. Dan listened.

At some point, and it always happens, Kyle said, "Ladies and Gentlemen, please give a round of applause to a very special guest. We're so glad he's here and it's a surprise to me and our team as it might be to you, but he's one man that is downright impossible to ignore. Georgia native, Mr. Dan Johnson. C Man, please stand and take a bow. Don't hit your head!" The crowd all turned, smiled, and applauded. Dan stood and gave a quick, embarrassing wave, although he has done this 1,000 times by now.

After the event, Dan and Melanie simply turned to leave, when a young man ran up to him and said, "Mr. and Mrs. Johnson", Kyle would love to say hello. Would you mind? Kyle was an inspiration to Dan, but Dan was possibly the most famous man in the world. He needed to act the part and put away his personal demons, so he did.

Kyle was on a chair surrounded by his family, drinking water. He said "Mr. Johnson", it is so great that you're here. We all admire you so much." "Hey, call me Dan," the Canyon said. I'm just a local Marietta guy. I admire YOU. When I saw you were speaking, I told my wife that we had to come see you. Everybody, this is my wife, Melanie." They chatted for a few minutes, wishing each other well. Dan wanted to tell Kyle's parents one thing. "Mr. and Mrs. Maynard, more than anything, I admire you two, for the way you raised Kyle. It should make all of us think about getting the most out of your life. Makes me think." That was the most pity Dan was going to let on about. What Melanie was thinking, Dan didn't know. The group probably thought it was a perfectly normal thing to say.

Dan and Melanie left and drove up to the Marietta Diner for dessert, before heading back to the lake.

# Solving the World's Biggest Problems

Tony and Dan drove the two miles down Main Street and up Eagle Rock Avenue to the Reservation. It was a cold, crisp October night. It was so clear that even with all the lights of the city nearby, several stars could be seen. They cracked open a couple of beers. Tony, a can of PBR, as usual. This time, Dan chose a bottle of Kirin, which he discovered in Japan:

Tony: Another choice from the "Crappy beer of the month club", huh!?

Dan: It's a great beer.

Tony: Is it made in the U.S. of A?

Dan: You know it's not.

Tony: Then it's a crappy beer.

Dan: You're a crappy beer.

Tony: That doesn't even make sense.

Dan: When you don't make sense, why should I?

Tony: Hey, look, there are stars in the sky.

Dan: There are always stars in the sky.

Tony: Not if I can't see 'em.

Dan: Even when you can't see them, they're there. It's like God.

Tony: No more God questions.

Dan: Let's go back to the stars.

Tony: Yeah, let's.

Dan: There are billions of them.

Tony: You count 'em all. You can't see them.

Dan: Now don't go there again. Scientists have methods.

Tony: and they all have little green men.

Dan: Not on stars, they don't. They're too hot, but some have planets revolving around them, and some might be able to sustain life.

Tony: Like eight-foot monsters?

Dan: Eight feet, eleven

Tony: Now you're finally making sense. Anyway, there are more pressing issues right here on Earth.

Dan: Like what? War? Poverty? Famine?

Tony: How come my thermos keeps my hot drinks hot, and, the same freakin thermos, keeps cold drinks cold

Dan: That IS mysterious.

Tony: Throw me one of those "crying" beers.

Dan: It's Kirin

Tony: Can it get me drunk?

Dan: It got me drunk in Tokyo.

Tony: Then throw me one
"You know what we've never talked about" Tony asked. "Whether or not leisure suits will ever come back in style?" Dan replied. "Well, will they?" Tony answered. "You're picking up on my style of humor," Dan answered him. "Yeah, what's that, the dumbness method?" "No, I retired that method a couple of years ago. Ok, what haven't we talked about?" Dan finally relented. Tony said, "politics". "Yeah, and we never will." "Why not?" Tony asked. "Because nothing destroys friendships, families, institutions, and someday, the world." "Well," asked Tony, why is it such a big subject? Why do we build giant buildings for politicians, and it's discussed all the time?" "Because" said Dan. "Politics is the ultimate paradox," "Why do you say that?" Dan replied, "Anything I say about politics from this point on would cause some people to define everything there is they want to know about me, for the good or bad." "Well, why the hell do you say that." "Because" said Dan, just by my saying, "We need less politics, or worse, substitute government for politics, and millions of people will tell you everything you would ever

want to know about me, and either like me or dislike me, without me saying another word. It's no different if I said, "we need more government. Don't see the volumes that speaks?" "Nope," said Tony. "Let me see," Tony counts on his fingers. "That's four words."

"My views stay with me," Dan said. "Judge me on my actions, and not my political comments, of which you've just heard the last of."

"Besides," Dan said. "Most people don't want to share their political opinions. They realize the polarization and division it causes, thankfully." "Eh, do you really think so?" asked Tony. "Oh, absolutely," said Dan. "There is still some common sense left in society."

The two spent the next several minutes discussing whether a nice set of breasts on a woman was hotter than a nice ass because they realized that carried more intellectual value.

Finally, Tony said, "Ah, screw it, and he put on some rock by a Jersey band. Dan could have used some Frank or Dean at the moment. "Hey", Dan said, in a fake angry voice, "This sounds like rock and or roll." Tony looked at him, "I just don't get you, sometimes."

# Reluctant Retirement

Dan, ever the master daydreamer, had been thinking about this ever since he had hired Mike. "Dan, win yourself a championship, or simply have a stellar first year with the Knick's, and you'll make a lot more money in endorsements than you will playing ball. A whole lot more. But it's all contingent on winning. So do us all a favor and win it all. Then, the companies will come knocking at your door. My door, and I'll do the work to sort through the offers.

Dan, at that point, began to think of his parents. His Mom loved being a vet, but he wasn't so sure if his dad wanted to stay in the rat race. He had a demanding job as an engineer. True, he was only 58, but that was old enough. Time to enjoy life, but would they do it? Forget the time. They were also proud. Would they look at this as Dan supporting them? That was silly, but there would be resistance. He planned on making it too hard to walk away from.

A year later, with the massive shoe endorsement beginning to pay staggering amounts, Dan and his parents came to an agreement. Neither felt they could leave their co-workers in the lurch, so there will be a two-year plan. Perhaps even Cathy would just work part-time. At an anniversary dinner in New York, a year later, with the Minnelli's there to help "push along the deal", Dan begged his parent's to allow him to "share the wealth", and awarded them with a sizable "retirement" monetary gift that chocked them up while possibly embarrassing them, but early retirement did begin to sound better all the time, and Dan even made a deal to include them in on the endorsements to where they would have a steady income every year, and Dan wouldn't feel the pinch at all. It was setup with Larry and it was a done deal. But it wasn't a done deal until Dan had a "come to Jesus meeting" with Chuck, in private.

"Dad, look at all the hours you drilled me, you prepared me, you and mom nurtured me. You've always been a straight shooter. Now it's my turn. The money I'm making is staggering. Well over $400 million a year due to the shoe deal. If you can't feel comfortable taking 2%, that's $8 million this year, from your son, after all you've done, as a well-earned "thank you", then I'm embarrassed for you. It's not a handout. It's a "thank you" and it should be more. I would have nothing without you and mom.

So, to make it official, Larry, not me, will make the payments four times a year. I won't see it and I'll never be able to spend the money.

Chuck realized the absurdity and amazement of the whole thing, so he took the retirement deal.

# We'll Always have Ann Arbor, Ann

Tomorrow, Dan would be taking a private jet from Teterboro to Gibbs Executive Airport, six miles north of downtown San Diego, then take a limo to the Del Coronado. He was lucky, the groom never seemed to plan weddings. They're told to show up, and maybe for some, that's effort enough. Not for Dan. Melanie was his love. He had a few girlfriends and crushes, but nobody else was the "whole package" like Melanie. Still, considering all he was doing was waiting, he was nervous and was tired when he went to bed that night. He stuck in a DVD of the Dean Martin Celebrity Roasts until he fell asleep just a minute after hearing Don Rickles tell Milton Berle, "Milton, the home called. You have to be back by 9 PM."

Dan "woke" to find himself in a fog-covered airport, wearing a trench coat. A few feet away stood a Lockheed Electra 12A, propellers churning, and time was of the essence.

A beautiful woman stood by his side that looked a lot like, Ann Karlsson? Dan began to speak.

Dan: "You're getting on that plane"

Ann: "I don't understand, what about you? Last night we...."

Dan: "Last night, we said a great many things. You said I was to do the thinking for both of us. Well, I've done a lot of it since then, and it all adds up to one thing. You're getting on that plane to Minneapolis, and I'm marrying Melanie. Do you have any idea what would happen if you stayed with me?"

Ann: "You're saying this to make me go."

Dan: "I'm saying it because it's true. If you're not on that plane, you'll regret it. Maybe not today, or maybe not tomorrow, but soon. You've got a great art career ahead of you, and I'll be watching, rooting you on."

Ann: "But what about us?"

Dan: "We'll always have Ann Arbor. And I've got a job to do, too, and where I'm going, you can't follow. I'm not good at being noble, but it doesn't take much to see that the problems of three little people don't amount to a hill of beans in this crazy world. Someday you'll understand that. Now, now. Here's looking at you, kid."

Dan rolled around in his enormous bed and would only remember bits and pieces of this pre-wedding dream. It wasn't cold feet as one might think. It was strictly human.

# Del Coronado

Dan had proposed to Melanie in April 2003, just days before the NBA playoffs in Dan's 6<sup>th</sup> season. The Knick's, of course, were five-time defending champions, and the expectation was that Dan would never leave. But he wanted to leave in five. He'll leave after season eight. He was already getting a little achy after games, even though he never really felt that a single player ever got the best of him. Nobody ever hurt him. Oh, they tried. Damn straight, they tried, but Dan knew in his heart that he showed more restraint than any player who ever played the game. He felt as strong, quick, and skillful as ever. When he was in the paint, he never missed. Well, almost never. His 42 point per game average would, after his eighth and final season, give him over 27,000 points. That wouldn't be the most, but it would be in the top ten, and what matters more is that nobody had averaged 42 points per game over multiple seasons. The leaders, all great players, had, in most all cases, played many more seasons, and some, more than double the eighth season that the CANYON was swearing to stick with. Eight seasons, a top scorer, among the most assists and rebounds, and eight championships, if he could swing that. That's a pretty resume. Then, he and Melanie would find something else to do.... for a lifetime.

They talked about where to marry. Traditionally, a wedding would take place in the bride's hometown, and they discussed a lavish wedding at the Del Coronado. But they had lived in New York. Of course, they could find a great place in New York, like the Waldorf, or the Plaza. Even the

Garden, which Dan mentioned. After all, Dan knew the owners. But Melanie, feeling traditional, decided that the Coronado would be awesome. Then there was the problem of the guest list. If they were to only choose close friends and relatives, they could get by on about 75 people. But there were business associates, former players. It was going to be hard. However, there was no financial pressure. Melanie's parents made a nice living, but Dan and Melanie, worth perhaps $1.4 billion, approached them and said "We're paying for our own wedding. After all, let's not be silly. It might be lavish, out of necessity. Whatever we spend, and we mean, whatever, won't break the bank."

By the time they were done, they had pared the wedding down to 350 guests. Dan invited all the Knicks players, their spouses, or girlfriends, and about 30 people from the front office. He invited the Mayor and the NY Governor. He also invited some, but not all his Michigan teammates. He hadn't kept up with all of them. He invited about two dozen people from companies that paid Dan to endorse their products. Of course, all the Minnelli's would come. Tony's girlfriend Brittany. A few assorted others, like "Double M", Marvin Middleton and his girlfriend, and a few other media types, and Dan had about 125 people on his list. Melanie made up the difference through many assorted friends from home, Old Dominion friends, and some work and local friends.

Dan was happy to stay away from most of the planning. They would have the ceremony on the beach, weather permitting (but usually perfect in San Diego) and then the reception inside. Dan didn't want to skimp on the music and wanted a large band that could play big band, some jazz and popular dancing music. He wanted a male and female singer.

Dan was basically told to show-up, as is often the case with the men. And of course, sign several checks. His best man was Tony. How could it not be? Tony hid his excitement, but it was there.

The only thing Dan did, and it was a surprise that nobody understood except for Melanie, so it was a risk, was to tell Debbie, his new personal assistant, to hire two classically trained actors, or voice actors, whatever she wanted to do. Put them in an upscale attire. One of them would get the crowd's attention, while Melanie looked and Dan like "what the hell is this?" Dan just smiled and whatever it was, she knew he was up to it, and the crowd knew nothing.

"Ladies and Gentlemen", in honor of Melanie and Dan, we have been asked to recite a poem written in England over 150 years ago, about love, written by well-known thespian, Allen Konigsberg:

"To love is to suffer. To avoid suffering, one must not love. But then one suffers from not loving. Therefore, to love is to suffer, not to love is to suffer, to suffer is to suffer. To be happy is to love. To be happy, then, is to suffer, but suffering makes one unhappy, therefore, to be unhappy one must love, or love to suffer, or suffer from too much happiness".

Melanie went to the mic and told the confused audience. OH, this is a quote from a Woody Allen movie! We love movie quotes and this crazy man I married KNEW that ALL OF YOU would look around thinking "WHAT THE HELL IS THIS", but I and I alone would get it. This is the essence of the man-child named Daniel Johnson, and this craziness is one of about five million reasons I love him. Now THAT the guests understood and wildly applauded.

One of Melanie's best friends gave a speech about Melanie's amazing "goodness", her caring about others, her wicked sense of humor, her competitiveness, her zest for life. Then it was Tony's turn. "You know, I've only known this very tall man since we were both 22, so that makes, let's see, seven years. Usually, you get lifelong friends up here. Sorry to disappoint you all. But Dan and I have spent enough time to be those lifetime friends people speak about. I feel that way. The guy that coined his nickname, Canyon, did it because a Canyon is big. It's enormous. But it's also deep. He is deep. The last thing that impresses me about Dan Johnson is his athletic ability, and the world knows how big that is. No, what's bigger is the depth of his decency, his caring about others, and as you can see, he has found his soul mate in Melanie. We may have fewer drinking sessions back in Jersey, but people were talking about us, so at least I get that monkey off my back."

After the wedding, the happy couple flew off to an island in the Caribbean that nobody would manage to find, somehow.

# The Assumption

In 2003, Dan would seek the assistance of the Rheumatologist that from Knicks team doctor. Not surprisingly, one of the premier experts in the business was in New York. It was never hard for Dan to get into restaurants, get tickets for shows, or other events, like doctors, based on his immense fame, and this was no exception. The Knick's team doctor went, and when Dan was asked what the problem was, he simply that it was a "consultation."

"I always found you to be an interesting case," Dr. Richard Leffers told Dan. Dr. Leffers was widely regarded in his field. The strain on your joints, all of them, should be extraordinary. Are you having problems now?" "Well", Dan said, I have soreness in several areas, yet. Some pain in my knees, sometimes my hips and back, and sometimes, my shoulders. They come and go. Sometimes, my feet are very sore in the morning, and then once I walk around, stretch them out, they feel much better. Some days I have no pain and other days, it's more significant, but I would say it's occasional and it doesn't interfere with my game. Once I'm playing, I never feel anything."

"Well, let's get you an ESR test and see if you've got any inflammation." Dan's test showed moderate levels of inflammation, obvious due to the pounding his body had taken on the court as well as on the mat. Dr. Leffers gave him some suggestions and asked him to come back in six months." "You're a professional athlete and knocked around, running up and down that court. It's inevitable that you're a candidate for some joint problems. Let's keep an eye on it and see what happens. We'll watch it.

Four months later, Dr. Leffers called him to tell him that the American College of Rheumatology, or ACR, would be having its conference, and would Dan like to be a so-called "guest of honor". No speeches, just come and meet some smart physicians, have a good meal. Dan and Melanie thought, "why not". Plus, there would be a band playing swing, which is what probably convinced Dan. The meeting was a ten-minute drive right in Manhattan.

The conference was a little bit boring, although Dan didn't come to for the opening event and certainly not for the breakout sessions. He came on the last night, which was composed of a cocktail hour, dinner, and music and dancing. Once Dan gave Dr. Leffers his assurance that he would come, the organizers put that information out on their website, "Special Guest, Dan "The CANYON Johnson of the NY Knicks". That helped reverse some last-minute cancellations as well as have a few people call at the last minute whose suddenly became available to attend."

Dan was never a dancer, not in the least, and Melanie, while at one time, loved to dance, she had bad hips that weren't getting any better, and Dan had his good days and bad days. But the band was great and played some Glenn Miller and Benny Goodman stuff that Dan knew, and the place got swinging, the more the alcohol started pouring.

Dan, at one point, went out to the lobby to use the restroom. On the way back, a doctor introduced himself. He was a little bit tipsy but compared to what he had seen in college and at some various parties, he was stone sober. Still, Dan could hear the very slight changes in his voice, and his slightly jovial personality. Nothing to write home about, though.

The Doctor introduced himself as Ken Petrovic, and said that he was a Geriatric Rheumatologist, Geriatric rheumatology is the branch of medicine that studies rheumatologic disorders in elderly (joints, muscles other structures around the joints). Sometimes it is called Geriatric Rheumatology. The Doctor said, Mr. Johnson, you're still young, but I would imagine that by now, with your size and the burden of playing professional sports, that by now, you have signs of arthritis in key joints." Dan said, "Well, there are days I feel pain in my feet, knees, shoulders, on and off. Sometimes, I'm pain free. I imagine it's very common for guys that play basketball. Even my wife may be headed toward hip replacement surgery, maybe in a few years. "Well, yes, that is to be expected, but I'm sure you're aware that virtually no human has ever reached your height, and those that do have short life expectancies." "Well, Doc, thanks for brightening up my evening." "Oh, I'm sorry about that. No doubt, it's the scotch and sodas." "No doubt", said Dan. "But Doctor, that bothered my parents a lot more than it does me, until recently. I probably have arthritis, and it'll probably get worse. What's your assessment, then? Do I have a short life span?" Even a drunk doctor seemed trained to answer. "Well, Mr. Johnson, I haven't examined you, and there's simply not enough evidence to point to any degree of certainty, but if you're already expecting some pain now, I think you're in for more difficultly later, but one can't tell anything for certain." Doctor, off the record, what do you think?" The doctor, perhaps feeling a little under pressure from Dan, simply said. "Mr. Johnson, I do not know, but off the record, the human body has limits, our growth has limits, the heart, lungs and organs have limits, and a man who is almost nine feet tall is testing those limits in many ways; testing his joints, his bones, his skeletal system, his heart. We weren't meant to be that tall, but here you are, and you don't only exist, you've excelled, so nature can surprise us. Take care of your body and see your doctor regularly. You are the world's tallest man. I would not predict that you will one day become the world's oldest man, to be perfectly sincere. Do you understand what I'm trying to say? That's the best I can do."

Dan wasn't crazy about the encounter, and only served to feed his imagination with dark thoughts, which he had had since he was a little kid and teased about his mammoth size. Nobody is meant to be this big, and mother nature has its ways of dealing with species that can't adapt.

# The Man-Cave and the Birth of Canyonville

Melanie and Dan had been married two years. It was September 2005. So much had changed in the last three years, it was astounding. Both good and bad.

Melanie had been to Minnelli's and game nights enough times now to be part of their family. Just like Dan. She loved their closeness and even their combativeness. They had so much life, but they couldn't escape tragedy. Nor could the world.

It seemed to all happen so damn fast. September 11, then the life-changing sale of Metro Holdings to Kaufman homes in the spring of 2002. Then, Gina's passing, only a month later, with a financial future set. Paul and his family would be leaving for Italy and Greece the next May and contemplating their future. Money no longer being a consideration. Tony, the same. With a few million in the bank, Tony's biggest problem was deciding what to do, but he decided to simply get as involved with P.A.L., the Police Athletic League, as much as possible. It came to believe that it was his calling, to help kids, just as Dan would do.

Grandma Luccia passed away in May of 2003, at 86 years of age. Gina's death took a terrible toll, nearly as bad as it did on Joe and Carole. Her wise cracks all but ceased. She began to live in her own, shattered world. Quiet, withdrawn. Tony tried to cheer her up, but it wasn't her. That zest of life seemed extinguished. Still, she would hug Dan and quietly say, "Thank you, Danny. You're a good boy."

For Joe and Carole, they planned a long holiday in Europe, but then what? What good is money when you are in such pain? Joe was fifty-eight, Carole fifty-five. Would they be able to find purpose in life again? Dan had no answers. He wanted Joe to perhaps direct his Canyon Foundation business, but as smart a businessman as Joe was, Dan was advised to hire a longtime industry expert. It wasn't anything like construction.

As for Dan, he had reached his eighth year and by the spring of 2005, his eighth and final championship with the Knicks. In a city that had experienced huge sports idols and personalities, Ruth, DiMaggio, Mantle, the Canyon was the biggest of all, because success was measured not in charisma, although that could help. Look at Ruth. Look at Broadway Joe. No, it was measured in championships. And Dan was part of the commercial success of the Canyon shoe franchise that has made him a billionaire. In 2001, Vickers sold 45 million pairs of Canyon shoes at an average wholesale price of $55. Dan's commission last year was just over $123 million. Even Stephon Williamson received $8.6 million, as the architect behind Canyon. Anne Karlson took in a half percent, or $12.3 million, forever pinching herself for approaching Dan that day at the UM dining hall. She continued to run her three galleries, successfully. Her Ann Arbor gallery was a close partner with the UM Stamps art school, helping students exhibit their work. She even allowed the school to use the phrase, "The Ann Karlsson Gallery at the University of Michigan." It was still owned by Ann. She brought artists' work from all over the world to her New York and Beverly Hills galleries, as reaped a sizable commission. When asked (and because Dan had ALWAYS had a crush on "Annie", and she knew it, Dan would come by to events, exciting the crowd and driving sales). Plus, friends matter, and Dan would influence many an exhibit when he was overseas, strictly by telling a head of state, "We would have to have some of your talented painters exhibit at our famous Ann Karlsson Galleries." "Oh, of course, always the response. I will see what I can do." When Queen Elizabeth or the President of France asks around, things happen. And Lisa Sawyer Vickers? Well, it is easier to be magnanimous when Wall

429

Street considers you the "Savior of an American institution." Along with line extensions, like the "Coldstone Women's Basketball Shoe", and the "Canyon Kidz" shoes, the maker of Canyon shoes", the company had worldwide sales of over $5.0 billion in 2001.

Dan had retired from judo and wrestling in 1996, in Atlanta, but was as popular as ever in countries that celebrated those sports. He travelled when he could. Of course, "the Iran trip", when he snuck into Iran, at the request of their government, as an "ambassador of wrestling" really put Dan in hot water with the U.S. state department. It was one time when Dan was really fooled. Yes, he was there only for two days and yes, he visited a national wrestling training center and only talked about wrestling, the Iranians tried without success to have him make negative remarks about the "Imperialistic Americans." It was the video of him stating his love for America that the White House and State department ultimately used as an excuse to simply give Dan a slap on the wrist.

Yes, the Knicks notwithstanding. It was a tumultuous two years.

With Dan and Melanie spending all summer at the Lake Lanier house, "the lake house", and Dan swearing that 2005 would be his last year, Melanie wanted to build the ultimate mancave, "the cantina" that Dan himself had mentioned more than once, even choosing the location on their six-acre property, facing the water about 200 feet away from the house. This would put a stamp on the six-bedroom house, now with a pontoon boat and 8, yes 8 jet skis. Dan loved to take guests on "trail runs" through the nooks and crannies of Lake Lanier. Nearly every Knick's player and many others, had been to the Lake, but this cantina, or "man-cave" that Dan would always mention, wasn't there yet, and Melanie had decided that there would be no better 30th birthday present. Imagine a "man cave" where money was no object! Well, now, it wasn't. Melanie just had to become a little sneaky.

So, Melanie had to let the cat out of the bag, at least a little, when discussing with Dan. "Honey, I want to give you a great birthday present next year, but I'll need the money to do it." "Well, babe", Dan said, it's our money, not mine. "Yes", she continued, but it's a lot of money." "What's a lot?" Dan asked? "Ha, ha, millions?" "Well, it's all relative, right?" Dan smiled and said "Maybe". "Well, you can trust me. It might be maybe half a million. I don't know until I begin to plan it, but I want to keep it a secret from you." "Does this mean you'll be at the lake house more during the season?" "Ohh", shouted Melanie. "You're gonna ruin everything!" Dan laughed. "Ok, ok. I'll speak with Larry, and you have fun." "Thank you, honey", she said, and that was that.

The next day, Dan called Larry. "Larry, I think Melanie wants to build me this man-cave I always talk about, at the lake house, and she'll need money." "Ok", Larry said. "How much?" "I have no idea, but I have given her enough hints about this thing. I want it big; I want it furnished. I want games, music, a big bar, the works. What'll that cost?" "Dan", Larry said. "Your wife wants to build you the ultimate man cave, and when it's done, I'm coming. You've got about $1.4 billion in assets, and it's gonna grow." "Well, what would a dream man-cave cost, and a mean the works? A million?" "Dan, how about I give her a line of $2 million, to pay contractors and for all the toys and gimmicks she wants? That's a fraction of 1% of your assets, Dan." "Ok, $2 million. Anymore and I'll call you." "Wow, laughed Dan. World's worst secret!" "Yeah, said Larry," but it has to be done this way." "Oh, and Dan? Fish it out of her. If she forgets Ms. Pac Man, I'll need to know. And the fast version, not the slow one."

Two days later, Melanie called Larry, "So," Larry said, you want to give Dan some kind of amazing birthday present, what is it?" "Oh, come on Larry," Melanie joked. "Number one, I'm certain he has a very good idea of what it is, minus, just maybe, a couple of details, and what would you tell him." "Hey," Larry said, why would I say anything? Dan already told me to get you up to two million dollars. I mean, it's in your name, too. He trusts you." "Yes, maybe so, but normally, if I'm spending this kind of money, we discuss it. Hell, when he spends $150 for dinner, he comes to me first and says, "I don't know, should we drop $150 at this place?" Larry laughed at said, "That'll go away. It wasn't long ago when he was in Ann Arbor eating ramen noodles. I meant, 15 boxes at a time, but he was poor, and he's NOT poor now." "Okay, Larry, swear to me you won't give him details, but he knows of this anyway. We picked out a piece of the property to build a man cave. We'd call it a cantina. Big, with a real bar inside and game, lots of games; a couple of pool tables, air hockey, ping pong, and then a bunch of classic '80s video games, like Ms. Pac Man, Space Invaders, Caterpillar (Larry knew she meant "Centipede"). Maybe a dozen of those. An old, classic juke box, lots of beer on tap plus liquor, cool posters on the wall, and I want it open with one of those big barn doors that opens to a cool patio. I want it to be so good that magazines want to feature it, and I want it done in 9 months, for his birthday. I don't want to tell you everything because I still don't trust you and I want you to be surprised, too." "Okay, well what will something like this cost." "Oh," said Melanie, I don't know, and that's what worries me." "Ok, listen," said Larry. "He just MIGHT have a vague idea, and you two talked about it, then make it his dream cantina. You do understand that even if it cost $2 million, that is a tiny fraction of your assets, and I mean far less than 1%. Trust me, it's all relative and Dan will love it. He won't be surprised but I want him to be thrilled. will be surprised but not shocked. Make sense?"

432

Larry called Dan. "Okay, I spoke to Melanie. How much do you exactly want to know?" "Well," Dan said. I'm curious as hell. I'm dreaming of this man-cave. I'm gonna bring everybody down there." Larry said, "Notice how I'm not discouraging it? I'm still a man and I'm jealous. The money's nothing and I want to go see it when it's done. I'm gonna be as anxious as you are."

# Canyonville Debut

"Okay", Larry said, "it's what you think, no holds barred, totally cool and I don't know everything. Might run you a mil-five, but let her do this, Dan. She quit her job last year and she's stir-crazy and she wants to make you happy. This is a good investment in your happiness. Both of you. When I think you're blowing your money, I'll let you know, but you're a billionaire and this is a couple of mil. You're worried?" "Only that she'll forget about a juke box", said Dan.

Melanie was in her element. She spent much of the next seven months in the Atlanta area. First, the architect. They decided on a 3,000 square foot building. They discussed a budget. She wanted it to be "very innovative, but very safe and sturdy." It should have a huge barn door, custom if necessary, opening one of the short sides, to let in plenty of sunshine and air on nice days, great insulation, metal with a wooden exterior to make it look old and rustic. She wanted, of course, great heating and AC unit, top of the line, so that everybody can party year-long. She wanted a long bar on one side, and space for games on the others side. She wanted about 20 large tv monitors all around the cantina, with one large one, as big as can be found, and a good area. She wanted no unsightly cords. She would hire an interior decorator to find great, very large, and comfortable furniture for guests to enjoy. She wanted a large, custom neon sign on the wall that said, "Canyonville". She had finally decided. That would be the same, and the more she thought about it, the more certain she was. It would be epic. Famous. She wanted a band area with lights. Maybe a small stage in the corner, a platform of some kind.

The architect asked for two weeks to prepare drawings. In the meantime, Melanie made calls and had meetings. When she said, "Hi, my name is Melanie Johnson, and my husband is the basketball player, Dan Johnson," you wouldn't believe what doors it opened. "Oh, my God, you're married to the CANYON?" "Yes, and I am building him a man-cave that we'll calling Canyonville, and I need help." "Oh my God, the world's greatest man cave?" Men she spoke to simply freaked out. Melanie hit on a nerve with men. A special little kid's dream that never died, and the builder's she spoke with wanted to be a part. The women, too. It's the like the "fort" you built as a kid with blankets, but a grown-up version where money didn't matter. Are you shitting me? She found a seller of vintage '80s video games and ordered 15. The seller told her they were the top sellers, and yes, the "fast" Ms Pac Man was there, because Larry sort of let that slip to Melanie, if you want to call it a slip. She sat with the interior decorator, and they were going to decide on sofas, tables, chairs, of all sizes but some very big, long versions, strategically placed. She found a cement contractor for a large patio and got help in making the ultimate outdoor party area, with an industrial barbeque, a gas line underground with six outdoor table firepits, massive outdoor refrigerator and stove, all with a covering to keep them dry. Outdoor speakers, and Melanie wanted the best security system that money could buy. Nobody could get anywhere near the property without being videotaped. The doors were thick, the entire building with motion detectors and loud sirens. Even warning signs that told any trespassers that they were already being filmed if they could read the sign. She found a seller of vintage juke boxes that could hold seventy 45's. Rock/oldies, jazz, and of course, Dean, Frank, Tony Bennett, and even a few country songs, although Dan wouldn't be listening. Even some rap because she knew his likely guests, and besides, Dan could always change the records over time. There was a top-rated sound system and radio for tuning in to stations.

CANYONVILLE would be for Dan. For them. Melanie found all kinds of movie posters, and they would go on the wall. Finally, plans was done. Melanie was ecstatic, and construction would begin in 4-6 weeks once licenses were acquired, and the tasks and timetable all figured out by the contractors. Furniture, games, and all inside décor would come last. Despite her concerns, and with all the bells and whistles she could think of, the bill would come in at about $800,000. That turned out not to be a secret among the three players, and everybody was satisfied. It wasn't exactly the world's best-kept secret. Even Tony Minnelli and Charles Winfield were told to "clear some time to come down to the lake house," and Dan, while daydreaming, put a mental list together of whom he might invite down to see something he "wasn't supposed to know about."

May 2004 was here, and the playoffs would be over mid-June. The Knicks were once again wiping up the competition, and Dan was as serious as ever. His incredible stats were up, and he seemed to be on a mission, even in his seventh year. He ran harder, he jumped higher, his passes had more zing to them, somehow, and the Knicks made quick work of the Spurs in four games. It wasn't even fair, and many in the league wished he had stuck to his word to retire in five seasons. Whether they believed it or not, Dan had one season to go. He would turn 29 in September.

Melanie attended the playoffs, all four games, but her mind was somewhere else. Making calls, getting commitments. Eleven days after the final game would be the opening of Canyonville, and even if Dan was a homebody, Melanie wanted the world to know just what they were missing by not being a friend of Dan Johnson's. Quietly, invitations were made by phone, with the day up in the air until the Knicks final victory was secured. She finally told Tony and nearly had him sign his name in blood to keep it all a secret. To make sure Dan himself would come, she once again had to basically admit what was going on. She said she was going to take some friends down to the house. An early birthday celebration. Players were taking vacations and camp would start again during Dan's birthday, so June was best. Dan wasn't fooled, so he went right alone. He could already feel his fingers on the Ms. Pac Man Machine.

Melanie hired a team of 20 caterers, security, and "party managers" to make sure everything was set up ahead of time. She hired two photographers and a videographer. She even invited "Double M", Marvin Middleton from basketball tonight, and his partner, whose name Melanie had forgotten. Marvin was the handsome guy with charisma, Melanie secretly thought, with all the fun nicknames for Dan. All twelve Knick players, the three coaches, and the GM, Rod Dorfman, and his wife, although with vacations in the wings, only three players attended, and no coaches or front office. They all took an oath of secrecy and asked for pictures. They would all make it down there in due course.

She blocked-off hotel rooms and paid for them in advance. Melanie had Dan arrive a day early so she could show him Canyonville. He drove up from the airport. She had a temporary banner in front of their long driveway that said "Welcome to Canyonville. Dan got out and he could not help but see the building. "Oh, my God", he said. "Of course, you knew all along, didn't you." "Yes, I figured it was the man-cave we talked about, oh, 20 times." "Well, for the cost and all the work, I suppose it is better to give you something I'm pretty sure you'll like." They walked over to the building, about 200 feet from their large, 6-bedroom house. The outside was covered in rustic wood, like a barn, in a gray color. He said "It looks all homey and rustic. It's perfect. He gave her a big hug." On the outside was an amazing cement patio that you would find surrounding a pool behind a mansion. A roof covered an outdoor kitchen with four TVs. The patio had several tables, umbrellas, and chairs. And then Melanie pointed a remote control at the building, and the big barn sliding door began to open. "You haven't seen the inside." And then Melanie pointed a remote control at the building, and a big barn sliding door began to open. Dan walked inside and was simply amazed. "Oh, my God, oh my God." The sign CANYONVILLE was in bright red, flashing, with a small platform stage under it. And then, a few feet away, across the backside of the building, the highlight, a 24-foot mahogany bar, with cabinets for holding liquor, taps for 8 kinds of beer, leather stools and TVs across the top. Dan couldn't imagine where she had that shipped in from. Over the top were industrial metal chandeliers running the entire length of the bar. In front of the stage was enough room for several couples to dance. The middle of the mancave had various hi-top and low-top tables. Across from the bar were leather sofas, extra-long, running down the entire 30-foot building, except for the corner, where there was a vintage, old jukebox and two bathrooms. On the opposite corner was an exit door, as per the Hall County fire code. Melanie walked over to the juke box, pushed a button, and a pre-chosen song came on.

> How lucky can one guy be.
> I kissed her and she kissed me.
> Like the fella once said
> Ain't that a kick in the head.

Dan was beaming from ear to ear. "Don't worry," Melanie said. There's Led Zepplin, AC/DC, Foreigner, The Beatles, the Beach Boys, Sinatra, Sammy, Hank, Willy. Even Tupac, Eminem, Ice Cube and Jay Z. "Well, forget it, then. You can take it all away now!" "Well, Melanie laughed, I'm counting on you bringing all your friends, and they all have different musical tastes." "Yeah, mostly bad taste."

Behind the furniture were two billiard tables, and then along the final wall, maybe the best thing of all, were fifteen of the best 1980's video games ever made, including Pac-Man, Ms. Pac-Man (fast version), Missile Command, Punchout, Centipede, Gorf, Donkey Kong, Tetris, Frogger, Joust, Galaga, and Rally X.

Wherever there was space on the walls, there was sports memorabilia and great movie posters, the Godfather, Casablanca, Manhattan and Love and Death, Blazing Saddles. Every table had napkins emblazed with "*Canyonville* – **Flowery Branch, GA"**

Now tomorrow, all your guests are coming. Well, about a dozen, but they'll put this place on the map and then you'll get calls from friends you've never met. You'll be retiring and I can have you here all alone with me, bored all the time. Dan said, "Well, if things go the way I want, I'll have a second career for a few years, and then I can slow down, but this is the most amazing present anybody can have."

The next day, Tony and his soon to be wife Brittany would be here, Paul and his wife, his agent, his financial planner, Charles Winfield and his girlfriend, Marvin Middleton (Double M) and his wife, and twelve lakeside neighbors that couldn't help but hear the construction, and Melanie calmed their fears by promising to invite them to the "soft opening". She also promised that they weren't loud partiers, that Dan is really a boring stiff, and that they would be invited to more parties and just to hand out. "We want to be good neighbors. Not just famous and annoying.

The guests stood with their mouth open, while a staff of workers served food, and a band played. All the guests quietly, and not so quietly said that between the house, the cantina, and the lake, they would do just about anything to be invited back to the

Lake House, which would forever be called "the Lake House" by Dan, Melanie, and probably Tony and Brit, but forevermore, Canyonville by everybody who had ever heard of it, and that would be everybody.

They hoped to be able to have some events and parties but would never anticipate the fame that CANYONVILLE would acquire. Not yet.

# Bushwhackers and other Delights

After the Knick's seventh NBA Championship, the Knick's owner called Dan and told him that a very influential supporter and minority owner wanted to treat him and his friends to a weekend of fishing and partying near his home, on a private Island called Ono, and he could invite some four other friends. It made Dan a little uncomfortable, plus, he'd rather be back at the Lakeside and amazing CANYONVILLE, but the owner said, "Dan, do this as a favor to me. He wants to do it." Dan had heard of the area from visiting his grandparents in the town of Lillian, the last town in Alabama along Perdido Bay, just across from Pensacola. His parents had met at Rosie O'Grady's in Pensacola, during a Thanksgiving visit when the grandparents felt like hosting, naturally, Chuck and Cathy had to show Dan where the courtship started. Dan also got to see the Naval Base and the museum. But Ono was an exclusive Island down on the coast, closer to Perdido Key and Orange Beach, and Dan had simply never been there. It appeared to be partly in Florida, but the border conveniently skirted around it, leaving all of it with an Alabama address.

It was an easy situation, because Dan and Melanie had been dating for a few months, and Tony had recently begun dating Brittany. They decided together to invite Dan's Wolverine buddy Charles Winfield and his wife, to complete the group.

Dan wasn't sure if this "supporter" knew what he was getting into, because Dan didn't fly commercial. But Dan would be at his lake house anyway, just built the year before, with Melanie, so Charles, Tony, and the ladies flew from Chicago and New York, on commercial flights, to Atlanta, and from there they all flew, the six of them, from DeKalb Peachtree Airport to the Jack Edwards field in nearby Gulf Shores, a small airport for private planes. They all decided that they "could get used to this." Dan, of course, had, already.

Upon landing, a limo immediately pulled up to the plane and drove them approximately 8 miles north to the Hotel Magnolia in the town of Foley, a quaint, historic bed and breakfast hotel in the middle of the town, built in 1908 by John Burton Foley of Chicago. Once there, there was a reception by the supporter, Rick Whiteman, and his wife and about six other friends, just beside themselves at the prospect of meeting Dan. Rick and his wife were then leaving for another house they owned in Vermont.

Tony said to Rick, "I never heard of this area. It's beautiful." "Well, where do your friends or people up there go?" Tony said, mostly Florida." Well, you can do us one small favor and not tell them about us." Tony asked Rick if went to school in Alabama, noting that he'd never met anyone who did.

Rick said, I got an undergraduate degree at Cornell, and a law degree at Duke." So that seemed to explain both houses. We discovered the Alabama gulf coast and Ono years ago and decided to have a place here.

After the very pleasant, private lunch, Rick and his friends left, and the limo took Dan and "team CANYON" to Ono Island, across from Orange Beach and about twenty minutes away. They went through a guard's house, where their name was on a list, and then stopped in front of a beautiful four-bedroom home. Dan was given a set of keys from Rick at lunch, so he opened the door, and of course, ducked down, but the home was nicely appointed. There was a letter which Rick told him would be there.

Dear CANYON and friends,

Welcome to our little Alabama getaway. We hope you have a fantastic time, and this is our thank you for bringing the Knicks another championship. I felt this is the least that we can do, and we'll be rooting you on for another banner next year.

Below are the names of a few restaurants and who to ask for if you go. You will get preferential treatment, I promise you. Don't forget the marina on the list. There's a boat as well as jet skis for you. Even the grocery store there knows you're here. Your money is NO good, so have a great time, and the limo will pick you up Sunday afternoon at 1:00 for your flight back to New Jersey. Have a great time!

The group went to dinner that evening, and then to the well-known Flora-Bama to listen to several bands and drink, and then the next day, a marina took them out on a boat in the Gulf, Bayou Saint John, and Perdido Bay.

They had their fill of bushwhackers, a frozen alcoholic drink made with Kahlua, rum, creme de cacao, and cream of coconut, famous in the area.

# Starting the Foundation

In January 2004, Dan told Larry that the annual process of dividing up charitable donations would be changing in a year, if Dan was able to successfully accomplish two things. One was to retire. He had told the Knicks this time, it was final. He had sore joints, which he was sure would heal and improve once the regular pounding on the court was in the rear-view mirror. Frankly, he didn't give a damn anymore if fans complained, just because so many other players of his caliber played for twenty years, and not the eight that Dan would end his career at. He had one word for that. "Eight championships." Okay, two words. Knicks fans can go find themselves another messiah.

The other task he was already asking about for his entire career. Dan wanted to control where his donations went. He thought about it all the time. Of course, the $20 million dollars he donated to charity last year went to very deserving charities, and many of them would continue getting money, perhaps even more, but under a new system, the CANYON Foundation system. Several athletes in different sports, in New York alone, had foundations, and Dan had mentioned it casually to them. "Hey, how did you start your foundation. When I retire, I want to start mine." "Why wait?" was sometimes the answer. "Well, said Dan, I'm still playing. I can't give it the time it needs." "Hey man, everybody says, I have an executive director, a staff, and a board." "Aren't you involved?" Dan asked. He got many different answer to that. Some did little more than lend their name and get an occasional overview. Some went to meetings two or three times a year and had input as to how the money was spent. Others were a little bit more involved than that. One way or another, all gave money and some time. There was nothing but praise for these athletes. They made a different, and Dan wanted to think HE made a difference in the money he was donating, but once he retired, he thought that would be his everyday job, and that was squashed pretty quickly.

Running a non-profit was a career. It was hard, and the more money involved, the more complicated it was. It needed a seasoned CEO or director. It needed legal counsel, it didn't administrators, it needed accounting assistance, and more accounting and tax assistance. It also needed marketing. It seemed crazy, but you have to spend money to make money, and you have to pay people a decent wage, even in a non-profit. There were crooks, but for the most part, these people who chose this path wanted to help.

Dan was going to do everything different, and while he had a little bit of a wakening experience, and had to compromise, he learned that even the best people could be made to feel more secure and work very hard when you took care of their family.

Eight months after asking Larry to "quietly" ask around, he came to Larry and said, "Dan, I have found a CEO of a major charity organization, with 35 years of experience, that isn't happy where she is. She wants a new experience and wants to go out having tried something new. She may be the one and she's in New York.

Larry arranged a meeting between Dan and Marcy Goodman, at a nice restaurant on the upper west side. Marcy was excited because her husband was a big sports fan. She was 56 years old and in the prime of her professional career, but she was skeptical. She was a no-nonsense, non-chatty person who was very direct and didn't want to beat around the bush with Dan.

There was virtually no small talk. "Well, Mr. Johnson, I was certainly surprised to hear that it was you who wanted to meet me. My lawyer knows Larry FitzPatrick, your financial planner. I hear you want to start a Foundation. Let's get right to the point. Give me a two-minute overview so I can see if this is something worth talking about further."

"First of all, call me Dan. May I call you Marcy?" Marcy was already impatient. "Actually, I prefer Mrs. Goodman." "Ok, Mrs. Goodman, I can see what you want. Keep it short. I give a lot of money to charity every year. Larry and I choose worthwhile causes and he gives the money. Nothing to be ashamed of. It was $20 million last year, but now I'm retiring, and I want to know where my money is going. I don't want it spread around. I want it laser focused on up to 20 charities that I think are most important, and I have already chosen them. They are to be children's hospitals and food banks. Now, I am going to give you exactly what you want if you give me 60 more seconds. This process won't change. If you don't like it, you can get up and leave now. I hear you're unhappy. Sorry to hear that, but if money makes any difference. I'll pay you more and give you more benefits. I'm so fucking rich that I can't spend it enough. I already know you make $385k. I'll pay

446

you $600k plus a bonus if you keep expenses down to a level we agree on. You hire the staff and they'll make a lot more money, too. If I hear you're the wicked witch of the east and treat anybody with anything less than complete respect, I'll have your ass on the street that same day. You'll get a generous severance, but you'll never touch my money, and it IS my money, not yours. I won't be in your face because I hate that. You execute my plan and you'll be happy. I'm talking to you straight like this because I respect your advice. I don't want a yes man, or woman, in this case. You have a lot of experience, but my word is the final word, or you can go back to your miserable existence with a charity you hate, if you don't like that. Now, I'm leaving. Don't say another word and I mean it. Think about what I said. Call Larry in two days or I'll assume you have no interest. I'll find somebody else very easily at this income level. You know it and I know it. If you're interested, we'll sit down again and talk in greater length. That doesn't mean you'll have the job, but we'll talk. Goodbye, Mrs. Goodman.

Marcy Goodman looked at Dan, and said, quite sincerely, "I've never had anybody talk like that to me before." "Well", said Dan. "You've heard of 'fuck you money? I have 'fuck you times 1,000 money. I'm a very nice guy but I found out the unpleasant fact that if you have enough money, you can be an asshole. But honestly, Marcy, and I'm not calling you Mrs. Goodman, I would rather be nice. I want a professional. An expert, and I'm convinced that's who you are. But, maybe for the first time in your life, you're going to have to realize that I'll be your boss.

Oh, and Marcy? I'm much nicer than this and I don't appreciate you setting the stage with your bitchy attitude, and putting me in this situation of being a little nasty right back, but it doesn't mean you don't have the job. Not yet."

And Dan walked over to the restaurant owner, said something to him, and walked out the door.

"Wow," Larry said to Dan. "What the hell happened?" Dan said, "Her attitude sucked from the very beginning. She challenged me to give her an "elevator pitch", you know, a two-minute speech, so I did it. Larry, I have a certain way I want this Foundation to be Run. It'll have my name on it. I never thought I'd have a nickname of Canyon, but when people in Uganda chant my name, and China, and Scotland, well, Canyon is the name people know me by. If it's the Canyon, then it's going to reflect my desires. I've listened to owners and coaches now for a very long time. Now it's my time, and money talks. I don't want my money going to 100 different causes, where I can't keep up with it. That might be fine for a mutual Foundation, but not for the Canyon Foundation. I made a choice. Children's hospitals and food banks. Twenty, max. Spread out from coast to coast. We need one in the three core markets that have been there for me. Atlanta, Ann Arbor, and New York. Take care of them and we can then spread out.

And also, last week I was having a couple of beers with my friend." "Tony?" Larry said, as in "no shit." "What's wrong, Larry, you want to come drink PBR with us in New Jersey?" "No, I don't." "Ok, then." Dan said. "Anyway, I want to have a special hurricane division of the Canyon Foundation." "I'm listening," said Larry. Dan continued, "Every year there's a hurricane or natural disaster. I want a fleet of trucks waiting in a warehouse, all packed and ready to go. The Executive Director will need to run that. Maybe an east and west coast program. Find a warehouse and drivers. I want those trucks rolling before that storm gets out of town. Our Director needs to speak with experts on what to supply. Water, batteries, generators, clothing, food, whatever is needed.

The final part is the support program for Ann Arbor, West Orange, and Marietta. I want the police, fire, and first responder emergency Foundation set, and the annual picnic planned.

So I assume our Ms. Goodman is no longer on the short list". "You'd assume wrong, my clueless friend." Larry said. "You really ARE sounding like Tony Minnelli. Bustin' my balls." "I went to Yale," Larry said. "That phrase isn't in my vocabulary. "Well, laddee freakin' dah," Dan said, "I know you Yalies are too good to watch Chris Farley. It's beneath you." "Anyway, Larry said. You seemed to somehow impress Marcy Goodman. Apparently, she admires your fortitude, your ambition and you passion, and is willing to meet with you again, and with a 'change in attitude', to use her point. "She likes the $600k" and Larry said, "You ain't just whistling Dixie, my Georgia friend." "That's what I thought." Dan said. Okay, book the meeting. Two days, because Melanie and I have a date with a travel agent. "Yeah", Larry asked. "Where you going?" "Far away from you." Dan said.

It was three evenings later when Dan and Marcy Goodman sat down at the same restaurant. This time, they met at the bar, so there would be no misunderstanding that Dan did not want to entertain Ms. Goodman with dinner. "Well, Mrs. Goodman," talk to me.

"Well, first of all," Marcy Goodman said, in a conciliatory tone. "I apologize if I came off a little rude." Dan said "No, I understand. I like directness. It's hard to find. I don't normally like to talk much. The whole world has tried to dissect my head, so I don't talk much, either. Ms. Goodman," Goodman interrupted and said, "Oh, call me Marcy. Nobody actually calls me Mrs. Goodman." "Good," said Dan. "Everybody calls me Dan. Well, I guess that's not even close to the truth. Very few people call me Dan, but it's what I prefer." "I've heard Presidents and the Pope call you The Canyon, but the Queen didn't." "No", said Dan. "Her majesty called me Mr. Johnson." "Did you like that?" asked Marcy. "Oh, very much," said Dan. It was dignified. "Did you call her Liz?" "Ha, hardly." "What did you call her?" Dan said, "I called her 'Your Majesty'" "Do you know what her husband calls her?" asked Marcy. "Her calls her, 'Your Majesty'" "I believe it, said Dan.

Dan took out a piece of paper, a newspaper article. "Marcy, I found this four years ago." The article was from the non-profit industry's key trade publication. He read from it. "Judging Marcy Goodman on her personality may not put her at the top of the non-profit executives list but judging her on her ability to change the lives of needy people around the world in a positive way leaves no doubt that she is deserving of her third Non-Profit Executive of the year in the last fifteen years." "Where did you get that?" Marcy asks. "I have been looking for people to help me form a foundation since I joined the Knicks eight years ago. When Larry gave me your name, I was relieved because I wanted to see if he'd mention you. You see," Dan said somewhat sarcastically, you were already on a list of people, but I didn't know if you'd be interested. Larry discovered that you might be."

Dan went on the explain how he wanted to support a network of children's hospitals, from coast to coast, as well as a network of food banks, from existing organizations. A map would reveal hospital recipients in every region, east coast, New England, middle Atlanta, Southeast, middle America, Southwest, Northwest, Pacific. With food banks, the same thing. Nobody would have to travel too far. He envisioned massive warehouse organizations that collected food and maybe even grew their own. He envisioned steps in place to distribute food efficiency and to eliminate waste. Healthy food. Hospitals were more complicated due to the type of care provided, but in fact, it was all complicated. "Marcy, I want a strong person in charge. Not a girl scout. I want results. I want you in charge of my vision. Does that make sense? My vision, your management. I've had enough coaches and bosses running my life. I would like updates, and more importantly, I would like results. I want a board of directors. I want Larry on it, the rest, you can decide on, as well as the staff.

Are you interested?" Dan finally asked, "Yes, I've been wanting this for a very long time. What do we have to do." Dan said, I would like you to write me an outline. It's not a test. I want to see how you envision the organization. The direction, the methods, the budget, the staff and why you need them, how you plan to raise money. I would like it in two weeks." Then, I will sit down with Larry and my wife.

# PART FOUR

# The Next Phase

# Friendly Territory

Marvin Middleton himself called Dan just a day after the CANYON'S historic retirement press conference. "C Man, why don't you come on the show for an hour, talk about your Foundation, future plans, and so forth. Nice and easy, man. No curve balls. Good for the foundation. Dan thought about it for a week, and then agreed. If Dan passed on a question, that was it. They moved on.

What happened on that set was tv history, in a way. Unlike other attempts to get dirt on the mysterious Dan Johnson, the Simmons's and Middleton "we don't give a shit" attitude seemed to open it.

"Good evening everybody and welcome to very special edition of Basketball Tonight" with the man himself, possibly the greatest to ever play the game, you all know who we'll talking about, that's right. The CANYON, the C Man, the now officially retired, and he means it this time, Dan Johnson. With me, as always, the Canyonville Crasher, Double M, Marvin Middleton." "Hey man." Marvin demanded, "I'm no crasher. C tell them." "Dan went along, "You did just show up once or twice, if I recall." Double M objected, "He's lying', he's "lyin."

"So, C Man, what's next in your life?".

For the next hour, and it didn't seem like nearly enough time, Dan Johnson explained his Foundation. At first, it was merely an exclamation of certain events, musical events at Canyonville, but that turned into an exclamation of the Foundation itself; his need to give back. In the control room, the producer smelled history, smelled excellence, smelled Emmy. In the earpiece of Simonds and Middleton, Bill Crestwood, the producer, talked slowly. "Ok, don't interrupt him. Ok, now ask him how that made him feel. Ok, ask him if he would change anything about that, ok, ask him if they thought that was the right thing to do."

Dan discussed his need to do more than sports. Use his fame for something, if he only knew what. His regrets.

Ed Simmons struck gold. "You go accused of bringing women up to your apartment. That's nobody's business, but at 23 years of age, isn't that more or less the dream of all men?" Dan came as close as he ever did to coming clean. "Well, you would think so. I wasn't any different than a regular guy. I liked to date, I was well known. I liked to meet women and I never hurt anyone, period." And then just as fast, that window closed, "and that's all I'm saying about that." And into both earpieces went the producer's voice, move on, move in."

Dan went on about having a few beers in a New Jersey Park a lot, but wouldn't say where. That was the worst-kept secret in West Orange, but for some reason, the people there not only left him alone, they almost seemed to guard his privacy. The attitude seemed to be, "The CANYON wants to be, of all places, in West Orange. Let's not fuck it up." Even the police looked the other way with respect to the beer. The cans and/or bottles were always thrown away.

Dan talked about his college days in Ann Arbor, South Quad, parties at the Student Union. Of course, games at

The Big House, some funny moments in other countries. Hearing "CANYON" said with different accents was always a hoot. "In Japan, I'm known as kyoukoku" "Is it true a very famous band wanted to rehearse for an upcoming tour at Canyonville?" "Oh, sure, but that happened other times. We also got calls from celebrities that wanted to part there. We tried to limit that, keep it for special benefits."

They asked about C's hobbies. He brought up his interest in jazz and how it was unappreciated by the masses, and he talked about how he liked movie quotes. "C'mon man,", Double M persisted, "share a few." Dan was more than happy to. Now, he was on a roll.

"Oh, there's some great ones," we began with. Of course, his favorite "Mongo only pawn in game of life", from Blazing Saddles and Alex Karris, and written by Richard Pryor. Dan used it constantly. There were Godfather movies. Woody Allen movies, especially from Love and Death, a movie that "you had to be intelligent and weird" to enjoy, Gary Cooper quotes. He loved John Belushi's "Was it over when the Germans bombed Pearl Harbor?" speech. Even more current movies, like Sigourney Weaver's line in Galaxy Quest. "I don't think I can say this one," Dan said. "Ok, just say it", Ed said. "We'll bleep it out." "Well FUCK THAT!!", and they laughed. If that's not the most perfect quote for so many things in life, then I don't know what is." Dan talked about his love for The Andy Griffith Show. "That's the show you watch to learn about life and how to parent." He talked about his admiration for Jack Benny, and his comedic timing.

As time was running out, Ed asked Dan, and he reminded Dan that many people got the same question. "Dan, what do you want people to remember you for." Dan thought, but only for a couple of seconds. "I'd like them to know that despite my size, I always did my best, I never took it for granted, but more important than that, that I used my fame to help others, and I'm just getting started with that. I hope I'm here a long time to do that."

# The CANYON Foundation

It was the spring of 2004. So much has happened in the last few years. September 11th, Gina has been gone nearly two years, Grandma Luccia for a year. Dan was worried about Jimmy. A daughter and a mother within the span of a year. Luccia was 86 years old, but it seemed like she'd live forever. Gina's death took so much out of her. The little comments, the gleam in the eye, came less frequently, and when they did come, they were labored, forced. Life was a struggle now. A chore where it had been a joy. Dan loved his movies. He'd get lost in them. Why? Because a writer could control the script. "Oh, wouldn't it be great if that guy could get the girl right around this time? And in the movies. He could. Anything was possible. Oh, sure, so much was possible in the real world. How many people would say, "How dare you, you, Mr. Canyon. Everything has gone your way. Championships, money. The women. We ALL know about the women. We know about her. Movie star. 36 years old. The stuff of the Playboy Forums. Then there were the others. Handpicked, eager, curious, the adventure of a lifetime. The thrill of spontaneity. The allure. The "bad boy" feeling you had. You, the quiet, unassuming, shy, "nice" young man from the genteel south. "Frankly my dear, I would be happy to screw the hell out of you." Your biggest fear was letting down the people that cared about you. He could just imagine Grandma, "Oh, Danny. I hear such stories about you. That's a shameful thing you do." And he's already heard, in his worst dreams. "Mr. Dan Johnson, you're not a good boy after all." What do people expect from a 25-year-old? It was a phase."

It had been just a few nights since Dan had had a dream. That dream. He was walking with a lame horse and a small wagon. The road was made of mud. Dan was dressed in a beat-up old outfit, with ramshackle homes nearby. On the wagon was a metal milk container. He stopped. So weary, so sad. He looked up to the sky. "Dear God. Did you have to do that? What did Gina do to you? To anyone? Oh, I know, she could be a little difficult, but who couldn't be? Finally, you allowed her some happiness. Love. It's a new concept. A new world. Ok, so you put her with that putz (Dan looks around as if to say "did I just say PUTZ?"). Maybe a better matchmaker. Oh, I'm sorry, it seems you were the matchmaker. He wasn't here to make the rest of us happy, was he? No, he was here to make HER happy. And he did. They were a good match after all. They fit like a glove. Like they were made to order. He looked back to God and then waved. Ok, I'll stop speaking like a tailor and get to the point. Golde always says the same thing to me.

First Gina, then Grandma. It was too much for Grandma. That spirit. That wonderful, wonderful spirit that was Grandma Luccia.

But you know, it started with the wedding. Well, the wedding that never was. Ok, Gina. Marry that man. Marry for love if you must. But give your family the wedding. Allow them that joy. Carole had such plans. Our Lady of Lourdes would have looked so beautiful. So beautiful. Don't throw away the tradition. Dan looked up to sky and yelled out. "TRADITION!"

"But God" Dan continued as Tevye the milkman. "Look what you did to Jimmy. A good man, a good man and yes, a rich man, but what does that matter now? A broken man. All the riches cannot bring back his little Gina. They cannot bring back his mama, and yet, you, you allowed these things to happen. You, who have given us The Ten Commandments. I know, I know. We haven't exactly been following them to the letter. I'm sorry God. Sorry for the ways of the world, but what am I, a poor milkman, supposed to do about that? I know, I know, it's no shame to be poor. Maybe if I were a rich man, I could solve all the problems of the world. Or solve one or two. That would be nice. But no song and dance right now about that. I'm too depressed.

God, all I ask, is please, be kinder to this Minnelli family. Smile upon them. They love each other so much, and they love you. Give this man, Jimmy, something to take his mind away from his grief. He walked into the sunset as violin music played.

Jimmy continued to visit the Minnelli's. Tony had his place now. Still in West Orange. Up Stanford Avenue. That steep street up from Pleasantdale Elementary School. Dan said, "Have fun on the snow days." Tony said, "I don't care. I gotta be close to Mom and Dad." The Llewelyn house seemed so bare, now. So sad and lonely. The music that filled the house. Nobody bothered with it now. Dan missed that. No Dean, no Frank. They used to take walks after dinner, right past Glenmont, the estate of Thomas Edison. You'd never know that the bustling roads of downtown, Orange, Newark, were just outside those gates. Nobody bothered Dan. Even Tony, restless as he was, seemed to enjoy those Llewelyn walks. Gina came, too. Jimmy, in his quiet way, was proud. His dad who never said much. Never told he loved him. Never said he was proud of him, would be proud. Jimmy always took care of his family. That was a man's job. His duty. He could hear his father. "You get a good job, and you work hard. Keep your head on straight. Don't a mess up. Don't stray. Take care of your family. This is what matters in life. That is a man's job. You love God and you appreciate this country. Your momma and I, we come here with nothing. We work hard but we have a chance, and we have freedom. Nothing is promised to you, Jimmy. Remember that. Nothing. God can give and God can take away. But you must take on this responsibility." Billy said many of the same things, in a different way, but it was the same. So much seemed random, a crap shoot, but on the other hand, we had to make our own luck, do the best with what was provided for us, and get back up when we were knocked down. That was the important thing. Because rest assured, we would get knocked down. Except for Dan.

Dan hadn't been knocked down. Many others were. Dan hadn't done enough to help others. But he wanted to really help. Not just tell his financial guy to give the same percentage out this year. They pick a few places. The Knicks have charities. He gave to New York. He gave to Ann Arbor. He gave to Atlanta and nearby Cobb County. He bought new scoreboards for the Wheeler Gym and to the Football team. He gave money to help renovate the gym and they wanted to rename it the Canyon, but Dan asked them not to. He gave to the 9-11 memorial at the Reservation.

For more than a year, Dan had spoken, here and there, to his agent, his financial guy. He had spoken to the Kaufman Family. He had a few informal meetings with a hospital or two, a food bank. It was never a problem. His appearance always drew attention. Sign a few autographs. Shake some hands.

Dan asked questions. He spoke to a few athletes that had foundations. How did they do it? Get started? What did he need to know? He spoke to two lawyers that had that experience. Then, the season started, and he had to play. This was going to be the last season. That's what he said after season five. This was eight and the big contract. The "contract to end all contracts" took place. He didn't feel too bad about it any longer. Seven straight championships, and Dan was working harder than ever, but his body was beginning to speak to him. His knees, his sore hips, his sore shoulders. The permanent scars were fingernails dug in. Nothing major, but they were there. All over.

# Take 1

In a Secaucus, NJ studio, Dan Johnson stood in front of a camera, with a blue screen behind him. His Foundation would be spending $7 million on a 30-second commercial during Super Bowl XL, between Seattle and Pittsburgh, in 2005, just a few months before Dan's retirement.

The blue screen showed a variety of hungry people on the streets.

"Hello, I'm Dan Johnson. My nickname, CANYON, represents to many people a thunderous slam dunk in an NBA game, but there's another word heard around the country that's far scarier. That word is hunger. Did you know that up to 30 million Americans go hungry every day? Many are just like you and me. Hard-working, good people of every background. People who had a bad break, a medical dilemma. People suffering. No American should go hungry.

At the CANYON Foundation, we work hard to help feed hungry Americans. Our goal this year is to buy 500,000 tons of food. That's enough to feed 30 million people for a month. It's a start. We also work to reduce all the waste of food that occurs.

Think of what it would mean for a family to have a nutritious meal every day. You can make a difference. Please donate to the CANYON Foundation and ask your employer to match your donation.

The CANYON Foundation, feeding the hungry and treating sick children, every day."

# Kid in a Candy Shop

The height of Dan's career might have been around 2003. He was married, had his lake house and Canyonville, and the Knicks had just won their sixth title. But in 2006, he was newly retired, just thirty-one, and even though he had arthritis pain, it wasn't to the degree it would be ten years later. He could walk without a limp and could explain to people who asked, "Sure, I've got plenty of bumps and bruises from my playing days." No sweat. He was travelling and the CANYON Foundation was starting to get its act together. Dan had always given millions to charity, but now he had an organized team that answered to him. Well, he had an organization that answered to an Executive Director, and she answered to him. Perfect.

For the next ten years, maybe eight, Dan came into his own. The arthritis was there. A little worse each year, but manageable. There were plenty of Rheumatologists that quietly believed Dan to have only a limited amount of time left, but Dan himself wasn't sure. In any case, he could live out some of his dreams that so many of us wish we could do, that is, if money was absolutely no object.

He had celebrities and regular people to Canyonville, and one that was so amazing, and yet so risky, he did his best to keep it quiet, and for the most part, he succeeded. Dan hired a promotional group to run a contest for parents of kids in one the cancer hospitals, and he called it "ultimate man cave weekend." Any parent with a child in treatment could enter by listing something they'd put in their dream mancave, and the most imaginative idea would win. One of the hospitals in the group was the Cincinnati Children's Hospital, a very special place, and a very special husband in wife, clad in Ohio State gear, entered the competition. Whatever they know or thought about Dan, they disregarded it entirely when sending in the form. From the name CANYONVILE, to Dan's popularity, it wasn't lost on them when the Dad, Charlie Maxwood, said that no Mancave would be complete without a signed Jersey of Archie Griffin, the only two-time Heisman Trophy winner and star for the Buckeyes, but also the hated rival of the University of Michigan Wolverines. Dan himself would pick the winners, and he couldn't wait. Then, he got this request. "What are you going to do?" "You don't understand, I can't have Ohio gear put up to contaminate this wall. "Oh, give me a break," Melanie said. "No, it's a very big deal," Dan said. "Grow up," Melanie said. What about the hospital? "Oh, the hospital is great, top-notch. Fantastic. You don't see me keeping a top hospital from getting the necessary care because they're in the state of Ohio. I'm talking about that school." "Well, here's your chance to act like a man instead of a little kid." Dan thought about it, and several days went by. Finally, he said something to Melanie. "I made some calls and I gave the promotional group the name of twelve winners." "So, how is it going to work." Dan said, "Well, they're doing all the work. They are contacting the winners and sending them a very nice, customized card. Our regular photo, you know the one of you and me, will be on the card. They are arranging the hotels nearby, the airfare, the meals, the transportation, and then on a Saturday night in about six weeks, we'll have them in, Friday afternoon, dinner somewhere in Atlanta at night. Then VIP treatment at the Atlanta Aquarium, lunch over there, and then back up here and a two-hour break. Then, to Canyonville. We'll make them both, each couple, a nice gift bag each, we'll have a couple of local bands here, little rock, little country, BBQ, of course, drinks, and I'll make a small speech about wanting them to have a good time for themselves because they give so much. I'm really excited about it. If it works, maybe we'll do it every year." "That's great, honey, but what about the special mancave prize?" "Look, hon, that guy from Ohio? Good guy, and he won, he was chosen, ok? Terrific couple. They cheer for the wrong school but we want to help their kid get better. That's what it's all about." "Hmmm", said Melanie. "I suppose."

The festivities went off without a hitch. "How great is it," thought Dan, to snap your fingers and make all your little daydreams about helping people come true? All it costs is money. And this one cost around $125,000 for ten couples. "They even flew commercial and were more than thrilled." "Well, not everybody can fly on a private plane all the time, 'Mr. Rocks on Rocks'" (referring to the fictional Millionaire from "The Flintstones" that Melanie and Dan liked to kid each other about.).

The group arrived at CANYONVILLE, most wearing just what the invitation recommended. "Wear anything you/d like to be comfortable and ready to have a great time. We'll be wearing jeans and T-shirts if that helps guide you! Melanie and Dan. The group entered from a nice bus with people standing outside on the patio with champagne cocktails and hor doerves. Dan and Melanie there to greet them.

About an hour and half later, after cocktails, dinner, and some dancing, Dan came up to the group and gave a short speech. He was improving, Melanie noticed.

"Well, everybody, thank you so much for coming tonight. Already Melanie and I count you as friends. You know, we've been so blessed. Things haven't been perfect, but I've been blessed to be able to help others, but it wasn't until my playing days were over that I wanted to get personally involved like what you're seeing tonight. You know, you can give money, and that's wonderful and so needed. For many years, I did just that. But I was hoping for the day when I could put a personal touch on that giving. This was an experiment. Let's see how others would design a man-cave, or what do they call it, Mel? Melanie said "a she-shack". A couple of the men gave out a playful 'yell' but mostly everybody laughed. "And" Dan said "you all gave some great answers" and that's why you're here. We can't put ourselves in your position, but if we can give you just one weekend where you can find a little relief, we want to do it. We know your minds are NEVER off of your little one, and neither are ours. We will keep giving, and giving, until there's never a sick child in this world." The audience applauded and a few wiped tears.

"Now some of the man-cave and she-shack entries were interesting. A Barbie-land inside the she-shack, a full-size basketball court, I like that one, hot tubs, massage chairs, all kinds of art on the wall and old-fashioned ads. And then I got a request that was so outlandish, so obscene, so full of nerve, that I considered stopping the whole contest. Charlie and Sue Maxwood, get on up here!" Charlie and his wife Sue, already laughing, already aware, came up front. "Ok, now I'm going to explain what's going on here. I thought, I thought everybody knew that I was a proud Michigan Wolverine. See that Maize and Blue banner over there. The neon sign across on the other wall that says, "GO BLUE?" Charlie and Sue are laughing. And Charlie's contest proposal? That we put up a Jersey signed by none other than Archie Griffin. ARCHIE GRIFFIN! Just shoot me in my Achilles tendon, man! Now, to anybody born on Mars, Archie Griffin is the only two-time Heisman Trophy winner in history and one of the greatest college football players of all time, who happened to play for Ohio." "Charlie says" "The Ohio State University". Dan chuckles but still says loudly, "OHIO!". "But Charlie", the CANYON Foundation means so much to so many people, and the Children's Hospital of Cincinnati, where your son is, is so important and precious to us, that I am willing to look away while we place, at least for tonight, a signed jersey of Archie Griffin on the wall, and who better than to present that Jersey to you, than Archie Griffin."

Archie Griffin walked out, huge smile on his face, wearing a beautiful suit. Charlie Maxwood fell to his feet in tears, sobbing like a baby. Because yes, it was his hero, Archie Griffin, but because it was a release. Months and months of pain, of watching their little boy go through chemo, suffering. Hell, he was every Buckeye's idol. Charlie had to be helped up while Archie gave him a hug. Now Sue stood, hands over mouth, tears streaming down her face. The tears flowed. It was Archie, it was everything. It was the months of chemo, the pain their son had to endure, his bravery, his smiles and "don't worry Mom and Dad, I'll be okay." The pain that no parent should have to endure.

There was a microphone. Archie came to the microphone. You know, when Dan Johnson personally called me and explained what he wanted to do, I couldn't say no. I just wish your son has a lifetime of running with the ball. Even though the CANYON here is from 'that school up north', as we loved hearing from Coach Hayes, he's doing a good thing, and yes, some things are more important than a game.

Dan said, "Charlie, that Jersey is for you. Aside from the fact that I can't let it hang here at CANYONVILLE, it deserves with a couple of true Buckeye fans. Folks a big hand for Archie Griffin, a class act if there ever was one." We will hang instead a photo of Archie with all of us and put it in an honored place here at CANYONVILLE, where all heroes are welcome. Archie stayed for the remaining hour and half as an honored guest, one of the most honored ever to walk inside CANYONVILLE.

Dan looked at Melanie, who was beaming, dried tears on her face. "This makes it all worth it." He said. "Everything".

Dan could cite dozens of examples of kindness he had the ability to bestow on people, and that's what he called it the few times he had to give a speech and talk about his charitable donations, many of which went unpublicized. He called it "the blessing of being able to bestow kindness on people," but he often changed that or said that "we all can bestow kindness, it didn't take money," and he was right, but medicine and research, and new hospital wings, and donations, containers and truckloads of food, that DID cost money. The taunts, the mockery, maybe it was all worth it, after all.

# The Dream

Dan opened his eyes and found himself walking down a road, somewhere in the desert. In the distance were some mountains and rock formations. It reminded him of many westerns or photos. The sun was just beginning to set, and the western horizon was emitting a burnt-orange hue.

Suddenly out of some shrub walked Billy Barty, just like he had never left. "Billy?" Dan said, shockingly. "Sure, kid, it's me." "I, I don't understand. What's going on?"

"Let's take a walk." "Billy, am I dreaming? Are you really here?" "Sure, kid. It's a dream, AND I'm here. It can be both, you know."

"Billy, if it's a dream, then this is all my imagination." "You, see" Billy lamented. "That's the problem with people. They think they know it all. But, kid, people know very little. One day, you'll see that."

Kid, people can see life. They can experience it. You breathe, you talk, some more than others. That's one reason I like you. You never talked too much. I, of course never learned that lesson too well, but anyway, people can see life, and they can see death, but they don't understand it. Oh, some think they got it all figured out. Life, death, God, the stars and planets, and they've got some of it figured out, but they're just scratching the surface, kid. There's so much they don't know, and it's cause they're scared, kid. I was there, once." "I'm there right now, Billy." Dan said. "Sure you are, kid. And it's normal, but you don't know anything either. So, the secret is controlling what you do know. Worry never solved anything, kid. It's time you learned that." "Yeah, but Billy, isn't it normal to be afraid of the unknown?" "Sure, kid, it's normal, but what does that matter? Does it help? Is being almost nine feet tall normal?"

"No", it's not, Billy, and I've been reminded of that my whole life." "Look kid, I love ya, but cry me a river. You're one of the most exceptional human beings ever to live on this planet." "But what did I do. I was born freakishly tall." "Yes", Billy said, and I was born freakishly short, but it was the stuff between my ears that determined my happiness."

"That still doesn't answer the question about death, Billy." "Nope, and kid, you're not gonna get that answer in this dream." "Then why are you here? You're no longer alive." "Kid, you're thinking of me right now." "I think about you every day, Billy." "I know you do, kid. So, I'm alive because your memory keeps me alive. I'm in your mind, in your heart. Gina, she's alive, and others, because you and others keep her alive." That's the best example of everlasting life that I can give you."

"Anyway, kid, I see you finally found your purpose." "Yes, Billy, I think so. There's so much work to do. I wake up and I'm busy all day." "Well, I'm happy for you, kid. Scoring baskets and winning medals and having secret rendezvous with beautiful women is nice", but so is helping people have a meal, or helping a young cancer patient." Billy was mortified, "Billy, you know about the women?" "Look, kid. It's your dream. You wanted me to know. Don't worry, I forgive you. I don't approve, but I forgive you."

But Billy, are you real? Are you really here, in my dream? I thought you were gone." "Kid, Billy said. Does it matter? I'm in your thoughts, your dreams, and your heart. You keep me alive. So do others. My family and friends. I'm lucky, I can be found in movies and videos. 65 years' worth. So, the way I look at it, I live.

Anyway, kid, I know you've always struggled to find purpose. But now you're helping people in need. I've been watching. And because you love it, you speak up more. You've transformed yourself. Keep pushing for more."

"Hey kid, I've got to go, but I wanted to let you know that you've made a difference. Think about it for a minute. All the records, the medals, the fame, and one day people might just remember you more for the Canyon Foundation, and that will still be around after you're gone."

"Thanks, Billy."

"Bye, kid, and Dan?" "Yes, Billy?" Dan asked. "The pies in your face? That was fun".

Dan awoke, took a deep breath, and felt more at peace than he ever had in his life.

# Tony's Hometown

Tony said something out of nowhere, but it became obvious it was to be something he had been thinking about for a while.

"Hey, Mr. Big thinker. I wrote something yesterday. I was bored. Maybe I'll be a speech writer." "Oh yeah?" asked Dan. "About what, beer?" Tony snarled. "No, wise ass. About West Orange." "Am I supposed to listen to it?" Dan couldn't tell that Dan was secretly serious about this. "I wouldn't waste it on someone like you. You're too big for your britches nowadays. Too big to listen to the little people in life." "Ok", Dan said. "Sorry, I want to hear it, really." "Eh", said Tony. "I'll think about it." "Oh, c'mon", said Dan. "Now I'm curious." "Ok", Tony said. "You laugh and this can flies your way."

"Aren't you going to stand?" Dan said "No", said Tony. So, he stayed lying down, looking up at the sky, handwritten paper above him.

*West Orange has been a town to many. It's in the shadows of a great city, a city that can be seen from our highest peaks. A city that's famous, with big names and bright lights. A city that beckons for the world.*
*But West Orange is a refuge. A place to call home. To unwind, to raise a family in peace and safety. It doesn't advertise its boundaries. In fact, before you know it, you're in Verona, or Roseland, or Livingston. It's just another small town, here for a long time and then grew in the years following World War Two, the "good war."*

*But West Orange is much more to its inhabitants. A place Edison chose to call home, and Edison gave light to the world. A place of Astronauts and actors, musicians, and Olympians. Raised to be good citizens, good Americans. A place of Turtle Back and Eagle Rocks, parks, reservations, and "Pleasant Valley Sundays".*

*West Orange will never acquire the luster of Paris, Rome, or that famous island we can see from atop our Reservation. But it doesn't want that. It just wants to be a quiet home that perhaps helps launch the dreams of ordinary people, to something great.*

*I asked a wise old resident.*
*To whose words, I will defer.*
*Who said, there are two types of people in the world, my friend,*
*Those who are from the town of West Orange,*
*And those who wish they were."*

Dan paused and then said, "That's called 'West Orange, town of wonder.' I read it at your library last month when I was bored." "HEY!! I don't like that! I poured my heart and soul out". "Hey Tony?" Dan said. Tony looked away, somewhat embarrassed that he "opened himself up". "Screw you" Tony said. "No Dan, seriously. That was excellent". The way Dan said excellent. That choice of words, for some reason, convinced Tony that Dan was sincere. "Yeah, thanks."

"Send it to the library on Main Street. They'll want it. Maybe they'll put it in a book." "It'll never go in a book," Tony said, realistically.

"No," Dan agreed. "But it was damn good."

# It's Canyonville II!

Canyonville surpassed any dreams that Melanie had for Dan, for her, for their friends, and for others. What started out as a fun little present with lots of extra stuff that lots of extra money could build, turned out to be nearly as famous as Studio 54, and the best thing of all, is that it became known primarily as an event center for benefits, for The Canyon Foundation. So many stars had been there already in only three years. First, Dan was as famous as them all. Secondly, it was for a great cause. How could anybody say no? It was great publicity, and often, it was a "benefit", as Dan made sure that regular working "stiffs" made excellent money. The Foundation would pay for it. Marcy Goodman demanded that, but Dan always found a way to pitch in one way of another. If it wasn't money, it was a gift of some other kind. "Live and Canyonville" raised millions, put hospitals and food banks on the map. There was nothing but love to Canyonville.

Dan came to joke, while strolling along their lakefront property, that Canyonville was so popular, that "wouldn't it be fun if we had a smaller shed out of sight, where we could "REALLY" have a good time? It wouldn't be nearly as fancy. People could smoke cigars, or "whatever". It would be run-down but extremely cool. There would be absolutely no tv cameras, no live events, no benefits. The kind of "man-cave" that normal people had. "Yeah", said Dan, but normal or not, I would still make it cool. Dan had bought some extra video games that he had to store two miles away at a storage facility, that he was "rotating" out.

He had developed into an amateur collector of classic '80s video games after making friends with a few guys in the industry. They did it for money. Dan did it for fun. He would love to place 3-4 of those games in the beaten-up, smaller mancave. "What would we call it?" Melanie asked. They stopped and smiled at each other. So many fun examples, and this was the fun part of their marriage:

- ➤ Here's looking at you kid, lounge.
- ➤ The family cantina.
- ➤ The Wolverine Cave
- ➤ The he-man woman haters club
- ➤ The dog pound (or "dawg" pound)
- ➤ The Caddy Shack
- ➤ Tara (Dan didn't like this one)
- ➤ "Tora, Tora, Tora" (Melanie hated this one)
- ➤ The Reservation
- ➤ Down the shore lounge
- ➤ Pal's Cabin South (Tony would like it, Melanie didn't)

They decided that the best, simplest name should, and would be, "Canyonville II".


Dan asked Melanie if he could "head up the job" this time. He contacted the same builder as before and they sat down. They would be a 2-week job. This really could be bought "off the lot" of a home improvement center, and that's what they did.

Dan decided on a 30x30, or 900 square foot barn. CANYONVILLE was 3500 square feet. It would be new, sturdy, well-insulated, with heating and air, but inside, it would resemble nothing like what Melanie did. Dan was excited and got to work.

Two weeks later, Dan unveiled it to Melanie. "Now, you can make changes to anything. This is not CANYONVILLE." "Quit stalling, let me see it!". "This has been so much fun!" Dan said. "Quit stalling!!" Melanie yelled.

Dan opened the door and turned on the lights. There were leather chairs and couches. None of them new. All totally worn and comfortable looking as well. She saw four video games that meant nothing to her. Space Invaders, Asteroids, Tron, and Crystal Castles. Dan said he had about 15 more in the storage space and of course, 15 at Canyonville itself.

Along the wall was a large humidor cabinet. Dan didn't smoke but this would be the real talked-about item by certain athletes and celebrities. Dan would soon get it stocked after visiting a store in Atlanta that could help him. Along the other wall was a bar, but a home bar that any honest, hard-working guy that was "doing well" might buy for his basement, for $2,000-$3,000. It had some scratches on it here or there. It was worn, and perfect. You could fit plenty of bottles behind it. Right behind it was a worn but perfectly fine refrigerator. There would be no beer kegs or taps. Hell no. This was a real man-cave. Inside, Dan would stock cans and bottles, and plenty of liquor for the bar. On the wall were two TVs. Next to that, an old-fashioned white projector screen and the pièce de resistance, on a simple, brown table, about eight feet in front of the screen, a BELL & HOWELL 8mm Projector - Model 253A -

with Take Up Reel, just like his dad and Jimmy Minnelli would have had in 8th grade U.S. History class, watching "Victory at Sea". It was beautiful. Dan added a stereo, and a beat-up, old phonograph. There was one of those little racks that stocked 45's, and here is where he got lucky and found a dealer in New York that sent him 50 of some of the best bands from the '60s and 70's. Okay, Dan overpaid the guy, $5,000, because he knew it was Dan, but Dan had to have it. Among the tunes:

➢ Slow Ride, Foghat
➢ Ride, Captain Ride, Blues Image
➢ In the Summertime, Mungo Jerry
➢ Woman, Woman, Gary Pucket and the Union Gap
➢ Spinning Wheel, Blood Sweat and Tears
➢ Gypsies, Tramps, and Thieves, Cher
➢ The Wreck of the Edmund Fitzgerald, Gordon Lightfoot
➢ Crocodile Rock, Elton John
➢ One Bad Apple, The Osmond's
➢ I want You Back, The Jackson Five
➢ Easy Come, Easy Go, Bobby Sherman
➢ There's a Kind of Hush, Herman's Hermits
➢ Indian Reservation, Paul Revere and the Raiders
➢ Billy, Don't be a Hero, Bo Donaldson and the Heywoods
➢ Band on the Run, Paul McCartney and Wings
➢ Candida, Tony Orlando and Dawn
➢ There's Got to be a Morning After – Maureen McGovern

It should be noted that most all of these songs were recorded before Dan was even born, so this wasn't of songs in "his era", but this was vintage Dan. This wasn't a concert hall. This was the "real deal". Something money couldn't buy, although it did. A place Tony and Dan could have come to if the Eagle Reservation was too crowded, or it was raining. On the wall were some vintage posters that Dan found. There wasn't a lot of room, but a few movie posters, including Caddy Shack and Blazing Saddles. Melanie loved it.

In two weeks, Tony and Brittany came down and Dan and Melanie surprised them. "Guys, CANYONVILLE belongs to the world. It has outgrown us." "Ok", Tony said, "Something's coming, what is it." "We're closing CANYONVILLE down." "What?" Brittany screamed. "But you and Mel love this place!?" Tony didn't buy it for a second. "Brit, there's full of crap. What's going on?" They said, "Walk this way." Around the trees about 30 feet, done deliberately, where you wouldn't see it, was the new shed. "So," said Tony. "You keep your riding lawnmower in this?" "No", said Dan. "This is CANYONVILLE II. Come inside. Honestly, it wasn't overwhelming compared to CANYONVILLE, that was point. Melanie said, "Can I explain? This is the real mancave. Away from the crowds. Nothing fancy, but everything you need and want. Something we would scrimp and save for. Second-hand bar and refrigerator. Cold beer in cans. An old projector poster, like we were back in middle school. Where a couple would splurge for a couple of old video games. Not the mega-rich husband of mine, but a hard-working, great guy and his great wife or girlfriend. To them, this would be it! They made it! It's where they would come to confide in each other, to bring real friends, not corporate sponsors. Where YOU can come. It's all here, but it's not bathed in spotlights. It's real.

CANYONVILLE is fabulous. It's bigger than all of us now and it isn't going anywhere. This is for family. You are family. It's for close friends. Brittany finally got it and yelled out as only Brittany can do. "Holy crap. I'm shitting in my pants. This is genius. I love it and we're the first to see it?" Tony said, "Brit has a way with words and that's why I love her. You're right, this is a stroke of genius. Of course, we won't tell anyone."

In a year, everybody knew about CANYONVILLE II, and the joke went like this:

"You're not really anybody, until you've been to CANYONVILLE.
But only a chosen few
Get to see CANYONVILLE II.


The only thing better than CANYONVILLE II was the urban legends that came out of it. There were the sex stories (but Dan and Melanie got first dibs on that). There was the story that one of the biggest trades in NBA history was settled by two owners and two GMs in CANYONVILLE II while a large benefit was going on at CANYONVILLE (Dan knew that one was true). There were proposals and break-ups. There was some damage done now and then which pissed off Dan. Much of the time, people just wanted to see it, and admire the simplicity of it. Dan would sometimes take them, turn on the light, say "well, this is it,". At first, people seemed disappointed, but they were the elite, the wealthy. When Dan felt like it, he'd explain how it was simple, like they all used to be, before they could afford the Bentley's, the vacation homes, and then, they got it. Then, the light would go off, and everyone would return to the lights and glamour, and stress, of CANYONVILLE and the world that they lived in.

# The Long Road

Dan began to experience the earliest effects of rheumatoid arthritis (RA) as a player with the Knicks, only he didn't know it, and while doctors may had suspected it, given his size, it wasn't disclosed or discussed in great length until Dan retired in 2005.

Playing in the NBA was a grind. An 82-game schedule, all the practices, and the day-to-day battles against very big, strong men, even if Dan was the biggest of them all. Normal aches and pains were part of the game, and later, the life, as with other sports.

Dan's longest, most painful, and most private battle was with RA. It wasn't something he discussed outside of a doctor's office except for the very general and obvious, canned response. "C Man, how's your health, those joints of yours?" "Well, any player can tell you that the years of pounding on a court, or a field, or a mat can have an effect on your body that haunts you for the rest of your life, and I feel it like most anyone else." "Yes, but many believe that your extraordinary height has only exasperated the situation." Dan would only go as far as saying, "No doubt." Since he rarely gave interviews, during his playing days or after, few reporters had a chance to even ask the questions, and it was obvious enough that Dan's height may be hiding a host physical ailments that were finally showing up, at his old age of thirty-five.

Dan had seen a rheumatologist as early as 2002, his sixth year with the Knicks. Through the years, he had been prescribed NSAID's like ibuprofen and diclofenac. Later, a host of Disease-modifying anti-rheumatic drugs, or DMARDS, biological therapies, and JAK Inhibitors, to reduce inflammation and pain. Some had serious side effects, and Dan felt like he was forever doing a balancing act between pain relief and side effects.

Even Melanie didn't get a lot of information from Dan, but the grimaces leading to poor sleep, sweating, and even soft grunts of pain became a daily occurrence by the time Dan turned forty. Melanie understood and would eventually have two knee replacements from her days at Old Dominion. But Dan seemed to have pain everywhere. She also knew that RA could have damaging effects on the body's organs, including the heart, but Dan said little. But she always suspected that he knew more than he was leading on to.

She urged him to spend as much time as possible at the lake house. The foundation was in good hands.

Still, at 43, Dan had a very youthful face, and his major endorsement money was as strong as ever, in fact, some stronger. Ads for a major financial investment company and liquor company only benefitted from Dan's retirement status. He seemed more charismatic, mature yet still youthful. Not the awkward and clumsy twenty-two-year-old.

When Dan limped into the studio, well, he was a former championship athlete who now had arthritis, like many of the best. Nobody was asking him to post up and shoot. He had an impeccable reputation. Hell, he should have been doing commercials for pain relievers. Who could speak more personally about it than the CANYON?

But Dan was fighting a personal battle, and even Tony didn't hear much about it. By the time Tony's third child was born, around 2011, the Eagle Rock hangout was history, but for Tony, Britt and the kids, the trips to North Georgia and the Lakehouse continued. The music concerts at Canyonville also continued, stronger than ever, but without Dan as a presence, usually. As he aged, he let loose the reigns of control more. Canyonville was legendary.

The occasional "A look back at the CANYON: Dan Johnson" reminded the old and young alike just how dominant he was, and interest simply popped right up again. The more anyone would revisit Dan and all his championships, it was almost too good to believe, and Dan himself wasn't that old, just retired. So dominant at such a young age. Dan didn't talk much but there was no shortage of former Judo players, wrestlers, and basketball players. Many seemed almost desperate to convince the audience how great Dan was, and that was coming from the experts.

The CANYON Burger still sold like hot cakes at The Brown Jug ("Home of the CANYON Burger") in Ann Arbor, as did Wolverine and Knick jerseys. A sign on Cobb Parkway in Georgia and on nearby Interstate 75 proudly announced. "Welcome to Marietta, home of the CANYON, Dan Johnson."

Dan did a free commercial for the "Historic Preservation Commission" of Marietta, GA, walking around the Square, passing the fountain at Glover Park, the Strand Theater, mentioning various businesses by name, walking into the Gone with the Wind Museum at Brumby Hall. The interest in everything Marietta, and especially the Square, skyrocketed. Visitors from as far away as Japan suddenly wanted to learn more about anything that Dan Johnson, the CANYON, found interesting. Businesses began to call the rise in business around the Square, "The Johnson effect." Dan was pleased that he could help his hometown.

But by his late 40s, the pain advancing, and the joys of life severely diminishing, Dan rarely left his Flowery Branch lake house. He kept the New York apartment more for Melanie and trips for her and her friends, for Tony to come into the city, but for few others. By now, there weren't many others, anyway.

At one time, a few years earlier, Melanie had dreamed of a big 50 birthday bash for Dan at CANYONVILLE, but not anymore. Little good could come from that now.

# The Trip Around the World

Dan had told his agent and publicist nearly a year in advance that when he retired in late June of 2005, that he and Melanie wanted to travel the world for several months, beginning spring 2006, perhaps ten months out. Maybe they could combine it with some business, as in endorsements. It would be a lot of work, but they thought, also fun. "Remember all these things are a way for you to earn more money, so unless you suddenly have a dislike for the stuff, let's start working it out.

They began to put the word out. First, Vickers had hired a smart new ad executive who came up with what they all thought would be a winning campaign. It would be a series of commercials under the working name of "New Career" in it, Dan would announce retirement and announce that he had always wanted to try a new career.

The first was to be called, "Run for the Hills." Dan would tell his commercial "agent" that he wanted to be a jockey. Of course, nobody thought that would be a good idea, and when he got to the track, it should horses lined up by a horse trainer and "talked to", suddenly they all bolted, running away as fast as they could. The trainer tells another guy at the track, "they were told that one of them would be The Canyon's horse."

In Another, Dan is told to slow down and do something less taxing, like bowling. He breaks pins and people go running for cover, so another bad idea. Others were being written up. Ballet dancer, swimmer, bobsled rider, surfer.

They appreciated the heads-up because they wanted to start taping in three months. That, plus some shorter print ads and a few more commercials, and they'd have more than a year's worth of marketing while Dan travelled. The CANYON shoe campaign was never to be interrupted. It was a meal ticket for too many people. So, this problem was solved.

The "New Career" series was a huge hit. People everywhere talked about, and there was a new one released every three weeks, which is what media experts said was just the right amount of time people would wait in anticipation before beginning to forget. Then, a new commercial would come, and everybody would get all excited again. "What sports this time will the CANYON try to play?" Other celebrities added to the commercials, in boxing, baseball, football, hockey, even non-athletics like acting, singing, dancing. They had a team of comedy writers because the commercials were driving sales up to record numbers. Everybody was happy. Even Dan was having a good time. It was an acting job, and Dan loved the arts. He'd love to be an actor if he only "looked normal."

Dan had a deal going with a Japanese liquor company that paid handsomely, and they would be happy to accommodate Dan. In fact, they had an idea for a "CANYON visits Japan, month-long trip, sponsored by Ikari, the liquor company. Ikari translated roughly into "Fury" in Japanese. The Marketing Manager for the Ikari brand would put together the schedule, line everything up from TV appearances to even a game show. Dan said, "no Judo matches, or anything physical." Ikari was a major partner in

"Canyon Productions", the endorsement and entertainment arm of Dan's portfolio, handled by his agent, his publicist, his lawyer, and Dan himself. The Japanese absolutely loved it, asking "where will the CANYON be next?" People loved the CANYON because he was so different, because he was a judo champion, humble in victory as well defeat. His Ikari endorsements were doing wonders for the brand." Dan brought about $250,000 worth of gifts with him, for the various dignitaries he would meet, from the Prime Minister to other celebrities. Simply meeting and being seen with Dan was a big feather in their cap with the Japanese public. Dan took more than one course in proper etiquette, so that he would always say the right things.

Dan and Melanie would travel to China for pleasure (unless a business venture could be included, to India, Greece, Italy, and other countries in Europe). They would come home and then travel to Russia, for pleasure and business, to Norway and Sweden, to Iceland, and then home.

Dan told his agent, publicist and some music people he knew that he wanted to "stock pile" a few "Evening at Canyonville" specials that could benefit charities. Dan and Melanie would be at the Lakehouse and make their normal appearance. Dan liked to introduce the evening's festivities, briefly, and then get out of the way. There might be an MC for the night.

One he loved was something he himself put together, the HBCU Showcase. Dan loved jazz, and he called the President of a major Historically Black College and Universities President. People were amazed that the

CANYON would be calling them for anything. They always got excited, and few people knew of Dan's love of jazz. Along with his agent and some Presidents, an evening of jazz was conceived and would take place at Canyonville. One or two colleges would be featured, typically with their jazz bands, then professional musicians, then a chance for the college bands to play with professionals. The hour-long special would include a commercial on the school, and a contribution to their scholarship fund. Since it was only a conception, Dan called everybody back and told them that he wanted to "fast-track" the series, so that they could have eight taped over the next year, and air four each year. Plans were put in place, a producer was chosen, and a timeline was put in place.

There would be a "Canyonville Comedy Showcase" with major and upcoming starts, so Dan wanted eight of those taped before they left on their travel. All in all, there were plans to have 24 specials over ten months. That meant about 2-3 per month over the next ten months.

Dan wanted to maximize his earning potential from July 2005 to December 2010, when he was 35. He would assess all of this in June of 2005, which seemed to always be the month of decisions on things. Melanie would laugh at how he planned out his life. She told friends, "He's always in a rush to get all these big projects done and then move on to the next. I don't know what his rush is."

Dan, letting his infinite, fertile mind stretch out, asked Melanie about places to travel to. Melanie mentioned Paris, Israel, Amsterdam, Egypt and the Nile, Ireland, all places of great beauty, intrigue, and historical significance.

Dan, on the other hand, got a little more adventurous. "Well, I would like to see all those places. I would also like to visit Point Barrow, Alaska and swim in the Artic Ocean, Iceland, Nuuk, Greenland." "Where?" Melanie asked and chuckled. "Well,", Dan said. "If not right in Nuuk, then in the greater Nuuk metropolitan area." He continued, Victoria Falls, Zimbabwe, in Africa, take a boat through the Panama Canal, ride a dune buggy in the Saraha Desert, and Antarctica." "Is that all?" asked Melanie, with her head cocked "Oh", said Dan, excitedly. "Explore the caves in the rock of Gibraltar and see if the monkeys will try to pick pocket me. They aren't monkees." "Oh, no?" Melanie asked. "No", said Dan. "They're Barbary Macaque Apes, and they're very important to the history of Gibraltar, which I'm sure you know is a territory of Great Britain but is on the tip of the Iberian Peninsula. The locals say that "if the monkeys disappear from Gibraltar, so will the British. Mel, did you know that?" Danny, Melanie said, did you know that you are the only person who can score 50 points in an NBA game and then lecture the entire arena of 19,694 on the significance of monkeys on Gibraltar?" Melanie asked. "Apes", Dan corrected.

In any event, they had a lot to do in the next year. Foundation business, endorsements, and travel plans. Dan felt happy and busy. He hoped Melanie felt the same way.

# Spread the Wealth

The Canyon Foundation was more work, and more rewarding, than Dan could ever have managed. Politics remained the biggest challenge. "Scratching backs" in order to get commitments, and grow the Foundation, was something very alien to Dan's personality, and now, 94% of all donations made their way to twenty organizations: Ten hospitals and ten food banks. Naturally, this opened a can of worms. Groups were left out. What did the Canyon have against the greater Columbus, OH food bank? What could you expect from a guy that attended "that school up north?"

Dan chose the institutions based on his own research. He took ten of the largest cities and ten of the leading research hospitals devoted to finding cures for cancer and for treating children. This meant that many fine organizations were left out, but Dan realized that he could not save the world all by himself, and gradually, he learned to dismiss the politics and give some very direct answers. "I want to control where the money of this Foundation goes. I want it to be concentrated among twenty very well-run organizations. They are held to high standards as to how they use the money. If they do not meet certain annual criteria, they will be replaced. But even that would yield to executive decisions made by more knowledgeable people, in non-profits and in medical and food distribution areas. If Dan wanted results, he'd have to meet people halfway, and get advice, and he learned to do that.

But if Dan wanted Fortune 500 companies to offer employee withdrawals to help the CANYON Foundation, they wanted to see that money go to work in their communities. Eventually, the list went from 20 to 53 organizations, over the course of ten years. Dan didn't like it, but his board had many discussions on the topic, and took a pragmatic approach. It was an honor to be a board member of the Canyon Foundation. Dan asked for, and got, some of the nation's finest leaders to make up the 12-person board. This included CEO's, a retired General, and a former Presidential Cabinet Member. The Foundation took on a political element in spite of Dan's naïve thinking, but it also paved the way for a massive influx of money over the years, and that DID come from the "CANYON" name. People wanted to be associated with Dan and his efforts.

Dan became a different person whenever his actions would benefit the Foundation. He would go on television talk shows and have humorous stories about sports ready to go, with the prior agreement that all appearances included an on-screen note about how to give to the Foundation. "The Canyon Foundation is saving lives, Jimmy", Dan would say. Nothing I ever did as an athlete can compare to feeding people and fighting cancer in children."

Dan made commercials and print ads. He'd easily poke fun at himself if it raised awareness. He had an ongoing campaign, "Fighting hungry and disease is a tall order," he'd very willingly admit. With your tax-deductible gift to the Canyon Foundation, your dollars buy food, help take care of young children, and Foundation research." He donned a generic basketball uniform in another spot, and said, "Some charities waste money. At the Canyon Foundation, 94% of our money goes directly to food banks and hospitals. We audit their activity personally and BLOCK any waste." Of course, he blocks another's shot. We report where all our money, YOUR money, goes. Ask your employer to join the cause and of they'll match your donation. The Canyon Foundation, because fighting hunger and disease is a tall order. Won't you help today?"

There wasn't a day the Dan didn't speak to his executive director, and he continued to push hard for endorsements, even as his playing days were long over.

Dan put a prominent Black rapper on the board, expressly for the purposes of appealing to the Black community. When new recipients were added, there was usually a political element to it, but at its core, the bottom line was that if the Foundation could feed another hungry person, would it matter if they were in Oakland or Mobile?

Dan was happy that his board wanted to give back, and no personal request was denied. "Your grandson's birthday party? I'll be there. Your son's high school reunion? I'll be there." The Foundation was taking on a life of its own.

The Canyon shoe line was earning $3 billion a year, which meant that Dan and Melanie were taking in $150 million annually. When that was added to other endorsement deals, when Dan reached 40, ten years after his retirement, he was earning over $175 million a year, and had a net worth of $1.6 billion dollars. His budget for the Canyon Foundation was 10% of his gross salary, to pay for salaries and expenses, so he donated over $17 million a year. His original five employees were now at eleven. The board was paid for 100% of expenses, travel to meetings and all accommodations for their quarterly meetings. His employees were handsomely paid. Dan also paid bonuses based on several factors. Of course, the ability to bring in more money was one. Controlling expense was another. If they could move that 94% rate to 95%, they would get more money. Dan gave them opportunities to double their pay , all coming from Dan's account. Treating their staff so well made them incredibly loyal to Dan.

Dan got to be the "good cop", but he nodded two bad cops, and both of those fell to women. Dan's Executive was Marcy Goodman. A Harvard graduate, with a reputation for organization, the Foundation was her baby, and she ran it with a passion almost surpassing Dan's. It was Dan's Foundation, but not if you asked Marcy Goodman, and if Dan ever dismissed Marcy for any reason short of criminal conduct, it would cost Dan dearly. If any company had a significant request, they had to run it be Marcy, and Marcy had her own assistant, so depending on the group, they first had to go through Amy Riggins, and she was no cakewalk, either. Amy was herself, a Duke graduate and at 42 years old, was sick of the bullshit of the corporate world. At a salary of $275,000 a year, plus bonuses and perks, it was a nice package for an assistant, but after all, what's in a name? Amy had been a group Vice President for a major corporation before she landed at the Canyon Foundation, and now she was fulfilled.

Dan made such a ridiculous amount of money, and it was only increasing. Paying 10% for his Foundation, was like ordinary people having a daily coffee habit.

Eventually, other countries wanted to be associated with the Canyon Foundation, even adopting the name, outright. The Board, of which both Dan and Marcy were members, decided that it would be impossible to properly audit and prevent malfeasance overseas. Yet, they saw the appeal of how an international group could benefit them, so Goodman asked, "Why can't we expand by choosing groups ourselves?" So, a test began in Canada. A Canadian Director would be chosen with the task of putting together a listing of hospitals and food banks. They didn't want to stray from that. In addition, it was decided that Dan could not and should not pay any more of his personal wealth, so that international groups had to be "self-funding" with an administrative rate not to exceed 8% of its donations.

The Canyon Foundation got to be so large that Dan could not control all its moving parts. He learned that helping people on a massive scale took a lot of work. Changes in the bylaws were made as needed, and Dan's own authority had been compromised in an effort to make the Foundation more successful. What he would not budge on was the name "Canyon" itself. Even though he was against the name originally, and always wanted his friends to call him Dan, that name told the world who he was. The Canyon WAS Dan Johnson, and he owned it. Dan took care of his own, but he owned that name. Therefore, there was a paragraph in the by-laws that just stipulated that at any time, for any reason, Dan could remove the name "Canyon". He could not stop the Foundation from operating thereafter, under a different name, however.

Dan and Ann Karlsson shared the proceeds from the logo. She invented it, and now she was wealthy from that. Dan made over $10 million a year from revenue generated from that logo, and he took that money and split it evenly among the towns of West Orange, NJ, Ann Arbor, MI, and Marietta, GA. That was over $3 million per year to Foundation emergency medical services for every cop and fire fighter in those towns. If a cop had a sick child, the Canyon police and fire Foundation paid their expenses. He extended this program to Flowery Branch, GA in the third year and chipped in enough so that each town received $3 million per year.

Once a year, Dan hosted a police and firefighter's appreciation weekend in West Orange, Marietta, and Ann Arbor. There would be a 3-hour BBQ on both Saturday and Sunday, to allow everybody to attend. The entire immediate family could attend. There was a band, and the favorite part was the raffle, in which there were about 50 winners. Each weekend cost Dan about $125,000, a drop in the bucket for him that Dan looked so forward to, that Melanie had to yell at him the days before to "calm down". Each weekend was exciting in its own way. In West Orange, the event was held, where else, at the Eagle Rock Reservation. The Minnelli's were honored guests, as were the mayors and town councils of each town, like John McKeon in West Orange. Dan was always able to get a couple of celebrities to come. The dress code was strictly jeans or shorts, and t-shirts. It was catered, and with a "team building" staff for games.

The raffles were so much fun that Dan sat down with a paid group to plan it. Some prizes were simple, some in the middle, with the grand prize being a trip for the family, up to eight, all expenses paid to Hawaii. The winners all cried, and even Dan held back tears. Everybody there got a "Canyon Cap", and Dan Johnson was an absolute hero in all three towns. Let's just say that nobody can recall him getting a speeding ticket. Plus, Tony, and later his family, went to all three parties. The media covered the event, which gave more free publicity to the Canyon Group's main charity arm.

# The Best Decade

Dan, for the few people that knew him best, and that was an extremely short list, was a thinker, often to his own detriment. He lived part of his life in a constant dream state that was part Hollywood, part history, part reality, and part of his own mind. Symbolism and words meant a lot to him. It's why he was constantly applying movie quotes to his life, almost always in private, for he had little confidence that people would have the decency and intelligence to be able to apply it. These were his own quiet thoughts, as he wouldn't dream of insulting anyone unless he thought they had it coming.

This is why Dan could understand the code of respect and honor in the Godfather, even if it was about organized crime. It's why Gary Cooper choked him up every time he recited Lou Gehrig's "luckiest man" speech, even though he had seen it 100 times, and it's why young Roddy McDowell clanged his silverware on his plate, so Donald Crisp, playing his father, would understand that even if his entire family left the dinner table in objection to a family quarrel, young Huw, his youngest son, was still sitting there, at the end of the table. That was in the movie "How Green was my Valley", and Gwillyn Morgan, played by Donald Crisp, said without even looking up, "Yes, my son, I know you are there." Roddy McDowell's character smiled, knowing that his show of respect to his father was recognized. Dan could not watch that scene without feeling the emotion rise in his throat and his eyes mist. Most others could not understand the importance of symbolism, of small acts. It is why Jimmy Minnelli once told him in private, just off the cuff, "You see, Danny, this is my family, and I am the leader of this family. I owe my children my guidance, and they may not always understand it when they are young, but I must have faith that it is still for the best, and maybe they WILL understand it someday, and even use it when they raise their own children. But what I have to say to them stays here, within the family. I have never made a practice out of embarrassing them in front of others, whether it's their friends, or teachers, coaches, strangers, whatever. Discipline out of love is being a good parent. Discipline in public is humiliation. Understand the difference for when you are a father someday." It's something Bill might say, or Scott Maynard, or his dad, for he could not remember his dad ever embarrassing him in public. Good people often shared the same, universal thoughts.

Dan felt like he understood his life. Maybe not so much when he was younger, but by his teens, he would daydream about it. He would dominate in the three sports he chose. He could tell how dominant he was. If anything, he would have to make "accommodations", especially in the one team sport, basketball, so that others wouldn't "feel bad". It was why he preferred wrestling and Judo, where he could control outcomes better, punish his opponents more, and not have to "share". Alone on the mat. He liked that. But the big money was in basketball. He dreamed of Olympic Gold, NCAA championships, pro basketball greatness, all of it, by the time he was twelve. He knew he would play a full four years in college against the advice of many, and he decided he would only play five years in the NBA. This was changed to eight years, due to team and peer pressure, and pressure from fans.

Once Dan retired from the Knicks, and he had the money he needed to totally direct his own life, he was able to find the happiness he seemed to lack, despite his fame. Most of that time was devoted to travel and to his Foundation. Melanie could visit the popular places more often, like London, Paris, Rome. Dan could visit Alaska, Greenland, Russia, the Amazon, the Panama Canal, and he took three weeks to hire a group that took him all around the islands in the South Pacific, to visit the sites of World War Two battles; Guadalcanal in the Solomon Islands, the Bataan Peninsula, Okinawa, and even though the tour group told Dan that he wouldn't be able to visit Iwo Jima, Dan made a few calls to Japanese contacts, and it was arranged. It was all done under the agreement that Dan "wanted to show respect" to all the fallen, which certainly wasn't a lie. It was just a matter of trial and error. The Japanese stationed on the island were ecstatic. Dan asked some questions and found a way to bring the proper gifts. In between, Dan would stay in touch with his agent, Mike, about dates for endorsement deals. Those were important for Dan to continue. More money meant more security, more contributions for Dan, more help for friends and "new" friends.

Dan was only in his thirties, and was on regular pain medication, but could still get around reasonably well, but it wouldn't last for long. These ten years, with Melanie, and free from all the competition, would wind up to be the best in their lives.

# Live from Canyonville

Canyonville, in the next few years, became legendary. Little would Melanie know that her man-cave idea would be perfect for benefits as well as a place producers and bands would love taping in. The platform stage fit about eight musicians, there was already professional lighting on the ceiling, it had the games, even the beautiful lake background that tv cameras could pan out to. The patio was loved during warm or cool nights. The grills, the fire-pits. It was where everyone wanted to be.

Dan's height and basketball career was the catalyst for much good. That was something he and Melanie would discuss lying in bed, or at the boat dock, where they had twelve Adirondack chairs sitting inches from the water, for themselves or guests. The dock itself had a quiet guest room on top that many people loved to use. "Well, some good things finally came out of my freak show appearance."

Some of the biggest bands in the world found their way to Canyonville, usually for a benefit, as Dan's Canyon Foundation poster was put up on the wall. Even in interviews, reporters would say "Have you played Canyonville?" A British band from Manchester replied, "Oh yeah sure, once for a benefit, and the other for a private party. Bloody amazing place. Ian ran naked into the lake there one time."

It became common to hear an announcer's voice, music playing in the background, saying quickly, "From the sensational Canyonville, on the banks of beautiful Lake Lanier in North Georgia, USA" …. Dan never got tired of hearing it. That became a slogan by itself. If Frank, Dean, and Sammy were alive, they would love playing here, Dan often thought. Dan had a dream one night that Bob Hope did a special here, with Ann Margaret,

503

Brooke Shields, Dean Martin, Joey Heatherton, Steve and Edye, and Jerry Colonna.

On many occasions, Dan and Melanie would allow Canyonville to be rented out for private parties. There was always security, as there were for all events except small gatherings for family or friends. There were local sound ordinances which the Johnsons and bands had to adhere to, for the comfort of the neighbors, who were always invited for open house events. Dan got a special kick out of letting neighbors use the event for birthday parties for the kids, or a few wedding receptions. Dan's only hangup was security, so there always had to be a team of security, which is why Canyonville never had more than an accidental broken bottle or plate. He was known to pay his security detail top dollar, and they loved to watch the place, because most every event was quote "tame". Every year, like he did up in Jersey, he let the Flowery Branch police and fire squads have a summer picnic or Christmas party, and Dan picked up the tab.

During Christmas, Melanie had a blast, smothering the place with decorations, and a giant tree. Of course, the Canyonville had 15-foot ceilings. Why should the owners have to duck? It was so great that one year, a production company from Nashville asked if they could arrange a "Country Christmas from Canyonville." Now this one was exciting, even if Dan wasn't a big country fan. The main reason was that Dolly Parton came to town, and she was as famous as Dan. He had met his match, and she was delightful. There was a short meeting about how monies were to be dispersed because Dolly has some of her own. Dan pitched in plenty to Dolly's find, and other big names. came, like Reba Macintyre, and the group Alabama. They liked the intimate setting and the controllable, 100-person crowd.

Dan and Melanie realized all the good Canyonville could do, but that didn't extend to the house.

There was even a comedy benefit two years after the opening of Canyonville, which was a children's benefit. It was a roast of none other than Dan himself, MC'd by the hysterical Larry the Cable guy. Dan had to put up with jokes ranging from timid to "blue", but all in the name of children.

These kinds of events made Dan very happy, mostly because they raised a great deal of money for good causes, and because, at least for an evening, they helped Dan forget, a little bit, about his now constant joint pain, and it wasn't unnoticed by anyone. Dan had a pronounced limp. People said nothing, but would sometimes whisper to Tony, those who knew about their close friendship. "How's the C Man holding up?" That was the typical expression. Tony would answer differently. It made no sense to lie, so Tony might say "He's trying to hang in there", to "he's working with doctors on the pain. Not much success, yet."

# Surviving COVID

It was December 2021, and COVID 19 was about to hit its peak. Dan was in Flowery Branch on a permanent basis. There were no events presently at CANYONVILLE, although fans wanted to hear music, and Dan agreed to have them do some events with no audience, and small bands spread out over the floor, like some venues were doing. It actually became very therapeutic for fans, and Dan relied on a popular female personality to be the host, as she had been for some others. Dan, of course, was never really the Master of Ceremonies for any events, though he might introduce the evening or give a speech.

These days, Dan didn't need COVID. It had been sixteen years since he retired, and every step Dan took was painful. He was happy to have the internet to conduct business, here are there. He did some voice-over work, and even a "Zoom" style of commercial, where he didn't have to walk. COVID actually helped cover up his pain, although he decided long ago to admit to having arthritis, "as a long-time athlete.". He never let on too many people about how serious it was, so the public simply saw him as an aging, famous celebrity who did commercials for financial companies, some food companies, his own foundation, and o course, seen everywhere all the time, The CANYON shoe. Most of Vickers advertisements didn't need Dan at all. They used young athletes, men and women, of all backgrounds but especially ones with an urban feel. Some might use a voice-over from Dan. "The CANYON basketball shoe, when you want peak performance." That, and five or six others using Dan's voice, could play for the next hundred years. Imagine a baseball bat company with a model called "The Babe", and Babe Ruth himself could be heard saying, "If you want power, turn to the Babe". How the hell do you think that would play? Arthritis or not, someday, the C Man would be old, even die, and it the brand was marketed well, it wouldn't have to end, but Laura Vickers remembered what happened to the company after World War Two, and she was always on the lookout for the next Dan Johnson, but was that even possible. They had a secondary brand for women named after Connecticut Huskie Great Kyra Coldstone. Stephon had the idea of Dan introducing "the Coldstone Shoe," through a voiceover, with Kyra, in uniform, holding the shoe and nodding confidently. It was a great start, and the shoe had a breakout year. It would never do the $4 billion of the CANYON, but it was never meant to, but it did add $400 million to the bottom line, very pleasing to Vickers. In terms of "equal pay", well, Kyra received 5%, same as Dan, or $20 million a year for the WNBA All-Star. Not exactly small potatoes, and when Kyra called Dan, it was he himself that said, "Just ask, don't demand, ask for 5%. That's the going rate, and you can tell them. Any less and well, is that fair? Of course not. Anymore and well, not fair to me, I suppose, right? Ha ha).

So, endorsements were doing well, considering the pandemic, but others, well, others were really suffering. After Dan saw a commercial about restaurants struggling, he called two of them in New York from what was now his "old neighborhood". He still owned the unit at 77 West, but Melanie was there a lot more than him, and even Tony and Bridget, splitting time between West Orange and Jupiter, FL, used it more often than Dan, who simply couldn't move around without pain. Tony was still working part-time, for the Police Athletic Union Offices, right in Jupiter, although has never needed money since the Kaufman sale many years ago. Britney loved it and wanted him to sell the Jersey house, but Tony still loved going back and hanging out with whomever was left there. He told Brit, "When Star Tavern opens a Florida branch, I'll consider it. Until then, I need my pizza fix every few weeks."

Dan called his friends, Rich and Mike, owners of Luther's the upscale steakhouse on the upper west side, only two blocks from 77 West. Luther's was about the classiest steak house anywhere, constantly mentioned on the list of the nation's best steak houses, and Rich and Mike were not only proud about that, but they also insisted on it. From paneled walls to the music, to the internally-renown wine list, to, naturally, the very best cuts of meat, to some of the most famous pastries in the country, Luther's had no weaknesses. Rich liked "Gladston and Madison" as the obvious name, but for some reason, Mike thought Luther's sounded interesting, but the truth was, Mike was a movie buff, and Luther's was named after the fictional Character, "Luther Coleman", from the movie, "The Sting". He was played by Robert Earl Jones, father of James Earl Jones, who, coincidentally, was one of Dan's favorite actors. It didn't take long for Mike and Dan to connect the dots over a drink in the early days. Eating at Luther's was expensive, and even harshest critiques, always questioned if the bill of the restaurant "was worth it", could never, ever question the quality of the food, the ambiance, or the professionalism of the staff. And speaking of the, but staff, they wore the finest clothing and memorized the menu, which wasn't a large menu, on purpose. There was no chicken, and just one seafood dish which would change week for week, and they put a lot of time into the seafood dish, but beyond that, it was about the steaks and the desserts. There was even the famous "dessert" room, which stayed upon late, which had the famous desserts designed by Chef Mike Gladston, who honed his craft at The Restaurant School at Walnut Hill College, with degrees in Pastry Arts. His partner, in business and in life, was Rich Madison. Rich was the meat expert and nobody, but nobody had a word to say about the desserts by Mike. Mike oversaw all pastries, "The Dessert Room at Luther's," and the city-wide distribution of desserts that their sales manager sold to restaurants around New York, in Philadelphia, as well as the "Dessert Room at Luther's" Mike and Rich owned at the Venetian Resort in Las Vegas, which specialized in Italian desserts and drinks. As a matter of fact, when Tony and Bridgett went to Las Vegas, around 2002, Dan called Mike and arranged a "special treat" for "Tone and Brit", which they raved about.

It was time for Dan to pay both Mike and Rich back for all the service they'd given to Dan and his friends. To the private rooms, to the special "off the menu" items, Rich and Mike always treated Dan like royalty. Plus, as picky and demanding as they were about their business, but had a great, wicked sense of humor, always a soft spot for Dan, even when Dan brought a can of "Chef Boy-ar-Dee to his table, telling the chef to tell Rich and Mike that "the food has slipped a little." He's still not sure if Rich and Mike thought that was funny or not, but Dan kept coming back, for many years, and they brought an unimaginable amount of business to the restaurant. As a matter of fact, the restaurant paid for an ad that was often plastered on buses and taxis, with a photo of Dan eating a steak, a nice glass of red wine next to him, with the quote, nice and simple, "The city's finest steakhouse." Dan Johnson. Dan wearing, naturally, a nice suit, standard for the guests. You want the best, you dress well, and jackets were mandatory, and the staff kept a close with no less than a dozen men's jackets of various sizes, primarily in dark navy. Dan did that ad for free. Needless to say, Dan never waited for a table. Never.

"Luther's, this is Katie, may I help you?" "Katie, it's Dan Johnson." "Hey, Dan, are you? How are those sore legs of yours?" "Katie, pretty rough but I'm hanging in there." "Well, Dan, it's very bad here. We must cut back, maybe close. Rich and Mike don't want to do take-out of any kind. Can you imagine our steakhouse packing our cuisine in brown paper bags? Frankly, we'd rather close than lower our standards, but I need to eat, and I need to pay the bills." "Katie, I'd like to speak with Mike or Rich." Katie said, "Rich is here, I'll get him."

"C Man, how are you? How are you feeling?" "Forget about me, Rich. You must stay open." "Well," said Rich, "I don't think we're going to have a choice. We're not going to become a sandwich shop, but we've got a staff, and we can't afford to bankroll the staff." "No, but I can", said Dan. "What are telling me, Dan? Don't play with my emotions here." "Rich, I'm not getting any younger or healthier, my friend. I have more money than I can spend. Do me a favor. Make me a spreadsheet. Remember, or maybe you don't know, I'm a finance man. Make me a spreadsheet. I want to see every employee and what they earn each month. Call Mike. Do it today and call me tomorrow. This is not going to put you out of business. Rich, this is what long-time friends do for each other." "Oh my God," was all Rich could say, and he promised to call Dan the next morning."

Dan called his financial guy, Larry, and explained what he was doing. "Dan, you are worth about $1.7 billion. I mean, give or take $200 million. It is your money. You want to bail out the world, that's your choice." "Larry, first of all, I'm not bailing out the world, and I can't spend my money when I'm dead, and I won't be around to argue with you when eighty, let alone in five years." "Dan, you're forty-six. Cut it out." "Larry, I'm not cutting your commission or fees. Don't question me. I'm tired of your bullshit." Larry replied, "I'm here to protect and earn you money. If you want to waste it, that's your problem." "You think saving people's livelihoods is a waste? You've been my financial planner for twenty plus years. How many millions have you made? I'm not saying you haven't earned it, so I don't want to hear that as your next words, but neither you nor I have had to serve people in a restaurant while living in one of the most expensive cities in the world. They're scared shitless. They've busted their butt for me for a long time, and I want to remove their stress. Is that okay with you." "Dan, doing my job." Dan said, "Well then do it. I'll be helping my favorite restaurant and favorite bar, and I don't care what it costs, because I have nothing to cover, and then some. I'll be back."

Dan could fire Larry. There was a contract. It would cost Dan somewhat, but he could do it, anytime. But he wasn't going to do that, and Larry knew it. It had been too many years, and Larry was loyal and hard-working, and would never cheat Dan. It wasn't in his nature, and he wasn't that stupid. He had the meal ticket of his life. Also, when all was said and done, Dan knew he "needed a Larry" to keep him from falling apart for every sob-story he heard, which is why, 90% of the time, the standard response to requests had to be, "please call my financial advisor." But there were always exceptions. Larry, on the other hand, needed to understand Dan's nature, and even $10 million wasn't going to put a dent in Dan's (or Larry's) bank account. Plus, Dan's most emotional decisions were usually on the scale of $100,000-$250,000, a pittance to Dan, and Larry knew it.

Dan placed a call to his other "favorite location", Dan's bar, also around the corner from 77 West. The owner's name was not Dan, but Glen Howard, who bought it from Dan Temple several years back. He had a similar phone call. "Call me tomorrow," Dan said to an equally shell-shocked Glen.

The following day, Mike and Dan went over the 23 employees they had, and their estimated salaries, including tips. When it was all said and done, Dan told them, and Glen over at Dan's Bar, to "add 20%, just in case", and the money would go out monthly. He wanted a letter, something, giving each employee a guarantee that they would have 12-months of pay. If they worked, they would make the additional pay above and beyond. They could work elsewhere if they wanted as well. The same offer went out to Dan's Bar.

It didn't take long for news to get out about Dan, and of course, some criticized him for "not doing more". He could empty his bank account to help others, naturally, but Dan didn't like others making decisions for him. He took care of people that were taking care of him, and his foundation took care of thousands that Dan would never meet. He didn't have anything to apologize for.

A week later, due to the fact that Mike and Rich knew his staff would want to thank a Georgia-ridden CANYON, they had a Zoom call, and all the employees were given the good news. It was fun to see everybody smiling and laughing through their tears of happiness. Dan simply said, "Guys, what's happening is rough and I can do this. My days now are all about helping others. You want to work, but if you can't, you're covered. Mike and Rich said that they would take the costs typically associated with payroll, and put it into an insurance Foundation, in case the pandemic and closure went past a year. Mike said, "We will not become a take-out restaurant. We will not lower our standards. You work in the nation's finest steakhouse, whether we can stay open or not." The reaction at Dan's, a hole-in-the-wall bar that Dan loved equally, was the same. Fancy steakhouse or bar, both were important to Dan, and both had employees that had to survive.

# The Chickens Come Home to Roost

It's ironic that the most rewarding time of Dan's life was condensed into the shortest amount of space. If we allowed it, there would be enough stories to fill a vault, or a wagon. Something big, like Dan and his dreams.

Dan's dilemma and his solution were, on the surface, quite simple to explain. As he said to Tony, in one version or another, in many ways, and over many years, was that he was given tremendous athletic advantages. He did as Billy Barty said, he put in his maximum effort at mastering judo, wrestling, and basketball, and so did the top players in that sport. Nobody poured more sweat into their craft and spent more hours in the practice room than Dan. However, the added benefit of size, plus his skill, was the difference. His size alone may have been conquered by motivated opponents, but not size and his abilities together. And Dan could have mastered other sports as well. In just the few times he "fooled around" he showed immediate results in volleyball, in the shot put and javelin, and course, in boxing, but he had enough trouble scheduling bouts and tournaments in just three sports. He was given accommodation when it came to moving practice times and competitions around that were not always appreciated by fellow competitors or even teammates.

Dan questioned why he was granted this advantage in life. But was it an advantage? Was his size worth the stares, the comments, the health risks? Who's to say? But what it did mean was that to the kind of man Dan was, the kind of person, sensitive, always questioning, the importance he placed on loyalty, honesty, and something not easily defined but we will call the "symbolism of life", what every word, thing, event stands for.

Dan put more work, more passion, into raising money for the Foundation than he had put into any of these athletic endeavors. He had found his passion, and between himself and the Foundation's board, it was quickly determined how best Dan could help his foundation, and that was through fund raising. Dan was, arguably, the most famous man in the world. CEOs acted like little kids whenever Dan arrived. He was bigger than life. What Dan wanted to do was to get Fortune 500 companies, as many as possible, to make the Foundation available for all employees to contribute to, through payroll deductions, and for the corporations to match. This success, his legacy, allowed the Foundation to bring in billions of dollars, which went exactly where Dan wanted it to go; to the development of a "National Food Bank Network" and to a select group of children's hospitals. Bigger than it sounds, but earmarked for what Dan had dreamed about since he was a teenager. No, it wasn't as simple as all that. There were disputes over the use of money. It was bound to happen, but the Foundation gave 94% of its contributions to their causes. That wasn't Dan's dream. That dream was 100%, but the Foundation got high marks from watchdog groups.

Dan then gave himself the luxury and "title" of "Ambassador". Dan was the face of the Foundation. It was Dan that met the children and the parents. Dan that met

515

the CEOs, that shook hands, and got up inside Canyonville to welcome the stars that decided to perform so that more hungry people could eat, and more sick children could be treated and perhaps, more to be cured and live a long life. If Dan didn't stop to finally accept his worth on this planet, it was simply because he was so busy doing that work.

Foundations began in other nations and Dan did what he could to travel. The first ten years, 2005-2015, were the "golden years", as he and Melanie would say later. Dan had arthritic pain toward the end of his playing career, but what player didn't have the occasional sore knee or shoulder? Once he stopped, in 2005, the running, the elbows, the pounding up and down court, he felt some relief for a while. Those ten years. And the change didn't come once the calendar reached January 1 of 2016, but right about that time, the pain got progressively worse. Right around Dan's fortieth year. He started to ease up on the travel, apologizing more and more for having to excuse himself from events on behalf of the Foundation, or to repay favors to executives and others for the work they had done for him. How to do that without saying to them, "I'm sorry, but my time has come. Nobody is meant to be this tall and the success, the idol worshipping, the championships, the admirers of women, men, children. I'm now paying for it all. The chickens had come home to roost.

The accolades for Dan continued. With his playing days over, fans, media, experts in those sporting fields had the time to examine in greater detail Dan's performance, and if anything, the lack of his presence now resulted in only more shock and awe. There was no shortage of programs devoted to his accomplishments, translated, or produced in a multitude of languages. Dan was busy accepting awards. Halls of fame in his three sports by unanimous vote, awards in other nations. Eventually, some dared to propose that his humanitarian work was beginning to catch up with his sporting accomplishments. I mean, how impressive is buying tons of food when compared to a slam dunk? But it was. His athletic accomplishments served as a springboard, as a tool, for helping millions of people live better lives, and THAT, THAT was Dan's legacy, and he knew it.

In 2021, a more frail, less sturdy Dan Johnson nevertheless walked under his own power in the Rose Garden of the White House, to receive the Presidential Medal of Freedom, the highest civilian award in the United States. The President joked that it was fitting for Dan to finally get this award, as "he had won everything else in America that could be won." In private, his staff suggested the President move on this action. Nobody was more deserving, and "time could be running out."

# Pain

Nobody knew for certain when Dan's large size began to fail him, because he didn't tell many people. Eventually, Melanie could hear him, sweating, legs or arms moving. She knew pain, too. Her years of top-level court play eventually resulted in two hip replacements.

Melanie believes Dan started having problems while in the NBA, and perhaps he retired just in time. It started with his feet. First, he had arthritis in both large toes. He had plantar fasciitis that was so bad that most mornings, he simply couldn't walk until they were thoroughly stretched. His knees hurt, his shoulders. He even had pain in the cartilage between his ribs, and he had to try to stretch them out.

Doctors could never quite find the right pain medication. Either it didn't work, or it was addicting and dangerous, or worked for a time and then stopped working. It all began to get worse when Dan was about forty, and Melanie believes he really suffered in silence for the rest of his life.

Then one day, at diner north of Atlanta, when Dan was in just 41, he had chest and arm pain, and doctors discovered a 95% blockage in his main heart artery, what his cardiologist said was his left anterior descending artery, or LAD. He had 95 blockage, and 80% blockage in another artery. Angioplasty and two drug-eluting stents saved his life. He went on a blood thinner, aspirin, and metoprolol, to help lower his blood pressure.

Melanie wondered if all the "perfect specimen" crap was just that. No human was meant to stand over eight feet tall.

# Bubba and Billy

Bubba and Billy had a three-hour talk show on WSB Radio, a station Dan liked all his life, and a simple call at just the right time, when Dan was in a decent mood, resulted in an evening with the CANYON. Dan was rarely in a pleasant mood at this stage, but the pain wasn't bad that night. He had the right combination of meds in his system so that he could sit somewhere comfortably. Dan was letting the foundation board have more control, and Dan's travel schedule was significantly down. He had begun to hunch-over slightly, and limp, but he did several voice-overs, telling people that he had now preferred to stay-put at his lake house. He and Melanie still had the NY apartment for trips to NY, whenever it was  important, but weren't there often anymore. Tony had a key and stayed there whenever he and Britt were in the city and felt like staying the night. No permission necessary.

Melanie liked the playful banter of Bubba and Billy and even chimed up a few times, to the broadcast. Dan and Melanie were situated at the lake house, in the large family room, on a crisp late October night in 2022.

WSB, the South's first radio station, went on the air on March 15, 1922. Its call letters later provided for the popular slogan "Welcome South, Brother." It had come to represent the very best in talk radio for people not only in the Atlanta area, but throughout the south and into the Midwest and beyond due to it being a "clear channel" station of 50,000 watts. Its history is deep and celebrated, as it celebrated its 100th birthday this year.

Bubba was really Bobby Dean Booth, a big ole boy from nearby Buford, a strong football program. He was born in 1966, nine years older than Dan, and played football for Coach Vince Dooley from 1985-1988, his last four years. He was not related to the infamous John Wilkes Booth, but Billy loved to slide in a joke about it on nearly every broadcast. It was good for jokes. Billy was nothing like Bubba, and that's what made the show so much fun. Billy was Bill Landers, a New Jersey native born in 1971, from South Orange, and attended Columbia High School and then the University of Maryland. But Billy took a job in Broadcasting in Columbia, SC, with WVOC AM radio, in 1987, before coming to Atlanta in 1991. He liked to consider himself a southerner at this stage, which was more fodder for on-the-air jokes, since Bubba would claim "once a Yankee, always a Yankee". Well, about ¾ of Atlanta at this stage were from somewhere else, but the boys used whatever they could for funny material. They would often slip in sound effects and sound bites from, well, anywhere. They were goofy and but then again, they were successful.

Billy and Bubba were above all, humorists, and had been together now for sixteen years. They could be serious and knowledgeable enough to discuss politics, history, virtually any subject, but they were there for ratings, and they were expert entertainers, bouncing comments off each and making their guests feel at home.

What was to be an hour with Dan and Melanie became two hours. During a commercial break, Bubba said, "Hey y'all, this has been fun, you wanna keep going? Mel looked at Dan and they shook nodded heads. Hey guys, Melanie said, this is fun. We don't have much of that, lately. Bubba and Billy knew that. Everybody sensed it or knew it outright.

"Ok, Billy said", in the NBA, you travelled a lot, a grueling schedule, we know you also traveled a lot afterwards, went overseas to sporting events, for charitable events, I mean, you've been all over." Bubba interrupted, "What he's saying is, he wants to see your frequent flyer points, and I told him, now Billy, these hot-shot celebrities do NOT randomly give out those points." Dan smiled, "No, I'm NOT trying to ask that," then he said safety to Dan, "what do you have, like three million? Get one of those plaques for the wall?" Bubba said, "What exactly are you trying to ask him?" "Well, Billy said, lots of things, like, did you ever throw one of them salmons at the big market in Seattle?" "The Pike Place Market?" Dan asked. "Well, I've seen THEM throw it, and I also thrown a mullet at the Flora Bama." "Where's that" asked Billy. "C'mon Billy," Bubba said, think about it, Flora-Bama. "Ughh, that's down in Birmingham, right, CANYON?" Dan chuckled, "No, guys, it's Perdido Beach, near Pensacola, right on the Florida-Alabama border. "Wow, that's cool, said Billy." "What other places do you like in NBA cities? Bubba asked." "Oh, wow, too many to mention," Dan said. "What do you think, Melanie, trying to get Mel to join in." "Well, she said, you mentioned Seattle already, I like Miami, Boston, Denver," she said. "Good food and shopping. Interesting places to shop and see." Billy said, "food's important, there are some famous food places. What do you think, Dan." "Well, Dan said, I like Portillo's up in Chicago, great hot dogs and beef sandwiches. Good chowder in Boston, Cuban food in Miami, Tex-Mex in San Antonio on the Riverwalk, good cheesesteaks in Philly." "Oh, Bubba said, I'm glad you mentioned Philly Cheese steaks. You know, you gotta order them a certain way, or they cut you." "Cut you, Melanie said, laughing?" "That's a slight exaggeration, what we called in Buford as a tall fish tale." Bill fixed his story. "Ok, you don't get cut, but they don't like it." So, how DO you order it?" Melanie asked? "Ok", said Billy. A good cheesesteak, you know, one you get at Pat's or Geno's, the two across the street rivals, has the roll, the steak, cheese whiz, and onions, which are optional, but to me, it's not a real cheesesteak without them. "So, the Philly way to order a cheesesteak is to say, "one whiz wid", as in one cheesesteak WITH cheese. "But what if you want two?" Bubba asked. Billy said, "See what I gotta deal with every day?" Billy said. Dan talked (finally). "One time when we played the Sixers, one of the local tv stations did a segment with me and had me stand in the parking lot of Pat's and Geno's, while they both yelled at me to come to their place." "It's a toss-up, said Billy."

Dan talked again. "Now, I have to speak up for New Jersey, because they don't have a team anymore, not since the Nets left East Rutherford." "Nets?" Bubba said. "Never heard of 'em", which he did of course because he was speaking to the one and only Dan Johnson, hero of the crosstown Knicks. "Well, NJ, gets a bad rap but I spent a lot of time up there. You're got some of the best pizza." "Yeah, the deep-dish stuff, right?" "Don't even joke," said Dan. "Thin and crispy. The best cheese," said Dan. "It's the water," Billy said. "What I've heard, anyway," "Well, Dan said, "Great pizza and then there's the Italian Hog Dogs, like Jimmy Buffs in West Orange, Charlie's in Kenilworth." "Down by the Boulevard" Billy, the NJ native, sings. "Say what?" Bubba asks. "Oh, never mind, it's the main drag in Kenilworth. Melanie knew, right?" "Uh, no," said Melanie." "Oh, sure," said Dan. "David Brearley Bears. I went to three or four judo tournaments there." "Hey, Billy", Bubba asked, "wasn't David Brearley that guy you got arrested with down in Daytona on spring break, back in '84?" "What the hell are you talking about?" complained Billy. Dan interrupted. "He signed the U.S. Constitution." "Oh yeah, Bubba said. He did that. It was that or Daytona." "You're thinking of Dave Durley," Bill finally said. "We don't talk about Daytona, remember?" "Hey, Melanie," Bubba asked. "Remember the Seinfeld public urination episode? In the mall parking garage? I think that was in NJ." Melanie just laughed. Billy said, "No more Daytona talk, man," feigning anger.

"Hey," said, Billy, you got Portugues food in the Ironbound section of Newark." "The Portuguese have food?", Bubba asked. "The best," Billy said. "You know nothing, you know absolutely nothing. And they don't feel the need to throw grits on top of everything." "Hey", Bubba, said sternly. "That's the national food of the south. Don't mess with my grits." "Well, Melanie said. "Dan here loves collard greens." "It's true, I do." "Well, Billy said, back to New Jersey, the best state for food." "Ha'" Bubba laughed. "

"Well, there are a lot of great areas for food right in the U.S. Dan, before we move on to some other areas, tell me what Southern Foods you like. After all, you're still Georgia born and raised. "Wow," Dan said, there's a lot. "Ok, there's fried chicken, of course, hot Nashville fried chicken, BBQ, namely, pork, brisket, and ribs, the three staples." "Quick", Bubba said. "Maybe sausage". "You're in Memphis. You going to Rendezvous or Corky's?" "It's a tie". "OHHH, he bails on the tough question!" "No," Dan said, I'm just smart. "No sucker punches." "Dan likes food, period," said Melanie, not telling the group or ANYBODY that Dan's consumption of food had been falling steadily from his one-time 8,000 calories regiment. He was skinnier and a little sickly looking, but Melanie would protect Dan's image come hell or high water. She'd like to see somebody enjoy their meals with the pain and inflammation of rheumatoid arthritis attacking every joint. "Keep going" Bubba said. "Ok," said Dan. "grits, of course, if they're prepared well, biscuits, collards, of course, simmered with ham hocks and hot sauce, Brunswick stew, fried okra, and for dessert, peach cobbler, blackberry, cobbler, sweet potato pie, and pecan pie."

"Ok, everybody," Bubba said. "A moment of silence, or better yet, appreciation. The man knows his southern cuisine." "Oh," Dan interrupted. "I can't believe I missed this." Billy said, "Shrimp and grits? Mac and cheese?" Dan said, "Those are fine, but no. I left out boiled peanuts". "Oh, well I take back that moment of silence." "Why? Dan asked." "Those are the ultimate." "No, just, no", Billy said, "Melanie, help me out here." "Well," Melanie said, I don't eat 'em either. They're wet!". "I rest my case," Billy said. "No", Dan said you guys don't know what you're missing." "See" said Billy, he says "you guys" but then he eats boiled peanuts." "Well, said Dan, my mom is from Alabama and my Dad from Cleveland." "He's a mutt", said Bubba. "From a mixed marriage."

"Ok, besides Bubba, "What foods can you not eat? Melanie, you go first. "Well, besides the aforementioned wet peanuts," Dan could be heard in the background, "Not wet, boiled,"" I don't like caviar or beer." "Well, okay everybody, thank you for listening to our broadcast. We seem to have some interference jamming up our signal.

You can't come on this show and say that you don't like beer!" "Well, I don't!" Melanie said. "Shameful" Bubba said. "There should be a reform school for people that don't like beer. Well, let's move on." "C man! What say you! Foods you don't care for." "That's a nice way to say it, Bubba," said Billy. "See, said Bubba, I'm improving." Dan continued, "I don't care for mayonnaise or raw oysters." "Bubba just shook his head and said, "What we've got here, is failure to communicate,' joked Bubba, reciting the famous line from "Cool Hand Luke". "Everybody likes mayonnaise, C Man." "Well," Dan said, I didn't get that memo. Mayo on a burger, just horrible. I don't get it." "Melanie," said Billy, you like mayo?" "Oh, love it," said Melanie. "It's a mixed marriage," said Bubby. "I understand the raw oysters". "See", said, Dan. "We can agree on the raw oysters." "Oh no we can't, said Bubba", I love 'em." "From a man who's been turning sand into pearls his entire life, I give you a man who won't eat oysters," Billy joked. "Raw oysters," said Dan. Not steamed or fried. "Nope, doesn't count, Bubba said."

Ok, enough food. When we come back, we're going to talk more to Dan "the CANYON" Johnson, the pride of Georgia, Michigan, New York....well damn, the pride of everywhere, and his lovely wife, the lady Monarch, which we need to talk about." "What's a Monarch" asked Billy. "She's gonna tell us where we return," Bubby told the audience.

"Hey Melanie and Dan," fantastic job. You doing, okay?" Melanie whispered to Dan, "Honey, you doing, okay?" "Sure" Dan said. I've gotta be doing something, and it's fun." "Want to keep going another half-hour." "Well," said

Dan. "We can't quit in the middle; people will talk about anything."

It was the top of the hour and time for a newsbreak and several commercials. The Dow was up 17 points, the President was meeting with King Charles in London, and this week marks the first-time heart patients will receive a nano-technology treatment that that will remove plaque from coronary arteries. This nano formulation directly targets plaque cells and shuts down the intake pathway. Backers are hopeful that it will greatly reduce sudden death from coronary heart disease.

Bubba looked at Billy, "Hey, this is a great show. Dan is speaking more than usual. Let's open things up and get him to talk more. I know the guy probably doesn't want to be on the air. I've heard the same as everybody else, but I know he likes movies. Let's go there. He gets enough sports questions, and everybody has heard all of that. Are you okay if I get things pointed in that direction?" "Do it", said Billy. "Hey, we sink or swim together. Just bring me into it."

"Okay, welcome back to the Bubba and Billy Show here on WSB. I'm Billy and with me as always is Bubba, from Buford." "Well, damn", said Bubba. "Get it, Buford Damn." "I get it, it's just not funny." "It's very funny. I heard it in a movie." "You did not hear that in a movie. It would go straight to video now." "Like Blockbuster?" "Yes, said Billy, your local one there in Buford." "Hey, don't laugh. I think there's still one in Alaska." "Well, what else can they do at night in Alaska?" "I have to tell you?" "Hey, well anyway, we have a very special edition here, we've got the C Man himself, Dan Johnson with his lovely California wife, Melanie Johnson, here to talk about, what?" Billy asked. "Any damn thing we want to talk about." "That's right and the world talks about basketball when they talk about Dan Johnson, but you know what? We can look all that up, and you know what, man." "Tell me" Bubba said. "Well, I'll tell ya this, how do you change perfection? What is there to talk about? Four straight state basketball championships, four straight collegiate championships, and eight straight NBA champions." "Insane," Bubba said. "You know what?" Bubba said? "The man's a bore. I mean, how about losing and then coming back. Way too routine and predictable if you ask me." "Well, I hear he's well rounded, but he's never proven it," Billy said. "Well, he's got that Candyland Bar up in Flowery Branch, the one he never invited us to." "Hey man," Billy said, but Bubba continued. "You look at a map? Buford's the next town over and I've never been invited. Hey C Man, what's the deal." Dan laughed and said, "Hey, both of you guys have been to Canyonville. You went to an Eagleston Hospital Benefit." "Did we?" asked Bubba? "The man could be right," said Billy. "Well, I forgot about it but that means I must have had a good time. Oh wait, did it have Ms. Pac Man AND Gorf?" "As a matter of fact, it did and still does," said Dan. "You see, Bubba said, that's just what I've been sayin', you just can't find Gorf anymore. I remember it now. You know why I liked it?" Bubba said and proceeded to answer his own question. "I was only a private in the army but in Gorf I was a "Space Colonel."

"Anyway, let's talk movies because every show we talk movies. Dan, first. Favorite movie. "That's impossible."

"Oh, c'mon," said Billy. Dan said, "what genre?" "Now listen, C Man, half our audience don't know what "John-Ray" even means. Okay, this is a fun show. Let's start with comedy." Dan said, "Okay, I'd say "Love and Death." "Who?" Bubby asked, "Love my breath?" "Ha, ha, no. It's a Woody Allen movie." Billy said, "Melanie, you know this movie? "Oh, yeah, it's my favorite, too." What's it about, and I mean the 10-second version. "Ok" Dan said. "Woody Allen plays a Russian in Czarist Russia during the French Invasion of Russia of 1812. He falls in love with Diane Keaton's character, his 2nd cousin, and they try to assassinate Napoleon. It's filled with a lot of jokes along the way. Some slapstick and some based on literature and more dry wit. It's not for everyone but it's very funny." "Ok", Billy said. "Well," said Bubba, "You're right about one important thing." "What's that?" asked Bubba. "It's not for everybody. How about a movie scene that breaks up Melanie every time." "Oh, that's easy" said Dan, "the pool scene in Caddyshack." "Ok," Bubba said. "NOW you're talking". That's good 'ole Spalding and Bill Murray cleaning out the pool." "Oh my God", Melanie said, I lose it every time." "That's a good one!" Bubba said. Dan yells out, "Spalding, NOO!", You can hear Melanie screaming with laughter in the background. "Listen to this," said Dan. "Will you come LOOFAH my stretch marks". "No, stop!" Melanie was howling in the background. "Well,", said Billy. We got a winner. The Johnsons like Caddyshack, and so do we. "Ya'll were beginning to sound like movie snobs," Bubba said. Caddy Shack saved you."

"Ok, last movie question", Billy asked. "One movie, name it." Melanie said "Gone with the Wind," and Dan said "The

Godfather". "Ok, Bubba, said, let's talk TV. We've got just enough time."

"Melanie, funniest show," Billy asked. "I Love Lucy". "Ok, fair enough". "Dan, same question." Dan said right away, "Andy Griffith Show." "Hey," Melanie said. He's gonna tell you it was the best show about everything. The perfect show." "No, not really," Dan said, but it was one of the funniest and also, one of the best show about teaching lessons." "Oh, yeah", Bubba said, Andy and Opie, life's lessons." "It's true", Dan said. "It reminded me of my dad." "Okay, Billy said, we're almost out of time, give me a few quick lessons from The Andy Griffith Show." "Ok, fast," Dan said. "Opie runs in a race and loses and won't congratulate his friends who won. He's very bitter about it and Andy teaches him the concept of being a good sport" "Next," says Billy. "Ok, Aunt Bea's Pickles. Aunt Bee's Pickles are awful. They call them 'kerosene' pickles. So, they throw them out and use store-bought pickles which taste good, but in doing so they realize they are cheating Aunt Bee's friend Clara who wins every year the fair and honest way, with her own pickles. Opie also learns that a little white lie is okay if it spares somebody's feelings." "Ok", Bubba says. "Opie is taught to lie." "You liked this show?" Dan laughed, "Moving on, Andy and Helen are stuck in a cave but only briefly and find a way out in the back. Barney still thinks they're stuck there, and he organizes a huge rescue party. Andy and Helen find out and realize that Barney will, once again, be the town laughingstock if Andy and Helen simply show up in town, so they have sneak back inside the cave. Then there's the episode when Opie kills a bird and Andy makes him raise the mother bird's babies until they are old enough to fly off on their own." "Opie the birdman", said Billy. "Even I know that one."

"Touching stuff," Bubba said, "Hey," Melanie said. "Don't mess with Dan and the Andy Griffith Show. I've had to hand him tissues too many times."

"Okay, real fast. Dan, Country or Rock?" "Can I say jazz? "No", Billy says. "Okay, rock." "Melanie, same question, "Ummm, country." Okay."

"Hey folks" Billy said. "We are out of time, but on a serious note, from both of us here and the entire staff of WSB. "Dan, we've all watched you since the time you were a teenager from Marietta and won a gold medal in a combat sport and then a 2$^{nd}$ sport, and then captivated the nation." "He wrote this down," Bubba said. "It's true, I did, because I want to get it right. Then the nation stood still while you made your choice to play basketball in Michigan, and became forever etched in Wolverine lore, winning four straight championships. Then, you joined the '96 Atlanta Olympics Dream Team as the only collegiate, and brought smiles to your hometown Atlanta fans, and then you took on the Big Apple and made a name for yourself in the Big Apple by winning eight straight NBA championships. But if that wasn't enough, you've saved your best performance for last but starting a foundation that has raised billions for cancer research and programs to feed the hungry. You know, we're humorists and we kid around. That's what we do, but we share in the amazement of everything you have achieved in your life, and we wish you only the best in the future." That last line was particularly difficult for Billy to say."

"Well,", Dan said, "Melanie and I appreciate those kind words, and we had a very good time tonight. I think I can speak for Malanie." "Yes," Melanie said. Thanks to both of you and your entire staff." "Ok, so from the WSB Studios, and from the Johnson home, just outside of the fabulous Canyonville, we say to you, goodnight."

Inside the programming room, a voice said. "Nicely done, guys." And inside their Flowery Branch Home, Melanie kissed Dan and said, "Nice job, Honey," let's go to bed.

# Sunset

A bucket of beers sat on the dock at the Lakehouse, along with a bowl of boiled peanuts, wings, and boiled shrimp.

On the speakers was the Wings "Band on the Run" Album. Britt and Melanie had the wave runners out. It took Britt a couple of years to ride solo, but little by little, she learned to keep up with Melanie. Mel loved the wave runners. Fast, exciting, and no wear on her knees.

So, the big 5-0, Tony said. "Well, Dan answered, you're only two miles behind me, said Dan." "Wish you were going back to Italy with us again", Tony mentioned. "We're finally going to the Pompeii ruins. That's totally your thing," Tony said. "Two-thousand-year-old bodies, buried." "Well,", said Dan, I feel like one of those two thousand year old guys every day," Dan said. "So, the new medicine is no help?" "Not much", said Dan, "and the side effects of some of these drugs might kill me, anyway." "Well, Tony said," "Don't leave this place anymore. Make these companies come to you. You rest those joints, and they'll heal." "C'mon, Tony. Nothing's gonna heal. Cartilage is gone, bones are wasted. It was all inevitable for me. The last guy who was my height died at twenty-two. I'm fifty. I gotta consider myself lucky. Here I am, cracking open a Summer Shandy, with hot boiled peanuts and wings, and all of this around me. I've been very lucky. Just like Lou Gehrig." Tony shook his head and gave Dan a disappointed look. He got the relevance to Lou Gehrig and didn't like it. Instead, he said, "Summer Shandy, yes. Holy shit that stuff is good. Wings, count me in, but boiled peanuts I'll never understand."

"Look", said Tony. "People have bum knees and arthritis all over. They still live to be eighty and ninety years old. They just aren't running marathons, and neither will you, and the difference is, you're a hall of famer, Olympic Champion, retired jerseys in college and the pros. You couldn't pay for a meal in West Orange, Atlanta, or New York. Or that po-dunk college town, whatever it's called."

"Po-dunk", yeah. Says the man from Bethlehem, PA." "Hey, you leave my Mountain Hawks alone." "Fine", said Dan. "It's actually a cool name."

"Tony", said Dan, quietly. "I think I've lived enough years." "No," said Tony. "God decides that, not you."

# Gossip Mill

Melanie was in her regular run of errands on and off of Spout Springs Road. A little grocery shopping, a couple of household items. When she approached the cash registers, she never used the self scan, she saw it, and she couldn't avoid her gaze. There, on the cover of the worthless rag was a grainy photo of a large man, bent over about two feet, walking with a cane. You couldn't see the face clearly, but nobody needed to. It was evident enough. The I vet said "The CANYON'S final, sad days."

"Sons of bitches," Melanie thought. "They have no fucking right." But, of course, it WAS Dan and what was she going to do? Sue them? Make an even bigger spectacle in the public eye? Force Dan into a courtroom in his state? That's what those scumbags are betting on. That'll I'll just turn away while curious onlookers looking for smut gladly pay for a copy. Maybe hearing about the pain of a good man will somehow make their pathetic life better. They should only experience his pain for one day. None of them, finding glee in Danny's pain could comes close to his all achievements, of all he did to help others around the world. She thought of walking out, leaving the groceries behind, but she'd only have to come back. They still needed to eat.

At a barber shop in Calhoun, three elderly men were sitting around at a barber shop, newspapers in hand. Calhoun was nearly 100 miles from Flowery Branch, just outside the forever sprawling Atlanta Metropolitan Area. It was northwest of Atlanta and a little more than halfway to Chattanooga. A place where, if you looked, you could still find remnants of the old South, the slower pace of life now all but gone within 100 miles of downtown Atlanta. But, as "super suburbs" like Cumberland, Smyrna, Kennesaw, and Woodstock were woken from their once peaceful, southern slumber, these places were seeing their last vestiges of their old times. That wasn't all bad, and yet, it wasn't all good, either.

"That Dan Johnson is a good boy," an 81-year-old said, describing the now 51 CANYON. You know, I went into a Waffle House down in Marietta, way, way back around 1992. Marietta was already way too big, and there was the CANYON with two other fellers. I'd say it was about a mile south of the Big Chicken, on the opposite side, near the loop. I had to pick up something from Sam's Club. Anyway, I went over to their table and said "That was some game you Wheeler boys played in that championship game." Wouldn't you know it, that boy, the CANYON, he stood off and took off his cap and shook my hand, and said "Oh, thank you very much, sir. It was thrilling." "What was he wearin', a Michigan cap?" "No, the man said". It was a Purdue Boilermakers cap." I asked him, "So have you decided where you want to go to school? You know that Bobby Cremins, he runs a pretty tight ship down the street at Georgia Tech." "What did he say," a second man said, "I'll tell ya what he said,". He said, "To hell with Georgia Tech, go Dawgs." "No, he didn't say any of that." He said, "Yes, sir. Coach Cremins is an excellent Coach and great guy. I just haven't made a decision yet. And then I left.

"Well, all I can say is, it's a shame. Good local boy. I hope it's not as bad as they say."

Across the world, there were small articles, here and there, citing the difficult challenges for Dan. The degree in which people stared into space and said a silent prayer to God to spare Dan of his pain, to others who found pleasure in it, is unknown.

# Welcome Home

It was a Sunday morning in March. Still some crispness in the air. Melanie and Dan watched "Horse Feathers," one of the great Marx Brothers films. It wasn't the first time, and from time to time, just because he wanted to, Dan would ask Melanie, "what's the password", and naturally, Mel would answer, "swordfish". At about 11:45 PM, Dan rolled over in bed, facing Melanie, and said, "I'm calling it a night. Love you, babe." Melanie said, "Me, too, but here, remind me, in the morning, I had an idea for our next trip." Dan gave her a sleepy look, and true to Professor Wagstaff, he said, "Whatever it is, I'm against it."

Dan fell asleep, and found himself walking on a canopy road, just like many he had seen driving around the Georgia countryside as a kid.

There was an old-looking building. It looked like a stone house, old, pretty, European. Warm lights inside. Suddenly, an attractive older woman walked outside, as if she was waiting for someone.

Dan looked, stared. Paused. "Grandma Luccia, is that you?" Luccia answered in a voice somewhat familiar, with a beautiful European accent, but very polished. Yes, Danny. It has been a very long time. Do you still think about me?" "Of course, Grandma. All the time. Especially when I need a lift, something to cheer me up." "Oh, I'm glad", Luccia said, looking so elegant. "You look beautiful." Dan said, not meaning that to sound disrespectful, Luccia smiled, "Oh, Danny, thank you. You were always a nice boy. A nice man.

You worried about things, but things have worked out for you.

You know, Danny, you could not have been anyone except Danny Johnson. Sometimes, you wanted to be someone else. We all think that way, but you were a very good Danny Johnson. We're all proud of you and a lot of people are waiting for you."

"I don't understand," Dan said.

"We will see you soon," Luccia said. Gina and Jimmy are waiting to see you, too."

Melanie turned to Dan at around 7:45 the next morning.

Dan? Dan, honey?

She felt Dan's forehead.

It was cold.

She checked his pulse and felt nothing.

Dan!! Dan!!!!

Oh, honey. Oh, honey.

No more pain, no more pain.

Oh, oh.

I love you so much.

I love you so much.

Oh, my baby!

No, oh nooo!

Please, God, nooo.

She pulled Dan up to a sitting position with all her strength and hugged him and continued.

Oh, baby, oh, my baby.

I'm sorry, sweetheart.

Oh, sweetheart, I'm sorry.

There's nothing I can do.

Oh, honey, what will I do?

What will I do?

Dan Johnson died in his sleep on September 24, 2026, at 51 years of age. He had coronary artery disease and a host of joint problems. Some doctors felt that despite a healthy life, and a proportional body, the toll on his heart, such a large body, could have contributed to his death. In recent years, he had shown signs of heart trouble, as well as almost daily joint pain that he didn't mention very often.

The news outlets seemed to have their stories ready within hours, as they either anticipated the event or simply stockpiled these stories due to the inevitable. It was bound to happen sooner or later.

It had been twenty-one years since Dan last laced up his famous Canyon Sneakers, but continued commercials and commercials endorsements kept him in the news almost the entire time. In the last three to four years, the pain from his arthritis had him hunched over and unable to perform, but there was a library of his older videos and voice-overs that easily substituted.

Every network and internet site addressed his death. There were tens of thousands of comments.

"There will never be a greater athlete" was the most expressed comment." Worlds like humble, kind, strong work ethic, even gentle, flowed out. Former players and even a few elderly coaches told stories for the cameras. His shyness, his love of music and movies, when the occasion occurred. His unselfish restraint.

Fifty-eight-year-old Hiro Nukiyama said that he cried upon hearing of the Canyon's death. He told cameras in Japan that "Dan Johnson is famous as a basketball player, but he was a great, great judo player. He practiced very hard. He had great respect for the sport and is one of its greatest champions. He made me a better player and all of Japan mourns the death of this great man."

Now that Dan was gone, there was an entire newsreel of stories having to do with his real passion, the only thing that seemed to give Dan some semblance of peace. The Canyon Foundation. His organization that raised over $22 billion dollars to help the two causes he concentrated on, children's cancer and food banks. Enough stories to fill a library. About Dan's fierce tenacity to making sure the Foundation's money was spent wisely. To him doing anything he could to raise money. Personal appearances, company banquets, gatherings at his sanctuary, his love, his Lake Lanier home, and Canyonville his ultimate man-cave that he preferred to reserve only for friends and special events.

Whatever it took to make sure there were more Wendy's in the world who got to live a full life, one not brutally cut short by cancer, and fewer children and families going hungry.

The Canyon Foundation saw a huge increase in donations, and Dan had discussed, at one time, the Foundation being disbanded when he died, but Melanie realized that Dan's reputation would ensure that his Foundation helped the care for sick children, and helped thousands upon thousands to get a meal, and she knew that Dan would approve. She had the ability at any time to close down the Foundation if she didn't like it's direction.

Melanie would have two knee replacement surgeries and lived quietly until the age of 86, passing away at a local hospital in Hall County, GA, thirty-eight years after Dan.

Tony Minnelli, his wife Brittany, three sons and seven grandchildren all attended the small memorial service at a hotel in Alpharetta, GA. Melanie had kept the number down to Tony, of course, and a few people that Melanie knew he would want.

The Minnelli clan had enough Dan Johnson artifacts to fill a museum, and none of it would be sold. Tony had financial security and most important, the peace in his heart that both he and Dan had chased and chased together for all those years.

There were only a few brief eulogies. One was from Jim Danley, a well-known sports columnist and announcer. Jim was known nationally as a well-spoken, articulate sports journalist and somewhat of a sports historian, who talked about Dan's success and legacy and a couple of humorous stories that took place when Dan was an athlete. The other was from the President and CEO of the Canyon Foundation, Marcy Goodman's replacement, who talked about what Dan said about was his life's passion, the real reason he played sports and accumulated wealth. Robert Ryan mentioned the staggering figures, of the tons of food served and people helped, and of the medical miracles helped along by the necessary money of the Canyon Foundation. Things Dan would never tell the public would now come out.

A police officer from Marietta, GA made the short drive, and spoke to how money from the Canyon Foundation specifically pegged for Marietta, West Orange, NJ, and Ann Arbor, MI, paid for the expensive surgery and longtime treatment for his son, as an infant, treatment that the insurance company rejected (Dan and Melanie later added Flowery Branch, GA to this list and helped pay for many projects in their lake house town). Treatment that his son would have surely died without. This police officer was a weight trainer, and through his uniform, you could see the massive shoulders, the huge forearms. The large man's voice cracked as he spoke about his little boy, now an 18-year-old honor student at all places, Wheeler High School, now a magnet school for exceptional students, and how he planned on studying engineering at Georgia Tech. "My son, my wife and I, our son, is alive, and has a wonderful future, because Dan Johnson decided that he wanted to help children. The combination of the man's size, the tough guy look, with his sincerity, his tears, led to quiet tears from the entire audience. Quiet. Dignified. And yet, somehow, happy.

"Ryan", the police dad said, please let everyone know who you are." The embarrassed son, tall, handsome, in suit and tie, stood up and gave a small wave before sitting down." A typical 18-year-old. "Dan Johnson was a famous athlete, and maybe he was many other things, but to us, he was an angel. God bless you, Dan Johnson."

Finally, and Melanie planned it this way, Tony got up to speak. Tony spoke about how the excitement of finding out that the Canyon would be living in the building he worked at would turn into a nearly thirty-year friendship. How they came from such different backgrounds but how they both had their doubts and fears about life. How Dan always stuck by him, encouraged him, and then how good he was to his children. Dan had already retired by the time his kids were born, but Dan was so famous that Tony's kids felt very special to be in his life. Dan and Melanie could not have children, and so Tony and Brittany's kids were like their own.

The ripples from the life of Dan Johnson would be felt for a very long time. Just as people still talked about Babe Ruth, the exploits and the records surrounding the life of Dan Johnson would reverberate. Melanie would give money to the things that she and Dan held special. Different things from the Canyon Foundation. She would give money to aspiring screenwriters and musicians. She paid for a plaza, called, appropriately, CANYON Plaza in Atlanta, a city which was now a thriving tv and movie destination that was larger than Hollywood. On the plaza were the 100 best movie quotes, on a low-hanging wall, only two years after Dan's death, and Melanie said how much Dan would have loved it. The plaza had comfortable benches, lots of trees for shade, and music speakers. It was a place Melanie felt that Dan and Tony would have liked to hang out at and talk about the world. Tony came to the unveiling and said, while different, would be a "Southern Eagle Rock Reservation." He joked and said, "the scenery may not be quite as good, but the music makes up for it." He then smiled and said, "Both places were beautiful, and Dan would love "Canyon Plaza" as he loved "the Reservation." Over the next several years, all kinds of events, including speeches, small musical concerts, and rallies for noble causes, were held at the CANYON Plaza. It would not be uncommon for speakers to use Dan's name as a rallying cry for their cause, "Just as Dan Johnson, The CANYON, fought for the well-being of others, for good health and to feed the hungry, so do we gather on this plaza, named for him, to fight for our cause."

Yes, the splash that Dan Johnson made would reverberate for years, but like all great events and people, those ripples, like a smooth stone falling in a pond, would grow more faint through time, opening the way for another Dan Johnson, another dreamer, another person yearning to make a difference in the world, to love, to laugh, to cry, to find themself.

# Hiro's Message

The image came up on a screen at Madison Square Garden. Dan thought a lot of Hiro, although many people would not know him, especially basketball fans. But he was able, frantically, to reach Dan's agent through the Fury Liquor people in Japan that knew Mike. He desperately wanted to record something because he could not make the trip to Japan. So, his brief tape was run during the Knick's memorial.

When word got out, three memorial services were planned because Dan was simply too big a figure for a single funeral. For one thing, Melanie wanted a small funeral, only for a selected few that she knew to invite. The Knicks and the University of Michigan wanted a service as well, so each would plan one, using their own spokesperson and video of Dan that they had playing in college, and for the Knicks, in the NBA. There were tributes in New York and Ann Arbor, to Dan's tremendous sportsmanship, and video highlights of his playing days were shown. A few fellow teammates said a few words, representatives from the police and fire department, and a few people who benefitted from the CANYON Foundation's donations.

The tape began; "My name is Hiro Nukiyama. I was a gold medal winner at Atlanta USA Olympics, where I defeat Dan Canyon Johnson. I lost to Canyon two times before when he won the gold medal in Spain, and during World Championships.

Defeating the Canyon was the greatest victory in my life, and I retired right after. I studied his fights for many years, and I was lucky to win one time. Nobody else ever beat him before or after.

The Canyon then comes to Japan many months later to honor me. I was overcome with emotion. To me, he is the world's greatest sportsman. When I hear that he has died, tears flowed from my face. To me, he is a man too big to die. I know he has helped many others. Small children and the hungry.

In Japan, Dan Canyon Johnson is revered and honored as a man who practiced the Bushido code of honor, which includes • Justice, Courage, Benevolence, Politeness, Honesty and Sincerity, Honor, Character and Self-Control.

Goodbye to my friend and respected opponent, Dan Johnson."


In Ann Arbor, Eric Dudley's widow, Janet Dudley, stood up and told the full capacity at Crisler about how Dan saved her family, and by not just giving her money, which he did, but saving her dignity. Janet Dudley was able to place her two children in an upscale apartment complex, while she completed her college education at Washtenaw Community College in Ann Arbor. "Dan didn't just give me money. He became a friend. He pushed me to make more of myself but without having to worry where my kids would sleep or get their next meal. I was a young widow. I felt sorry for myself, but Dan never did. He said "Ok, let's roll up our sleeves and improve your life". He paid for my tuition and today, and I am certified Dental Hygienist. I am financially independent. I will ever forget what Dan Johnson did for me.

Charles Winfield, who attended services in Atlanta and Ann Arbor, stood and quietly went to the mic. "You're Little Cazzie's wife?" Janet, through tears, nodded yes. "He was an excellent basketball player and a good man. He didn't deserve his outcome, and I know Dan felt the same. You deserved a chance.

Imagine how good the C Man felt knowing he could help "Little Cazzie's" family.

Madison Square Garden took over as the service where the celebrities I sports, politics, and acting community came to be seen and recognize the CANYON. Videos were shown, speeches were given. The major of New York, spoke, the Governor, the Vice President, celebrities that Dan got to know personally, all giving example of Dan's prowess, his competitiveness, his incredible sportsmanship, and his humanitarian work. An entire contingent from West Orange, NJ arrived, so big that they seemed to take up the entire lower ring. Police officers and fire fighters, all in uniform, civic leaders. The Mayor spoke about a statue would, in the near future, go up at Eagle Rock Reservation, as soon as the right artist could be chosen and funding acquired. There was no charge to attend the "Celebration of Life", and 19,000 fans poured in, a capacity crowd, to pay their respects to the CANYON, the greatest Knick every to play the game, and the game's greatest humanitarian, let alone, a man who delivered eight championships to the Knicks.

# Melanie's Eulogy

The Mayor of Marietta, GA called Melanie, offering any type of service or facility in the city. Like he did for West Orange, Ann Arbor, and later, Flowery Branch, Dan provided a great deal of financial support to the city, primarily, to the police and fire Foundation. Dan's money had saved lives in Marietta. Individual stories of medical miracles could easily be cited. The mayor offered the Cobb County Civic Center, near the beautiful Marietta Square, and Melanie accepted. While she only wanted a small service with family and friends, it became impossible not to allow grateful fans, the police, firefighters, and others. Before she knew it, 2,500 people, the building's capacity, filled the Center. In the few short days they had, Melanie said she was exhausted and took up the mayor's offer to plan the ceremony, with the help of his staff. Dan was larger than life and was known around the world. How does one even plan anything like this? Melanie refused to allow Dan's elderly parents, now in their 80's, to be bothered, and they chose not to attend. They didn't need a service to remember and honor their only child.

Tony Minnelli and his family came only to the Marietta service, along with Paul and his family. Jimmy passed away in 2021, at the age of seventy-four. Carole was down at their south Florida home. Ann Karlsson and Charles Winfield attended just the Marietta services, and a number of other acquaintances, too large in number attended. Too many wished to speak and the Mayor had no choice but the consult with Melanie over the list of speakers. Surprisingly, though, Melanie herself told the Mayor that she wanted to give the eulogy, and it had to be the last speech at the service. People needed to hear about the real Dan Johnson, about who he really was.

It was an overcast day in the city of Marietta. Scores of cars were attempting to find a place to park around the Marietta Parkway, also known as the "Marietta Loop". If Ann Arbor was the Wolverine celebration, and New York, the big celebration, Marietta was the hometown celebration. Dan was a product of Wheeler High School, only four and half miles away, and still, a basketball powerhouse. People spoke to how proud they were that Dan Johnson was born and raised in the Atlanta area, a fellow Georgian. They loved his athleticism, even if he did choose to play for an out-of-state school and for the N.Y. Knicks, which he really had no choice in. Dan never forgot Marietta, but his tremendous support of the police and fire fighters. He also gave money to Wheeler, for scoreboards, and much more. More, always more, than what people ever knew about. And many liked that he retired to Lake Lanier. There was just something about "coming home" after a job well done, and if anyone did a good job for others, in making dreams come true, or by just helping others get back on their feet, it was Dan.

A Methodist Reverand said some words, including a poem by Gretta Zwaan based off of Matthew 25:23:

> "I may not get credit from earth's selfish crowd;
> I may not hear accolades spoken out loud,

*No recognition for things I have done*
*Until I meet Jesus, God's only Son.*

*That will be glory! A wonderful day!*
*When I am promoted my Father will say:*
*"Well done, faithful servant; come sit with the Lord,*
*You have been faithful, you've earned your*
*reward."*

Melanie, the final speaker, stood up to the podium. The date was November 3, 2026:

"I wish everyone could have known Dan Johnson the way I knew him. His height and even skill and determination were the least of his attributes. You expect to hear a spouse, or a friend say that. After all, all athletes have a life of some kind, but we've also learned to hear things like "he lived for his sport. He was consumed with being the best".

Being an athlete was thrust upon Dan because of his tremendous size, and oh sure, he came to enjoy it. And he hardly just went through the motions. I don't care how big you are. He was taught by some of the top people that you have an obligation to give your best, and I promise you, Dan always gave his best. My God, every basketball season from high school to the pros ended in a championship. Think about that. It has never been done before and will never be done again. But I suppose I could be bitter about that.

And then Dan was a world and Olympic Champion in two other sports. I don't think the world will ever again see the likes of Dan Johnson. Even the great Jim Thorpe cannot approach the success of my husband.

But all these things came second to Dan's passion for helping people. That was his dream. He never wanted to be an athlete. It's simply what he gave to the world that expected it from him. Giving through his foundation was the life event that finally made him happy. Rings and medals never did. In fact, if Dan could have lived the life of his dreams, he'd be a crooner. Oh, you all know that old fashioned name. A man who sings beautiful music, love songs, like his idol, Dean Martin. You see, Dean not only could sing, he could act, but it wasn't that. Dean had charisma. He was comfortable in his skin. My Dan did not have charisma. No, no. He didn't. He had great empathy for others. In fact, he spent his athletic career in conflict with his inner self. A man so powerful, so large, and yes, he wanted desperately to win. He loved to win, oh yes. But he also wanted to quiet his critics. He was so sensitive, Dan. He had this inner conflict because he wanted to win but he didn't want to hurt anybody. He only wanted to hurt one person in his life, a man that attacked him in Central Park. I wasn't there but I do know he almost killed a man with one punch. Had it been second punch, he would have killed him. But Dan wanted to do good and spent years doing all he could financially, and gaining stardom, so he could give the way he wanted to, and help people live better lives. Remember Dan as the athletic marvel that he was. I played college ball. I know what it was like. But, if you want to remember the real Dan Johnson, remember him as a man who desperately wanted to help others.

Dan never got to be Dean Martin, but not for a lack of effort. I had to listen to that scratchy voice for several years at home (that brought some chuckles). But Dan got to be so many things that it's also hard to feel too sorry for him. My husband, my best friend, Dan Johnson, lived a most extraordinary life.

Dan lived inside a magical world of emotions right within his own mind. He was a thinker and a dreamer. In his mind, he flew to magical places, laughed like no human being was possible of laughing, loved like no human could love, and in his fertile mind he conducted beautiful symphonies.

Oh, not the musical kind, even though he adored good music, trust me, no, symphonies of kindness. Dan Johnson wove in his mind, a symphony of life. That's what I would call them, for even I could have but a glimpse of what Dan could see and feel in that mind. In his mind, he could do what his long-bodied frame, all eight feet, eleven inches could not do, and that is, to reach the stars. Through his magnificent imagination and through his love and kindness, Dan Johnson, not the CANYON, but just Danny, to me, reached the stars.

I'm sorry to tell you that he suffered terribly these last few years. All the doctor's amazed findings when Dan was very young, that a human could grow to just under nine feet tall and live a normal life, well, it just wasn't true at all. The fact that Dan lived as long as he did without complications was a miracle. But it caught up to him, this gentle man. But in Dan's 51 years, he accomplished more than any person I can imagine. I feel so blessed. I will miss him. God, will I miss him, but now, he is home, and out of pain. I love you, Danny.

"Dan was a jazz lover, and in his day with his contemporaries, that was not a popular thing, as you know. But that was Dan. That fit him. A little unusual, a little artsy, a little nerdy, open to a lot of interpretation, off the beaten path. But he loved other styles, and he admired musicians because he never acquired that skill. Did you all know, the two people that Dan Johnson admired the most were men who both stood under four feet tall? One was in over 200 movies, Billy Barty, whom Dan met on the Tonight Show with Johnny Carson, and became a great friend and mentor. Dan looked up to him so. And then, as a high schooler, Dan discovered a great jazz musician named Michel Petrucciani, who was from France but lived right in New York, and Dan heard him play several times. Michel stood about three and half feet tall and was born with a brittle bone disease called Osteogenesis imperfecta.

He was in constant pain for many years. He and Dan had a unique, if distant kind of bond, even though their afflictions were different from each other, with Dan suffering from rheumatoid arthritis in virtually joint of his body.

Michel appreciated seeing Dan the few times he made it to a club to hear him play, always sitting in the back. Michel was a wonderful person with a great wit to match Dan's. One time, Michel was speaking to the audience as he liked to do and Dan was looking around, not really interested, and Michel said, 'Dan', all sometimes he would 'the tall man', isn't listening, he has his head in the clouds.' That was Michel. Sharp, witty, and one of the greatest musicians of our time.

Both men were so accomplished, as was Billy Barty, always hopeful, despite their pain and challenges. Mostly happy, always looking up, and of course, everybody looked up to Dan. This is why it is so wonderful that Dan's favorite song is one from Michel called, what else, but 'Looking Up.' I ask you to bask in the beauty of this song, just for half a minute or so, and think about not just Dan Johnson, but of hope, of happiness, of possibilities, of looking up. Then, please get up and mingle around. After all, its jazz, it goes on for a while.

And when you listen, remember that Dan Johnson was able to do things nearly everybody else can only dream about. He was able to help so many, financially, on a large scale, yes, but also on a personal scale. His resources fed people, helped treat people. It's true. Billions and billions of dollars, and it will continue. But he touched people on a personal level. I could not begin to tell you of the dozens of times he changed people's lives, in an instant, by pulling them out of despair, giving them a helping hand, putting them back on the road to success. Giving them not a handout but giving them back their dignity. Dan personally gave out millions of dollars, aside from his foundation, but he never threw it on the ground, so to speak. He spoke to people, encouraged them, helped them, in many instances, came up with a long-term plan to change their lives, but first, he pulled them from the depths of hell. That was Dan's real dream. Not medals or championships, but to inspire, to make a difference, and by doing that, it was his greatest personal victory and because of that, while we mourn his passing, we can celebrate his life. He really suffered the last couple of years, but I can tell you that he also died a happy man. Without pain, without sacrifice, we would have nothing".

The song started playing, the delightful, upbeat song, and regardless of what the audience may have thought, their affection or even disdain for jazz, every face had a smile on it, because they knew it was Dan's favorite song, and most would agree, for reasons maybe hard to explain, that it SOUNDED like Dan, somehow. When Melanie began to walk around after a minute, the group took her cue, and did the same, and the service was over.

# Landing in Newark

Tony landed in Newark, with the document in his jacket pocket. He brought very little, just a small overnight bag, as the ceremony lasted two hours and then they returned to the airport to make their way home. Tony never got to know Atlanta, or the south, except for occasional trips to Florida. He could easily afford a nice home there, but rented or just went to "Canyonville" down at Lake Lanier. Tony was one of the very few that Dan allowed to visit the house, and both he and Melanie told him to consider it the Minnelli's second home, and Tony went there often. The cool lake waters felt great in the hot Georgia summer, and the weather was far milder than the northeast, at almost any time of the year.

He was able to bypass the always slow baggage claim area, and head for the parking lot, where he and his wife drove back to their North Caldwell home.

Tony said, "I'll be in the family room. Do me a favor and leave me alone for a little while."

The color-faded manilla envelope was dated 12-31-2007. Whatever was in this envelope was nineteen years old. He opened it up, a little nervously, and began to read the single sheet of paper.


12-31-2007

Tony,

Somebody once wrote a letter like this to me, and I read it after he died. I thought I would do the same thing, so I wrote this when I was thirty-two. I don't know how long I'll last but at least the letter was done.

It wasn't always easy being so different. A lot of people thought that if I wasn't so tall, I wouldn't have achieved much in my life, and I spent a lifetime trying to show them that they were wrong. I don't know if I succeeded or failed.

I do know that you and your family didn't care about my height. You welcomed me into your home and gave me the love that I had only from my parents, and then from Melanie. That's really all I had in my life. Everything else was simply about money and power. I suppose that's good up to a point.

You always felt different, too. Different than the rest of your family. Given less respect, but I want to tell you that you are just as good as anyone in your family. You were just slower to find yourself, just like me. A late bloomer. You're a smart and funny guy, and other than my wife, I am more comfortable with you than anyone in the world. Maybe more than my wife, as there are some things a couple of guys want to talk about that women can't understand or don't want to hear.

I like you exactly the way that you are. I like the way you talk; in a way I wish I could be like. I like your sense of humor. You spoke the truth about a lot of things, only sometimes, people didn't want to hear it.

I was lucky and underserving, that because I was this incredibly tall guy, I could meet Presidents and movie stars, and wealthy businesspeople who thought it was cool to have their picture taken with me, a freak of nature. But what I really liked was sitting around in the dark, at the Reservation, looking out at the city lights of New York, where we could talk about anything, and drinking a cold beer. It wasn't Paris or some exotic beach somewhere. Maybe it's fitting that it was in New Jersey, a place always fighting for respect, called names, called ugly and worthless, yet a place with great beauty, if you know where to look. Maybe it's not always the place, but the people that inhabit that place. I think that in its own way, Eagle Rock Reservation is the most special place in the world.

You are in a good place now, with a family that loves you, and nobody is happier for you than I am. Maybe today, I am in a good place, too, where I am liked for who I am, instead of what I am. Maybe, somehow, we will see each other again, and be able to lay back on a hill, watching clouds or counting the stars, asking about the many questions a person has about life.

You helped make my life better, and I wanted to tell you that. You were my very best friend.


Dan


Tony stared at the letter while tears silently rolled down his cheeks. His profound sense of emotion, his tremendous feeling of loss, now began to take hold. A whimpering sound began to come from Tony, this grown man, this tough man, a "man's man" insofar as how that term is most understood. The whimpering evolved to a moan, and then to an audible series of sobs, getting louder as the seconds ticked by. This man had not cried in this way since he was nine years old, on the football field of West Orange High School, playing for the P.A.L. or Police Athletic League Mustangs. Everyone thought he had broken his leg, but it was simply a bad bruise. Up to St. Barnabas Hospital he went and missed a week of school. He was alone and could let all his feelings out, and Anthony Minnelli, recognizing the death of the greatest friend he ever had in the world, put his face in his hands, and sobbed.

# Life in Review

ATLANTA, GA - The interest in basketball and sports legend Dan, the CANYON Johnson has reached epic proportions, following his death this week at the age of fifty-one. The CANYON had been experiencing a long list of ailments common to athletes, including arthritis and other joint problems, but he passed, according to medical experts familiar with his health, from heart failure. He went through angioplasty five years ago for blockage in his heart arteries, and received two stents. However, it is undetermined if that situation contributed to his death. An anonymous doctor, unfamiliar with Johnson's records, said, "Dan Johnson was an amazing physical specimen, but his heart may have simply given out due to the demands of pumping blood to a such a large body. A person of lesser physical condition might have succumbed at an even younger age."

The CANYON leaves a list of records that seems impossible for any human to equal:

1. Olympic Gold medals in Judo and Wrestling, along with numerous national and world championships.
2. An Olympic team Gold in basketball, a member and key contributor in four straight NCAA titles for the Michigan Wolverines and eight straight NBA championships with the New York Knickerbockers, ever year he was in the league.
3. Founder of The CANYON Foundation, for which he had said was his greatest achievement, which has raised an estimated $22 billion, for the eradication of childhood cancer and hunger. In contrast to his shy demeanor, Johnson took on the role of spokesman, salesman, and when needed, sergeant at arms. He said himself, "There was a time when wanting to be accepted and liked took precedence over everything else. But I matured through

the years and realized that if I had to lose a few friends to fight cancer and feed people, then so be it."

4. A Presidential Medal of Freedom awarded just four years ago, for his selfless acts of humanitarian work, awarded by President Rafael Diaz.

During one of his few interviews, he quoted Churchill, saying "You have enemies? Good. That means you've stood up for something, sometime in your life. It took me half a lifetime to understand that."

Later, another news report aired. "It has now been six months since the passing of sports legend and humanitarian Dan Johnson, and the Smithsonian Institution has just announced a future exhibition entitled: 'CANYON, The Extraordinary Life of Dan Johnson.' Thanks to tremendous cooperation from Johnson's widow, Melanie Johnson, the exhibit will feature a huge collection of artifacts, from clothing, sports attire, videos, the stool used for years in the elevator at his New York Apartment, even his specially designed car. There is a special area showing all the medical breakthroughs brought to the world based on his fund raising, and even his collection of vintage jazz records.

Attendance is free, but there will be a staggered ticket program designed to control what is expected to be record-breaking attendance. "

Finally, the city of West Orange, NJ has awarded the bid for a special statue of best friends Dan Johnson and Anthony Minnelli, to be unveiled on a future date at the Eagle Rock Reservation Area. The statue will celebrate the joys of friendship, dreams, and the joys and serenity of the Reservation, which overlooks the New York skyline. Friends and onlookers said that the two friends spent countless hours discussing many stories and subjects, while enjoying the beautiful overlook.

The University of Michigan and The New York Knicks have both previously erected statues of Dan Johnson outside of Crisler Arena and Madison Square Garden, respectively.

When asked for a comment, Anthony Minnelli said that the 77 West building gave him the treasured elevator stool as a keepsake, where Anthony once served as a doorman. It would be going as well to the Smithsonian for the exhibition, but that later, it would reside with the Minnelli family.

"We considered Dan an honorary member of the Minnelli family, and we all loved him," Anthony Minnelli stated.

# The Final Visit

Tony Minnelli stood staring out toward the island of Manhattan. It was an overcast day, with a 70% chance of rain by the afternoon. It was a Saturday morning and he decided to get out early. A stop at the Caldwell Diner, and then he promised Brittany he'd get a dozen bagels at the Bagel Box right on Eagle Rock Avenue. Jeez, it has been there forever. The students at Mountain High School, and then West Orange High School, they'd buy them and get away with it because they'd bribe the teachers. He only ate everything bagels. The Jews got it right. Everything bagel, toasted with cream cheese was majestic in its simplicity.

On this same road, there was once the E.J. Korvettes variety store (rumors that it stood for "Eight Jewish Korean Veterans were unproven), Walter Bauman's, where he bought Brittany's ring, Gary's Restaurant, two swim clubs he once snuck into, now condominiums or office building, Pal's Cabin, maybe other places he once thought would stand forever, but if he didn't understand, he finally did today, that even the mighty eventually fall. That everything comes to an end.

He'd come to understand so much in his life, it only took fifty years. Many more things would remain a mystery, and maybe that's how some things in life were meant to be. Would it really be best if we knew everything? He had one true friend in his life, the others were nice acquaintances, and that was okay. There's nothing wrong with nice acquaintances, and in a day where everyone is listed as a friend, there's nothing with having just one. Some never have even that, and some only think that they do. His dad one said, "Have a friend who would stand alongside you in a war, in the foxhole." He had just one like that, even if that friend had to duck down all the time.

He had worried about so many things. Bad things that never happened. Some others did, but life still went on, and he learned that he could never satisfy everyone no matter how hard he tried. He remained in many ways, the goofy, foul-mouthed kid who never grew up, leaning on this wall with a beer, arguing about music, food, sports, women, with a man from another place whom he had nothing at all in common with. A man he didn't deserve the friendship of, but a man that for some mysterious reason, felt otherwise.

So many people he loved were gone, just as thousands of people whose names were now inscribed on this wall, a monument to the lives lost on a September 11th morning, in Manhattan, in Washington, and in a field in Pennsylvania.

He had a family of his own, a wife, and children. One day, God-willing, some grandchildren. He had more to do, even if that "more" was a smile, a hug for his kids, sitting and listening to the Four Seasons or Bon Jovi. When he was younger, he sometimes cursed life for not going the way he wanted it to, for not knowing what God intended for him, and he still wasn't always sure, but he didn't let it bother him anymore.

He held in his hand a can of Pabst Blue Ribbon and an urn. There were instructions, written long ago. Very specific, right down to the PBR. Melanie understood.

About a quarter of the beer was gone. That's as far as it would go today. He couldn't drink like he used to. The rest of the beer, on this gray Saturday, 9:30 AM, with an empty parking lot, would be poured out.

There was no speech, just a deep breath and the job was done. A mild breeze and the ashes took to the sky momentarily, and then vanished into the air.

The car slowly drove out, turning left onto Prospect Avenue and then onto Route 280 for the short drive home. Britt was waiting for the bagels. As he drove away, the soft refrain of "Imaginary Lover" by the Atlanta Rhythm Section drifted over the speakers. The CD was a gift from his friend.

"When all the others turn you away, they're around."

# The Little Boy's Box

Melanie asked Tony to help her go through Dan's things. It had been six weeks, and she was shocked when she got a call from the curator at The Museum of American History at the Smithsonian Institution.

"Tony, the Smithsonian wants to know what I can donate to their museum. I never thought about anything like that. Danny's life in a museum." "Well," said Tony, "We were so close to him. He was Danny to us. I never called him C Man. I'd never live it down". Melanie said, "I called him C Man out of pretend contempt, like "Ok, C Man, get your dirty clothes off the floor." "Yeah", said Tony.

"Will you and Brittany come down to the lake house, please, and help me out? I can't go throughout the 'Little Boy's Box' alone. I'll lose it, I know it." "The what?" asked Tony? "You'll see", Melanie said. "In three days, Tony and Brit were on a flight to Atlanta."

Tony rented a car for the hour and a half drive up to the lake house. It was a Saturday, so the traffic up Georgia 400 wasn't too bad. It had been a month since the Minnelli's had seen Melanie, but Melanie asked for some time alone.

After hugs and a couple of tears, Tony said. "Ok, what can we do, and I'm to hear about this toy box thing." "Not toy box," Melanie said. 'Little Boy's Box'. Dan loved collecting things. What I called crap, he called, 'items that carried sentimental value'". "Yeah, sounds exactly like something he would say." "Well, get ready. I know he collected stuff like game programs, napkins, matches from restaurants, tons of other stuff. His entire life. Tony, you didn't know that?" He said, "No, but that's something a wife would know. Think I care what a guy stuffs in his pocket?" Ok, well, I don't think the Smithsonian will want a napkin. I've got a Michigan letter jacket and some trophies and things like that. I need your help in deciding. The museum wants it for a year and maybe, they said, two years."

The "Little Boy's Box" was a big box, about the size of an extra- large microwave oven. It was filled all the way to the top, with paper and other things just thrown in. "I told Dan that this was his box, like a little boy would put his toys. It was in the corner of the man-cave, covered up. Nobody ever noticed it. I don't know what's in it beyond a few things I saw him collect and throw in there. It goes way, way back because he used to just keep it all around, in closets, in junk drawers. I told him "No more" when we got married. Choose a box and store it. Well, the box got bigger, so, ready for some fun, or tears?" "Let's open some beer and wine." Tony said. "And put on some jazz," said Melanie. "Let's not get carried away," said Dan.

They put out a blanket and about four empty boxes, for sorting. It was four in the afternoon and at 11:00, they went to bed, still unfinished, because many items had stories behind it. Some items made perfectly good sense, Dan's Michigan graduation program, but other items were just so totally random that it turned out the be great fun while it also made them realize that a day wouldn't go by when they wouldn't think of Dan, for as long as they had days left.

1. Napkins that said, "Eagle Rock Bowling Lanes". Another that said, "Jimmy Buffs". "The 40-Watt Club", Brown Jug, "Home of the CANYON Burger, "Taco Mac", "Blind Willie's".
2. About fifty matches with logos: "The Manor", "Coach and Six Restaurant", "Tavern on the Green", "Clyde Frazier's Wine and Dine", "Crestmont Country Club", "the Tic Toc Diner", "Star Tavern."
3. A Knicks commemorative program, "1998 Championship Season".
4. A crushed cup that said "The Varsity, Atlanta-Athens. No food over 12 hours old."
5. About ten Olympic pins from assorted countries, including one that said "Izzy". "Now that was one dumb mascot". Tony said.
6. A book that said, "100 Best Movie Quotes." Melanie said that he had bought that book about four times and wore it out. This was an extra one."
7. A CD case of Michel Petrucciani, empty on the inside. "Well, that's no surprise", Melanie said.
8. Three keys of no designation or value. "Who knows?". They agreed to throw them out.
9. A button that said "Go 'liners". Again, nobody knew, but they kept it. Maybe they could figure it out later.
10. A football program for a Michigan-Ohio State game.
11. A napkin that still had the faint smell of perfume that said, "Thank you, honey." Nobody said anything but it went in the trash.
12. A Sports Illustrated Magazine dated "June 25, 1996" with a cover photo of Dan standing in the front of the "Big Chicken" Kentucky Fried Chicken restaurant in Marietta, GA. A caption said. "Atlanta 1996. The CANYON comes home. Can Dan Johnson

capture gold in three sports?" Dan was on the cover of Sports Illustrated 31 times. Not a record, but "up there". The last cover was three weeks ago with a close-up of Dan smiling, and a caption that simply said. "DAN JOHNSON, 1975-2026. The curator, with assistance from the magazine, was already working on a "Sports Illustrated Wall", with all 31 covers.

13. Another Sports Illustrated with Dan on the cover, Dan grabbing a rebound in a Knicks uniform. The caption read "Never in question. The Knicks crush the Lakers in four-straight."

14. A TV Guide from 1971 with a picture of a boy playing a toy flute. The flute had eyes and a mouth. The caption said, "Jack Wild of H.R. Puffenstuff." "Now that's what I'd call random", Tony said. "It meant something to Danny. I can promise you that," Melanie chuckled.

15. Among the items were over 20 birthday cards from Melanie to Dan. "I never knew he saved these", and Melanie started to cry. Some Valentine cards were found as well. More crying. A Christmas card from Johnny Carson. Everybody thought that was cool, even if Johnny's staff sent it. "Season's Greetings from Johnny and the Tonight Show family." A Christmas card from Billy Barty. Inside, he wrote, "Merry Christmas, kid. I'm proud of you." "This card would have meant the world to Danny," Melanie said. White House holiday cards, several from famous celebrities, to where each one brought out a "wow, look at this one", from all three of them.

16. A children's size t-shirt that said, "Uncle Floyd. Channel 68". "Oh my God", said Tony. "Melanie, please, may I have that shirt?" "Yes, of course,

Tony. That shirt means something to you?" "Oh yeah, a lot." Melanie said nothing.

17. A birthday card from Dan to Melanie that she thought was lost after a couple of years. On the front was a black and white still from "Casablanca", with Bogie and Bergman on the cover, the final airport scene. Inside was, of course, the words, "Here's looking at you, kid." Melanie was laughing while wiping tears, "He didn't trust me! I know him, that son of a gun! He knew I would love this but eventually, throw it out. I hate clutter. To him, this was priceless." Brittany asked, "Are you glad he kept it now?" "Oh God, yes. So, so glad." Tony said, "Jesus, even for me, this is draining." Melanie added, "This card is 30 years old."

18. A card that was white with an orange T on the cover. Inside "Dear Melanie, we enjoyed your stay in Knoxville. Best of luck. Coach Pat Summit." "Tennessee recruited me. Great coach and school. I don't why he kept stuff of mine like this." "Because "Brittany said "It's obvious. He knew that one day, you would cherish these little things. Sometimes it's the little things that carry big meaning. Oh, my gawd", Brit said in the strongest New Jersey accent possible. It was wonderful. "That man loved you so much." More crying and hugging.

Finally, Tony dug something out. It was a can. Tony yelled out confused and at the same time, hysterical. "A can of cheese whiz." Tony and Brittany heard Melanie curse for maybe the third time in their lives, "What the FUCK???" Then Tony shouted, and he was laughing as he said it, barely getting out the words, "Break out the crackers!!"

"Wait" Brittany asked. How old is that can. Melanie looked underneath and simply put her hand over her mouth. "Are you ready?" "Tell us", Brittany yelled. "There's a stamp that says 11/99". Brittany said "Holy shit. Hey Tone, how many years is that?" Tony and Melanie thought. Brittany could easily do it, but this was always her way. Finally, Melanie said, slowly, "That can of cheese whiz is 37 years old." All three started to laugh and couldn't stop. Three minutes later, they were bent over. It was one of those laughs you're lucky to have once every ten years. "Oh, my Gawd," Brittany said. "I can't breathe." "Why?" Melanie asked. Brittany punched Tony in the arm, "You're a man. You knew him. What kind of sick shit were you guys into on that Eagle Run playground?" Tony composed himself, "It wasn't 'Eagle Run' and it wasn't a playground. "Go back to Kearny." The Cheese Whiz meant something, but even Melanie didn't know. Everything Dan said, did, and COLLECTED, MEANT SOMETHING. So did the 37-year-old can of Cheese Whiz. Something.

It must be noted somewhere that Brittany Minnelli was a person you wanted in your life, even if it seems that she didn't fare that that largely in Dan's story. That wouldn't be true. To quote Tony himself at their wedding in 2008. "Brittany is a good Italian girl. She's very protective of people she loves, and there's no 'like' with Brit. If she likes you, if you're a good person, then Brit loves you, and that's the greatest endorsement in the world. Nobody can love like an Italian girl. She loves with all her heart; with everything she has. She will fight for you like nobody's business. And she will forgive, eventually. Because she truly wants to love. But God help you if she hates you. The lord himself shakes in terror at the sight of an Italian girl who you've done wrong." Of course, this was largely done for effect and entertainment purposes, and the crowd and Brittany loved it.

Also, if Brittany liked and cared about you, you had a pet name. It wasn't Tony, it was "Tone". It wasn't Melanie. It was "Mel." She called Dan, Danny, like all the Minnelli's. Yes, Brittany added spice to everyone's life.

The list of items went on and on. Almost everything was kept. A napkin with no writing on it at all but what appeared to be a dark brown streak was on it. Melanie picked it up, shrieked, then dropped it. Tony picked it up and smelled it. "It's chocolate," said Tony. Nobody could figure that one out and into the garbage it went. There were other things like that, that would remain a mystery. Finally, a beer cap that said "Pabst Blue Ribbon" was found all the way at the bottom, bent almost in half from a bottle opener. Melanie handed it to Tony and said,

"This was meant for you". Tony got very quiet while Brittany put her hand on Tony's shoulder. Tony nodded and put it in his shirt pocket.

Melanie found a piece of paper, folded over once. "Hmm." "What is it?" asked Brit. It looks like a poem. I never knew Dan to write poetry. He loved all those movie quotes, but never mentioned poetry. I think he wrote this, too. "Read it, Mel, read it," said Brittany.

## The Winds of Change

*The seasons come and then they go*
*The babies born, and then they grow*
*You love, you beg for time standing still*
*But in your heart you know, it never will*

*You see their faces, feel warm embraces*
*As if just taking place, just yesterday*
*You look at gray skies, feel the wintry blast*
*When did the spring pass, the warm rays of May?*

*You can never go back*
*You must live for today*
*But the memories they last*
*In your heart to stay*
*So cherish them*
*Pass them on, to the ones for whom you care*
*And form today, new memories, sentimental friend, if you*
*dare*

*Daniel M. Johnson*

"What does "M." stand for?" Tony asked. "McGinnis",
Melanie told him. His mother's maiden name.

"Oh my God", Melanie whimpered, and started to cry.
"You're crying at that?" Tony asked. Brittany, clearly
irritated, punched him in the arm. "The fuck, Anthony.
Don't tell a woman what she should cry about!" Tony,
realizing the seriousness and the situation, simply said
quietly, "sorry". "It's okay", Melanie said, and then laughed
a little bit. "I'm a mess. I don't know what will make me
cry. But I thought I knew him, but something would always
come out." "Yeah", Tony said, but it's just the kind of thing
he would do. Just when you expect one thing, bam, there's

something else. Right now, he's laughing at the three of us, thinking 'gotcha'," and the three of them laughed.

# The Exhibit

Fourteen months later, Melanie, Tony and Brittany, Charles Winfield, and many other guests and dignitaries stood in the reception area of the Smithsonian's Museum of American History, with an actual 8'11" poster of Dan Johnson, encased in plastic. Over the top, in large letters, was a sign that read. "CANYON: The Extraordinary Life of Dan Johnson." People were said to travel from all corners of the world to see the exhibit, and it shattered Smithsonian attendance records.

Policemen and fire fighters, in uniform, from West Orange, NJ, Marietta, GA, Ann Arbor, MI, and Flowery Branch, GA, all arrived during the first month, with signs and banners, stating things like, "Thank you, CANYON". Families told the press amazing stories of how Dan Johnson personally called to thank them and to check on those that he had helped. That was part of the Foundation's "Constitution", written instructions for the Director to meet with Dan and provide contact information for Dan on a regular basis. He couldn't call everyone, but every month, Dan chose a few to call, check up on them, and wish them the best. That went on until just the final few months when Dan was quite ill. But for over twenty years, Dan called hundreds of families, and none of them ever forgot it. But it wasn't just emotional support, it was specific monies earmarked under "special projects" that went above and beyond the mass distribution of foodstuffs and medical payments to hospitals. This was the "personal touch" that Dan had dreamed about, to affect the world on a large scale, down to a personal level, and he achieved it. Dan died knowing that dads would once again be throwing a baseball in the front yard of their home with their son, Mom's would be going to a concert with their child, families would be on the highway, counting license plates from different states, and raising a toast to the new bride and groom. Celebrating the arrival of grandchildren. At least some of them.

Dan had made a difference, and he could now rest. Maybe there was to be another journey of some kind.

There were cocktails and hor d'oeuvres. They picked up a glass of champagne in a small circle. Charles Winfield raised his glass for a toast and said, "Well, folks, the world celebrated him, but we knew him," and their glasses clinked while the VIP's made their way into the exhibit.

Over their heads were a great many well-lit, large photographs. Melanie, at first, thought "how could Dan's life fill part of a museum?" It was only now, here in Washington, that the full impact of Dan's life hit her. Dan in his Knicks uniform, Dan cutting down a net in his Michigan uniform, without the aid of a ladder, huge grin on his face. Another photo of Dan wearing a Michigan uniform, holding a trophy and raising four fingers to signify the Wolverines' 4th straight national championship, Dan on a wrestling mat, on the Olympic podium in his Judo Gi, a photo of Dan at a Japanese high school, in Moscow's Red Square, receiving the Presidential Medal of Freedom, cutting a ribbon on the new wing of a children's hospital, Dan crying at the funeral of a young girl, serving turkey to the needy during a Thanksgiving dinner, at the annual meeting of a Fortune 500 company that reached a record giving level for the Foundation, Dan meeting every living President, Dan meeting the Queen, and far in the back, a photo of Billy Barty on a ladder, with his arm around Dan's shoulders. More than 500 photos, large and small, were displayed around the large hall. Dan with the healthy, the sick, the famous, and ordinary. Dan with people representing nations around the world, from all walks of life. Famous musicians playing their music at Canyonville.

A black and white photo of Dan eating boiled peanuts with Jimmy Carter, at the Carter Center in Atlanta. There was nothing fake about that. Dan loved his boiled peanuts.

And throughout the exhibit, in glass-enclosed cabinets, were awards, written stories, and yes, the Smithsonian wanted every scrap from the "Little Boy's Box". Menus, scrap pieces of paper. All the things, large and small, that summed up the man.

The Smithsonian made a movie, a 15-minute video that ran on a loop and played in a makeshift theater setup inside the exhibit area. It was narrated by a celebrity, with short comments by people from all walks of life, the famous to the ordinary. It showed his beginnings, his growth, his athletic accomplishment, and very heartfelt interviews by people that Dan felt. Many viewers walked out teary-eyed. Even Melanie and Tony said that there were things they didn't know about Dan and learned at the exhibit. The attention to detail was extraordinary.

Dan's greatest gift, many spoke about, was his humanity, a concept that can be hard to clearly expound upon, but it was his decency, his honest desire to treat people with respect. To honor their dignity, even as he showed during his life that he was an imperfect man.

Melanie came to realize that a person's character, their legacy, their "essence" was not measured by any one thing. It wasn't only measured in championship trophies, or Hall of Fame Inductions, or even charitable donations, but in all those things, and in many more. From Presidential medals down to a small piece of paper. She realized that maybe that was why Dan held onto that box.

# APPENDIX

# Double M Nicknames for Dan Johnson

These are nicknames all created by Double M (exception being "CANYON", "C", and "The C Man") on the air during segments of "Basketball Tonight".

The CANYON
The C Man
"C"
Big Johnson
The Wolverine Warrior
The Sensei
The Knickerbocker Nemesis
The Man with his head in the clouds
Mr. Excitement
The Georgia Peach with extra Reach
The Man Too Big for your Cousin's Volkswagen
Mr. Limo
The Secret Weapon
The Man Who Made Red Auerbach Cry
Dan the Man
The Man too Tall to Walk Around in the Mall
The Only Man Chuck Norris is Afraid of
The Man who Lives in Two Zip Codes
The Only Man Bigger Than the Big Chicken
The Only Man That Can Be Seen from Space
The Only Man to Bench Press a Greyhound Bus, Twice
The Mister Who's Undefeated at Twister
The Johnson Women Fear
The Wheeler Wonder
The Marietta Magician
The Mean Wolverine
The Commander in Chief
The Post-Up Prince

Mr. Slam
The Pest of Central Park West
The Manhattan Assassin
The Minister of Dunk

# Key Excerpts from Dan's Journal

> 9-16-1987: "This is my journal's first entry. Little girls have diaries. A word is a word. It only carries meaning when meaning is assigned to it over time. Only then does it matter. A diary has come to mean a cute little book of thoughts for girls. A journal, as one thinks FAIRLY about it, is the same exact thing, but I believe in symbolism, so this is my journal.

> 9-17-1987: I am twelve years old and 7 feet tall. I am a freak. I am following in the steps of Robert Wadlow. My parents might not think I am aware of his predicament and early death, but I looked it up at the library. He died at 22. Will I? I don't have a pituitary tumor, so maybe I will live longer, but I'd better not take any chances, and make my mark now, early in life. There is just something abnormal about me. That's obvious enough.

> 12-24-1987: We went to visit Grandma and Grandpa in Lillian, Alabama. We drove from Marietta. They live on a farm, but they aren't farmers. There's nothing around them but farms. Dad showed me where he learned to fly in Pensacola. Then we drove around more of Alabama, to Orange Beach, and ate a place called Hazel's Nook, for fried chicken. We were in Gulf Shores and drove up to the town of Foley, and then back to their place. Grandma said it would always be a farming area, and that the country needed

that. Mom said Marietta used to have lots of farms, and I laughed.

- ➤ 9-19-1987: I like Judo because I can't be certain I won't be thrown. I know I am going to be stronger than everybody. I can already feel it. But they might use my strength against me, trip me up. Throw me. But they won't let me compete because they're afraid I might kill someone. I not allowed to fight a 12-year-old, a kid my age. I know I can kill them. I wonder what that would feel like…. stop! I would die myself, but I like throwing people around. When the kids laugh at me when I walk by, it would be fun to do a harai- gosh on them and watch them fly. Not die, because I would throw up, but bruised. Yeah, bruised, and ashamed for mocking me. I CAN'T HELP MY SIZE!

- ➤ 11-2-1988: I love girls. I love the way they look, and talk, and smell. I know kids make out at parties, but they look at me like the freak that I am. I wish they were taller. It's funny how the boys are even shorter than the girls. I wish I could be a lot shorter so maybe girls would like me.

- ➤ 8-23-1990. I can't believe I'm in high school. I wish I could drive. Everybody says hi to me and asks me about basketball. Nobody ever mentions wrestling. Wrestlers are tougher and nobody cares. But they all seem to like me because they think we're gonna destroy everybody in basketball. We will. They can't stop us because they can't stop me. I must pass so that the other guys will feel important, but I can score every time I want to. I'm not stupid and neither is anybody else. But I would feel bad, so I'm glad I can help the other guys to look good. But I don't think I'll make friends over it. They only like me because I can help the team win.

➤ 5-4-1993. We never lost a game at Wheeler and coaches have been calling the house for, it seems, a million years. I like Duke but Michigan has a good wrestling team and a great basketball program. It'll be cold. I don't like snow. I like Indiana's campus, and Dad would like me at Purdue. I would feel good. I would like that for a little while longer, nobody knows where I'm going. I'M IN CONTROL!! Yay for me.

➤ 5-22-1993: I picked Michigan. GO BLUE! It was SOO hard, but what's done is done. I hope the girls are hot. I visited so many campuses that I can't keep everything straight.

➤ April 4, 1995: We beat Duke by 17 points and won the NCAA title. I played like crap. They swarmed me all night and stole a bunch of my passes. I don't know what happened. The reporters called it a "valiant" effort by Duke. I was supposed to dominate. I scored 39 points. It doesn't seem to matter that we won. That is always expected of me. Even when good players have a little success, I am supposed to be perfect. We're national champs, so why don't I feel so great? I guess I suck and if I suck at basketball, I suck as a person. I'd like to see them play without me for once.

➤ March 2000. I'll make over $100 million from sales of a shoe. I can't even fathom that. Larry will help me once again give millions away, but as soon as I can get out of this uniform for good, I'll help people my way.

➤ February 11, 2002. I just met the most beautiful girl in the world tonight. Her name is Melanie. I can't put my finger on it. I've been with beautiful women before. Sometimes, it was easy. They banged on my door. Fun. If my high school self only knew some of the women, I'd get just for being so tall. I know the answer. She's beautiful on the inside. Nobody will know quotes from Woody Allen movies like that. I like her mind but what I wouldn't give to have some fun with that body, too. It's a sign, I know it, but why should she feel that way about me? DON'T BLOW IT!

➤ June 11th, 2006. Melanie just gave me my dream man cave. We decided to call it "Canyonville". It came to us at the same time. I want it to be a famous location for charity events. "Live from Canyonville." It's just amazing. I love her so much.

➤ November 2, 2024. I don't know if I can take the pain anymore. Nobody can help. I know they mean well. Anything that works a little bit screws me up in other ways. I can't think straight. I don't want to be a Zombie, but God, help me. I can't take the pain anymore. I keep thinking of "Old Man River", "I'm tired of livin' but scared of dyin". Please God, let me die already.

➤ May 3, 2025. I saw a butterfly out the window a few minutes ago. They start very ugly, a centipede. Nobody is especially fond of that little insect, and then later, everybody is in awe of its beauty. What does a butterfly think about? Does it think about love? Does it think about finding its purpose? Does it experience envy, sorrow, excitement, fear? Pain? Are the victories and beauty of life worth the pain? I wonder.

That was the last entry in Dan Johnson's journal.

# Canyon Copyrighted Logos

**(designed by Ann Karlsson)**

**The CANYON Foundation Logo**

**The official CANYON Logo**

**The CANYON Foundation**
**10 Year Anniversary**
**2015**

**Brown Jug Restraurant**
**Ann Arbor, MI**
**CANYON Burger Logo**

# Where Dan Liked to go in Marietta and Atlanta

1. Marietta Square and Glover Park
2. The Strand Theater on the Square – "A cool place". Dan once watched a silent movie, and a man played the huge organ along with it.
3. Dobbins Air Force Base – Dan was driving south on Cobb Parkway when out of nowhere, a stealth bomber flew over his head and landed on the runway.
4. Marietta Diner – Didn't open until Dan was nineteen, but he got there often enough. How can one diner make 200 dishes and make them all well? He found out later when he went to the Tic Toc Diner, Caldwell Diner, and other diners in Jersey. There's something special about them but rarer in Marietta.
5. Kennesaw Mountain National Battlefield Park – Dan liked climbing to the top of Kennesaw Mountain and seeing the cannons used there during the Civil War, and trenches built by the soldiers.
6. Chattahoochee National Recreation Area – Dan rafted there many times and even jumped off a high rock naked, before he was famous and the whole "Johnson" crap would follow him, and nobody took a photo because they didn't give a crap. Everybody did, even girls.

7. Bagelicious – On Johnson Ferry Road. Good stuff. Very good stuff, even if the staff acted like New Yorkers. Helped him get ready for New York living.
8. The Big Chicken. Just a local KFC, but the best for using at giving directions.
9. The Fox Theater. Look up and stare at the twinkling stars, and where the Broadway shows would play here.
10. The Georgian Terrace Hotel. Across the street from the Fox Theater. When Gone with the Wind Premiered in Atlanta, (but at Lowe's, not the Fox), many of the stars stayed there, but nobody, Dan always thought heroic than Helen Keller from Alabama, born deaf, blind and dumb, and yet graduated with honors from Harvard. Has any human ever been as miraculous?

# What Dan Knew About West Orange, NJ

1. Thomas Alva Edition. You really must mention him as number one. His factory was still there and the home, Glenmont, was down the street from the Minnelli's in the exclusive Llewellyn Park. Dan liked to think the Minnelli's might knock on the door. "Hey Tommy, have you got an extra light bulb," or "Edison, WTF, turn down those lights and go to bed already. A man can't work 24/7, you know."

2. Eagle Rock Reservation. A place to drink and think. And gaze. Dan solved a lot of problems here and learned absolutely nothing about many other things.

3. Pleasant Valley Way. I mean, hello? Carole King, anybody?

4. A town where David Cassidy grew up. Dan listened to their records but didn't tell anybody.

5. The Manor. He would have gotten married here, but Melanie chose the Del Coronado in San Diego, her hometown. Okay, he figured that was nice, too.

6. Star Tavern. Ok, it was in Orange, but like what, 500 feet? Let's not get so technical. World's greatest pizza or not? Who was better, thought Dan? End of story.

7. Jimmy Buff's – For Italian Hot Dogs. Sometimes, you just need a double. They were never impressed with Dan's height, either. They said, "what do you want?", but the food was the thing.

8. Degnan Park and Vincent's Pond – Even though Dan didn't have skates that fit his size 22 foot, he still loved walking around and listening to stories from the adults that grew up going there.

# What did Dan Like Most About Ann Arbor?

1. The UM campus. The Hatcher Library and Michigan Law Quad top the list.
2. South U.
3. The Big House – Where the word "iconic" was invented. Can 107,000 people be wrong (adjust number as needed)?
4. Brown Jug – When a burger is named after you, well, you know.
5. Pinball Pete's – Where nobody stood in line for "Gorf" (more plan time for Dan).
6. Crisler Arena – The "House that Cazzie built". Did Cazzie ever lose a game there? The C Man didn't.
7. Fleetwood Diner – When you just must have 12 Coney Dogs at 3:00 A.M. Everybody knows that feeling.
8. Museum of Natural History – Lots of bones. Rumor was that Dan's bones would go on display one day.

# Tour of Canyonville

Dan felt bad that every guy couldn't build the ultimate man-cave. He had up to about $1.4 billion to do it, but his wife Melanie had to stay within a budget of just $2 million. She pulled it off in grand style.

1. Canyonville was built to look like a barn, all in wood. It had a large barn door-style opening in front, and due to Flowery Branch fire codes, another regular exit door in the back. It was 3,500 square feet. Dan would have made it larger, but it was still "cozy" and he never told that to Melanie.

2. Outside of the building was a large concrete patio, a covered kitchen with a commercial refrigerator, grill, smoker, cabinets for glassware,, three outdoor firepits, two gas-lit and one that wasn't.  There were several tables and chairs, and area for three games of cornhole, outdoor speakers and an area for live music when the weather was nice. The shore of Lake Lanier was twelve feet away.

3. The house, about 125 feet away, had a dock on the water, with twelve Adirondack chairs, a pontoon boat, a furnished guest room upstairs, and downstairs, a storage area for the Johnson's six wave runners and two kayaks.

4.  Inside Canyonville was an 18 Ft Inlaid Beechwood / Walnut Commercial Bar, with mirrors and shelves. Space underneath where Canyonville typically serves 12 beers on tap and several others in bottle and cans. A local beer distributor would come by when requested before special events or whenever called.

5.  Lighting – Melanie was consulted by a premier lighting company that was flown in from California to view, take measurements, and lay-out an amazing lighting experience. First were stage lights, and then a series of ceiling spotlights and soft lights that could be made bright or soft as the situation or event required. There were colored lights, rotating lights, even a large disco ball which could be taken down when the crowd felt it was "overkill", like at country music nights. The lights made it possible to stage events properly, if it was rock, jazz, country, classical, a comedy night, or any combination of the above. Sound and lighting engineers were flown in or brought in from nearby Atlanta for most events. Other, more intimate time, Dan and Melanie could "wing it", having been taught a few tricks of the trade. In tandem with the lighting engineers, were acoustic experts, who worked to install materials on the ceiling to provide the best possible sound for what was essentially, a "souped-up" barn.

6.  Flooring – Tile was used on the floor, with a removable wooden dance floor.

7.  Furniture – Melanie hired an interior decorator, who lined a full side with vintage sofas and chairs, and behind the dance floor, both hi-top table and stools, and several tables and chair sets. The glass covered tables were "lightbox" tables, each decorated with different-themed memorabilia. One had 50's rock and roll decoration like Elvis and the Big Bopper. There was a 60's table, 70's, 80's, and 90's. Programs from concerts, 45's, CD's and more.

8.  Juke Box – An M100A Seeburg, holding 100 45's. Melanie hired a collector to load the machine with music she knew Dan liked, and then music the "masses" would like. There was early rock like Elvis, plenty of Motown, of course, Sinatra, Dean, Sammy, then 60s and 70's rock, and country. There was a secondary sound system for other kinds of music, like jazz, classical, even rap.

9.  Billiard tables – Two Brunswick Gold Crown VI Tournament Slate Pool Table in Mahogany

10. Video Games – Along the back wall, 15 of the best '80s games, including Pac-Man and Ms. Pac Man (fast version), Centipede, Galaga, Missile Command, Gorf (Dan's favorite), Beer Tapper, and a few others.

Made in United States
Orlando, FL
21 October 2023

38103378R10324